Dianne Blacklock has been a teacher, trainer, counsellor, check-out chick, and even one of those annoying market researchers you avoid in shopping malls. Nowadays she tries not to annoy anyone by staying home and writing.

Also by Dianne Blacklock

Call Waiting
Wife for Hire
Almost Perfect
Crossing Paths
Three's a Crowd
The Right Time
The Secret Ingredient
The Best Man

False Advertising

Dianne Blacklock

First published by Macmillan Australia in 2007
This edition published in 2017 by Dianne Blacklock

Copyright © Dianne Blacklock 2007

dianneblacklock.com

False Advertising

EPUB format: 9781925579666
Print on Demand format: 9781925579673

Cover design by Red Tally Studios

Publishing services provided by Critical Mass
www.critmassconsulting.com

To my family

Helen

'Bugger!'

'What you say, Mummy?'

Helen looked down at Noah, whose big round eyes were gazing guilelessly back up at her.

'Butter,' she lied. 'We have no butter, and no milk either. We'll have to go up the shops later.'

'We haffa go uppa shops later!'

'Mmm.' She peered into the empty carton one last time in the vague hope that even a little milk might materialise through sheer force of will. But no, there was no milk for her first coffee of the day, yet again. Why was she the only one to think ahead? To realise that when you used the last of the milk, a new carton did not magically appear in the fridge? Nor was the empty carton refilled if you put it back in the fridge. Why was she the only grown-up in the house?

Damn David and his damned vagueness. It drove her mad sometimes. How long had she been working nights? David knew she rarely got home before midnight. She wasn't expected to check the milk then, was she? Couldn't he just make sure there was some milk in the fridge so she could have coffee in the morning? No, that would require a little thing called empathy, and David didn't appear to possess much of that particular trait, except when it came to the starving masses in Africa, the plight of the East Timorese or victims of a tsunami, but then, he didn't have to do without coffee first thing to help them out.

Helen stepped on the pedal and the lid of the bin sprang open, but she hesitated, the milk carton poised above it. She let the lid drop, then stepped on the pedal again and like the beak of a baby bird waiting to be fed it sprang open once more. If she wasn't getting her morning coffee, the landfill of the world could suffer one lousy milk carton. She stared down into the bin, sighing as she slipped her foot off the pedal and allowed it to close. Sometimes a conscience was a pain in the proverbial.

She turned on the kitchen tap, careful to tuck the lip of the carton under the spout first. Mustn't waste water either. Apparently there was a drought, despite the fact that it had rained all week and there was a pile of dirty washing almost as tall as Helen waiting for her in the laundry. She would have to work out what they needed for the next day or two and put a load through the dryer. David frowned when she used the dryer. Helen didn't like to use it either, but sometimes when it had rained for five days solid, with one and a half jobs between them and a small child, drastic measures were required. And if that meant using a little extra coal-burning energy, then so be it. Besides, if she did the load early enough, cleaned out the filter, and put the clothes away in the drawers before David got home, he need never know.

'Phone ringing, Mummy,' Noah announced. Noah had been a quiet child, with a limited repertoire of essential words and phrases that had served him well through his toddler years. But when he'd hit preschool this year he'd discovered conversational skills he hadn't known he possessed. Now he revelled in providing a detailed running commentary of each and every moment of their day, with a special emphasis on the bleeding obvious.

Helen picked up the receiver.

'Good morning, Mrs Chapman!'

Damn. The accent sounded Indian, the tone insistently cheerful.

'We are not selling anything –'

Of course you are. Why couldn't she just hang up? What did she care if this man thousands of miles away in a call centre in New Delhi thought she was rude? She could hang up and it would make no difference at all. He would simply move on to his next random call, and she could get on with the important task of sorting laundry. Life would go on in a perfectly reasonable manner for all concerned. But Helen could never bring herself to do it; she felt some overwhelming obligation to allow this person his due portion of her time. What that constituted was a little difficult to determine, and Helen frequently found herself trapped inside a never-ending phone call, like Alice after she fell into Wonderland, only not as much fun.

'How old is your current mobile phone?'

'Oh, I don't need a new mobile phone.'

Wrong answer, she realised too late, as the man launched into his spiel about how he was going to give her a brand-new phone. That's right, a gift all the way from India. She'd actually be happy with just a little milk right at the moment.

'Sum'n atta door, Mummy,' Noah announced urgently.

'I'm sorry, I have to go, there's someone at the door,' Helen said, promptly hanging up. He'd had his quota, she'd been fair, wasting an appropriate amount of time for the both of them.

Noah stood in the doorway to the hall, arms outstretched, clenching and unclenching his hands. His pyjamas were getting too small for him, as evidenced by the soft little strip of belly gaping through where the top didn't meet the bottoms. She hadn't cleaned him up after breakfast yet, so his face was smudged and his hands were sticky, still clenching and unclenching, waiting for her to pick him up. But how could she resist? Helen scooped him up to perch on her hip as she heard the knock again, a little more insistent this time.

'Coming!'

'Coming!' Noah parroted.

She noticed David's coffee cup on the arm of the sofa as she passed through the front sitting room, inciting at least three reactions: first, the arm of the sofa was not a coffee table; second, he hadn't put his cup back in the kitchen; and third, and most annoying, he had got a cup of coffee this morning with scant regard for the fact that his wife would have to go without. It wouldn't have even crossed his mind. Was it a man thing or just a David thing?

Helen arrived at the front door and paused, smoothing her hair back. As if that was going to make a difference. She glanced down at her daggy tracksuit. She hadn't slept in it, though it looked as though she had. It was the first thing she pulled on every morning so that she was not actually in her pyjamas for the rest of the day. It was a fairly transparent ruse.

She took a deep breath and opened the door. Two uniformed police officers were standing in front of her: one man, one woman. Their faces were grim, unsmiling. The woman moved first. She reached for her hat with her right hand, removed it from her head, and tucked it into the crook of her left arm.

Gemma

'What did you say, I can't hear you?' Gemma had her finger stuck in her free ear to block the announcement playing over the airport PA system. She thought Luke had just said that he couldn't come to pick her up, either that or passengers for Flight 77 were boarding now. He probably hadn't said the latter.

'I, ah, I'm not going to be able to make it, Gem,' Luke said, loudly this time. 'You'll be right getting a taxi?'

'Yeah, sure, no worries,' said Gemma, still straining to hear him. It was a terrible connection. Ever since she'd changed to this telco she'd had nothing but trouble. So much for their slogan, 'Keeping you in touch'.

'See you at home?' Gemma virtually shouted, assuming Luke was having as much trouble hearing her.

'Ah, no . . .'

Of course: if he was at home, he should have been able to come and pick her up. He must have been held up at work. 'I mean later, after work?' she said, stepping out through the automatic doors to the taxi rank.

'No, I can't . . . I won't be there,' he said.

'Oh? What's going on?'

'Bye Gem.'

And he hung up. Or the line could have dropped out, Gemma supposed. But he did say 'bye'. He sounded odd, she decided as she dragged her backpack towards the queue of taxis. She really hated those middle-aged, middle-class wheelie bags, but she had to admit she'd kill for a pair of wheels on her backpack right now. Lugging it around like this was soon going to get pretty old in her condition.

Gemma opened the back door of the first taxi. 'Where do you want me to put my bag?' she asked hopefully.

His reply was the boot of the car popping open. The age of chivalry was not just dead, it was extinct. Gemma heaved her bag around the back of the taxi and over the edge of the boot, letting it drop in. She retrieved her wallet and phone before slamming the boot shut again.

Gemma recited the address automatically as she climbed into the back seat. She usually sat up front with the driver, but she couldn't be bothered being assertive or making conversation today. She was exhausted. She rested her head back against the seat. If Luke wasn't going to be home, maybe she'd take a bath when she got in. She pictured the poor excuse for a bath that graced their tiny flat – it was really no more than a glorified shower tray – and thought better of it. She wished he was going to be home. What could be holding him up at work? He was a labourer at a marina for godsakes. Maybe he was working an extra shift? Not exactly Luke's modus operandi, but perhaps he was beginning to take the whole baby thing seriously, seeing as she had just made the trip down to Sydney to announce it to the family and all. On her own. She'd been so annoyed when Luke had piked; he said they couldn't afford for both of them to go, especially as he'd have to lose a couple of shifts as well. He insisted it was better if she went by herself. Truth was, Gemma knew Luke was a little scared of her parents, which was faintly ridiculous. Her parents were certainly to be avoided, but hardly feared. Then again, Luke seemed edgy around anyone who could even vaguely be identified as an authority figure. He still strutted around like a rebel without a cause, which was a little odd for a man past thirty years of age, especially one who was about to become a parent himself.

So Gemma had had no choice but to front up to her dad's Sixtieth Birthday Spectacular, pregnant and partnerless. This was not how she'd envisioned her visit. It would have been the perfect opportunity for the two of them, arm in arm, to announce they were getting married and having a baby. Her mother would be running around like a chook with her head cut off and she'd only stop long enough to knock back some champagne and make some predictable comment about not looking old enough to be a grandmother again, before returning to the fray in her favourite role of Hostess Extraordinaire. Her dad, meanwhile, would be hunkered down with all his old cronies, desperately trying to forget they had reached the age at which they had officially called their own parents 'old'. They would listen to the Rolling Stones and reassure themselves they were still a couple of years younger than Mick Jagger, while ignoring their spreading girths, their thinning hair, and the part about them not being rock stars. At the end of the weekend, Gemma and Luke could have disappeared back up to Brisbane and out of reach before her parents had really processed the news. Or had a chance to vent their opinions about it.

The taxi pulled up outside the small block of units where Luke and Gemma had set up home. Actually it was Gemma who had begun to set up home. Luke had got a bit antsy when that had involved spending money.

'But we need some stuff, Luke,' she'd defended herself. Gemma only wanted to be comfortable, for the place to feel more like a home, instead of temporary lodgings. It was probably some kind of weird nesting instinct kicking in, but she didn't want to feel like she was staying in a backpackers' hostel any more. Besides, a couple of extra coffee mugs and a doona could hardly be considered extravagant.

'We don't need all this stuff, babe,' Luke had shot back. 'How are we gunna cart it up north when we go?'

Their plan had originally been to get jobs on one of the islands, or further north, up in the Daintree perhaps. They'd heard there was plenty of work in the resorts, with accommodation included. But they'd only made it as far as Brisbane before they ran out of cash. Perhaps it had been somewhat shortsighted not to pace themselves, but planning too far ahead was an anathema to Gemma, and obviously to Luke as well. Besides, they'd both picked up casual work easily enough when they'd arrived in Brisbane; Luke at the marina and Gemma in a cafe, at least till the morning sickness had made it impossible for her to work around food.

She walked up the chipped terrazzo stairs to the second floor and dropped her backpack in front of their door, bending over wearily to find her keys in one of the pockets. The stairwell was a little cooler but Gemma knew the flat was going to be like an oven if it had been closed up all day. However, when she unlocked the door and stepped inside she was surprised to find it wasn't closed up at all. The sliding doors to the balcony were open right back, the sheer nylon curtains dancing about on the breeze.

'Luke?' Gemma called tentatively. She walked across the living room to the bedroom. 'Luke?'

He wasn't there. Gemma scanned the room: the bed was unmade, but the place looked neat. Too neat. Something wasn't right. There were no shoes on the floor around the bed, not even a pair of thongs. She crossed to the wardrobe and slid back the door on Luke's side. A few wire coathangers clanked against one another. His clothes were all gone. She pulled open a drawer: nothing; the next drawer: nothing. She knew she wouldn't find anything but she kept going until all four drawers hung halfway out of their sockets, sagging listlessly, empty. Gemma crouched on the floor, breathing heavily; she felt herself beginning to tremble. What was going on? She got up and went into the bathroom, opening the mirrored door of the cabinet. No razor, no toothbrush. Gemma took a step backwards, her leg bumping against the edge of the toilet seat. She closed the lid and slowly lowered herself to sit, staring at the hideous pattern on the wall tiles. Where the hell was he? What the hell was going on?

He'd gone north after all. Obviously. That had to be it. He was going to find work and send for her.

Then why wouldn't he tell her if that's what he was doing?

He wanted to surprise her?

Now she was clutching at straws.

She jumped up and strode determinedly back out into the living area, picked up the phone and called Luke. It went straight to voicemail.

'Luke,' said Gemma, trying to keep her voice steady, 'what's going on, babe? I'm feeling a bit freaked out here. Call me, okay? Call me when you get this. Whatever it is, we'll work it out, Luke. I love you, babe. Just call me.'

Gemma hung up. She bit the edge of her thumb, thinking. She picked up the phone again and dialled the marina. Val in the booking office answered almost straightaway.

'Donnelly's Charters.'

'Hi, Val, it's Gemma, Luke's Gemma. I was wondering if I could have a word with him?'

'You're not the only one,' she replied. 'Haven't seen him all weekend. Ted's ropable.'

Gemma couldn't say anything. She couldn't speak. Her heart was doing this weird irregular beat.

'You still there?' said Val.

Gemma cleared her throat. 'Yeah, sure.'

'When did you see him last?'

'Um, well, I've been away for a few days.'

'That'll be the end of him, then,' said Val.

Gemma's head began to spin. She felt sick. 'Okay, thanks for that, I have to go, bye.'

She slammed down the phone and ran back to the bathroom. Lifting the toilet seat, she dropped to her knees and threw up into the bowl.

A week later

Helen remembered every detail of the visit from the police, though she didn't admit it when people asked. It was easier to say it was all a blur. No one ever pushed it. They accepted whatever she said, put it down to grief. Grief – Helen had learned through all the events of the past week – was the universal justification for all kinds of behaviour. People would let you get away with a lot on account of grief.

They had sat in the front room, the police officers and Helen. She had quickly snatched up David's coffee cup and offered them a seat. Constable Alison Hammond and Constable Michael Murray. They had looked genuinely upset. Later Helen thought how hard it must have been for them, making that trip in the car, pulling up outside, walking to the door, facing her. It was hard on doctors too. She'd stood beside enough of them as they told family members of a negative prognosis, of an adverse outcome after surgery, of the death of a loved one. To be the bearer of bad tidings must be a heavy load indeed.

And it would have been extra difficult considering what had happened to David. Helen was amazed they'd kept a straight face. Not that it was funny. Of course it wasn't. A person getting hit by a bus was a tragedy. But it was also a cliché, with unfortunately comic overtones. So much so, Helen wondered for a second if they were joking. Not that they just came out with it like that: 'Your husband's been hit by a bus.' What they said, or what Constable Alison Hammond said, after she'd removed her hat, after she had verified that Helen was who they expected her to be, that she was in fact the wife of a 'David Alan Chapman', of this address, what Constable Hammond said was, 'Mrs Chapman, I'm sorry to have to tell you there's been an accident.'

Now there was a cliché.

Helen allowed Noah to slide from her hip down onto his feet. 'Sweetheart, I think it's time for *Playschool*,' she said, leaning down to his level. His little face lit up and he clapped his hands together. Helen cupped his face and kissed his forehead, holding him for a beat longer than normal before releasing him. She watched him scupper off down the hall, before turning back to the ominous visitors on her doorstep.

'Please, come in,' she invited Constable Hammond and Constable Murray. Once they were seated in the front room, Constable Hammond did the talking.

'Your husband, Mr David Alan Chapman, was standing waiting to cross at lights on George Street at Broadway at 7.28 this morning. He stepped from the kerb directly into the path of the 422 bus on route to Railway Square. The driver was unable to stop. I'm afraid your husband was killed instantly.'

Helen often wondered how they knew that. Killed instantly. Was there an instrument that measured it? What was an instant anyway? Did he turn to see the bus coming towards him in that instant? Did he flinch; did his life flash before his eyes? What did he feel when it hit? Was there an instant before the instant he was killed, when he felt the impact of several tonnes of metal and glass colliding with his body?

She had of course remained calm as they told her. She didn't get hysterical; Helen never got hysterical. She was a nurse, for crying out loud. She was trained to handle emergency, sickness, death, without fuss, to take them in her stride.

But she had felt something well up inside her. She couldn't name the feeling. Perhaps she'd never had it before. It wasn't grief yet. It wasn't even particularly sad. Helen knew it was going to hit her, probably soon, but not in front of the two officers. She was protected right now by the silicone coating of shock. She had to focus, get the information she needed, and then she'd have some calls to make. Or at least one call. And that was going to be the hardest.

'What happens now?' Helen asked finally.

'Pardon?' said Constable Hammond. She looked bereft, white; Helen noticed her eyes had teared up. God, this was probably her first time, poor thing. Helen wondered if she ought not go over and sit by her, pat her hand in that consoling way she did for the relatives of very ill patients.

'I'm not sure of the procedure,' Helen explained. 'I guess there's something I have to do, that I'm supposed to do . . .' And then it occurred to her. 'Wouldn't someone need to identify the body?'

'That's correct, Mrs Chapman.' It was Constable Murray speaking this time. 'Under the . . . circumstances,' he said carefully, 'it might be better if it was someone else, another family member. Is there someone we can contact for you?'

That was thoughtful. They probably didn't know she was a nurse, that she'd seen hundreds of dead bodies. Sometimes they didn't look scary at all; they simply looked as though they were sleeping. Many who died in the hospital were at the end of long illnesses, so they were emaciated, pale and bloodless, but strangely at peace. The only ones that did upset her were those who were gruesomely twisted and deformed in accidents so they didn't even look human any more . . .

Helen caught her breath. Her heart was palpitating. Not yet, keep control. She cleared her throat. 'If you could leave it with me. How much time do I have?'

*

After the police had left, Helen picked up the phone and called Jim and Noreen without pausing to think about it. It just had to be done. David's parents were both retired and they barely ever left home before ten in the morning, there being no longer any need to be the early bird catching the elusive worm. Jim Chapman had enjoyed a successful and highly satisfying working life, he liked to remind everyone, frequently. He'd started out as a bank teller but before long was made branch manager, and then area manager, and eventually some complex and very specific title to do with superannuation that Helen could never recall. He'd achieved all of this with no fancy qualifications, he liked to tell everyone, frequently. Not that he didn't realise things had changed, and that a university degree was now a compulsory entry visa into the ranks of white-collar professionalism.

Eldest son Steven was halfway through a commerce degree when David finished school and announced he wanted to do Arts. 'What, painting?' Jim had frowned. 'You haven't got an artistic bone in your body, boy.' David had explained that he wanted to study humanities; sociology and archaeology in particular. His father had laughed. 'Commerce is good enough for your brother, it'll do you.' But of course it didn't, and after failing his first year, David took off overseas on money he'd made working part-time jobs when he should have been studying the Dow Jones. His parents couldn't do anything to stop him, and from the omniscient perspective of middle age, they counted on him getting it 'out of his system'. What exactly he was supposed to be getting out of his system was not clear, and David befuddled them further by landing himself in South America and working as a volunteer with a non-government aid agency.

Helen often wished she'd met him then, when all things still seemed possible, when his enthusiasm apparently knew no bounds. Not that he didn't have fervour when they met, but it was on the wane. He'd come home from his stint overseas and was living with his parents while he continued to work for various overseas aid agencies, for little or no money. His father ranted and raved that he was throwing his life away, that he would never have a career. David said he wasn't interested in a career; he was interested in making a difference. What about making a living? Jim countered. How did he expect to support a family and buy a home by 'making a difference'? David said he would worry about supporting a family when he had one, and he didn't care in the least about buying a house. That was incomprehensible to Jim. How could he not care about buying a house? Where was he getting these crazy, communist, leftie ideas from?

Clearly, it was an untenable situation. In the end the only way David could get out from under their roof and support himself was to take a job as a base-grade clerk in the public service – ironically, exactly what his father had wanted. David remained involved in his various causes, and he planned eventually to go back to university and get the qualifications he needed to find paid work in his chosen field. But other things got in the way. And one of them was Helen.

'Hello?' David's mother always sounded wary when she answered the phone, albeit with good reason today. But Helen knew she couldn't tell Noreen first. She had to give Jim control, let him 'handle' his wife, as he was wont to do.

'Hi, Noreen, it's Helen,' she said levelly. Noreen was a nice enough woman, but they'd never been close. She followed her husband's lead in everything, and as he didn't much care for Helen, neither did she. She was just a little more polite about it.

'Helen.' She said it like a greeting. 'Everything all right? How's Noah?'

Helen nearly replied 'everything's fine' on automatic pilot. 'Noah's fine, he's good,' she said. 'I was wondering if I could speak to Jim, if he's around?'

'Of course, dear.' Noreen would never question why Helen wanted to talk to Jim and not her. She would assume it was something important, perhaps a financial matter, that didn't concern her. 'Just a minute, I'll get him for you.'

A moment later Jim came on the line. 'Hello Helen?' He said it as though it was an accusation. 'What's up? Noreen said you wanted to talk to me?'

Helen took a deep breath. She suddenly realised what she had to say, and she hadn't even absorbed it herself yet. David was gone. Gone. He wasn't coming back. He was dead.

Nothing was ever going to be the same again. As soon as she said it out loud to Jim everything was going to change. It was almost as if it wasn't real yet. This last half-hour had been like standing in the centre of the hurricane, the calm before the storm, and every other cliché used to describe that inevitable, apprehensive, loaded pause that occurred just before everything started to fall down around you. A lump was rising again in Helen's throat. No, not yet.

'Helen, are you there?' Jim said impatiently.

She swallowed. 'Yes, Jim. Sorry.' She took a breath. 'I'm afraid I have some bad news.' She sunk into a chair, her legs suddenly not doing such a good job of holding her up. 'Perhaps you'd better sit down.'

'What is it?' he said guardedly.

'It's David . . .' God, this was so hard.

'What about David?' he demanded. He was beginning to lose it. Deep down, on some inexplicable, molecular level, he knew his son was gone.

'He's been in an accident,' she said weakly.

'What hospital is he in, where did they take him? Not that blasted St Michael's –'

'Jim,' Helen interrupted, 'he died instantly.'

There was silence.

'The police have just left,' Helen went on after a while. 'He was . . . he was run over . . .' She didn't want to say it. 'In the city, on his way to work. Um, it was a bus.'

'Oh God,' he breathed, barely audible.

Helen allowed him time to collect himself. Jim would not want to show any weakness, to appear vulnerable. He was the head of the family, after all.

After a while she heard him clear his throat. 'I would imagine in a situation like this they'll need someone to identify the body.'

'Yes,' said Helen. 'That's what the police said.'

'Okay.' He sounded resolved. 'I'll take care of it. I'll call Steven, and ah, look, I'll probably drop Noreen around with you when I go. She shouldn't be left alone.'

'Sure,' said Helen. He hadn't asked her how she was. She hadn't really expected that he would.

'You'd better give me the name of the policeman you spoke to.'

*

It was because of Jim that Helen and David had met in the first place. Helen had been Jim's nurse, or one of them, when he'd had his first heart attack, and she suspected that attributed to the fact that he'd never seemed comfortable around her. She supposed it was not entirely unreasonable – she'd had to perform various intimate, though routine, procedures on him when he was at his most vulnerable, a condition Jim was not exactly accustomed to.

Helen had been in the habit of taking her lunch or dinner in a public cafe, usually with her head stuck in a gossip magazine she'd borrowed from one of the waiting areas. While most hospital staff preferred to hide from the public and use the staff cafeteria, Helen usually preferred to hide from the rest of the staff, be anonymous, and absorb herself in the lives and loves of Hollywood celebrities. It was a guilty obsession. She would never actually buy one of these magazines herself; they were trash, completely fabricated and a load of rubbish. But Helen couldn't get enough of them. Perhaps reading about the trivial, so-called struggles of the rich and famous made her own situation seem not so bad. Perhaps they simply transported her to other worlds, other lives, lifting her out of her own. Helen didn't know, and she was not inclined to analyse it too closely in case even this small, harmless pleasure became tainted for her.

Then, on a particular day in the month of August, David Chapman had walked into the cafe and was making his way to an adjacent table when he recognised her.

'Hello,' he said, not exactly displaying a great deal of originality.

Helen didn't respond, she was too absorbed in her magazine. And she wouldn't have assumed anyone was talking to her anyway; the 'hello' would have been filtered out as background noise, directed at someone else.

But David had persisted. He'd cleared his throat and repeated, rather loudly, 'Hello there,' and then stooped to read her name tag, adding, 'Helen, I thought it was Helen.'

Which was when Helen had abruptly looked up, startled to see a young man – a family member of one of her patients if she was not mistaken – standing there looking expectantly at her. He smiled. 'Mind if I join you?'

That kind of thing never happened to Helen. At least not since she was a teenager. She'd been reasonably popular at school, certainly not unpopular; she'd had her share of friends, but they had all moved on, while Helen remained in exactly the same place. She couldn't remember the last time she'd been on a date. It had just been too difficult to maintain relationships while she cared for her mother. So there was no time for dating, little time for socialising at all. Work had become her only social outlet, yet she kept her distance from the rest of the staff. Helen didn't quite understand why she did that, but anything else seemed like too much work. Letting people in, giving explanations, opening up. It was easier, if lonelier, to keep to herself.

Only Mr Chapman's son obviously didn't know this about her, and he was still waiting expectantly beside her table. So Helen blushed, fumbled with the magazine to hide the article she was reading, then fumbled further to hide the cover of the magazine, then coughed and sniffed and finally looked up and met his eyes. They gazed steadily back at her, with what almost could have been described as affection. He didn't even know her. Why was he looking at her like that?

'Sure,' she offered as a rather delayed response to his request to join her. Then she glanced at her watch and added, 'I have to be back on ward soon.'

David had remained undaunted. He appeared to have thick skin, which he was going to need to finally win her over. Much later, when Helen had felt comfortable enough to ask him, David had put his persistence down to a longstanding fetish for nurses, or, when he wasn't teasing her, to something he'd seen in her eyes. She'd reminded him of the beleaguered children in the refugee camps overseas who looked to aid workers like him for hope. Helen had inadvertently tugged at his heart in a way he couldn't resist.

He sought her out every time he visited his father after that. The day Jim was discharged he asked her for her phone number, and a few days later he rang, and a few weeks later she finally agreed to go out with him. A few months later he moved in.

And then a few years later he died. That's how the story would end from now on.

*

The next time there was a knock on the door Helen froze momentarily before she remembered that it was probably Noreen. As she opened the front door she saw Jim's car pull away from the kerb. Her mother-in-law looked shaken; her eyes were red and swollen under the make-up she'd hastily applied as camouflage. Must keep up appearances. They exchanged a stilted hug, but Noreen held on firmly to both of Helen's wrists as they drew apart.

'Helen, I want you to know you'll never have to worry about Noah,' she said in a trembling voice. 'We are his family. He'll never do without because of this, we won't let that happen.'

The fog had descended soon after. For the next couple of days it was a blur of people in and out of the house, casseroles, cakes, so much food she and Noah could never have eaten it all. She packed up some and took it over to Brookhaven. Helen hadn't seen her mother since the day before the accident, when she'd called in on her way to work. Marion wouldn't have known the difference anyway. The staff clucked over the food as though they'd never had anything so special as a chocolate-chip muffin in all their lives. Helen wished everyone would stop being *so* laboriously nice: it was exhausting. She would be happy when things were back to normal and people could go back to ignoring her.

She walked into her mother's room, dragging a chair over to the bed. As she sat down Marion's eyes met hers expectantly. Helen knew that look: her mother had no idea who she was today.

'Mum,' she began, 'it's me, Helen.'

She saw the now familiar flicker cross her eyes, the confusion, uncertainty, doubt.

'Hello Helen,' she said politely, her expression suggesting it was Helen who was a few sandwiches short of a picnic and she'd best humour her.

'I have to tell you about David,' Helen pushed on. 'Do you remember David, Mum?'

She seemed to be thinking about it. 'Perhaps . . . I do remember a David. He was married to . . .' She looked up at the ceiling as though the answer might be written there.

'He was married to me, Mum, Helen. I'm your daughter.' Helen held her mother's hand in between hers. Please know me, remember me, just this once. 'We have Noah, your little grandson? You only have one grandchild, Mum. Do you remember Noah?'

'Of course I remember Noah,' she said indignantly. 'He built the ark and took the animals two by two, and then it rained, for forty days . . .'

Helen leaned her head down on her mother's hand as she continued her fragmented account of Noah and the flood. Helen wanted to cry, she hadn't been able to yet. She'd been frightened of tears at first, hadn't wanted to break down in front of Noah, and then she'd suppressed them so much they wouldn't come. Lying in bed that first night, alone, the smell of David still in his pillow, which she'd hugged to get to sleep, she still hadn't cried. She had hoped that telling her mother . . . if she'd just had a glimmer of recognition . . .

'Do you know Tony?' Marion said suddenly, breaking off her narrative.

Helen lifted her head. 'Yes, I know Tony.' Her elder brother, living blissfully free of responsibility in London, following his apparently never-ending dream of becoming a theatre director. When Marion couldn't even remember her own name, she always remembered Tony.

'Will Tony be coming today?' she asked hopefully.

'No, Mum, Tony won't be coming today.'

Marion paused, the disappointment plain in her eyes. After a while she looked back at Helen. 'Do I know you, dear?'

*

The funeral had taken place the next day.

Jim had insisted there was to be no viewing, which left Helen with the unspoken horror, every time she closed her eyes, of the way David must have looked when Jim went to identify his body. Jim and Noreen had taken over all the arrangements for the funeral. Helen appreciated their help; she couldn't have managed it herself anyway. How was a widow with a young child expected to plan a funeral in a few days? How was anyone who was grieving? So Jim and Noreen chose the order of service, the readings, hymns, everything, without so much as running it by her. Helen didn't have the strength to fight with them, but she finally put her foot down when Jim informed her where David was to be buried. That much she knew with absolute certainty – David had always said he wanted to be cremated and have his ashes scattered off the headland at Garie Beach in the Royal National Park. Jim said that was romantic nonsense and that David was to be buried in the family plot Jim had purchased on his retirement. He'd spoken to David about it. 'Yes,' Helen agreed, 'and he told you no thanks.' They'd tried to insist, but Helen held the power this time: papers had to be signed and she was the closest next of kin. She won, but they weren't finished. Jim and Noreen sat her down and told her in no uncertain terms she was irresponsible to allow Noah to attend the funeral. He was too young, he wouldn't understand, they insisted. That was right, Helen had replied calmly, but it would help him understand, it would give him a chance to say goodbye to his daddy. They were appalled. He was only a child, he didn't need to be exposed to this. Besides, didn't she realise how much his presence would upset everyone at the funeral? That, Helen told them, was not her problem.

'You're being a little selfish, dear.' Noreen had finally spoken up; she'd been sitting in silence the entire time. 'You're unnaturally attached to that boy, Helen. You're going to have to loosen the reins now, let some other people in. He needs more than just your influence in his life.'

*

David Alan Chapman's funeral was a farce. It was solemn, pious and sanctimonious and it would have meant nothing to David, in fact he would have hated it. Helen couldn't help feeling she had let him down in this, the last thing she would ever do for him.

She still hadn't cried. She knew everyone was watching her, waiting, judging. Maybe they thought she was keeping it together for Noah's sake; maybe they thought she was as cold as Lindy Chamberlain.

But no one could have known the remorse that had plagued Helen since that morning sitting in the front room, opposite

Constable Hammond and Constable Murray, clutching David's coffee cup in both hands. Since she'd woken up that morning she'd had a running commentary in her head listing his faults and shortcomings. He was being crushed, his body annihilated beyond recognition, while she whined about not having milk for her coffee. They were her last thoughts of him alive. She could not adequately describe how much she hated herself.

They hadn't even spoken since the Wednesday night. On Thursdays David knocked off work early to pick up Noah from preschool, getting home after Helen had already left for the afternoon shift. To make up the time, he started early on both Thursday and Friday mornings, leaving the house while she was still asleep. That was their routine. Every single week they didn't see each other for almost two whole days. Why didn't she wake up to see him off? She would have done when they were first together. When had she stopped that?

She had tormented herself trying to remember their last words to each other, the precise details of their last night together. Days and weeks merged in her memory. They'd watched TV, as usual, but Helen couldn't even recall what they'd watched. If she could jog her memory, maybe she could come up with what they'd talked about. She so didn't want her last words to him to be 'Did you remember to set the alarm?' but she suspected that's precisely what they were.

The wake was held at Jim and Noreen's place, of course, and that was just as well as Helen had no idea who half the people there were. She felt as though she was suffocating. Strangers kept thrusting their hands in hers, muttering 'Lovely service' with appropriate gravitas. She wanted to scream at them, *No it wasn't!* But she didn't. She just gazed blankly back at their earnest faces, nodding faintly, till they released her, visibly relieved to pass her along to the next in line. David's brother, Steven, could not even offer his condolences, but then, he'd never known what to say to Helen at the best of times. And these were clearly not the best of times. He was a nice enough man, a little colourless, but certainly not unpleasant. His wife Cheryl was of the high-need variety — often sick, or tired, or otherwise miserable, their two pale-faced girls the same. Steven had married a version of his mother, but he lacked the domineering nature of his father to bring some kind of balance to the relationship. Consequently Steve and Cheryl seemed like two people treading water much of the time, waiting for someone to come along and rescue them. David had tried to get along with Steve, but they simply didn't have much in common; they were more like acquaintances than brothers, their conversation reduced to polite observations about the weather, their work, the odd football game.

It had taken Helen half an hour to get to the kitchen. Everyone turned to gawk at her as she pushed through the door, catching her breath.

'What's the matter, dear?' It was Noreen's sister, Jeanette. David had always spoken fondly of his Aunt Jeanette; she had a little more verve and a lot more warmth than her elder sister.

'I'm okay,' Helen managed to say. 'I just, well, I was after a cup of coffee, that's all.'

'But the coffee's all set up out in the dining room,' Cheryl squawked , grasping Helen by the elbow to propel her back out of the kitchen.

'No,' Helen protested, yanking her arm away. Everyone gaped at her.

'I was just making another pot,' said Jeanette in a voice that was kind but not condescending. No one else seemed to be able to manage that. 'Come on, I'll pour you a cup before I take it out.'

Helen met her eyes and managed a weak smile. Cheryl backed away. Everyone returned to their various tasks, cutting and slicing and buttering; nothing to see here, folks. Helen walked steadily across the kitchen to where Jeanette was pouring the steaming coffee into a cup. She smiled, handing it to her. 'There you go. Do you take milk?' she said, indicating a carton on the bench.

'I'll do it.' Helen picked up the carton and was about to pour it into her cup when she realised it was empty. She looked automatically into the mouth of the carton. 'There's no milk left,' she heard herself say.

Looking back on it, Helen couldn't say what happened next, whether she dropped the cup before she fell or whether they both went down together. All she knew was that suddenly she was bent double on the floor, crying like a child, her chest heaving with heart-wrenching sobs. Everyone had gone into a spin, clustering around her, mopping up the coffee. She remembered the feel of Jeanette's hand on her back, soothing her. 'It's okay, it's going to be okay, love.'

Helen didn't know if everything was going to be okay. Ever again. But she did know that finally she had shed tears for her dead husband. And that was at least some relief.

Central Railway Station, Sydney

Gemma stepped out of the carriage, heaving her backpack behind her. She looked up and down the platform, straining to see past the clusters of reuniting families, friends and couples, all hugging and laughing and generally being delighted to see one another. But Gemma couldn't see Phoebe. It was unlike her younger sister to be late. Phoebe was nothing if not punctual. And precise, practical, pretty, perfect. She was just the kind of person Gemma would hate, if she wasn't her sister, and she wasn't also eminently kind and good-hearted. So Gemma tried to ignore the disappointment rising in her chest, the hint of panic hovering in her stomach. It was just that she had been so looking forward to seeing a familiar face, not only after fourteen hours on a train, but after weeks of being alone, weeks of staring down the barrel of the inevitability of her situation.

'Gem! *Gemma!*'

She swung around and spotted Phoebe weaving through the crowds towards her, and immediately she felt tears welling in her throat. Oh, this was ridiculous – damned hormones.

'Sorry, sorry I'm late,' Phoebe called before she got to her. 'There were roadworks on Park Street, I got stuck for ten full minutes and then I seemed to get every single red light, and then there were no spots in the parking area . . .'

She finally came to a halt right in front of Gemma. Perfect, pretty, fabulous Phoebe. Gemma didn't think she'd ever been so happy to see anyone in her whole life, and without warning she threw her arms around her sister, hugging her tight.

'Gem . . . *Gemma*,' Phoebe protested mildly. 'Come on, we only saw each other a few weeks ago. Get a grip.' She drew back to look at Gemma, noticing the glassy eyes. 'You are going to tell me what on earth is going on, aren't you?'

'I am, of course I am,' Gemma promised. 'But I've been sitting on a train for fourteen hours – I have to get out of these clothes and into a shower.'

'You can start with why you took the train in the first place,' Phoebe persisted.

'I couldn't afford to fly.'

'I didn't think there was much difference in the fares these days.'

'There is when you can get a concession.'

Gemma saw it: Phoebe's shoulders drooped noticeably.

'Which means you're on the dole again,' she said, the resignation heavy in her voice. 'Which means Luke is out of the picture, I take it?'

'Mostly right,' Gemma confirmed, trying to stay upbeat. 'But I'm not actually on the dole, you'll be pleased to know.' It was called something different when you were pregnant.

'Oh? So how did you get a concession?'

'I'll explain when we get to your place. Give me a hand with this, would you, Phee?'

Phoebe went to pick up her backpack. 'Oh my God, Gem, what have you got in here?'

'Just my life,' she said blithely.

'Don't you think it's about time you got over the backpacking thing and bought yourself a suitcase with wheels?'

Gemma opened her mouth to say something, but she realised she didn't really have a comeback. 'Come on, one strap each and we'll manage.'

*

Phoebe's eyes had become round and wide. Her mouth too. Gemma thought she was incapable of shocking Phoebe any more. Clearly she'd got that wrong.

'You're pregnant?' Phoebe gasped. 'How did that happen?'

'Do I really need to explain it to you?'

'Don't be smart.'

Gemma had felt refreshed and revitalised after her shower. While she'd never felt particularly at home in Phoebe's uber-sophisticated professional couple's apartment conveniently located in central Pyrmont, at this particular juncture a hot shower in a pristine bathroom was better than sex, especially as sex was not exactly in the offing anyway.

When she had come back out to the living area, wrapped in Phoebe's gorgeous cosy robe, her sister had already made her one of her trademark gourmet sandwiches – roasted vegetables and God only knew what else on Turkish bread – and a pot of fragrant coffee, the aroma of which was making Gemma nauseous. She'd had to tell Phoebe her news before she threw up all over the equally offending sandwich.

'And, now that you know, well, I'm sorry you went to the trouble, Phee, but I just can't eat that,' said Gemma, pointing to the sandwich. 'And, um, the smell of coffee makes me sick.'

Phoebe took a second to twig, before whisking the pot of coffee over to the kitchen and pouring it down the sink.

'You didn't have to do that,' Gemma protested weakly, nonetheless glad that she had.

'What about tea?' asked Phoebe, running the cold water to wash all traces of the offending beverage down the sink. 'Is tea all right? I have some herbal –'

'No, weak regular tea will be fine. Thanks.'

'So what do you feel like eating?' Phoebe went on, refilling the kettle.

'Just pass me a loaf of bread and some peanut butter,' said Gemma.

Phoebe turned to look at her. 'You haven't been craving peanut butter, have you?'

Gemma blinked. 'Not particularly,' she said vaguely. 'Why?'

'There have been some studies linking overconsumption of peanut butter in pregnant women to the increased incidence of anaphylaxis from peanuts in children.'

Gemma was not exactly sure what Phoebe had just said, except somewhere in there she was pretty sure she was being accused of being a bad mother. And the baby wasn't much more than a peanut itself.

'How do you know that?' Gemma asked her. 'Or, more to the point, why do you know that?'

Phoebe shrugged. 'I read an article about it.'

That still didn't answer the 'why' part. 'Well, Phee, I'm not drinking, smoking or using any illicit substances,' said Gemma. 'So if you're going to take peanut butter away from me as well . . .'

Phoebe was already at the pantry door. 'Say no more.' A few moments later she popped a funky resin platter on the table in front of Gemma, on which she had artfully arranged a few slices of bread, a small pot of peanut butter, a matching resin-handled spreading knife, and a tiny bunch of grapes with a couple of fresh figs for garnish. It was very Martha Stewart, and not a little disturbing. The bread of course was some kind of weird brown loaf impregnated with birdseed, when Gemma craved the soft white artificial stuff. But she wasn't about to risk another lecture from Phoebe about the possible harm she might be doing to her unborn peanut.

'So,' said Phoebe, taking the Turkish-bread installation back to the kitchen, 'I take it Mum and Dad don't know yet?'

'Don't you think you would have heard by now if they did?'

'That's an understatement.'

'I was going to tell them when I was down for Dad's birthday, but when Luke didn't come I chickened out.'

'That's why you were so subdued that weekend,' Phoebe mused as she busied herself making the tea.

'Yeah, and I didn't even know he was planning his great escape at the time.'

'What do you mean?'

'I mean, he took off while I was in Sydney.'

Phoebe frowned. 'What, just like that? Where did he go?'

'Don't ask me,' said Gemma. 'I haven't heard from him since.'

'But what was the last thing he said to you?'

'I believe it was something along the lines of "I won't be able to pick you up from the airport, *babe*",' Gemma said wryly.

Phoebe carried a tray with a teapot and cups over to the table. 'Hold on, I'm not getting this . . .'

'No kidding. Phee, he just took off. He disappeared. When I got back from Sydney all his stuff was gone. He didn't tell me anything, he didn't tell them at work, he just left.'

Phoebe was staring at her in disbelief. 'Bastard.'

'Yeah, well, they seem to be drawn to me.'

'But someone can't just vanish into thin air like that.'

'Apparently they can. His mobile went out of service completely after a few days; I wouldn't be surprised if he tossed it. I called around, but we didn't know that many people in Brisbane and no one had seen him or heard from him. If they had, they weren't telling me. I got in touch with some of his old friends here in Sydney as well, but they claimed they hadn't heard anything either.'

'So where do you think he could be?'

Gemma shrugged. 'At first I thought he might have gone through with our original plan and travelled further north looking for work. So I called every resort listed, and all the islands, but no one had heard of him. I realised after a while that he was long gone, and there was no reason for me to stay up there on my own. Besides, I couldn't make the rent. I had no choice but to come back.'

Phoebe was pouring the tea, mulling it all over. 'I thought you said everything was going great with you two?'

'I thought it was,' said Gemma. 'But I can see now, in hindsight, he'd been pretty twitchy ever since I found out I was pregnant.' But of course in true Gemma style she had ignored that and carried on regardless. God, she was an idiot sometimes. 'Anyway, clearly I'm better off without him.'

'Better off without a father for your baby?'

'Phee, he was hardly "father of the year" material. Like you said, he's a bastard. And I'm beginning to think I'm a bastard magnet. If there's one in range, he's drawn to me.'

'I don't know about that,' said Phoebe. 'I seem to remember it was you doing the chasing.'

'No . . .' Gemma said weakly. Had she?

'You were always complaining how you were the one who had to keep calling him. That he never returned your calls . . .'

'*Where have you been, Luke? I've been trying to get on to you since last week.*'

'*I didn't realise I had to report in, babe.*'

'*But don't you ever check your messages?*'

'*This conversation is totally not cool, Gem . . .*'

Gemma sighed, pushing the prize-winning peanut butter platter aside. She was feeling a little queasy again.

'So when do you plan to tell Mum and Dad?' Phoebe asked.

Gemma looked at her. 'I hadn't exactly planned –'

'Come on, Gem, you can't keep a baby from them.'

'Watch me.'

Phoebe was visibly horrified.

'Look, I just need some time,' Gemma explained. 'I have to get my shit sorted out before they find out, or else . . . well, you know what they're like, Phee.'

Gemma and Phoebe's parents were typical of first-wave baby boomers – the very model of a modern middle-class family. For Gary and Trish Atkinson life was for living; it was not meant to be a hardship like their parents had made out. Of course if they'd stopped and thought about it, they would have realised their parents had not chosen to live through two world wars and a depression, but that having lived through two world wars and a depression their perspective had been reasonably and irrefutably shaped by those experiences, particularly as compared to their children, who had very little experience of genuine hardship. First-wave baby boomers had a perspective all of their own. They could do anything they wanted, be anything they wanted, and have anything they wanted. And although they had scorned the conservative aspirations of their parents' generation while they were busy getting high and discovering the soundtrack of their own, they had quickly signed up for mortgages once their free university degrees had landed them plum jobs with nice salaries, thank you very much. They might as well be paying off a house for themselves than for some greedy capitalist pig landlord, after all.

And their children were going to be brought up differently too, with the freedom to be themselves, their self-esteem nurtured, not restricted by gratuitous discipline, knowing they were deeply loved and cherished just for being who they were. But they were also going to make sure those same children were given the kinds of opportunities they had never had. While they believed absolutely in the principle of public education, and did not begrudge supporting it with their taxes, if they could afford to send their kids to private school, why shouldn't they? It was the only guaranteed way to nurture each and every child's special and unique potential.

So the Atkinson brood was among the very first of the hot-housed generation of kids raised by the new breed of permissive, indulgent, 'modern' parents who wanted to give their children everything and not have them endure even the slightest inconvenience or hardship throughout their young lives. The same parents who were confounded when those same privileged, indulged children appeared ungrateful and barely spoke to them, or else never left home and were incapable of standing on their own two feet.

First-born Ben had done exactly what was expected of him and completed a business degree straight after school, providing himself with formal qualifications to step into the position for which he had been groomed all along in the family's property development venture. Gary and Trish were so proud of their handsome son they bought him a BMW on graduation, completing his transformation into the very model of a modern eligible bachelor. He dutifully played the role for close to a decade – skiing in winter, yachting in summer, the obligatory three-month Kontiki tour through Europe, the swag of girlfriends – until he found himself a pretty ex-model to marry. In truth her modelling career consisted largely of discount store brochures and shopping mall catwalks, plus a walk-on role on *Home and Away*, so she was more than happy to become known as ex-model Mrs Leisa Atkinson on the social pages for which they were frequently snapped. As a wedding gift, Gary and Trish had given them the deposit for their first apartment in Bondi, but once baby Jasper came along, Ben and Leisa decided to move across the bridge and raise their family in Mosman, a stone's throw from the breathless grandparents. Leisa grew her hair into a blonde bob, completed the set with a baby daughter, Emily, and had recently acquired a black Mercedes four-wheel drive to ensure her family's safety on the dangerous northern peninsula roads, particularly now with all the travelling involved getting Jasper to soccer on the weekends.

And then there was Gemma.

She was the black sheep her family had to have. There was no way she would ever reach the dizzy heights Ben had scaled. Not that she wasn't smart enough; she was smart enough to know that she didn't want to throw another log on the bonfire of their vanities. And she set about making it her life's purpose to prove it. She was asked to leave a couple of the best ladies' colleges, and finally was forcibly removed from another. She experimented with alcohol, drugs and sex, had brushes with the law, moved out of home at the tender age of fifteen with the first in what would prove to be a long line of no-hoper boyfriends, only to return after a couple of months and start the hoopla all over again. All the while Gemma seemed to take strange delight in watching her parents squirm and blanch as they continued to make every excuse under the sun for her. They were always there to pick up the pieces, or more correctly pick up the tab, paying her debts and her fines while continuing to finance her increasingly hedonistic lifestyle. It became almost a sport for Gemma: she really wanted to see if she could break them. When would they say enough was enough? Apparently never. They were either idiots, or, worse, what Gemma secretly suspected and even quietly feared, throwing money at her was easier than trying to have a meaningful relationship with the person she really was.

Of course she absolutely ruined things for poor Phoebe. The reins were wound in so tight around her younger sister she could barely sneeze without her parents knowing about it. But somehow Phee managed to survive pretty much intact while keeping everyone happy, which appeared to be Phoebe's specialty. She was school captain and dux, while excelling equally in sport and music, later graduating from university with first-class honours in law. Gemma didn't know how she did it all with such grace.

'You have to learn to work with them,' Phoebe used to tell her, 'not against them. They're not trying to control your life; they just want you to be happy.'

'I am happy,' Gemma always insisted. 'Very happy.'

'But couldn't you try being happy in a way that would make them happy too?'

Gemma doubted it. She sometimes felt as though she'd landed from Mars into this strange family where she just didn't fit. She knew she wasn't what they hoped her to be. Despite all their protestations, her parents expected their children to fulfil their own hopes and dreams. And Gemma was not going to give them the satisfaction.

The prospect of another grandchild would be too much for her mother to ignore. Her need to take over would consume her; but Gemma hadn't even decided what she was going to do yet – only that she would go ahead and have the baby. Keeping it was a whole other can of worms, one she was not ready to open yet. The only thing she was sure of was that the more people who knew about the pregnancy, the less chance she had of making her own decision.

'You can't tell them, Phee,' she said seriously. 'Not yet anyway, not till I've at least got a job and somewhere to live.'

Gemma was watching Phoebe closely, watching her put all the pieces into place, waiting for the penny to drop . . .

'Um . . . what are your plans in the meantime?' Phoebe asked tentatively.

'Well, I was kind of hoping I could crash here . . . just short-term.'

Phoebe missed a beat. 'Oh . . .'

'I know it's a lot to ask –'

'No, no, it's not,' Phoebe said weakly. 'It's not that . . .'

'It's Cameron, isn't it?' Phoebe's husband. The original man of steel. Or he'd probably prefer titanium or something more upmarket. 'I know he doesn't like me, Phee.'

'Maybe that has something to do with you throwing up on his shoes the first time you met him.'

'He still hasn't gotten over that, eh?'

Phoebe shrugged. 'It's just that he likes his privacy . . . likes things to be a certain way . . . He's very . . . particular.' Phoebe sighed heavily. 'What the hell. You're my sister and you need us. Cam's just going to have to handle it.'

Balmain

Helen was sitting on the back step nursing a cup of tea between both hands, gazing out at the yard, waiting out the time till she could pick up Noah from preschool. The lawn desperately needed a mow, the edges a trim; a passionfruit vine running rampant over the shed needed to be tamed. The whole yard was looking sad and overgrown. Not that it had ever been a picture – she and David weren't exactly your *House and Garden* kind of people. Helen thought it was probably because the house wasn't actually theirs. And now she didn't know how much longer she'd be able to hang onto it. It had been going round and round in her head for weeks now, and she was still no closer to a solution. Mostly because she hadn't really done anything about it. Except mull. And that was getting her nowhere.

So she cleaned. She cleaned out cupboards and wiped down shelves, benches, walls, architraves, skirtings, windowsills, anything listed on the back of the bottle of Spray'n'Wipe. It was full of useful suggestions. Helen had sprayed and wiped parts of her house she had never thought to spray and wipe before. And it gleamed. Even Noreen had remarked how immaculate the house was looking, although she'd said it as though it was weird. Or as though Helen was weird. Clearly she was not grieving the way Noreen and Jim expected, and they intended to do something about it. And for some reason they chose Noah's birthday, of all times, to bring it up. It was a hard enough day as it was; Helen felt it was somehow wrong that birthdays and holidays kept on coming after someone had died. Christmas was almost another year away, mercifully, and she fully intended to ignore her own birthday this year. But she couldn't ignore Noah's fourth birthday, and she didn't want to. She'd even bought him Wastelanders figures, a vexed issue that had been under discussion for a while. The Wastelanders were all Noah could talk about and all he wanted, but David had been ambivalent, despite the fact that Noah only knew of them at all because of a daily five-minute cartoon on the ABC. Surely if they were on the ABC they were okay? David was inclined to agree, except they were made in the US, and he had an inherent distrust of anything that came out of the US. However, Helen believed even David would have softened under the circumstances and she went ahead and bought Noah three figures and the DVD. The look on his face as he opened them was enough to convince Helen that she'd done the right thing.

Jim and Noreen were invited for lunch in an attempt to make it a little more festive, but as soon as Noah was absorbed playing with his presents, Jim had taken Helen aside. They were prepared to look after Noah, he told her, so Helen could go back to work and things could get back to 'normal'. She'd had enough time off, he declared, she needed to get out of the house, to have something to occupy her. Helen wanted to tell him she had plenty to occupy her. There were lots more surfaces to wipe for one thing; hadn't they ever read the label on the back of the Spray'n'Wipe bottle?

The thing Jim should have realised, the thing she shouldn't have had to explain, was that she cleaned solely because it gave her something to do during those long, dire hours after Noah was tucked up in bed. There was no one singing out, 'Put the kettle on while you're up'; no one to split an after-hours, adults-only chocolate bar with, before hiding the wrapper so Noah wouldn't discover it in the morning; no one to commiserate with about the abysmal shows on TV while they sat and watched them anyway. There was no one simply to pass the time with.

So Helen cleaned till midnight, and often much later, because she couldn't go to bed until she was completely exhausted. If she wasn't completely exhausted she'd just lie there, staring at David's pillow, still in the same pillowcase because she couldn't bring herself to change it, her mind drifting to an image of him, stepping off that kerb, probably daydreaming so he didn't see the bus coming, didn't even look. It made her so angry that if he were here she'd want to shake him and tell him what his momentary lapse of concentration had done to their lives.

And then she hated herself for being angry with him, and hugged his pillow and cried herself to sleep.

It was better to stay up late cleaning.

She couldn't explain it to Jim and Noreen. They had trouble enough understanding why she couldn't go back to work, yet it was obviously untenable. Nursing meant shifts around the clock, and she had no intention of leaving Noah for whole nights and days with his grandparents. She had no intention of leaving Noah, full stop. Except for preschool, where she hovered long after the other parents had left, and was first back in the afternoon to collect him. She couldn't help it: she was filled with an overwhelming sense of dread that something was going to happen to him. After all, it was becoming increasingly evident that something bad seemed to happen to everyone Helen cared about. She woke some nights with her heart pounding in her chest, the image of a bus still vivid in her mind's eye, bearing down on Noah, standing alone, his eyes huge and wide and terrified. Sometimes David was holding him, sometimes Helen was running towards them, but she never made it to them in time. Sometimes Noah was sitting beside her as she drove the bus straight at David, which made her break into a sweat, jumping out of bed and pacing, breathing hard, till there was nothing she could do but go and find the bottle of Spray'n'Wipe and get to work.

She wasn't going mad, and despite Jim's constant nagging, she didn't need a counsellor to tell her that this was not perhaps the most constructive expression of grief and that she had to learn to trust that nothing bad was going to happen to Noah. No, she just needed to be with him at all times to make sure. What harm was there in that? She'd get over it in time, and then she could think about going back to work. Not before.

'And how are you going to live?' Jim wanted to know, as though he had a perfect right.

'I'll manage,' Helen replied, which was close to the truth. There had been a modest payout from David's superannuation fund, and she was eligible for some government benefits. If she only had herself and Noah to worry about . . .

'And what about your mother?' Jim insisted.

There was the rub. David and Helen paid Marion's fees in the nursing home in lieu of board for living in her house. It was David who had originally encouraged Helen to place her mother in care, out of nothing less than concern and regard for the both of them. Their courtship had been floundering; David was persistent, but Helen was always making excuses not to go out with him. She didn't know how to tell him about her mother, and it was becoming more and more difficult to leave her alone. Helen had fought for the maximum respite care, but even that was paltry, and so she'd cut her hours at the hospital. But it wasn't enough. Marion could no longer be trusted near the stove, having burned the base out of nearly every pot they owned, as well as the electric kettle after she'd put it to boil on the gas element. She had let the bath overflow twice, and another time Helen had come home from a late shift to find the hose on full bore in the backyard, thrashing about like an angry snake. And then she'd taken to wandering. It was not like the old days in Balmain, when everyone knew one another, the shopkeepers called you by name and neighbours looked out for the kids playing on the streets. A time when roaming Alzheimer's sufferers would have been safe.

Marion was becoming a danger to herself and potentially to others, and Helen was out of ideas and overwhelmed. David had eventually wheedled the truth out of her and insisted on meeting Marion. They hit it off immediately. Helen wondered if he reminded her somehow of Tony, or if it was simply that she enjoyed the novelty of male company. There had certainly been a dearth of that for some time. Helen had lost most of her twenties looking after her mother, and she would have spent the next decade in much the same way if David had not come along. He said he didn't mind whether they went out or not, he just wanted to be with her. He even sat with Marion some nights when Helen had to work. And gradually, respectfully, David began to point out the hopelessness of the situation. Marion needed round-the-clock supervision; sooner or later, she would have to go into care. And it was getting sooner by the day.

Helen had finally been persuaded by common sense, but insisted that if it had to be done, she was going to do it right. With David's help, she set about thoroughly researching every facility within a reasonable distance: staffing, accommodation, programs, standard of care. They fronted up for inspections armed with checklists, grilled the staff, requested references. Helen would not allow her mother to languish in a substandard anteroom for people waiting to die. She was finally won over by the warmth of the staff at Brookhaven, the location, and the pretty aspect from most of the rooms. Marion would like that.

She just had to persuade Tony.

'Are you absolutely sure she needs to be in a home?' he asked on the phone from London.

Helen groaned inwardly. 'No, maybe not, Tony, if you want to come out and look after her –'

'Oh, and how do you propose I do that?'

'Go to the airport and get on a plane to Australia. I hear Qantas is good.'

'Very funny.'

Helen wasn't trying to be funny. The unpalatable truth was that Tony seemed more worried about his inheritance than the plight of his mother. And finally that was enough to get him on a plane home in an attempt to sort it out. The issue was how they were going to pay for a facility of this standard. Helen was disinclined to sell the house, holding onto a vague, she knew irrational, hope that her mother might get better and be able to come home. At least it would be nice to be able to bring her home for special occasions. Whatever, it didn't seem right to dispose of her mother's property while she was alive. David proposed the solution that he and Helen remain in the house, which was mortgage-free, and in return cover the fees at the home. But Tony had argued that possession was nine-tenths of the law, and if they occupied the house till Marion's eventual death, the legalities of the situation might become clouded. Although Helen tried to reassure him till she was blue in the face that neither she nor David had any intention of ripping him off, Tony remained unconvinced. Helen would never have expected this from her brother. They used to be close; she couldn't understand why he was making things so difficult.

'Then I guess we'll have to sell up,' Helen said, hurt and frustrated by the whole saga. Tony seemed particularly touchy about any input David had to offer, and Helen was tired of adjudicating between them. 'We'll put the money into a trust account to cover Mum's costs.'

But Tony didn't like that idea either. 'The house is worth a small bloody fortune, Hel. You don't just hand it over to a solicitor – it'll all be gobbled up by management fees.'

Helen sighed. 'Then what do you want me to do, Tony?'

He finally relented and agreed to have them stay in the house, though that didn't stop him from having complex legal papers drawn up, clearly detailing right of succession and God only knew what else, and presenting them to Helen for her signature. David thought she should have her own solicitor look them over, but Helen was heartily sick of the whole business by then. Besides, it didn't seem right to turn around and distrust her brother when she'd been so upset that he hadn't trusted her. In the end Helen was just anxious to get her mother settled and make sure she was going to be all right in her new surroundings. She signed the papers, Tony went back to London, and Marion was finally moved to Brookhaven.

At first Helen didn't know what to do with herself. She spent so much time at Brookhaven the staff joked they were going to have to give her her own parking space. Caring for her mother had been the focus of her life for so long, she'd forgotten what else there was to do. Her father had died when Helen was a teenager, and though clearly grief-stricken by her loss, Marion had seemed all right for a while, slowly coming to terms with living without her beloved Anthony. But when Tony left for overseas, things began to go awry. Helen had to be with her more and more. She had had no other life till David came along. And then the two of them had cocooned themselves snugly against the world. Helen wasn't sure why. David did find socialising a bit frivolous; he wasn't into sport or popular culture, he said he preferred to spend his time with intelligent people discussing important, or at the very least interesting, issues. But they didn't really do much of that either. Between work and Marion, and eventually Noah, there had been little time for socialising anyway. And no need, it had seemed. They had each other.

But now he was gone, and Helen had never felt so alone. She had no one to talk to, no old friends, no work colleagues, no one, it seemed. She felt isolated and adrift in the world. David had been her compass, and without him she'd lost direction.

Helen blinked back tears. She had to stop feeling sorry for herself. It didn't achieve anything; it certainly wouldn't solve her problems.

What would David do? What would he advise her to do?

He would assess the facts of the situation in a calm, rational manner, because that's how David did things, calmly and rationally. And the facts were that Helen could not afford to pay the fees at Brookhaven indefinitely, but neither could she give up the house. Not now, not right now. David would definitely have felt it was important for Noah to have continuity and to feel secure, but that was only the half of it. Helen had no idea where to go to from here, so staying put was the safest option.

The Ship Inn

'You didn't really expect to be able to waltz right back in to your old job, did you, Gem?'

She wouldn't have knocked it back.

'No, of course I didn't, Lauren,' Gemma dismissed the idea. 'I'm just putting the feelers out. I thought there might be something going, and you know what they say, better the devil you know.'

'I don't know if that'll work both ways,' Lauren said dubiously. 'You pissed off more than a few people, the way you upped and left like that.'

Gemma grimaced. She didn't have to be told she'd pissed people off; she was well aware of that. She had walked out of Bailey's on a Friday afternoon and not showed up for work on the Monday, or ever again – no call, no explanation. She and Luke had made a spontaneous decision over the weekend to take off. It was too exciting, too romantic, too wild. And it was the weekend – who was she going to call anyway?

That was why she didn't want to call anyone from her old team now, and certainly not Charlie, not till she knew the lie of the land. So she'd got in touch with Lauren instead, who she could totally count on knowing the lie of the land. Lauren knew everything that went on within the halls and offices and boardrooms at Bailey & Partners, and she told it like it was. She could be a right pain in the arse, her honesty bordering on plain rude sometimes. They had worked together when Gemma first started at Bailey's as an admin assistant, and Lauren was still in admin to this day – her comfort zone, as she liked to call it.

She had agreed to meet for a drink, though of course Gemma wasn't drinking. That was nearly the worst bloody part of this whole thing. She couldn't even get drunk that first night when she realised Luke had left her – the mere smell of alcohol made her queasy these days. Pregnancy was like an enforced good behaviour bond. Wasn't having a baby punishment enough? So Gemma insisted on buying their drinks, and Lauren had no idea that her friend's bourbon and dry had no bourbon in it. For as long as her body would oblige, Gemma intended to keep the pregnancy to herself. It would close too many doors, and she didn't have that many open to her in the first place.

She had worked at Bailey's for three years prior to her fateful meeting with Luke. It was the longest Gemma had ever stayed in one job, the first time she hadn't become bored. She'd never thought of advertising as a career option; truth be told, she'd never thought in terms of a career at all. She'd been doing waitressing and bar work on and off for years, and frankly she just got tired of working when her friends were partying. She wanted a day job. So she registered with a temp agency and went out on various typical admin gigs, answering phones, typing, filing, general dogsbody stuff. It was hardly stimulating, but Gemma didn't care. She didn't have to be on her feet all day, the carpet didn't smell of stale beer, and she could knock off work in time to meet her friends any night she pleased. And the weekends were totally, blissfully, to herself. It was a pity she seemed to spend them either inebriated or hungover.

Then she'd landed at Bailey's. It was a big, sexy advertising agency located smack in the centre of the city in vast modern offices of steel and glass, peopled by designer-label executives and uber-cool creative dudes. At first Gemma was immune to its particular charms, delighting in taking the piss out of the place when she was with her friends. But despite herself, she began to become fascinated with the whole process. She found herself working harder than she ever had before, staying late, showing initiative, offering ideas, being noticed. She became their temp of choice, her contract was renewed again and again as she was moved out of admin and around to virtually every team. Before long she was made permanent and became assistant to one of the production coordinators. Gemma loved it. It was dynamic and fast and fun; she was using her brain in ways she never had before and discovering skills she hadn't known she possessed. She had never imagined work could be like this. She was pushing thirty and for the first time in her life she had a real job that she wanted to stick at.

And then she met Luke.

He was a friend of a friend of a friend in her old crowd. Gemma hadn't been out with them in ages. She protested she was too busy, but they all knew she was drifting away. She finally made one too many excuses and they were beginning to feel slighted. So she vowed to make it to their next soiree, and Luke was there. She spotted him immediately. He had that offhand, effortless charisma that was sexy as all get-out. Gemma found herself completely entranced, and she found herself in his bed that same night. As they became entangled, work became mundane again. Luke made her think about what she was doing – selling people stuff they didn't need, helping to turn the cogs in the capitalist wheel, whoring herself at the altar of crass commercialism – for what? To work her guts out for someone else for the rest of her life?

Luke made her question, he made her doubt, he made her pack it all in and follow him up to Queensland.

And then he dumped her there.

'Personally, I could never understand what you saw in him,' Lauren said, after Gemma had recounted her sorry tale, albeit a tightly edited version. 'He was a bit of a drop-kick if you ask me.'

Gemma sat glumly, sucking her dry ginger ale through a straw. Of course he was a drop-kick. She'd never had good taste in men. The light of her infatuation tended to blind her temporarily and it was only when it faded that she could see them for what they really were. Unfortunately, it had taken a little longer to fade than usual with Luke.

What had she been thinking? Leaving a good job to follow him and go back to being a waitress? It had seemed like a good idea at the time. Maybe she'd known on some level that it would be her last chance to be foolish and free and do something totally on a whim.

And so life decided to bite back and teach her a lesson in being responsible. And what a lesson. No wonder Luke had done a runner. She would have run given the chance. But of course she was left holding the baby – if she ran, it came right along with her.

'So Lauren, do you know if there's an opening at Bailey's?' Gemma asked, returning to the reason she was here. If she thought too much about how she had got here, it was just depressing. 'Anything at all that might be coming up?'

Lauren thought about it. 'There might be something, but it's not on a team.'

'Doesn't matter,' she said. 'I just need a job at the moment.'

'Okay, well, the MD's assistant is about seven months' pregnant –'

'Hold on,' Gemma said, frowning. 'Liz is pregnant? I didn't even know she was seeing anyone. And since when did you start calling Jonesy the "MD"?'

Lauren blinked at her. 'Oh, jeez, I forgot. You must have left just before it all happened.'

'Before all what happened?'

'Jonesy was dumped.'

'What?' Gemma was shocked. Jonesy was the heart of Bailey's, the soul, the life of the party. His motto was that it wasn't worth doing if you weren't having fun. 'When . . . how . . . why?'

'Like I said, it must have been just after you left,' said Lauren. 'He totally stuffed up this major account, didn't meet the deadline, the budget blew out. The clients went ballistic and wanted his head, so the board presented it to them on a platter.'

'They made Jonesy the scapegoat?'

'Nuh,' Lauren shook her head, 'he deserved it. Turns out he'd been working over budget for ages. The business was in a mess and they were talking about cutting staff, even consolidating into one headquarters in Melbourne, which meant heaps of people would have lost their jobs. In the end they brought in this management whiz from the Melbourne office to clean up the mess. Now the reins have never been tighter, believe you me.'

Gemma was still taking it all in. 'What happened to Liz?'

'She didn't want to work for the new guy, so she left. Then he interviewed about seven hundred girls to find a replacement, finally hired one, and a month later she tells him she's pregnant. She reckons she didn't know when she went for the job. Anyway, he was going to sack her on the spot, but she pleaded with him that she needed the money, so he gave her a stay of execution. That was a few months ago. Kelly was only telling me the other day that he asked HR to start advertising again.' Lauren paused, thinking. 'You were friendly with Kel, why don't you give her a call? I reckon if she put in a good word for you, the MD would probably be glad not to have to go through all that rigmarole all over again.'

'I don't know . . .' Gemma's head was spinning. Opportunity was right in front of her, there for the taking, she could almost touch it, but she'd never get away with it. Would she? What was going to happen in a few months' time when she turned around and had to tell whatshisname she was also having a baby? What was this guy's name anyway?

'Why do you keep calling him the MD?' Gemma asked. 'Are things that formal now?'

'Not really,' Lauren said. 'His initials are MD as well, so that's what everyone started calling him, and it stuck.'

'What does the MD stand for?'

'*Something* Davenport . . .' Lauren was thinking. 'Malcolm or Myles or Marcus, something poncy . . . sounds like the captain of the rowing team at a private school.'

Gemma's heart was sinking so low she suspected her toes would register a pulse. 'So I take it he's not winning any popularity contests?'

Lauren shrugged. 'There's not really anything wrong with him, I guess, but he's no Jonesy. The whole mood of the place has changed. Like I said, he runs a tight ship now, he keeps an eye on pretty much everything. But otherwise, socially and that, he seems to keep to himself. I suppose it can't be easy for him.' She considered Gemma's strained expression. 'Seriously, give Kelly a call. Things are so tight, there'll be no new positions coming up for ages. You might as well go for this one. What have you got to lose?'

Balmain

'How are you going to afford to pay for the nursing home?' were almost Tony's first words on the phone from London. He'd swiftly dispensed with the 'how are you' plus a mumbled apology about not being able to get back for the funeral, before cutting right to the chase.

'Sorry to put it so bluntly,' he went on, 'but you have lost a wage.'

Was it possible for him to be more insensitive?

'Tony,' Helen replied levelly, 'I've lost a husband.'

'I know that, Hel, I'm just looking at the big picture, because I doubt that you are. I'm worried about you.'

No, he wasn't. Once upon a time maybe. But Helen didn't know what his agenda was anymore.

'How will you cope?' he went on. 'Those fees aren't cheap, and you're a single mother now.'

'I'm a widow, Tony.'

'Which is worse: you won't be getting any child support.'

Christ.

'How are you going to get by?'

'If you're so concerned,' said Helen, 'you could always contribute to Mum's fees for a while, till I get on my feet again.'

There was a significant pause. 'Hel, if you need anything, you only have to ask,' he said carefully. 'But you have to be realistic about your situation.'

Helen could feel a tightening in her chest. 'What are you suggesting, Tony?'

'I'm only thinking, do you and Noah even need such a big place? The two of you must be rattling around there these days.'

'Are you saying you want to kick your only sister and your only nephew out on the street?'

'Of course I'm not saying that.' He sighed. 'Helen, I realise this is an emotional time for you, but I don't know how you can even suggest that I'd see you out on the street. I was only thinking you might be much more comfortable in a nice little townhouse, without all the maintenance –'

'It's not a good time to sell,' Helen said flatly.

'On the contrary, I've been looking online and the market's quite strong at the moment.'

'Not everything comes down to economics, Tony! Mum is still alive. If we sold the house, that money would have to sit in a trust for her. You couldn't get your hands on it anyway.'

Her words seemed to echo down the line, all the way to London.

'That's not fair, Hel. I wasn't thinking of myself. I'm thinking of you and Noah.'

He sounded genuinely hurt, but then again it was hard to tell. He worked in the theatre, after all.

'Well, it wouldn't make any difference to my situation,' Helen said after a while. 'I either live here rent-free and support Mum, or I pay rent somewhere else. I'd be struggling to do either right now.'

There was silence for a moment.

'It sounds like you've found yourself in that most unenviable of places, little sister,' Tony said finally.

'Oh, where's that?'

'Smack bang between a rock and somewhere just as hard.'

Helen felt the lump rising rapidly in her chest, and a sob escaped before she could do anything to stop it.

'Oh, don't,' said Tony, but not unkindly. 'That's how you always got around me when we were kids. And Dad. Mum never fell for it though.'

Helen sniffed, collecting herself. 'That's because you were her favourite.'

'Mum didn't play favourites.'

'She still asks for you,' said Helen, 'every single time. She doesn't even know me most days.'

'There's nothing I can do about that, Hel,' Tony said quietly. 'It isn't my fault, I wish you wouldn't always think the worst of me.'

'I don't.'

'I'm really not the selfish bastard you think I am.'

'I don't think that –'

'I know it's been hard on you, with me living over here. And I'd send you money if I had it, but London is so expensive, you have no idea . . .' His voice trailed off, and then he cleared his throat. 'You know I'm sharing this place with three other people, and one bloke's just moved out. We're all struggling to cover his share of the rent while we find someone to take his place.' He paused. 'Hey, why don't you do that?'

'What?' Hadn't he just said 'find someone to take his place'? What was he suggesting . . .?

'Get someone in to share the expenses,' said Tony.

Helen felt queasy. 'What are you talking about?'

'A boarder.'

'What, a total stranger?'

'Well, not once they start living with you –'

'I don't think I could do that, Tony.'

'Look, I'm just saying it's an option, Hel,' he said. 'And you don't seem to have a whole lot of those.'

'Thanks for reminding me,' she said glumly.

After another pause, Tony said, 'Are you getting any counselling, Hel?'

'Why do you ask?'

'I just think it'd be good to talk to someone about all this.'

Helen didn't say anything.

'Look, I have to go,' said Tony. 'But, listen, call me, Hel, any time, even if you just want to talk. You should call me more often.' He paused. 'We've got out of the habit the last few years, and I miss talking to you. You know we've only got each other now, Hel.'

She breathed out. 'I know.'

Pyrmont

Gemma rolled over with a groan. Her bladder was giving her a nudge. Again. She'd already got up once at four. She'd heard somewhere it was nature's way of preparing the mum-to-be for interrupted sleep. After all, that's the only kind of sleep she'd be getting for the next three years, give or take. Mother Nature was a bitch.

Her bladder could not be ignored any longer. She opened one eye and squinted out. Daylight. Perhaps if she kept squinting the whole way to the bathroom and back again, she could trick her body into believing it hadn't actually woken up, and she'd be able to go straight back to sleep. She peered out through barely opened lids and climbed carefully out of bed, as though she was trying not to wake a sleeping partner. She crept from the bedroom, down the hall to the bathroom, lifted her nightie and sat. Aargh! Straight onto cold porcelain! She jumped up, looking behind, scowling at the toilet bowl as she slammed the seat down. She hated men.

Gemma sat back on the toilet, wide awake now. She turned to focus on the digital clock conveniently located at eye level on the vanity cabinet. Phoebe was a time-management freak and she had clocks in every room, sometimes more than one. She probably timed her toilet stops: forty-five seconds for ones, three minutes thirty for twos.

The vanity clock had just ticked over to 8.40. Gemma supposed it could have been worse. She listened for signs of life, but it was quiet in the apartment. Well, as quiet as Pyrmont could get. There was never any respite from the traffic noise; it was like living in the middle of a freeway. Which, come to think of it, was a pretty apt description of the suburb.

Phoebe and Cameron were probably still sleeping it off after their big night last night. And what an excruciating night that had turned out to be. Gemma had had to stay sober while a bunch of finance and law prats jostled verbally with each other to prove who was richest and cleverest and could drop the most designer names for everything, right down to gardening tools and cooking utensils, for chrissakes. Food was an obsession. Phoebe knew her stuff, and with thorough preparation and planning her menu had been a triumph of style over substance, incorporating the hippest, coolest ingredients sourced with varying degrees of difficulty from the hippest, coolest purveyors of foodstuffs across the city. Her guests had been suitably impressed, though quick to detail their own recent culinary feats to the oohs and aahs of their little coterie. They were like a bunch of preschoolers trying to outdo each other in the sandpit. It was nauseating, which Gemma found all the more annoying as she'd only just got over her morning sickness.

She stepped in front of the mirror and considered her reflection. Her blonde mop could do with a cut – she was getting a bit of a surfie-chick, bed-hair look about her, and even Gemma conceded she was too old to get away with that. She turned sideways. Did she look pregnant? She had to meet this MD bod next week and she didn't want to look even vaguely pregnant. She caught her nightie in close at the back so that the thin fabric clung to her silhouette. Her breasts were definitely bigger, which wouldn't go against her. She smoothed her hand over her belly. Although she felt bloated, there was really nothing to show for it yet. Gemma had been blessed – or cursed, depending on what style of clothing she was trying to fit into – with a pear-shaped figure. At its worst, too much on the bottom and not enough up top, but passable most of the time. She only hoped these so-called childbearing hips would live up to their name and provide the peanut with a nice little hideout where it could remain tucked away discreetly for the time being.

Gemma heard noises at the front door. She walked down the hall to the living area just as Phoebe and Cameron bounded in, their faces shiny with perspiration, wearing not quite matching, but certainly coordinated jogging outfits.

'You cannot be serious,' said Gemma, putting her hands on her hips. 'Please tell me you haven't been for a run?'

'If you want,' Phoebe panted, heading for the fridge, 'but it wouldn't be the truth.'

'You were both pissed as newts last night.'

'We weren't *pissed*,' Cameron denied.

'Were too,' said Gemma. 'I'm surprised you could get out of bed, let alone run anywhere.'

'Running's good for a hangover,' said Phoebe, passing Cameron a bottle of water. 'Gets the heart pumping and the blood flowing to clear all the toxins away.'

'Not that we were pissed,' Cameron added.

'You were all pissed from where I was sitting,' said Gemma. 'It was excruciating.'

'That's only because you're usually more pissed than anyone,' Cameron threw at her.

'Ah, those were the days,' Gemma returned, unfazed.

'I'm going to have a shower,' he said as he walked up the hall.

'So, last night,' said Gemma, perching herself on the edge of the table. 'Did you have a good time?'

'Yeah, I'd say it was a success.'

'No, what I was actually asking was whether *you* had a good time.'

Phoebe crossed her arms in front of herself. 'What are you getting at, Gem?'

She shrugged. 'Well, I was just wondering . . . would you call those people last night close friends, Phee?'

'I don't know . . . we have lots of friends,' she said defensively.

Gemma walked over to the fridge and opened the door. 'They just don't seem like your kind of people.'

'Well, maybe you don't know me as well as you think,' Phoebe said airily.

Gemma smiled, glancing at her sister. 'I know you used to eat snails out of the garden before you knew they were escargots and –' she straightened, flourishing one hand and affecting an accent, '– *so* 1980s, darling. Who was that prat Duncan?'

'Duncan Reynolds. He's senior partner at the largest law firm in the country. He's very influential and very rich.'

'Then why doesn't he go out and buy himself a decent personality?' Gemma said, picking up a bottle of juice and closing the fridge door again.

Phoebe slumped in defeat. 'God, I know, he's *such* a bore.'

Gemma swung around, her eyes lit up. 'Ha! You big fake!' She pointed a finger accusingly at her sister. 'What are you doing hanging around with people like that, Phee?'

'I don't *hang around* with them,' she said. 'Cam just likes to network with the right people.'

'He must have been thrilled no end to have me here,' Gemma said wryly. 'They all looked at me like I had a disease when I told them I was a waitress.'

'Yeah, well, you could just as easily have said you work in advertising, if you'd wanted to fit in.'

'Why would I want to fit in with that lot?' Gemma said, pouring herself a glass of juice. 'Besides, I wouldn't have a hope. I felt like Bridget Jones, only pregnant.'

'Bridget Jones did get pregnant in the final instalment.'

'Did she? Who was the father?'

Phoebe looked at her. 'Do you really want to have a conversation about the paternity of Bridget Jones's baby?'

'It'd be better than some of the conversations going on around me last night,' Gemma groaned. 'Work and real estate were all anyone could talk about.'

'Well, maybe when you have a job and you can afford somewhere to live, you'll feel comfortable sitting at the grown-ups' table.'

'Ouch,' said Gemma. 'I told you I'm going to start looking for a place.'

'And I told you it's not a problem you staying here.'

'Obviously it is.'

'I was only joking about the grown-ups' table, Gem.'

'I know,' said Gemma. 'It's not you. Cameron can barely stand having me here a few weeks, he'd have a stroke if you told him I was staying indefinitely.'

Phoebe started to protest the unprotestable.

'Besides,' Gemma talked over her, 'Mum and Dad are going to end up finding out if I don't get out of here soon.'

'They have to find out sooner or later, Gem.'

'I'm opting for later.'

Phoebe leaned back against the kitchen bench. 'They have a right to know –'

'Are we going to have this argument again? One thing at a time is the best I can do, Phee, and grandparents' rights are not exactly high on my list of priorities.'

Gemma picked up the glass of juice and sculled it back. Phoebe was watching her. 'You know you can see right through that nightie. Your tits are enormous.'

'I know, aren't they great?' said Gemma, smoothing the nightie over her breasts. 'The one time in my life I've really got a rack and I've got no one to appreciate it.'

'Gem!' Phoebe frowned.

'What?'

'You're pregnant.'

'So, I'm not a nun,' said Gemma. 'Do you expect me to stop having sex?'

'I expect you won't have a lot of opportunity, not while you're pregnant.'

'I've heard some guys really get off on the idea of doing it with a pregnant woman.'

Phoebe grimaced. 'Well, now that you've loaded me up with that mental image, would you mind getting dressed before Cam comes out of the shower?'

'Okay, okay.' She drifted off up the hall. 'Hey, I thought later you might want to help me find something to wear for my interview?' she said, turning halfway around.

'Sure,' said Phoebe. 'Where do you want to look?'

'I was thinking we could start in your wardrobe.'

Balmain

Helen had been trailing the bus for blocks now. Stopping, lurching forward, stopping again. It was Friday afternoon and the streets were clogged. She couldn't get around it, she couldn't get away from it, she couldn't do anything but sit behind it, staring at the garish ad for some kind of lolly-flavoured alcoholic drink, three bottles lined up doing the can-can, with leering big grins on their labels. Why not just say it up front? Come on, kids, try us, we taste like soft drink so you can get drunk really easily! How much more fun can you get in a bottle?

'Mummy,' said Noah from his car seat in the back.

'Yes, Noah?'

'Is atta bus what smooshed Daddy?'

Helen turned her head sharply to look at him. 'What did you say?'

She had struggled over telling Noah the actual details of David's accident, but he had to be told something, and she and David had always been honest with him. David was scrupulous about that. He would have told him, she knew in her heart, so it seemed only right that she tell Noah the truth. Jim and Noreen had been horrified when they found out. They more or less accused her of child abuse. She wished she could handle them the way David had, but she was completely out of her depth.

'Is atta bus what smooshed Daddy?' Noah was repeating insistently, in almost a singsong rhyme.

Helen tried to collect herself. He was a child, asking an innocent question. She had to hold it together. But she was beginning to find it difficult to breathe. She opened her window to get some fresh air, though how she thought that was possible on Darling Street at peak hour, she didn't know.

'Uh, I don't think so, Noah,' she answered finally, looking over her shoulder at him. 'That bus was in the city, near Daddy's work.' She turned to look ahead again. Her hands trembled as they rested on the steering wheel.

'Mummy?'

'Yes, Noah?'

'Did it hurt Daddy?'

Helen's heart froze. 'What, darling?'

'Getting smooshed.'

Her throat was dry. 'It happened too fast, Noah. Daddy wouldn't have felt anything.'

'Why didn't Daddy hold sum'n's hand?'

Helen turned around again. 'What do you mean, sweetheart?'

'Daddy did tell me one day that I always haffa hold sum'n's hand across a road or else I'll get smooshed by a bus. Why didn't Daddy hold sum'n's hand?

'. . . Mummy?

'Whata matta, Mummy?

'Why you crying, Mummy?'

One week later

'Actually, it was my husband's, um, my parents-in-law who thought I should come.'

'Oh?' said Jill. She'd told Helen to call her Jill. She was the bereavement counsellor provided through the State Transit Authority to the families of accident victims. It was a free service. She'd be mad not to take advantage of it, Jim had insisted.

'Have your husband's parents received any counselling?' Jill asked.

'I don't know,' said Helen.

'Well, if they needed you to come,' said Jill, 'you can tell them you came.'

'Pardon?'

'You don't have to stay, Helen,' she said plainly.

Helen was confused. Was she being dismissed? 'I'm sorry?'

'This is an incredibly personal and painful thing to have to talk about, and if you're not prepared to do that, if that's not something you want to do, or feel the need to do, well, you shouldn't have to do it because someone else thinks it's what you should do.'

Helen nodded faintly.

'Please, feel free to go. It's okay.'

Helen let a moment or two pass, and then shrugged. 'Well, I guess I'm here now.'

'All right,' said Jill. 'We can talk for a while if you like.'

'About the accident?'

'That's up to you.'

'But you do know what happened, don't you?'

'I've read the report from the inquest, if that's what you mean. That didn't tell me much.'

That's what Helen thought as well. The inquest didn't tell her anything, except too much detail about David's injuries, which only served to further fuel her nightmares. But it didn't tell her how something like this could have happened, much less why it happened.

'It certainly didn't tell me anything about you, Helen,' Jill went on, 'and you're the one sitting here in front of me.'

'What do you want to know about me?' Helen said warily.

'Whatever you feel like telling me.'

Helen wasn't so sure she felt like telling Jill anything about herself. Besides, what was there to tell?

'I think they . . . my parents-in-law expected that you'd fix me somehow, so that I can get over it and move on. They want me to go back to work.'

'Is that what you want?'

Helen shook her head. 'I don't feel ready. I'm a nurse; I don't think I'd be very good at taking care of other people at the moment.'

'That's understandable. People going through a bereavement often describe a "limbo" period where they just don't want to have to do anything, or make any decisions.'

Helen was listening. 'Is that one of the stages of grief? I remember learning about them during my nursing training. Um, somebody Kübler-Ross, wasn't it?'

'That's correct,' said Jill. 'But it's not really the accepted theory any more. Not that someone who's grieving might not have all the feelings Kübler-Ross described, but to fit them to prescribed stages is to ignore that we're all individuals and that we all grieve in our own way.' She paused. 'Have you heard of chaos theory, Helen?'

'When a butterfly flaps its wings there'll be a hurricane on the other side of the world?'

'Something like that.' Jill nodded. 'The theory is about cause and effect, but how, why, when and where a cause will lead to an effect we can rarely ever know, because of all the unpredictable variables.'

'I'm not sure what that has to do with me.'

'You're an individual, Helen. There are plenty of people who have suffered loss as great as you, there are people suffering the same loss as you now – your in-laws, for example. However, no two people will experience the same bereavement. There is no one with your precise history, in your precise circumstances, so no one can tell you how or what you should be feeling.'

Sometimes Helen wished someone would. Tell her what to feel, what to do next, how to go on.

'I guess I just want to know how to get over this.'

'Forgive me for being blunt, Helen, but why should you get over it? You've suffered an enormous loss. I don't imagine you'll ever get over it.'

Helen was taken aback. What Jill was suggesting was too frightening a prospect. If she couldn't get over it, she'd end up like her mother, and she simply couldn't do that to Noah. Somehow she had to stop herself from sinking.

'But I don't want to feel like this forever,' said Helen. 'My mother, she never got over the death of my father, and now she has Alzheimer's.'

Jill's forehead creased into a slight frown. 'Surely the doctors have told you that Alzheimer's is a physical deterioration of the brain, that it's not caused by grief?'

Helen just looked at her.

'But it worries you anyway?'

She nodded.

'Helen, when I said that I can't see you'd ever get over the death of your husband, I wasn't suggesting that you'll feel this intensely for the rest of your life,' said Jill. 'But this will change you immutably. You can't ever be the person you were before the accident. It's impossible. It's like saying to someone who's lost an arm, you won't be any different. Of course they will. But they can learn to adjust, learn ways to get by. They can still have a full life.'

With only one arm, Helen sighed inwardly.

'The point I'm trying to make,' Jill went on, 'is that if you only focus on trying to get over David's death, to move on, it will feel insurmountable because it is insurmountable. The reality is, his death will be a part of your life from now on. It's not the end of your relationship. You'll always have a relationship with him in your heart, and if you can come to terms with that, own this new reality, you can adjust and live your life within it.'

Helen was still doubtful. Her father's death had remained the defining feature of her mother's life, and Marion's reality had been altered forever, but not in a way Helen wanted for herself, or for Noah. Helen was frightened to let go, but holding on was frightening as well; it seemed she would remain in limbo for some time yet.

Sydney Airport

'As you can see from my résumé I've had experience across all aspects of the advertising industry,' Gemma said confidently.

'Yes, and all under the one roof, the very same one you want to come back and work under again.'

She had finally been granted an audience with the infamous MD, at four in the afternoon at the airport, take it or leave it. After postponing twice, he'd finally agreed to meet her in the business lounge between flights. Okay, he was a busy man, she got it. Five minutes into the interview Gemma was already regretting she'd come. The MD had the personality of a slab of granite but with less charm. And he needed a stylist. Badly. He was wearing grey pants with a white business shirt and a navy tie; he looked like he was a clerk in the tax office, not heading up *the* cutting-edge advertising agency in Sydney. And while his glasses had black frames in the latest profile, his haircut was a shocker; Gemma doubted he'd changed the style in a decade, possibly longer. Clearly the glasses had been a case of more good luck than good taste.

'You've had far more extensive experience waitressing and bartending,' he was saying.

'You have a problem with that?' asked Gemma, hanging onto her dignity by a thread.

'Not at all.' He glanced at her over his glasses. 'I'd just like to understand how all of your previous experience equips you to fill this position. You worked for a lot of years in the hospitality industry.

Then you started here in an admin role, and in no time you'd made it onto a team.'

'What can I tell you.' Gemma shrugged. 'I have a knack.'

'I don't doubt that,' he said. 'Your progress was almost as rapid as your departure.'

Bugger. He'd been talking to people.

'Look, Kelly has recommended you highly – it could only be an asset to have someone with your experience. But I want to make something very clear, Ms Atkinson.' He was looking straight at her. 'I need someone who will be committed to this role, not have their eye on another section the whole time. This is not a foot-in-the-door job. I need a stayer. Someone reliable, someone I can trust.'

Fuck. This was it. The man was asking her for something she couldn't give. Not long-term.

But on the other hand, how did anyone know what life held for them next year, next month, Christ, even next week? She certainly hadn't even expected to meet Luke, let alone get pregnant and then get dumped. She hadn't predicted any of what had happened to her in the past few months, so how could she predict the next few months?

Gemma had always held to the mantra 'Be true to thyself'. That didn't necessarily mean being true to every Tom, Dick and Managing Director, blabbing every last intimate detail about herself in a job interview. She was entitled to hold onto a little privacy; she had no doubt the MD kept plenty to himself. So she would do what she usually did: go with the flow and worry about the consequences once the consequences made themselves known.

'Mr Davenport,' Gemma began, 'this is the job I'm here for and this is the job I want. I'll be the best PA you ever had, and if you don't think so in three months, then you won't have to ask me to leave – I'll go of my own volition.'

*

Genius. That last stroke had been pure genius. It gave her at least one, albeit tenuous, hook to hang onto when and if she lasted long enough to have to explain herself to him. Now she had to find her own place as soon as humanly possible. Cameron had made it abundantly clear he couldn't abide living with her longer than he absolutely had to, and Gemma was only too happy to put him out of his misery.

She sang out as she came through the door of the apartment, but only the ubiquitous traffic noise greeted her. She glanced at the clock on the wall; it was probably a little early for either of them to be home. Gemma kicked off Phoebe's shoes and unzipped her skirt, breathing out with relief. God, she was going to have to start getting those ugly elastic-waisted clothes before long. She walked over to the sound system and slotted her iPhone in, brought up a playlist and pressed start, turning the volume up loud to drown out the traffic noise. She wiggled out of the skirt along to the music, stepping out of it where it had dropped, and slipped off her jacket, tossing it onto the sofa. She danced across to the fridge and opened the door of the freezer, where she knew she would find Phoebe's illicit stash of Caramel Toffee Crunch ice cream. Grabbing a spoon from the cutlery drawer and the phone from its cradle on the wall, Gemma sashayed across to the desk and plonked down in front of the computer. She put the ice cream aside for now: she liked to wait for it to soften. She should have been toasting her success with champagne, but Caramel Toffee Crunch would have to do. At least she didn't have to worry about her waistline, seeing as she barely had one to speak of anymore.

Gemma googled 'share accommodation Sydney'. She couldn't afford a place on her own, especially once the peanut arrived. Not that she was altogether sure yet that she was going to be bringing it home. She didn't like thinking about the alternative, but it was even worse when she tried to imagine herself with an actual baby, caring for it, being responsible for it. It was slightly terrifying, in fact. So she would continue to focus on one thing at a time. She had a job, now she needed a place to live. And sharing was her best option for the meantime.

However, half an hour and after nearly half the container of ice cream later, Gemma was rapidly getting nowhere. She'd sent off a dozen emails, but she wasn't having a good strike rate. Maybe she shouldn't have mentioned she was pregnant. Gemma didn't really blame any of them; if she was in their shoes she wouldn't want to live with her either. The prospect of sharing a house with a screaming, poo-shooting bundle of helpless humanity was daunting enough for Gemma, and *she* was going to be related to it.

'He-*llo!*' Phoebe and Cameron had suddenly materialised in the entrance to the living area. Gemma hadn't heard them come in, probably because of the music.

'Good news,' she announced loudly. 'I got the job!'

Phoebe gave her a weak smile. 'That's great,' she said, watching Cameron as he strode across to the sound system and flicked it off.

'Can't hear yourself think in here,' he muttered, shaking his head like a disappointed headmaster.

'Sorry,' Gemma chirped. She wasn't even going to let Cameron get to her today. 'You'll be pleased to know I'm looking for somewhere to live, as we speak.'

'Alleluia.'

'Cam,' Phoebe chided as she proceeded to pick up the pieces of her suit from the floor and the sofa.

'Hope you're enjoying that ice cream,' Cameron said to Gemma, crossing his arms and glaring at her. 'Seeing as no one else can now you've eaten it straight from the tub.'

She frowned at him. 'I'll replace it, okay?' Gemma glanced across at Phoebe for backup, but she apparently had nothing to add.

'So, have you found anything promising?' Phoebe asked.

'Plenty, it's just that they don't want me.'

'And to think, these are people who don't even know you,' Cameron sniggered.

Phoebe sighed quietly, returning her attention to Gemma. 'What do you mean, they don't want you? Why not?'

'What do you think? The peanut, of course.'

'Peanut?'

'The sprog, the spawn, the bun in my oven . . .'

Phoebe looked troubled, frowning and biting the edge of her lip. But Gemma had a feeling it didn't necessarily have anything to do with her.

'No worries,' Gemma said brightly. 'I'll keep trying. It's only the first time I've looked. Something'll come up.' She peered at the screen again. 'I was about to call this one actually . . . where is it . . .

Ah – "Quiet thirty plus pref. female to share three-bedroom house with woman and four-year-old boy. Board and bills."'

Cameron was making a low, chuckling sound. 'You, quiet?'

Fuck off, Cameron.

'I am a lot quieter these days,' she said squarely. 'I'm a nonsmoker and a nondrinker, at least for the next few months. And as of today I have a decent job. I think you'll find I'm quite the model housemate.'

'Except you're pregnant.'

'Except for that,' she relented. 'But if this woman's got a child of her own she might be more open to the idea. I mean, she'd have to like kids at least.'

'Having one doesn't automatically mean you like everyone else's,' said Cameron. 'She's got inside information, remember; probably the last thing she wants is another screaming brat running around.'

'Cam, don't talk like that,' said Phoebe. 'Gemma's baby's not going to be a screaming brat.'

He grunted. 'Why should it be an exception?'

Phoebe opened her mouth to say something, but she couldn't seem to get it out. She shook her head instead, made an exasperated groan, then turned and headed up the hall to their room. A moment later they heard the door slam.

Gemma looked over her shoulder at Cameron, but he just shrugged. 'I'm thinking PMT.'

Dickhead.

'If you don't mind,' he said pointedly, 'I've got some calls to make.'

'Sure,' said Gemma, sliding off the chair. 'I'll leave you to it.' She plucked up the bucket of ice cream, and Cameron gave her a look that could have curdled it.

'It's not as though you're going to want any with my germs all through it,' she quipped as she turned on her heel and walked up the hall, straight past her room to Phoebe's. She knocked lightly on the door. 'It's me.'

'Come in.'

Gemma opened the door holding the ice cream out ahead of her, like a flag of surrender. 'This'll make you feel better.'

Phoebe was sitting back on the bed, a pillow propped behind her. Their room was so pristine that the mere presence of a human being was like an unsightly stain. It was the type of room you saw in magazines that you could never imagine real people living in. Which was why it suited Cameron perfectly.

'Ice cream will only make me feel better for a minute or two,' said Phoebe, shaking her head regretfully. 'Then I'll just feel fat and guilty and loathe myself even more.'

'I think it's going to take more than a little ice cream to fatten you up, Ms yoga-pilates-run-ten-k's-a-day,' Gemma taunted, closing the door.

'I don't run ten k's *every* day.' She frowned, eyeing Gemma up and down. 'Are you wearing any pants?'

'Yeah,' Gemma said guilelessly, lifting her shirt up to reveal her knickers.

'I don't mean *under*pants.' Phoebe rubbed her eyes wearily. 'Could you please make an effort to put some clothes on when you're at home, especially when Cam's around?'

'You can't seriously think Cameron would give me a second look? He can't stand me.'

'Doesn't mean he's not going to perve at you given half a chance.'

Gemma considered her. 'Did you two have a fight?'

Phoebe sighed. 'Cam and I don't fight. We "discuss".'

Gemma climbed onto the bed next to her sister. 'So, did you have a "discussion"?'

She shook her head. 'No, not really. I just had a bad day, that's all. And my period's due.'

'Cameron said it was PMT.'

'Dickhead.'

They looked at each other and smiled. Gemma passed her the ice cream. 'Come on, you know you want it.'

Phoebe screwed up her nose, looking inside the carton. 'Ugh, it's gone all soft.'

'That's the way you like it.'

'No, that's the way *you* like it,' she returned. 'But hey, I could learn to like it,' she added, taking the carton from Gemma and scooping up a big, runny spoonful that she had to quickly pop into her mouth.

Gemma was watching her. 'Hey, Phee, I know you're a lot better at it, but I can do the big sister thing. I am older than you after all.'

Phoebe smiled faintly, dropping the spoon back into the container. 'We just had our quarterly staff evaluations. I didn't do so well.'

'But you work like a Trojan,' Gemma protested.

'Doesn't matter, it's never enough. Women have to be five times better than the blokes around them. They can't suck up to the boss over a round of golf. Don't worry, I tried. I even took lessons, and I'm not a bad player, but I'm never even invited, so that was a complete waste of time. And don't get me started on footy speak. Unless you have an intimate knowledge of the game, and not only that, the major plays from the last round, you can't follow anything they're talking about. They use it as metaphors in conversations about work. It drives me nuts.'

Gemma could not recall Phoebe complaining about working hard, ever, much less making excuses. She was not accustomed to Disgruntled Phoebe, and she wasn't sure how to handle her.

'It's a jungle out there, eh?' was her rather lame offering.

'It's a fucking war zone,' Phoebe said bitterly. 'Just as well we're not allowed to carry guns in this country or you'd be lucky to get out alive some days.'

Gemma looked at her. 'That bad, eh?'

'I don't know.' She sighed wearily. 'Sometimes I just feel like I've had enough. I'd like to drop out, move to the country and grow vegetables and sew patchwork quilts.'

Gemma pulled a face. 'Well, that's just weird,' she said. 'But honestly, Phee, why don't you quit if it's making you so unhappy?'

Phoebe looked at her sideways. 'We can't all go through life like you, Gemma.'

'Well, we all could, you know,' she declared. 'And the world would be a much more laidback place. But seriously, Phee, you're uber-smart and you have all this experience as well as a law degree. You could walk into any job you wanted.'

'Different bear pit, same animals.' Phoebe leaned her head back. 'You're lucky, you know, Gem.'

Gemma blinked, turning to look at her sister. 'I'm single, pregnant and homeless and had to lie through my teeth to get a job that I'll probably lose again in a few months when I'm found out. "Lucky" is not the word that springs to mind when I think about my situation.'

'You're having a baby,' said Phoebe. 'I mean, no matter what else is going on, *you're having a baby*. Doesn't that put a different perspective on everything?'

'Yeah, it does, believe me, it does,' Gemma said dryly. 'So what's stopping you?'

'From what?'

'From having a baby of your own?'

Phoebe's face fell. 'Oh, well, it's not a good time. We need two wages to cover the mortgage, and Cam's travelling a lot . . .'

'If you wait for everything to be just right, you'll never do it, Phee.'

She looked sheepishly at her sister. 'Cam's not very keen.'

'No kidding,' said Gemma. 'But what do *you* want, Phee?'

Phoebe appeared to be searching for an answer, but in the end she gave a little shake of her head. 'It's only the hormones talking. Aren't you supposed to be closest to pregnant right before your period?' She shook her head again, more purposefully this time. 'I'm being ridiculous. I have a bad day at work and my solution is to pack it all in and have a baby?' She thrust the ice cream at Gemma and jumped off the bed.

'What am I thinking?' she said, undoing the buttons of her blouse. 'I have a job and I have a mortgage. And it took us ages to find this apartment, and it's not exactly an ideal place to bring up a baby.' She tossed her blouse in the hamper. 'And I'm still young. I mean, I can hear the biological clock ticking faintly in the background, but there's no cause for alarm just yet.' She slid back the door of the wardrobe and took out her running shoes. 'I mean, I keep fit. I still have a decade of fertile years ahead of me if I take care of myself –'

'Hey, Phee, do you actually need me here for this conversation?' Gemma said.

She smiled, dropping the shoes on the floor. 'Okay, what about you? Are you going to call about that place?'

'I guess.' Gemma hesitated, staring into the container of ice cream. It probably couldn't technically be called ice cream any longer, it was more like Cream of Caramel Crunch soup. 'Let me just see if my self-esteem has room for yet another rejection.'

Phoebe looked over her shoulder as she changed into her running gear. 'Then don't say you're pregnant.'

Gemma frowned. 'I don't know. I got away with that at the interview, but I'm not sure I can get away with it with someone I'm going to live with. I don't want to be tossed out on my ear in a couple months.'

'I'm only saying don't tell her off the bat,' said Phoebe. 'Go and meet her first, check out the place, see if it's a fit.'

'Then what?'

'Then use your considerable powers of persuasion to convince her you're her new housemate.'

'You and Cameron are actually counting down the days, aren't you?'

'No,' she said. 'Well, maybe Cam is, but I'm going to miss you.'

'Don't worry, I'll never be far away. You're it, remember – you have the dubious honour of being my one and only support, little sister.'

Phoebe stopped in the middle of tying her laces. 'You never talk about him.'

'Who?'

'Luke. You never say you miss him, or how you feel about what he did.'

And that's the way it was going to stay. Gemma had pulled more than her fair share of stunts over the years, but finally her chickens had come home to roost. Only she was the chicken doing the roosting. She could hardly expect sympathy, so she just had to tough it out. She wasn't going to let anyone know how she felt – abandoned, frightened, embarrassed, ashamed. To be so unceremoniously dumped was pretty confronting. Gemma wanted to believe it said more about Luke, but she had the sickening feeling that it said an awful lot about her – and that was something she didn't want to explore right now.

So she simply shrugged, stirring the ice cream soup absently. 'To be honest, I'm so pissed off with Luke I haven't thought about whether I miss him.'

'That's grief.' Phoebe was nodding sagely.

'Hmm?'

'You being pissed off with Luke. Anger is one of the stages of grief.'

'I thought the stages theory had been debunked?'

'I didn't get that memo.'

'Yeah, I'm sure it has, I saw it on Doctor Phil.'

'Who's Doctor Phil?' asked Phoebe.

Gemma looked sadly at her sister. 'There's a whole world of daytime television you're missing out on. You really should stay in more.'

Autumn

Gemma pushed back the front gate and it protested with a feeble squeak. The path before her divided a slightly wild, though modest, patch of garden, and led to an unpretentious cottage: cosy, if a little shabby, which suited Gemma just fine. She was hoping it was not going to be one of those precious restoration jobs or, worse, a twee Laura Ashley doll's house. This was an honest worker's cottage, a Balmain original. If the owner was anything like her abode, Gemma was in with a chance.

She stepped up onto the verandah and knocked confidently on the front door. Showtime. This was it. Gemma had always considered herself a pretty tough person, but the last couple of months had knocked her about more than she cared to admit. And while she was all chutzpah with Cameron, giving as good as she got, it was not the most desirable of situations to be living where she was clearly not wanted. She had to get this place. She had a feeling her options were running out.

Gemma could hear footsteps approaching from inside. And then the door slowly opened and a woman peered out at her. She seemed wary. She was attractive, potentially even striking, with large dark eyes like oversized almonds, set off by cheekbones to die for, but she was pale and gaunt and visibly apprehensive, as though she was steeling herself for bad news. Gemma hoped this was the right place.

'Helen Chapman?' she asked tentatively.

The woman nodded, clearing her throat as she clutched her cardigan around herself. She seemed nervous, but why should she be nervous? She was the one in the driver's seat.

'You must be Gemma Atkins?' she mumbled, not meeting Gemma's gaze.

'Atkin*son*,' Gemma corrected. 'But call me Gemma, please. It's nice to meet you.' She thrust her hand at the woman, who considered it a little cautiously before unravelling her arms and barely placing her hand in Gemma's, only to withdraw it again a second later.

'I can't wait to see inside,' said Gemma, placing a foot squarely on the doorstep like a vacuum cleaner salesman. 'Can I come in?'

'Oh, um, okay,' said Helen. She seemed a little unprepared for that. Had she not expected a prospective tenant would want to look inside the house?

Gemma charged past her into a wide hall. 'This is great!' she declared, on what was, granted, very little information. There was a room either side of the hall, but both doors were closed. The one on the right was decorated with clown letters which spelled out 'Noah', the four-year-old boy, Gemma deduced. There was a doorway straight ahead to a sitting room, but the hall continued in a dogleg around it.

'The room, um, the room for rent, it's just around to the left,' said Helen in a small voice.

'Do you mind if I take a look?'

Helen seemed to hesitate, but then her shoulders sagged as though in defeat. 'Sure, of course.' She walked around the corner of the hall. 'That's the bathroom,' she said, indicating a door on the left. 'And this is the room here.'

Gemma stepped into a generously proportioned room with a single tall window above a double bed that was covered with a blue chenille bedspread. She couldn't remember the last time she'd seen chenille. A heavy, dark timber wardrobe stood against the opposite wall, next to a similar style dressing table.

'This is it,' Helen said, almost apologetically.

'This is all I'll need to get started.' Gemma turned to look at Helen Chapman. She was twisting her fingers together, seeming pretty anxious about the whole thing. Gemma suddenly felt an overwhelming compulsion to be honest with her. Lay the facts out before her and take it from there.

'Look, I've got something I need to tell you,' she said.

The anguished expression on Helen's face was a little disturbing. She really needed to lighten up.

'I'm pregnant,' Gemma said quickly. 'Going on about four months.'

She watched Helen's expression morph into relief, and then morph again into confusion.

'So, can I see the rest of the house?' Gemma asked hopefully.

*

Helen had made a pot of tea and they were sitting at the table in the large, sunny kitchen. This was the only room where Gemma could breathe; the rest of the house felt claustrophobic. It was crammed with ancient heavy furniture, and scores of knick-knacks cluttered every available surface. It was all very old-fashioned, but not in a good way. Doilies and cut-glass featured prominently, as did dark timber, dusty velvet and faded old florals. The place felt like an old lady lived here, not a thirty-something woman and her young child.

'I'm just wondering why you didn't tell me on the phone,' Helen was saying as she poured the tea. 'About your, um . . . your condition.'

'Would I be sitting here now if I had?' asked Gemma.

Helen glanced at her sheepishly, setting the pot down. 'Still, you must have known you wouldn't be able to hide it for long. I had to find out sometime.'

'That's right,' said Gemma. 'I wasn't trying to deceive you, that's why I told you straightaway. I just wanted to meet you first, have the chance to put my case to you in person.'

Helen looked at her, waiting.

'I didn't get past an email with anyone else,' Gemma explained. 'And I understand, they were all households of working people, no kids. When I saw your ad, I thought you might be more open to the idea, seeing as you have a child.'

'A baby's different.'

'I know, but, well, I assume you're on your own, like me.'

Helen dropped her eyes, nodding faintly. Sticky subject, obviously. Steer clear of that for the moment.

Gemma cleared her throat. 'Look, you're probably thinking that I'm some kind of hopeless loser –'

'I don't know you,' Helen said quietly. 'And I certainly haven't formed an opinion of you.'

'But a pregnant woman shows up on your doorstep needing a room?' Gemma raised an eyebrow. 'You have to be wondering what happened.'

Helen didn't say anything, she just took a sip of her tea.

'The pregnancy wasn't planned, I suppose you've figured out that much,' said Gemma, ploughing on. 'My boyfriend and I were working up in Brisbane when I found out, and it was too late to do anything about it.'

Gemma saw a flicker of discomfort in Helen's eyes. Move on, quickly.

'But we were solid, me and Luke, or so I thought. After we got over the shock, we decided we'd get married, and I flew down to Sydney to announce it to my family.'

'You have family here?'

'Sure, I'm crashing at my sister's place at the moment, but I can't stay there.'

'Oh?'

'Her husband's not exactly wild about the arrangement.'

D'oh! What the hell are you doing, Gemma? You're supposed to be trying to impress the woman.

'Don't worry, I'm perfectly housetrained,' she added quickly, 'but you know how it is . . . three's a crowd.'

Helen nodded faintly. 'So what happened between you and, um . . .?'

'Luke,' Gemma said. 'Well, when I got back to Brisbane, he was gone.'

Helen blinked. 'Gone?'

'Gone,' she repeated. 'Without a word. Oh, except he called me at the airport to say he wouldn't be able to pick me up.'

'Did you have any idea?' Helen asked. 'Were you having problems . . .?'

'We were having a baby,' Gemma said drily. 'It hit us both pretty hard but I thought we were getting used to the idea. Turns out he wasn't, so much.'

'That's what he told you?'

'He hasn't told me anything. I haven't seen or spoken to him.'

'Why not?'

'Because I don't know where he is. He was gone when I got home, he'd taken all his stuff, he wouldn't answer his phone . . .' Gemma shrugged. 'Anyway, eventually the number was out of service. I haven't heard so much as a word from him. Neither have any of his friends. He might as well be dead.'

Helen looked visibly stunned. Her face had gone white.

'It's all right, I'm okay with it,' Gemma assured her. 'I mean, not at first, at first I felt like I'd been hit by a bus.'

Helen fumbled her cup, spilling tea into the saucer and splashing it across the table. Gemma watched her clucking and fussing and apologising and berating herself as she blotted out the tea with a paper napkin. She certainly was a nervy type of person. Gemma was beginning to wonder how they'd get on living together.

'Look, the thing is,' she resumed when Helen sat down again, 'although I'm obviously better off without him, I never expected to be doing this on my own.'

Helen seemed thoughtful. 'And, um, and your parents can't . . . they don't have room?' she said awkwardly.

Gemma's heart sank. This woman wasn't a fool. She didn't want to take on her problems.

'I can't stay with my parents,' Gemma said. 'We don't exactly see eye to eye.'

She saw the bewilderment on Helen Chapman's face. Not surprising – Gemma was hardly painting a particularly appealing picture of herself. In barely a few minutes she'd cited a boyfriend who'd dumped her, a brother-in-law who didn't want her in his home, and parents she didn't get along with. She had to get her act together. She used to be in advertising, she could do better than this.

'Ms Chapman,' said Gemma, assuming the voice she used when she was doing a pitch to a client. A kind of confident confidante. 'May I call you Helen?'

She nodded faintly.

'Helen, okay, so I'm not in a particularly enviable situation. I hardly planned things this way, but you can't plan for everything that comes along in life, can you?'

Helen shook her head thoughtfully. 'No, you can't.'

'My parents are good people,' Gemma continued. 'I don't mean to suggest otherwise. But they tend to think there's only one way to do things, and that's their way. I need to sort this out myself. I can't do that if I live with them, and I can't afford to live on my own, at least not at the moment. So if you can possibly find it in your heart to allow us into your home, I'll make sure you never regret it.'

Helen's big dark eyes had grown bigger and darker as Gemma spoke. Good. Now bring it all the way home. If it worked for the MD, it'll work for Helen Chapman.

'But I certainly don't want to be anywhere that I'm not wanted. If it's not working out, you won't have to ask me to leave – I'll go of my own volition.'

Three days later

It had taken Helen a long time to get to sleep that night. What was she letting herself in for? Allowing a woman she didn't know – a *pregnant* woman with a tonne of baggage and no visible means of support – to live with her, and her young impressionable son. She must be mad.

Helen had decided once and for all that she couldn't face returning to work in the foreseeable future, possibly ever. Into nursing at least. With the help of the counsellor she had worked through her options, and she'd kept coming back to Tony's suggestion of finding a boarder. So she wasn't mad, she was desperate. Which could sometimes make you do mad things.

Truth was, Helen had barely had a response to her ad, apart from middle-aged men who were rather transparently after a ready-made family. She had politely responded, telling them she'd be in touch to arrange an inspection. But she wouldn't. She'd clearly stated 'pref. female' in the ad. She would have put 'only females need apply' but she had a feeling that was illegal. Discriminatory. She wasn't sure, so best be safe than sorry.

Only three females had responded, and the ad had been running for weeks. The first was a junkie. She'd tried to hide it: she'd showered and washed her hair and worn her most presentable outfit, but Helen recognised the signs as soon as she opened the door. She'd seen enough junkies in the hospital over the years – the sunken eyes set in a pale, pale face, the trembling hands, the impossible thinness. So Helen told her the room had been taken, just before she got there. She was sorry. The girl took the news on the chin; Helen doubted she had the strength or presence of mind to argue. However, that night as she went off to sleep, Helen felt a little uneasy, not least at the thought of the girl passing on her address to any number of her wasted druggie mates – she was a single mother, an easy target for a break and enter. But mostly Helen's uneasiness stemmed from the guilt she felt for turning her away. It was the nurse in her. Or the sucker.

The next female who replied to the ad was a lesbian. Helen knew this because the woman included it in her response. Thought it was better to be honest at the outset. Did she have a problem with that?

Of course Helen didn't have a problem with that. She and David were liberal in their views and intended to bring up Noah the same. In fact, it was probably good for him to be exposed to a wide range of people from the start so that he would never find it unusual or need to question it.

No, no hope of that. Noah questioned everything. 'Why?' was his standard response to pretty much any statement. What if the lesbian brought a girlfriend home? Would Noah's curiosity be embarrassing, intrusive? How would Helen deal with it? Then again, if their hypothetical boarder – and it was beginning to feel more hypothetical by the minute – was straight, and she brought a man home, wasn't that going to elicit a barrage of whys and wherefores too? What if the hypothetical boarder brought different men home every weekend, or more often? Helen had to ask herself how she felt about that, and the answer was that she didn't feel too comfortable at all. Did she have a right to make rules? It was her house, wasn't it? But the hypothetical boarder would be paying for her room so she had rights too, didn't she? So whose rights superseded whose?

Helen told the lesbian she'd get back to her, and then she thought seriously about abandoning the whole idea.

Until the email from Gemma Atkinson. She was thirty years old, she didn't smoke, she didn't drink, and she had a good job. Helen doubted she took drugs if she didn't smoke or drink, though anything was possible. There was nothing whatsoever to make

Helen hesitate, except her own inordinate fear of making decisions. David would have handled this kind of thing, but now she was going to have to do it herself. And she had to do it. Quite simply, she was running out of options. So Helen invited Gemma out to see the place.

Gemma Atkinson had showed up on their doorstep – the quintessential sun-kissed Australian girl, brimming with good health, leggy, blonde and gregarious. And also pregnant, as it turned out. She'd neglected to mention that rather important detail, that they would be getting two for the price of one. Helen had suspected she might be approached by single mothers, and she certainly didn't have a problem with having another child around per se. But a baby? Helen knew all too well how babies took over your house and your life, how their needs became paramount. This would be no quiet boarder who would keep to herself, that simply wasn't possible.

But she and David had been planning to have another child, soon. They'd talked about the impact it would have on Noah, and decided that all in all it would be a positive one. And they had intended to be very open about the whole process; they wanted Noah to learn the facts of life in a natural, normal way. Soon after the accident Helen had vacillated between desperately wishing she was carrying David's child, and being incredibly relieved that she wasn't left to raise two children on her own. Noah was clearly destined to be an only child, so maybe having a baby around was not such a bad thing; perhaps this would provide him with experiences he was otherwise unlikely to get.

Jim and Noreen were not going to like it one bit. Not that that was a reason not to do it; in fact, if David were here, he would say that was all the more reason to go ahead. But he wasn't here, and he couldn't tell her what was the right thing to do. Would he have taken a pregnant woman in? Of course. That was the kind of person David was. He probably would have welcomed the junkie with open arms.

In the end, it was what Gemma Atkinson had said about the controlling parents, about needing to make her own life, that had moved Helen.

And now she was moving in. Today. Helen had intended to arrange for Noah to meet any potential boarder ahead of making a final decision, but Gemma had jumped at the mere whiff of an offer, and before Helen knew what was happening, they'd shaken hands and apparently confirmed that Gemma was moving in the day after next. She was starting her new job next week and she wanted to be settled. Helen supposed that was fair enough.

'Mu-um, when's a lady coming?'

'Any time now,' said Helen, checking her watch.

'Whata lady's name, Mummy?'

'I already told you, Noah, don't you remember?'

He looked at her with that impish grin that always reminded her of Tony. Although Noreen had staunchly insisted that Noah was the spit out of David's mouth, in reality he hadn't inherited any of the Chapman features, and David had always been the first to say it. Noah was all Zelinsky – dark hair, dark eyes, standing there twisting his arms around each other, playing coy. Just like Tony.

'I don't bremember, Mummy,' he said.

'Her name is Gemma,' said Helen.

'Gemma!' he cried, throwing his arms out like it was the best thing he'd ever heard. 'Why is she's name Gemma, Mummy?'

'Because that's what her mummy and daddy called her.'

'Why?'

'Because . . . maybe she looked like a Gemma to them.'

'What does a Gemma look like?'

Helen heard a knock on the door. 'You may be about to find out, Noah. That's probably her now.'

'It's her now!' Noah cried. 'She's atta door, Mummy, you haffa hurry!'

'All right, all right,' she said, trailing him up the hall. Of course as soon as she opened the front door he whisked around behind his mother, wrapping his arms around her leg and hiding his face.

'Hi,' Gemma said brightly.

'Hi,' Helen returned as a taxi pulled away from the kerb out front. It had not even occurred to her the other day to ask Gemma if she owned a car. 'Is that all you have with you?'

'This is all I have, full stop.' She smiled, hitching her backpack up a little on her shoulder. She'd borrowed a wheelie bag from Phoebe so that she could distribute her belongings between the two bags.

'Really?'

'I got rid of most of my stuff before I went north.' In truth, Gemma did have some stuff stored at her parents', but she didn't need it that badly.

'You certainly travel light,' Helen remarked.

Gemma hitched her backpack up again. She wished Helen would stop being fascinated by her belongings, or lack thereof, and invite her in. 'Hey, hi there!'

Noah had peeked around to look at her but as soon as she acknowledged him, he shrunk back like a turtle into its shell.

'He'll put this on for a while,' Helen told her. 'But pretty soon he'll be talking your ear off.'

Gemma nodded, giving one more laboured heave-ho of her backpack.

'Oh, sorry, that must be getting heavy. Come on in,' Helen said. Finally.

Gemma followed her down the hall as Noah peeled away from his mother and made a dash for his room. Helen opened the door of what would now be Gemma's room and stepped aside. Gemma walked past her, glad to be relieved of her load as she dumped her backpack on the bed.

'I had some keys cut for you,' said Helen.

Gemma turned around to smile at her. 'Thank you.'

'Back door, front door,' Helen went on. 'The back door's the bigger key, and it's square, whereas the front . . . but look, I'm sure you'll work it out.'

'I'm sure I will.'

Helen put the keys down on the dressing table. 'I didn't know if you had plans for dinner?'

'No, no plans.'

'So I've made a lasagne –'

'I love lasagne!' said Gemma.

'Oh, but this, well, this is vegetable lasagne,' Helen apologised. 'I probably should have said . . . we're vegetarians.'

'Oh.' Gemma nodded. 'How vegetarian?'

'Don't worry, we're not fanatical about it,' Helen assured her. 'I mean, it's not a religion or anything, we just don't eat meat. Dairy's fine though, and eggs, as long as they're free-range. But you know, if you wanted to cook meat, I mean, I wouldn't have a problem with that or anything.'

Gemma smiled reassuringly. 'I'm sure I'll get by. I can always eat meat when I'm out. And it's not as though we'll be sharing all our meals.'

'No, that's true,' Helen said. There was so much to work out it made her head hurt thinking about it. 'Perhaps we'll need a schedule . . .'

'Let's play it by ear for now, shall we?' Playing it by ear was Gemma's preferred mode of operation. She had an aversion to schedules, much as Helen had an aversion to meat.

'Okay, good idea,' said Helen. They could much more easily come up with a schedule once they were aware of each other's movements, needs, preferences. 'So, I'll leave you to settle in. Call me if you need anything.'

'I definitely will.'

'Dinner's in about an hour.'

Gemma glanced at her watch.

'Sorry, we do eat early,' Helen said. 'You're probably not used to having small children around.'

'I'm going to have to get used to it,' Gemma said cheerfully. All this politeness was becoming a strain.

'Okay, I'll leave you to it,' said Helen.

'Thanks.'

She walked out of the room and Gemma plonked down on the bed. So, this was it, her domain. This was where she was going to cross the great divide into motherhood, a single room in someone else's house. Who'd have thought.

She flopped back, stretching her arms above her head and staring up at the ceiling. Bedroom ceilings were the most important ceilings in the house: you would spend more time looking at them than in any other room. Gemma was pleased that this one had a pretty ceiling rose and a rather ornate border, as well as flaking paint and a couple of damp spots. Plenty of detail to gaze at while she mused over life's big questions. And she had a feeling the coming months would provide plenty of fodder for that.

Gemma began to have that strange, inexplicable sensation that she was being watched. She turned her head to see Noah standing at the foot of the bed, staring unblinkingly at her.

'Well,' she declared, propping herself up on her elbows. 'If it isn't the infamous Noah.'

He shook his head solemnly.

'Aren't you Noah?'

He nodded. 'I'm just Noah. Not mimfimiss Noah.'

Gemma smiled, sitting all the way up. 'Right you are. I'm glad we got that sorted. And how old are you, Noah?'

He held up four fingers very importantly. 'This many is four.'

'So it is,' she said. 'My name's Gemma.'

He nodded. 'I already knowed that 'cause Mummy told me.'

'Good, well, it's nice to meet you, Noah.' She put out her hand, but he went coy again. 'That's okay, you don't have to shake my hand if you don't want to.'

'You're gunna live wif us, aren't you?'

'I am,' Gemma said. 'Is that okay with you?'

He nodded with a kind of resigned air. ''Cause my daddy can't live here anymore.'

'Oh?' Gemma thought she'd better not ask about his father, given Helen's skittishness around the subject.

''Cause he's been runned over by a bus.'

Gemma nodded warily. 'Oh, that's no good.'

'And so we haffa take him to a special place and let him go.'

Was he talking about a dog now?

'There you are,' said Helen, appearing in the doorway. 'Come on, out you come, Noah, I told you you're not to bother Gemma.'

'He's no bother.'

Helen glanced at her and then returned her attention to Noah. 'Come on, scoot. It's time for your bath.'

Noah turned and scuppered out of the room as Helen went to follow him.

'Helen?' said Gemma.

She looked back at her.

'Noah said a strange thing to me just now.'

'He did?'

Gemma took a breath. 'He said his dad had been run over by a bus.'

Helen's expression didn't change, nor did she offer any kind of explanation.

'Why would he say something like that?' Gemma persisted.

'Because that's what happened,' Helen said coolly.

Gemma stared at her. 'You don't mean . . .'

'Noah's father, my husband, was run over by a bus on his way to work three months ago. He died instantly.'

Gemma couldn't speak.

'So now you know, not that it's any of your business,' said Helen. 'I'd prefer it if you didn't grill Noah about it, if you don't mind. We may be sharing a house, but I fully intend to respect your privacy, and I hope you'll pay us the same courtesy.'

Bailey & Partners

When Gemma arrived at the reception desk on the ground floor, the daytime security guard remembered her immediately. Well, it had only been around eight months since she left, but he would have been unlikely to forget her anyway. Gemma was not someone easily forgotten.

'Ms Atkinson,' he said, beaming. Eddie had been with Bailey's for years and was approaching retirement. It was nice to know he hadn't been given the chop under Attila the MD.

'Eddie,' Gemma purred, 'it's so good to see you.'

'It's better from where I'm looking, love.'

Gemma had rather enjoyed dressing for the part again. She'd swiped a couple of Phoebe's suits to get her through the first few weeks; they probably wouldn't fit her after that anyway. And though she hadn't got around to having her hair cut, she'd discovered it was long enough to sweep up into a French roll. She felt quite the corporate PA.

'I believe my heart missed a beat when I saw your name on the list this morning,' Eddie was saying. 'Are you back for good?'

The 'for good' part was perhaps a bit hazy, but . . .

'I'm back,' Gemma confirmed.

'Then it is my great pleasure to present you with your security pass, and to escort you to the elevators.'

'Thank you, Eddie,' she said and, taking the arm he offered her, she walked with him across to the lifts. He swiped the card through the slot and handed it to Gemma.

'Welcome back, Ms Atkinson.'

Gemma stepped into the lift, turning to smile at him. 'Thanks, Eddie, I'll see you around.'

'I'll look forward to it.'

As the doors closed Gemma felt a slight sense of trepidation. She was excited to see everyone, but she was not so sure everyone was going to be all that excited to see her, or be as charming as Eddie had just been. She knew she'd done the wrong thing. Not only had she left without a word, but she'd also left them in the lurch with a major account close to a deadline. It was not the way to go if you ever intended coming back. But she had never intended coming back. And surely it was not unforgivable?

Gemma supposed she was about to find out.

She stepped out of the elevator at the twelfth floor. She'd be working another three floors up but she wanted to visit her old team first. See what she was up against. Gemma approached the wall of glass separating the lift bay from the office. There they all were, sitting around the long communal desk that was a Bailey's innovation to keep the team cohesive and break down the hierarchy. But there was still a hierarchy, no amount of communal furniture could take that away.

Justin was the team leader and no one disputed it. He did not possess enough talent or commitment to specialise in one particular area, but he certainly possessed the requisite amount of arrogance to feel comfortable telling others what to do. He proved the maxim – those who can't, boss everyone around to do it for them.

Marcus could give Justin a run for his money in the arrogance stakes, but he had a specialty. He costed the campaigns and controlled the purse strings, so even Justin had to defer to him at times. Mel coordinated production, and Gemma had been her assistant, so she assumed the little blonde sitting beside her was her replacement. Everyone else, Tom, Jen, Brooke and Nathan, were subsidiaries in one way or another to the big three.

Charlie would be upstairs. He was a creative – creatives were not attached to any particular account team. They had a floor of their own, and minds of their own. While everyone else was suited up, slick and professional, the creatives wandered around in grotty

Dunlops like aging uni students, wearing T-shirts with subversive, witty or just plain mystifying slogans, or else wildly patterned Hawaiian shirts. They sat in front of humungous, gleaming Macs and were surrounded by every dazzling new piece of CGI wizardry thus far known to man.

Charlie didn't wear loud shirts, he was more modest and unassuming, in every way. And he was patient and sweet and a little shy, despite being far and away the smartest guy in the place. If you wanted a group of twelve to become a crowd of twelve hundred, he could do it; if you wanted a scarf to turn into a snake and slither down from the neck of a model, he could do that too, without her ever having to come into contact with the reptile. He could remove somebody from a scene, or add someone in, make animals speak, change the entire colour palette, turn day into night, a half-moon into a full moon. There was nothing Charlie Lambert couldn't do.

And there was nothing he wouldn't do for Gemma. Everyone knew Charlie had a crush on her, Gemma best of all, and she'd used that knowledge to her own advantage, a little shamelessly at times. But she couldn't help it. She was fascinated by the workings of the creative department even though she didn't have a hope of joining the inner sanctum – she did not even approach their level of computer skill and it would take too long to play catch-up at this stage. At the same time she had discovered an innate talent for storyboarding. While everyone else was throwing around ideas and concepts, Gemma was already seeing them in pictures and narrative. And not only that, it appeared she had a knack for communicating this with the creatives. She didn't know how they did what they did, but she knew what they needed to know to be able to do it. She became the team's unofficial creative liaison, spending long hours perched at Charlie's side, talking him through as he moulded and crafted ideas into images on the screen. They became like a team unto themselves, excluding and largely ignoring anyone else's input, bouncing only off each other, pulling regular all-nighters, finishing each other's sentences.

That was until Luke came onto the scene. Charlie closed off after that; he became stilted and curt with Gemma, and they couldn't work effectively together anymore. By that stage she hadn't really cared – she already had one foot out the door. She stopped feeling part of the place for that last month or so, but standing here now, she was hard-pressed to understand how Luke had had such a hold over her. Why had she let this all go so easily, treated it with contempt when she had loved every minute of it?

Gemma suddenly became aware that all eyes were upon her. She smiled her most dazzling smile as she swiped her card in the slot and pushed through the door.

'Well, lookie here,' Justin drawled. He swivelled his chair around to face her and reclined back, one leg slung casually across the other. 'If it isn't the prodigal daughter returned.'

'Jesus, Justin, your originality is truly breathtaking,' said Mel. Mel said whatever she liked whenever she liked to whomever she liked. That's how she'd got to where she was, she used to tell Gemma, there was no point pussy-footing around. Gemma had liked working with her – you always knew where you stood with Mel. She called a spade a great big tool for shovelling dirt and she didn't take shit from anyone.

'So, Gem, what brings you here?' she was asking.

Gemma took a deep breath. 'Well, I'm back on the payroll.'

Marcus narrowed his eyes. 'I thought there was a moratorium on staff. The teams aren't supposed to be hiring.'

'I won't be on a team,' she said. 'I'm replacing Joanne Dwyer.'

'You're going to be PA to the MD?' Justin remarked, lifting an eyebrow. 'Ha, that should be fun to watch. What's that line about an immovable object meeting an unstoppable force?'

'Have you been reading the cliché handbook again, Justin?' said Mel. 'The MD's not so bad, Gem. You'll get on fine.'

'Yeah, if you're into tyrannical control freaks, he's a real doll,' said Justin. 'So what happened to your Prince Charming?'

Gemma decided to put an end to the gossip before it started by giving them nowhere to go. 'He dumped me,' she said simply. 'Obviously I wasn't good enough for him.'

Mel laughed. She got it.

'Hey, does Charlie know you're back?' asked Justin. 'Somebody buzz Charlie.'

'I already have,' came a voice from further down the table, either Nathan or Tom.

As if on cue, a pair of well-worn sneakers appeared at the top of the spiral staircase that unravelled its way from the floor above into a corner of the room. As the shoes descended, the rest of the body duly followed until his face came into view, and his eyes landed on Gemma with a thud.

'Hey Charlie, how are you going?' she asked, trying to be chirpy and warm and sorry all at once.

Gemma hadn't thought too much at the time about the effect her leaving might have had on Charlie, she'd been too caught up with her own issues – namely Luke. Now the brittle expression on his face was giving her a fair idea of how he must have felt. She'd never meant to hurt him.

'It's really good to see you, Charlie,' she said sincerely.

He swallowed. 'When did you get back?' he managed to say, though his voice didn't venture far from his lips.

'Just in the last month,' Gemma replied. He looked so guarded, so wary of her. She wanted to give him a big, reassuring hug, except he'd die if she did anything so demonstrative in front of everyone. But he was the best friend she'd had at Bailey's, and she could certainly use an ally at the moment. 'We should do lunch one day . . .'

Now he just looked embarrassed. Gemma turned around. 'Everyone, we should get together for lunch, soon.'

There was a lukewarm murmur around the table. Mel had replaced her glasses and was already focused again on the screen in front of her. 'Email me,' she said without looking up. 'We'll make a date. I'll bring you up to speed on what's been going on around here.'

'That'd be great.' Gemma looked at her watch. 'Well, I'd best go on up. I don't want to be late on my first day.'

A mumbled, automatic chorus of 'see you around' and 'good luck' followed her to the door. She turned to look at Charlie, but he was already halfway back up the stairs.

*

All in all, that hadn't been so bad. Charlie was going to need some work, but the others appeared more or less disinterested. Her dramatic departure had not had such a dramatic impact, apparently. Gemma supposed that was a good thing.

She took the lift up to the fifteenth floor, where upper management surveyed their domain. They got to have their own offices up here, communal desks and disbanded hierarchies were not for them. They were all very aware of everyone's position on the totem pole; how else could they know who to step on as they climbed their way up?

Gemma walked along the corridor past the strip of executive assistants, like battery hens in their little cubicles. She almost had to do a full circuit of the floor to get to the office of the MD, flanked on one side by the assistant's workstation. It was an open area, which didn't allow for much privacy, but on the other hand she wouldn't have to feel cooped up like a chook either. A tired, dark-haired woman glanced up from the computer screen in front of her as Gemma approached the desk.

'Hello, Joanne?'

'Gemma?

'That's me. Good to meet you,' she added, putting out her hand.

The woman heaved herself onto her feet, and Gemma was confronted with the full horror of late-term pregnancy. She resembled an over-inflated balloon with legs. And it wasn't only her stomach – her face and hands looked like they'd been inflated beyond the recommended capacity as well.

'Please, Joanne, don't get up,' Gemma insisted.

She dropped heavily back into her chair with a weary sigh. 'Thanks. And call me Jo.'

'Are you okay?'

'Oh sure, I'm just so exhausted these days. It's getting harder to sleep with this.' She patted the ominous bulge. 'I don't know how I'm going to make it through till the end of the week.'

'Look,' said Gemma, grabbing a chair and dragging it over to the side of the desk, 'I'm here now, and I'm a fast learner. Give me a day or two and I can take over if you like.'

Jo eyed her dubiously. 'I think it's going to take more than a day or two to show you the ropes. The MD has a certain, very precise way of doing things. I'm not even sure I've got it all down pat yet. But he said it was my responsibility to make sure you know what you're doing, seeing as I'm the one who made it necessary.' She sighed. 'Anyway, he doesn't want to have to waste any time – he said the changeover has to happen without missing a beat.'

What had Justin called him? Tyrant was putting it mildly.

'Well, at least don't go getting up and down so much,' said Gemma. 'I can be your gofer this week, make things a little easier for you.'

She smiled. 'Thanks. I just can't seem to get comfortable whatever I do. My feet swell if I sit for too long, but if I put them up I get really bad pains in my groin. And walking, or should I say waddling, is a whole other thing . . .'

Gemma grimaced. 'So this is what I have to look forward to . . .'

Jo looked at her, frowning. 'Pardon?'

'Um, you know,' she said, flustered. 'One day, that is.'

'If you have twins.'

'Oh, you're having *twins*,' Gemma exclaimed, unable to disguise her relief.

Jo was still frowning at her, not surprisingly. 'Okay, well,' she said, 'maybe we should get started?'

'Absolutely.' Gemma pulled her chair in closer.

'First up, the MD holds a lot of meetings, and I mean a lot. That seems to be where he spends almost the entire business day, and then he catches up on paperwork in the evenings.'

'So what are all these meetings about?' Gemma asked. 'Drumming up new business?'

Jo shook her head. 'A little, but mostly they're with staff. He meets with each team at least once a week.'

'What for?'

'He likes to keep his finger on everybody's pulse, if you know what I mean.'

'You mean he's a control freak.'

She shrugged.

'This'll certainly be different,' Gemma said. 'The guy before him was . . . well, let's just say he was a little more relaxed.'

'Yeah, and he almost sent the place to the wall,' Jo reminded her.

'True.' Though Gemma doubted it was because he didn't run seven thousand meetings every week.

'Anyway, the MD's very meticulous about his schedule,' said Jo. 'He uses a three-tiered system – daily, weekly and monthly.' She turned the monitor towards Gemma. It was open to a schedule divided into fifteen-minute intervals, with colour-coded entries written in some kind of shorthand.

'How on earth does he follow that?' asked Gemma.

'He came up with it,' Jo said. 'It's synced to his computer and his phone, so whenever he adds an appointment it sends me an alert, and vice versa. But don't ever commit him to anything without running it by him first, even if it's a meeting he always takes and his schedule is free at the proposed time.'

Gemma was gobsmacked. 'He really is a control freak.'

'I don't know,' she mused, leaning her chin on her hand. 'Sometimes I get the impression he's only trying to keep his head above water.'

Great, so he was incompetent as well.

'He's very capable though, don't get me wrong,' Jo added. 'He's certainly put this place back on track. But he works so hard, he doesn't stop, he won't delegate . . . It's almost like he feels he has to personally keep a handle on everything or it'll all fall apart.'

'That's a bit arrogant.'

'Oh, but he's not arrogant, that's the thing,' she said. 'I don't think he gets off on the power at all. In fact, sometimes I think it overwhelms him.'

Gemma was beginning to wonder whether Jo didn't have a little crush. 'Where is he, by the way?' she asked.

'Well, let's check the schedule, give you an idea how it works.' Jo traced her finger down one of the columns. 'As you can see, he's out of the office for most of the day.'

Gemma had no idea how she could see that.

Jo looked at her blank expression. 'Don't worry, you'll pick it up eventually. In the meantime, he said not to worry if he didn't catch up with you today, I should just get on with training you.'

They spent most of the morning unlocking the secrets of the schedule, but Gemma felt barely any the wiser. It seemed unnecessarily complex to her. She didn't know why he couldn't write simple, straightforward notes, instead of truncating everything into inscrutable codes and abbreviations. If she had her druthers she'd be dumping the whole system and starting over, but she wasn't going to have that choice. Her primary role here was to hold onto her job, which meant putting up with whatever he could throw at her.

At twelve thirty, Gemma shooed Jo off to lunch, insisting she take a long one. Jo accepted gratefully, but only on the proviso that Gemma answered the phone and nothing else. She must not alter or add to the schedules in any way, or commit to anything, or decide on anything. Just take a message.

That suited Gemma. As it turned out, there was only one phone call and that was from Jo's mother, who proceeded to apologise to Gemma for blocking the line with a personal call, but she didn't like to call Jo's mobile phone on account of the cost. Gemma assured her that the company had many phone lines and she was most welcome to call any time. Jo's mother reminded her that Jo would only be there for the rest of the week, and then they had a nice chat in which Gemma caught up on all the news in Jo's family. She didn't mind, it helped fill in some time at least. She had assumed this job would be a lot busier. Frantic, in fact. She was sure she remembered Liz being flat out a lot of the time. Being PA to the managing director had seemed to carry a fair amount of responsibility and not a little excitement. Liz had attended meetings along with Jonesy, as well as regular power lunches and ritzy cocktail parties, as Gemma recalled. Not that she was up to all that at the moment. Perhaps that's why the MD had taken to attending meetings alone – Gemma suspected Jo was not up to it either.

When Jo returned from lunch she insisted Gemma take the full hour as well. As there was apparently no chance of the MD showing up any time soon, she agreed. She didn't really feel like another scheduling tutorial, and there was little else to do. She'd finished all the filing.

Gemma decided her time would be best spent breaking down some walls, or one wall in particular, and she might as well do that sooner rather than later. She caught the lift down to the creative department and swiped her card through the slot to release the glass door. It was quiet; most of them would still be out to lunch; some even liked to take a nap at this time of the day. These boys – and they were almost exclusively boys – did not follow schedules. She wondered how they got along with the MD.

Gemma spotted Charlie at the far end of the communal table seated in front of his computer. She could see his sandy, perpetually ruffled hair poking above the top of the monitor, and hear the constant clicking of the keyboard. As she walked closer he glanced up, paused for just a beat, then returned his eyes to the screen and the clicking resumed.

'Hi, Charlie.'

He didn't say anything.

'I was wondering if you're free for lunch? My shout.'

'I've eaten,' he said gruffly.

'Oh, come on, Charlie,' said Gemma, perching on the edge of the table.

'I have work to do, Gemma.'

'Can't you take a break, just for a little while?'

'No.'

She considered him. 'You could if you wanted to.'

'I know.'

Gemma pulled a face. 'You can't stay mad at me forever.'

He glanced at her briefly then returned his attention to the screen. The clicking became banging.

'You can't keep ignoring me either, Charlie. You know how persistent I am.'

His shoulders lifted and fell again in a defeated sigh and he rubbed his eyes wearily. 'I really have a lot of work to do right now, if you don't mind, Gemma.'

'Just a cup of coffee?' she pleaded. 'I need to talk to you about something.'

He met her eyes. 'What could you possibly need to talk to me about?'

She leaned in closer to him. 'I can't talk to anyone else about this, not around here.' She dropped her voice. 'You're the only one I can trust.'

Charlie groaned. 'Oh, no way, not this again.'

'What?' Gemma straightened up. 'What are you talking about?'

'I'm not going to play your games this time, Gem – bringing me into your confidence, telling me all your little secrets . . .' He sighed loudly, and with finality. 'Enough, I'm not interested.'

She frowned at him. 'This isn't a little secret, Charlie, it's a big one. And it's serious.'

'Then you'd best keep it to yourself.'

With that he focused again on the screen, and the interminable clicking resumed. Gemma paced around behind him, then up the other side of the table, thinking. She hadn't expected Charlie to be so resistant, so stubborn. Maybe she deserved it, but once he knew what this was about, he'd be sympathetic, Gemma was sure of it. Charlie was too good, too kind to turn his back on her when she was in such dire straits. That's why she needed him now more than ever. She'd never had a better friend.

Gemma spotted a stick-it notepad on the table. She grabbed a pen, jotted down a couple of words and walked determinedly back to where he sat, peeled off the note and stuck it right in the centre of the computer screen.

'What the –' And then he stopped. Dead. Staring at the scribbled words 'I'm pregnant'. He slowly turned his head to look up at Gemma.

She snatched the note back off the screen, screwing it up tight in her hand. 'Now will you come and have a coffee with me?'

*

'And you haven't seen or heard from him since?' Charlie was asking her.

Gemma shook her head, taking a sip of her tea. She still couldn't drink coffee, but she could at least tolerate the smell of it now. They were sitting in a cafe up the road, somewhere they were unlikely to be interrupted. It wasn't quite fashionable enough for the Bailey's crowd. Gemma had just finished telling Charlie the whole sordid story. It was a relief to get it off her chest, especially to Charlie. She'd almost let herself forget what a good friend he'd been. He'd always listened, never judged, always made her feel okay about herself . . .

'So you must be feeling pretty foolish right now?' he said.

'Charlie!' she protested. 'I thought you'd understand.'

'I do understand, and I reckon you must feel like a fool, Gem, mostly because you acted like one.'

'That's a bit harsh.'

He looked squarely at her. 'Do you want me to butter you up or do you want me to be honest?'

She shrugged. 'Couldn't I have honesty with a little butter on the side?'

He smiled then. A proper Charlie smile. Not guarded at all.

'So, what are you going to do?' he said.

'About what?'

'About telling the boss you're having a baby, for one thing.'

'Oh,' she dismissed. 'I haven't even thought about that yet.'

Charlie shook his head. 'Same old Gem, worry about it when it happens, eh?'

'Well, what's the point of worrying about it before that?' she declared. 'In the meantime, I intend to be a model employee so he won't want to sack me when he finds out.'

'But what's he supposed to do while you're off having the baby?'

Gemma waved her hand. 'Oh, I'll come up with something.'

'Do you even want to be a PA long term, Gem?'

'No, of course not. I want to get back onto a team, work with you again.'

'But didn't you just say that he made it quite clear the job was not a foot in the door –'

'Okay, okay,' Gemma interrupted impatiently. 'I thought I could count on you for support. Why are you being so negative, Charlie?'

'I'm not, I'm being realistic, and you're not facing facts, Gem. It's like you're driving along in a car with no brakes, and you know there's a steep downward slope ahead but you've got your foot planted firmly on the pedal and you're pushing on regardless.'

She looked at him. 'So, are you coming along for the ride?'

'Ha,' he exclaimed. 'Do you think I'm mad?'

'A friend would,' said Gemma. 'Aren't you my friend anymore, Charlie?'

'A friend, a real friend, would be doing everything he could to stop you.'

'The wheels are already in motion,' she said. 'I just want to get as far as I can before it all spins out of my control.'

'Great plan,' Charlie muttered. 'Is this how you intend to approach motherhood as well?'

Gemma dropped her eyes, frowning down at her cup of tea. Okay, so she knew she'd make a hopeless mother, and the peanut would obviously be better off with someone else – that's why she was considering just that. Still, she didn't like having the fact rubbed in her face.

'Gem?'

She looked up and Charlie was gazing intently at her, his head tilted on one side. 'Sorry, I didn't mean . . .'

'It's okay.' She waved it away. 'I know I've made a mess of things, and I have no one to blame but myself. I'll find a way through it, I just thought . . .' She hesitated, biting her lip.

'What?'

'I just thought I could count on you, Charlie, like before. Like always.'

He seemed uncomfortable. 'I don't know what you expect from me, Gem.'

'Just friendship, that's all. You were the best friend I had here, Charlie. One of the best friends I've ever had.

'And you pissed off without so much as a goodbye or any word in all this time. I don't think that's how you treat a best friend.'

'No, it isn't,' Gemma said solemnly. 'And I'm sorry. I'm really sorry. I'm so sorry I could kick myself. In fact, I will kick myself if that'll make you happy.'

'What are you talking about?'

'I'll do whatever you want. You name it. I'll bring you those muffins you like, I'll let you beat me at your stupid video games.'

'I always beat you at my "stupid" video games,' said Charlie, unmoved.

'It's the thought that counts,' she said. 'I'm just trying to show you that I'll do whatever it takes to make it up to you. So we can be friends again.'

He looked across the table at her, his face set into a frown, but as she met his gaze steadily and openly, his expression eventually relaxed and finally he sighed, shaking his head with a reluctant smile. 'Banana nut, don't forget.'

Gemma let out a little shriek of delight as she reached over to hug him.

'What are you doing?' he mumbled. 'Cut it out.'

'I knew you couldn't stay mad at me forever.' She beamed, settling back into her seat.

'Yeah, well, don't push it.'

'I won't, I promise. I'll be the best –' Suddenly Gemma gasped. She'd just felt a strange flutter low in her belly.

'What is it?' said Charlie.

There it was again. 'Oh my God!' she breathed. 'I just felt it, Charlie, it kicked, or jumped or did a somersault, I don't know, it's probably only the size of a teabag . . . But it moved. All on its own.' She looked straight at Charlie. 'For the first time.'

Gemma suddenly realised there was actually a baby in there. In the beginning it had been a shock, and then a novelty, then when Luke left, it became a pregnancy – a 'condition', an inconvenience. The inevitable outcome was something she preferred not to think about. Now it was making its presence felt, literally, and Gemma could ignore it no longer. She was going to have a baby.

'How does it feel?' Charlie asked.

Tears sprung into her eyes, uninvited. This wasn't like her – she didn't get soppy and sentimental. She swallowed. 'Terrifying.'

He reached across the table and took hold of her hand. 'It's going to be all right, Gem, you'll see.'

Gemma wished she could be so sure.

Friday

Helen couldn't put it off any longer. She'd talked about it with the counsellor and it was time. After all, it was a simple trip into the city from Balmain, it was no big deal. Of course, a simple trip to the city took somewhat longer now because she had to drive, and that involved finding somewhere to park, so it was expensive as well. In the past she would have just taken the bus, but Helen had discovered she couldn't bring herself to get on a bus. It made no sense, she was well aware of that. David had not been a passenger on the bus that day, at least not on the bus that killed him. He'd caught a bus to the city as usual and arrived in one piece. Passengers on the bus that struck him were unhurt. So why should Helen be bothered about getting on a bus? If she was trying to protect herself, the last thing she should be doing was driving a car, which was by far the most dangerous of all modes of travel. But for some unreasonable reason, she just couldn't step foot on a bus. She hadn't mentioned that part to the counsellor, she didn't want her to think she was crazy.

Of course, the problem was, driving in the city involved being behind, ahead or beside a bus for much of the time, and that also made Helen uncomfortable. No, more than uncomfortable, it made her anxious, even frightened. By the time she found a parking station she was a wreck, and the walk to David's office only made her worse. She jumped every time a bus barrelled past her, and she had to circle around in a wide arc to avoid the site of

David's accident. She felt like a basket case by the time she arrived at the front entrance of the Railco building.

Going into David's office to pick up his belongings was never going to be an easy thing to do. Helen had been promising to go in for months now, not that anyone had hassled her. As if. Helen was becoming used to being handled with kid gloves. A contingent from the office had showed up at the funeral, and they'd sent flowers to the house as well. It was the right thing to do, the least they could do. David was a young man killed in a tragic accident before his time. They came because it could happen to anyone, they came because they felt guilty that they were glad it hadn't happened to one of them.

Helen caught the lift to the floor where David had worked. When the doors opened she stepped out and walked over to the reception desk. 'I'm here to see Mr Craven.'

The woman glanced up at her with a fixed smile. 'Is he expecting you?'

'Yes, he is.'

'And your name, please?'

'Helen Chapman.'

The woman's eyes registered. She got to her feet. Here we go.

'Oh, Mrs Chapman, I'm sorry, I didn't realise it was you.'

What did that mean? What had she planned? To roll out the red carpet, have a group of wailers greet her?

'I'll take you to Mr Craven's office,' she said, coming around the desk.

Helen knew visitors would usually just be given directions, but losing a husband obviously meant losing your bearings as well.

'I'm Sally,' said the woman.

'Helen.'

'I didn't actually know your husband –'

Oh, this was by far the worst kind. People who had never met David thought it was their duty to wax lyrical about his reputation. That somehow, hearing what he was like from people who didn't know him from a bar of soap was going to make her feel better.

'I started just before . . . but anyway, from all accounts he was a fine colleague. Dependable. Solid.'

Helen groaned silently. If David was still alive and this woman had been asked about him, she mostly likely would have said, 'Gee, don't know him really. Can't help you.' But instead she felt duty-bound to give a meaningless eulogy.

This wasn't like Helen, sniping at people this way, even if it was in the privacy of her own mind. She had to remind herself that people were only trying to be kind, they just had no idea what was the right thing to say. Helen had no idea either. That was the problem – there was no right thing to say to someone whose husband had been hit by a bus.

They arrived at the door of Paul Craven's office. It was ajar and Helen saw him look up, his eyebrows raised expectantly.

'Mrs Chapman,' Sally announced, her tone heavy with foreboding.

Helen watched his expression change to dread, and her heart sank. She should be getting used to it, but how do you get used to that? It was as though she was a marked woman, an emissary of the Grim Reaper himself, forever a reminder of the fate that awaits us all.

Sally held the door back as Helen walked through and Paul Craven got to his feet, composing himself. Sally closed the door as she left, relieved to be escaping, no doubt.

Craven walked around the desk and grasped one of Helen's hands with both of his, meeting her eyes directly. 'I'm so sorry for your loss, Mrs Chapman.'

Rehearsed, but nonetheless genuine. 'It's Helen.'

'He was a very decent man, your husband,' he went on. 'A good worker, reliable, never one to gossip or have an opinion, couldn't draw him on anything . . . even the football – David would never take sides.'

Helen wondered if he realised these weren't necessarily traits worth lauding.

'And reliable,' he said, releasing her hand and forgetting he'd already said reliable. 'You could always count on David to do the job and not ask any questions.'

Helen had half hoped she was going to find out that David was the office clown, or a brilliant problem solver, or a leader of men . . . not the reliable one who never had an opinion about anything. He'd certainly had enough opinions at home. He liked to talk everything out ad nauseum, to the point where it exhausted Helen at times. In the end she usually just agreed with him, but he saw right through her. He was not content till he was certain she was genuinely seeing things his way.

But apparently he'd kept to himself at work. He had told her he didn't feel as though he belonged. He didn't fit in, he had different aspirations, but it didn't bother him too much, he wasn't going to be there forever. Helen had never met any of David's work colleagues. Christmas parties were for staff only, and David had never stayed long anyway. She could probably count the number of times on one hand that he'd stopped in to have a beer with them on his way home. He said they were all nice people – he had a lot of respect for Paul Craven, felt he ran the place fairly, but Helen couldn't recall any other names. Of course he had mentioned people, but that was all, only a mention.

'Would you like a seat, can I get you a coffee . . . or something?' Craven said awkwardly, breaking into her reverie.

'No, no, I'm fine. I can't stay.'

He looked relieved. 'Well, let me show you to his things. I hope you understand, when you didn't come in right away . . . well, we had to clear his desk.'

'Of course.'

Helen followed him to a storeroom on the other side of the office. One or two people looked up as they passed, but as they had no idea who she was, they were uninterested. Helen was glad to be anonymous; in fact, she found her greatest relief these days in anonymity. Paul Craven opened the storeroom door and turned on the light, ushering her inside. It was about the size of a small bedroom, windowless, with shelves lining the walls either side, stacked with files, paper and other items of stationery. He stepped on a stool and reached up to the top shelf to a box with 'David Chapman' written on the side in thick black marker. He stepped down again and handed it to Helen. It wasn't heavy at all.

'If you'd like to have a look through first,' he said tentatively, 'I could find a desk for you outside, or you can use my office.'

'That's very kind,' said Helen, 'but just here will be fine.'

He frowned mildly. 'Are you sure?'

'Absolutely,' she replied, 'I won't be long.'

'Take all the time you need.'

He left her alone and Helen sat on the footstool and rested the box on her lap. The lid was taped down, and she peeled the tape away carefully so that it could be resealed. The inside looked rather forlorn. It appeared to be mostly stationery: there was even a pen clearly marked with the departmental logo. Perhaps there was a policy that on the death of a staff member the family inherited everything on their desk at the time. There was a notepad and a half-empty box of paperclips; a couple of old Christmas cards that must have been given to him at work, from Paul Craven, and from a Sue and family to David and family. And there was a framed picture of Noah at preschool; they had given him that last Father's Day to replace the baby photo, but that was still here as well. Helen picked up a packet of Tic Tacs that didn't look as though they'd been touched. Was that because someone had given them to him and he didn't like them, or because he'd only just bought them? And did it matter? What did it tell her about David? What did any of this tell her about him? Here was his whole working life in a cardboard box. It didn't tell her anything.

Helen realised she was finding it hard to breathe – there was no air in this tiny windowless room. She shoved everything back into the box and carried it with her out of the room, out of the office and out of the building. She didn't speak to anyone, or even make eye contact. And she didn't look back.

*

'So what are we going to do with this?' said Gemma, holding up the bottle of champagne Phoebe thrust at her as she opened the front door.

'Celebrate, you know, drink to your new place.'

'Except I can't drink.'

'Damn, I keep forgetting,' said Phoebe. 'I can't seem to wrap my head around the fact you're not drinking.'

'You and me both.' Gemma stood back as Phoebe walked past her into the hall.

'Wow, it's a great old place,' she said, gazing around. 'A bit shabby, but imagine what you could do with it.'

'I'd rather not,' said Gemma. 'I'm glad it hasn't been homogenised into some poncy designer's wet dream. It has character.'

Phoebe raised a dubious eyebrow. 'So, is your landlady home?'

She winced. 'Don't call her that. She's barely older than me.'

'So? She's still your landlady.'

'Yeah, but landlady makes her sound like a little old woman with hair rollers and an apron,' said Gemma. 'And no, she isn't here right now, but she should be home any minute. She sticks to a pretty tight schedule with Noah, and it's bathtime soon.'

'Tight schedule? Must be a challenge for you,' Phoebe said. 'So, are you going to show me around?'

Gemma took her on the grand tour, bypassing Helen's and Noah's bedrooms, and ending up in the family room at the back of the house. It had probably been tacked on sometime in the sixties, and the larger windows helped make it feel a little less claustrophobic than the rest of the place, but it was still cluttered and dreary.

'It's like a museum,' Phoebe murmured.

'Apparently she grew up here,' said Gemma. 'I think she's lived her whole life in this house.'

'And nothing's changed all that time, by the looks of it.' Phoebe wandered across the room, pausing in front of a closed door. 'Where does this lead to?'

An ornate but ugly hall table was pushed up against the door, filling the alcove. It was topped with a large cut crystal bowl stuffed with dusty artificial roses. The door, frame and architraves had been painted the same dirty green as the walls, as though to disguise they were really there.

'I have no idea,' Gemma said. 'Helen, my um, landlady, well, she's an incredibly private person. Obviously whatever's behind there, she certainly doesn't want anyone to see.'

'You're sounding like an Agatha Christie novel. It probably just leads outside and they wanted to block the exit.'

'No, there's definitely a room beyond there. I checked from outside.'

'Ooh, the plot thickens. It's probably just a storeroom or something.'

'Then why seal it up? Don't you think it's a bit strange?'

'No, I think you're a bit strange.' Phoebe turned her attention instead to the sideboard nearby, which was covered with framed family photographs. Most of them were quite old, stern black-and-white portraits of apparently humourless people from another era. But there was a wedding photo that was much more recent, of a striking dark-haired woman arm in arm with a tall, blond man. Actually, the only thing that suggested it was a wedding was that the woman was holding a bouquet; the couple were both dressed in fairly nondescript day clothes.

'That's Helen,' said Gemma when Phoebe paused in front of the photo.

'She's very attractive. How long ago was this taken?'

'A few years, I guess. She hasn't changed much.' Gemma leaned closer. She wasn't all that cheerful now, though oddly, for her wedding day, she didn't look all that cheerful then.

'He looks like the guy in that police show in the seventies,' said Phoebe.

'Yeah, right,' Gemma said dubiously.

'What was his name?'

'I have no idea who you're talking about, Phee.' Gemma rolled her eyes. 'Do you know how many police shows there were in the seventies?'

'Oh, but you do know,' Phoebe insisted. 'There were two of them, red car, one wore a big chunky cardigan all the time.'

'You think he looks like Starsky? Starsky had dark curly hair; he looks nothing like Starsky.'

'Well, it must be the other one then, Hutch.'

Gemma peered closer at the photograph. 'Mm, I guess,' she murmured. 'It's giving me the shivers looking at him.'

'Why, is he dead or something?'

Gemma looked at her. 'Yeah, actually, he is.'

'What?' Phoebe blinked. 'What happened? How did he die? He's so young.'

'It was an accident, a really tragic accident,' Gemma said gravely. 'You're not going to believe it.'

'Now it really is starting to sound like an Agatha Christie novel.' Phoebe turned to look squarely at Gemma. 'Did it happen here in the house? Is that why you're so interested in that room?'

'No, no,' Gemma said, pausing for effect. 'He got hit by a bus.'

Phoebe looked confused. 'What do you mean?'

'I mean, a bus ran him over.'

'For real?'

'For real.'

Phoebe winced. 'It sounds like a bad joke.'

'I know. Imagine having to tell people that all the time.'

They were silent for a moment till Phoebe sighed loudly. 'Well, I think I could use that drink now.'

They sat at the kitchen table, Phoebe sipping her wine and Gemma sipping orange juice.

'So when did it happen?' Phoebe asked.

'Just a few months ago apparently.'

'It's so sad . . . and tragic . . . I mean, what do you say to a person in those circumstances?'

'Nothing,' said Gemma. 'She doesn't want to talk about it.'

'No wonder,' said Phoebe. 'Does she seem okay to you?'

'I guess, but she doesn't have much of a life. She gave up work. She doesn't seem to do much of anything, except look after Noah.'

'He's the little boy?'

'Yeah. Poor kid.'

'Poor her. The kid's probably young enough to get over it. How's she supposed to get over it?'

Gemma wondered how she'd feel if she found out Luke had been hit by a bus. At the moment, she had to admit she'd probably throw a party. Maybe not right away. She'd put it off till she could have a drink at least.

'Moving on to less morbid territory,' said Phoebe, setting her glass down in front of her. 'How's the new job?'

'It's all right,' said Gemma. 'Jo left today – I'm on my own from next week.'

'You're ready for that?'

Gemma propped her chin on her hand, thinking. 'Yes and no. The MD has got this complicated scheduling system, you have no idea. But I think I've figured it out. I don't like it, but I can understand it. It's just that I'm not going to get much of a chance to impress him if I'm stuck at my desk the whole time.'

'What makes you think you'll be stuck at your desk all day?' Phoebe asked.

'Jo spent all day long, day in, day out, at the workstation. She didn't go to one meeting with him all week.' Gemma shook her head. 'Liz used to shadow Jonesy; that's what I thought a good PA did.'

Phoebe shrugged. 'Depends on the boss, what he needs.'

'Well, I've barely caught sight of him all week,' said Gemma. 'He didn't even show up on Friday afternoon to say goodbye to Jo, he just rang. I was beginning to think he was avoiding me.'

'I think you're being a little paranoid, Gem,' Phoebe said. 'If he was avoiding anyone, it would have been Jo. He wasn't going to have to see her again, whereas he'll be working with you from now on.'

'I suppose,' said Gemma, just as they heard the front door, followed by voices in the hall. 'That'll be Helen. Don't say anything about . . . you know,' she added, dropping to a whisper.

Phoebe pulled a face. 'Like I'm going to bring that up.'

A moment later Helen appeared in the doorway. She looked a little startled, or rattled. Something was bothering her.

'Hi Helen,' Gemma said brightly. 'This is my sister, Phoebe.'

Phoebe jumped up from her chair and offered her hand across the table. Helen seemed a little dazed, just staring at it.

'Pleased to meet you,' Phoebe said, her hand still hanging midair.

Helen appeared to shake herself out of her reverie, taking Phoebe's hand. 'Nice to meet you, too.'

'Would you like a glass of bubbly?' Gemma asked.

Helen glanced down at the bottle. She used to drink more; in fact, she went through a bad stage after Tony left and her mother sank into a fog of depression that never lifted, eventually becoming the confusion and disorientation that was Alzheimer's. As Helen was able to get out less and less, she found herself turning to the bottle more and more, until the night she passed out and her mother left the house, wandering the streets dressed only in her nightgown. It was the call from the police that finally woke Helen. Marion had been found curled up asleep in someone's front yard. On being disturbed, she apparently had one of her more lucid moments and was able to parrot off her name and phone number. The police were calling to verify before they drove her home. Helen tried to sober up quickly, but she never forgot the look on the face of the policeman who brought her mother to the door. Helen stopped drinking after that. She had enjoyed the odd glass or two of wine with David on special occasions, but he'd never been much of a drinker anyway.

'Really,' Phoebe urged her. 'I can't drink it all by myself.'

'No, um, no thanks,' said Helen, backing out of the doorway again. 'Noah's getting ready for his bath. I'd better go and help him.' And with that she slipped out of sight.

Gemma and Phoebe looked at each other. Gemma mouthed the word 'weird' and Phoebe shrugged her shoulders.

'Should I go, do you think?' she whispered.

Gemma shook her head. 'No way. Don't tell me I can't have people visit.'

In the bathroom Helen was filling the tub when Noah appeared in the doorway, his arms laden with a collection of toys.

'Noah,' she protested mildly, 'look at all the toys you have in here already.'

'But I haffa have these ones for my game.'

What did it matter? 'Okay,' Helen sighed wearily, turning off the taps. Noah emptied his conscripts into the bath with a splash and clambered in after them. Helen leaned back against the doorjamb, watching him but not really seeing him. All she could see was that sad little box of David's belongings, the sad little job that he'd never wanted. But neither had he summoned up the wherewithal to leave. Would he have stayed there forever? Would that have been his life? Maybe walking in front of a bus had been the best thing that ever happened to him.

Helen shook her head to banish the thought, horrified with herself that she'd even entertained such an appalling idea. 'I'll just be in the kitchen, sweetie,' she said to Noah, who was oblivious to whether she was there or not. She walked briskly down the hall, appearing rather breathlessly in the doorway. Gemma and her sister looked up at her, a little startled.

'Um, maybe I will,' she cleared her throat, 'maybe I will have a glass with you.'

Gemma smiled. 'Sure, come on in, join us.'

Helen nodded, crossing to the cupboard where the wineglasses were kept. She brought one back to the table and sat down, while Phoebe poured the wine.

'Thanks,' said Helen.

'So how was your day?' Gemma asked warily.

Helen took a mouthful and set the glass down in front of her. Just say it. 'I had to go into David's office today to collect his things. I've been putting it off . . .'

They were uncomfortable, clearly – she was making them feel uncomfortable. That was her role in life now.

Phoebe spoke first. 'Gemma told me what happened. I'm so sorry for your loss.'

'Thank you.'

More awkward silence.

Helen sipped her wine, feeling despondent. Apparently she couldn't even sit around with a couple of girls and have a drink and a chat without dragging everyone down. She missed the company of other women, the camaraderie, the shared experiences. But who was she going to find that shared her experience now? She had become a kind of freak because her husband had died in a freak accident. Maybe she could start a support group for people like her. She couldn't think of anything more depressing.

'Well, I'd better get going,' said Phoebe, standing up.

Helen looked across at her anxiously. 'Please, I didn't mean to break things up.'

'No, no, you didn't,' they protested in a chorus. 'There's ten kilometres of road somewhere with Phoebe's name on it,' Gemma added, but Helen only frowned.

'She's one of those people who jogs,' Gemma tried to explain. 'Not in her right mind,' she added in an exaggerated whisper.

'Actually,' Phoebe interrupted, 'we're going out to dinner tonight, so I really do have to get going. It was lovely to meet you, Helen.'

Gemma walked her sister to the door as Helen went to check on Noah. He was still immersed in his game. It usually took a bit of cajoling to get him into the bath, but once in, she couldn't get him out. He would happily stay till the water was cold and his skin completely shrivelled. Noah seemed content to play on his own, which was just as well, he wasn't going to have much choice. Seeing Gemma and her sister, the banter between them, made Helen think about Tony. They'd been so close as kids, and even through their teens. In fact she'd always planned to meet up with him overseas. That of course had never happened, and now it felt as though there was so much distance between them, and not the kind measured in kilometres. She really should make an effort to keep in touch, like he'd suggested.

'Is everything all right?'

Helen turned around to see Gemma watching her expectantly.

'Sure, everything's fine.'

Gemma nodded. 'It was okay? My sister coming –'

'Of course, don't even mention it,' Helen dismissed. 'Any time.'

'So, you are all right?' Gemma persisted.

'Yes, why wouldn't I be?'

'Well, it's just that it couldn't have been easy today, I would imagine.'

Helen took a breath. 'No, it wasn't.' She walked past Gemma and around into her room. She was still holding the glass of wine. She sat on the bed and took a sip. When she looked up, Gemma was hovering in the doorway.

'Do you want to talk about it?' she asked tentatively.

'Talk about what?'

'Today, going to your husband's office . . .'

'There's not a lot to talk about. They had a box already packed up. There was just stationery, a packet of Tic Tacs, not much to say about any of that.'

Gemma nodded. 'Well, if you ever did want to talk, you know where to find me,' she said with a faint smile.

'Thanks.' Helen watched her slowly turn away. 'Gemma?'

She turned back again.

Helen looked at her directly. 'Do you think . . .' She hesitated, searching for the right way to say this. 'Oh, never mind.'

'Go on, what is it?' Gemma urged, walking further into the room.

Helen took a breath. 'Do you think everything happens for a reason?'

Jesus, that was a bit of a delicate question, to say the least. What was she supposed to say to that?

Gemma decided to go with honesty. 'I don't know. I mean, it all depends on whether there's a god or not, doesn't it? And I don't just mean whether you believe in one or not, I mean whether there really is one or not. The people who believe in one tend to think everything happens for a reason, regardless. Sickness, health, good luck, bad luck, rain or shine. They pray that it won't rain on their daughter's wedding day, while a farmer somewhere is praying that it will. If it rains, who's right?'

Somewhere in there, Gemma realised she'd lost her point. The expression on Helen's face confirmed it.

'That's not exactly what I was getting at,' Helen said politely. 'I was just asking if you think accidents really happen, if there's not some kind of intent involved.'

Frigging hell. Her husband got hit by a bus. What was Gemma supposed to say? More to the point, what did Helen want to hear?

'Well,' said Gemma, going to sit on the bed beside Helen, who looked a little taken aback as she shifted to make room. 'You can't have an accident on purpose,' Gemma went on. 'That's an oxymoron. If there was intent, it wasn't an accident.'

'I guess I'm wondering if there isn't hidden intent in everything we do,' said Helen. 'I mean, most people would agree that adults are responsible for their actions and the consequences. So how can anything truly be considered an accident?'

'If that was the case, then it wasn't an accident that I got pregnant,' said Gemma. 'I had sex, so I had to be prepared for the consequences. Fair enough. But does that include the father pissing off? Did I somehow knowingly choose someone who would walk out on me at the slightest whiff of commitment or responsibility?'

'Maybe you did,' Helen said guilelessly.

Gemma blinked.

'I mean, it gives you an excuse,' Helen went on. 'You can bring a child into the world maintaining that it wasn't what you'd planned, it was an accident, so it's not your fault if it all goes wrong.'

Gemma didn't think she wanted to listen to any more of this. She stood up and walked to the door.

'Gemma, I'm sorry,' said Helen quickly.

She stopped and turned around in the doorway, waiting.

'I don't think that came out right. I wasn't meaning to imply . . .'

'You know what, Helen, I don't think everything happens for a reason, I think it's all random,' said Gemma. 'There's no plan, no purpose, no deep meaning. Shit happens, and unfortunately life seems to consist of shovelling it out of the way the best we can.'

Bailey's

'Come on, Charlie,' Gemma pleaded. 'Just show me what you're working on. I'm going to see it eventually.'

'Yes, you will,' he said, unmoved.

'So, come on.'

'My understanding of the word eventually is "at some later time".'

Gemma groaned. 'I just want to be up to speed before the meeting this afternoon.'

'But you're not invited to the meeting this afternoon,' he reminded her. 'You just got through telling me you're not invited to any meetings, and that you're going stir-crazy and you can't take it anymore –'

'That's why I'm not waiting to be asked this time,' she said. 'I'm gatecrashing.'

'It's not a party, Gem. What are you going to do when the MD asks you to leave?'

'He won't, or he might at first, but I'm going to impress him with my savvy knowledge of the campaign, dazzle him with my invaluable input and generally blow him away with my talent and insight. He won't ask me to leave, in fact, I'll wager he'll be asking me to every meeting from now on. Before long, he'll have me running meetings –'

'Is that before or after you have the baby?'

Gemma scowled at him. 'You know what you're like, Charlie? You're like a rusty bit of jagged steel on a country road, lying in wait to puncture me the minute I'm getting anywhere.'

He rolled his eyes. 'Please tell me you're not going into copywriting?'

'Maybe I will. Who knows what's ahead of me?' she declared archly. 'You know what, Charlie, I've decided I can do anything. Why should I let a pregnancy get in the way? I was almost not going to take this job just because I was pregnant. How shortsighted is that?'

'About as shortsighted as thinking a baby's not going to change your life.'

'I was only talking about the pregnancy,' Gemma said. 'I don't even know if I'm keeping the baby at this stage.'

Charlie's jaw dropped. 'Are you serious?'

She stood up and walked towards the window so she didn't have to look at the shock on his face. 'I'm serious that I don't know.'

He was right behind her. 'What are you talking about?' he said anxiously. 'You can't just give your baby away.'

Gemma turned to face him. 'Why can't I? It's Luke's baby too, but he got to run off and he doesn't even have to think about it again. I, on the other hand, have to carry it for nine months, stop drinking, smoking, or having any fun, and what do I get in return? Childbirth, stretchmarks, boobs that'll end up hanging to my waist, stitches where even the sun don't shine, probably incontinence . . . But wait, there's more – I'm also supposed to sacrifice everything to bring up a child that I didn't plan, that I didn't ask to have, when there are people out there who are desperate to have a baby and would give anything.'

Charlie looked stunned. 'But it's yours, Gem. You can't . . .' His voice faded away.

'I might not have a choice, Charlie,' she said. 'I can't look after a child if I don't have a decent job, some kind of future. If the MD thinks I'm indispensable, I might just manage to keep my job, then I can think about whether I keep the baby.'

He nodded thoughtfully. 'Come on then, let me show you what I have here.'

2 pm

'Thank you, Ms Atkinson,' said the MD, in a tone that suggested 'that will be all'.

Gemma had just shown Charlie and Mel and her perky little assistant into the MD's office. She had earmarked this meeting for a few reasons, not least because of Charlie being here. But Gemma had a good rapport with Mel as well; she knew she'd treat any contribution Gemma made with due respect. It was only to be a brief progress meeting for a particular campaign, which was why the MD was holding it in his office. That gave Gemma easy access, and she was staying put.

'I have nothing else better to do,' she said lightly, dragging a chair over to join the group. 'I'll take notes.'

'I usually take my own notes,' he said.

'So, I'll save you the trouble,' she persisted cheerfully.

'It isn't any trouble.'

'I know, I'm happy to do it.'

His eyes narrowed as he glared at her, before glancing around at the others. It was becoming awkward. The only way for him to proceed with a modicum of dignity was to allow her to stay.

'Okay then, let's get on with it, shall we?' he said, not making eye contact with her again. 'What have you got to show me?'

Charlie had been nursing a laptop, and he got to his feet, placing it on the desk in front of the MD.

'This is still a rough cut, but it should give you a reasonable idea,' Charlie said, coming around beside him. He opened the laptop and clicked on a series of keys. The advertisement in question began to play, and the MD sat back in his chair, clasping his hands behind his head. Gemma couldn't see it from where she sat, but she'd watched it several times over that morning. It had been an expensive ad to create. It began as a montage of filmed scenes: children climbing on a play structure in a park, a young couple dancing the length of a nondescript suburban street, a family running along the seashore trailing a kite. Charlie's magic came into play then, as the children morphed into adults looking through a new home, the street unfolded into a *rue* in Paris, and the kite transformed into an aeroplane, all to a nostalgic song by the Mamas and Papas as soundtrack. Until today's meeting, apparently the MD hadn't had much of a clue about what they'd been trying to achieve, Gemma had discovered from his notes. It seemed the man was not overendowed with imagination, which was unfortunate considering the industry he found himself in. What he did focus on was the cost, and he hadn't seen much for the huge production budget so far. Mel had asked Charlie to mock up something quickly to give him an idea of the end result. Of course, they usually had the luxury of working through this stage without someone second-guessing them, but that was another era. Things were different now.

The song faded out as the ad had played through to the end. The MD was still sitting in the same position, he hadn't budged. Finally he sighed loudly. 'What's it for?'

Charlie was speechless. He opened his mouth but nothing came out.

'I'm not sure what you're getting at, MD,' Mel said instead.

He brought his hands down onto the desk in front of him, leaning forward. 'What is it advertising?'

'Uh, you know, MD,' said Charlie, 'the State Bank.'

'I didn't see a bank.'

'MD, a bank is an entity, not a building,' Mel tried to explain. 'The fact is, more than seventy percent of the banking population never set foot in a bank from one month to the next anymore. Even people who don't bank online are paid straight into bank accounts and use debit and credit cards to pay for nearly everything, or else pick up the phone to pay the rest. People don't go into a bank if they can help it. It's not relevant to use bricks and mortar to represent a bank nowadays, MD.'

'I'm not suggesting there had to be a building,' said the MD. 'I simply want to know how that ad has anything to do with banking.'

'It's a concept ad,' Charlie blurted. He was still standing nervously beside the desk, like a schoolboy waiting to be dismissed by the headmaster.

The MD turned to look up at him. 'Why don't you take a seat, Charlie.' He paused while Charlie returned to his chair. 'So tell me,' he resumed, 'what is the "concept"?'

'Freedom,' said Mel, as though it was obvious.

'And what has freedom got to do with banking?'

'Well, MD, money is freedom,' she went on, throwing him the pitch she'd used for the client. 'So how we access our money, where we choose to store our money, who lends us our money, all affect our freedom.'

'But how does anyone get that idea from that ad?' he said. 'There's no information about accounts or borrowing, no details.'

'You can't bombard the consumer with a whole lot of info,' said Mel. 'They won't remember it, and besides, there's too much advertising clutter out there as it is. People are confused, overloaded. You have to find a way to break through the clutter and hit them hard with the core message you're trying to convey.'

'And wouldn't that include a few pertinent details, some selling points?' asked the MD. 'Or else how can the consumer decide if they want it, if it's any better than what they have already?'

'Spruiking is outdated,' Gemma broke in.

The MD glanced over at her as though she were an annoying insect that had just buzzed into the room.

'It's not as effective nowadays,' she sailed on, undaunted. 'You can't tell consumers that something is bigger, better, shinier – they don't believe you anymore, they're too sophisticated.'

'And yet they get confused if you try to give them details?' he shot back. 'You can't have it both ways – are they too sophisticated or too stupid?'

No one had an answer for that.

'Whatever,' he dismissed, 'I still don't understand how an image of a child on a beach with a kite encourages people to move their business to this bank.'

'Lifestyle,' said Mel. 'We're trying to sell them a lifestyle.'

The MD lifted an eyebrow. 'Last I knew, you didn't have to take out a loan to go to the beach, thank God.'

'You're intellectualising the ad, MD,' Mel said carefully, 'but we don't want people to respond intellectually. We want them to respond emotionally, to link the brand with the kind of life they want to lead, the kind of people they believe they are, or want to be. We want them to make an emotional, even a spiritual connection with the State Bank.'

The MD was listening thoughtfully. Maybe Mel had got through to him at last. He sat back in his chair and sighed again, heavily. 'So in other words it's bullshit, right?'

'Pardon?'

'This kind of advertising, it's all bullshit. Started by a bunch of advertisers having a wank, I'm betting to impress each other more than anything.'

Even Mel looked rattled, and she did not rattle easily. 'They test well at screenings,' she said in a voice a couple of sizes smaller than usual. 'People like them.'

'Sure,' the MD agreed. 'They like the music, pretty pictures, colour and movement. But how many of them actually go and buy the product? In fact, how many of them even know what the product is? There must be some research on this somewhere.'

'I'll look into it,' Gemma said crisply, jotting down a note, very indispensable assistant-like.

The MD opened his mouth to say something to her, but must have thought better of it. He looked at Mel and Charlie instead.

'The thing is, Australians love to send things up and they can't stand bullshit. Ads like these are entirely bullshit, and they take themselves too seriously. They might work in Europe, but think about it – what have been the most successful campaigns in Australia?' He paused. He was actually waiting for an answer. 'Anyone?'

'The big beer ad,' Charlie said finally, wistfully.

'Perfect example,' said the MD. 'Irreverent, hilarious, it actually sent up the idea of taking things too seriously.'

'But that was a hugely expensive ad to produce at the time,' Mel pointed out.

'Which achieved hugely successful results,' he said. 'The client won't mind spending the big bucks if it gets the big returns.'

'So what do you want us to do about this campaign?' Mel asked tentatively. 'I should point out, the client liked the concept, and we've spent a lot of money already –'

'We have to go with it now,' he said. 'But let's see if we can't come up with something better, something different, next time. I don't want Bailey's to be arthouse anymore. Let's start making ads that sell stuff.'

Gemma held the door open as the trio filed out of the office. Charlie looked shattered. Mel looked frustrated. The perky little assistant who hadn't said boo the whole time just looked bewildered. Gemma was about to follow them out when the MD stopped her.

'Ms Atkinson?' he said firmly.

She turned back to look at him.

'Close the door.'

She did as she was asked.

'Don't do that again.'

Gemma was tempted to ask him what it was exactly that she shouldn't be doing again, but thought better of it. He didn't seem to be the kind of person who'd tolerate pleading ignorant, or even a little humour. She had to take a risk, meet him at his own game, get him to respect her for being as bloody-minded as he was.

'Are you saying that I shouldn't sit in on meetings anymore?'

'Not unless you're invited.' He began to shuffle papers on his desk, indicating that she was dismissed.

'Well, maybe you should start inviting me,' she said.

He looked at her over the top of his glasses. 'Pardon?'

'I think you need a second chair.'

'What are you talking about?'

'Someone to smooth the way, give you feedback,' she went on. 'You're not going to win many allies with your approach.'

'And tell me, Ms Atkinson, when you were running an ad agency, what was your favoured approach?'

Gemma ignored the sarcasm and ploughed on. 'As you know,' she said, walking further into the room, 'I was here when Jonesy was in charge, and, fair enough, he almost took the place to the wall, but at least the staff were happy.'

'I'm not in the business of making people happy, unless they're the ones paying me. When I'm paying them, and losing money doing it, well, they can bite me.'

Gemma was aghast. 'Whatever Jonesy was doing or not doing with the books, that had nothing to do with the rank and file. They were working hard, doing their best for a boss who nurtured and encouraged them. Did you see Charlie at the end then? He was devastated. The guy is brilliant. Have you even seen any of his work? Do you know how many awards he's won for the agency?'

'Awards don't sell products,' said the MD, unfazed. 'They only impress other agencies.'

'And potential clients. You get an award, suddenly you get a whole load of new accounts.'

'But if all you get is awards and no results, the clients will march, and all you're left with is a very attractive trophy case.'

Gemma plonked down on a chair. 'It wasn't the staff's fault that Jonesy screwed up. They were all working hard. And you walk in here like an auditor and everyone's suddenly scared of losing their jobs.'

MD lifted his glasses and rubbed his eyes. 'No one has lost their job.'

'Yet,' she muttered.

'Right, I've had this,' he said, standing up and leaning over his desk. Gemma shrunk back in the chair, looking up at him. 'I moved heaven and earth so that not one job was lost. There were two, no, three people who left in the months after I came, and we didn't replace them, that was all. Where are you getting this information?'

Gemma was trying to remember where she'd heard that jobs had been cut, and then she realised she hadn't heard it anywhere. In fact Lauren had just said that there had been talk of staff cuts but that instead they'd brought this guy up from Melbourne . . .

'Sorry, I must have got it wrong.'

'You do everything you can,' he went on, apparently not hearing her, 'and people are still going to think what they like. They make things up, they actually make things up.' He raised his arms and walked away from the desk. 'You know, it wouldn't matter what I did. I could double their wages, put on free drinks every Friday, have staff meetings in a luxury resort, and they'd still complain because I'm not Jonesy. But what none of them seems to realise is that Jonesy nearly cost them their jobs. I saved them, but do you think that's the way they see it?'

Gemma stood up. 'I got it wrong, okay? I was mistaken. Someone did mention the possibility of staff cuts, but that you were brought in instead.'

He just stared at her.

'No one said anything bad about you,' she half lied.

He breathed out, nodding faintly.

'You should really lighten up,' she said under her breath.

'What did you say?'

'Nothing.'

He frowned at her. 'Well, I've got work to do. That'll be all, Ms Atkinson.'

'Oh, would you stop calling me that?' she groaned.

'What?' He blinked. 'Ms Atkinson?'

'It's so patronising. My name is Gemma. Please call me Gemma.'

He had an odd look on his face, almost as though he was embarrassed. 'I wasn't . . . I didn't mean to be patronising. That . . . wasn't my intention.' He cleared his throat. '*Gemma.*'

'Okay,' she said, a little bemused.

He nodded. 'We'd better get back to work,' he said. 'Please close the door on your way out.'

When Gemma returned to her desk an email had arrived in her inbox. It was from Mel. More of a summons really:

Meeting down at DryDock at 6:30.

DryDock was one of the team's favourite watering holes, down at east Darling Harbour. When Gemma arrived she spotted Mel straightaway, along with the entire team. Even Charlie was there, and he had never been much of a 'drinks after work' kind of guy, at least not with this crowd. The creatives and the ad execs were a little like oil and water, they tended not to mix socially.

The group had commandeered a couple of tables and already had a round of drinks in front of them. The mood, however, could hardly be described as jovial. Sombre was more like it, even grim.

Mel saw her coming first and immediately got to her feet. 'Hey, Gemma. I'll get you a drink – your usual?'

'No,' Gemma blurted without thinking.

Mel looked at her oddly. Gemma glanced at Charlie and he leaped up from his seat.

'She has a different usual now,' he said. 'That is, her usual is not the same as it was before.' He gave up trying to explain himself. 'I'll get it.'

Gemma threw Charlie a relieved smile, which he returned, before heading for the bar.

'Pull up a roost, Gemma,' said Justin. He was sprawled in his customary fashion, one leg hooked loosely across the other, arms spread out along the backs of the chairs beside him, regardless of the discomfort or otherwise of their occupants. Justin seemed to have a need to take up as much space as his lanky limbs afforded him.

Gemma walked around the table to where Charlie had been sitting; she knew he wouldn't mind her taking his chair.

'So what did you make of the MD's dummy-spit this afternoon?' Justin asked her.

She shrugged. 'Typical.'

'So he's said this kind of thing to you before?' asked Mel.

'Oh no,' Gemma assured her. 'He doesn't say much of anything to me.'

'What do you mean? You're his assistant,' said Justin.

'In name only. He's a one-man show. I just answer the phones.'

'We were hoping to get some inside information from you,' said Mel. 'Let us in on what makes him tick, or see if you know something we don't.'

Gemma shook her head. 'Sorry, he's not an easy person to get to know. He really keeps to himself. That's the first meeting I've been to since I started, and I had to push my way in.'

'The guy's an arrogant arsehole,' Justin declared, oblivious to the irony of him of all people making that remark.

Charlie returned to the table with Gemma's drink, trailing another chair behind him.

'I think we should take this straight to the board,' Justin announced.

'What are you suggesting?' said Mel, frowning.

'Mutiny,' said Marcus.

'Fuck off, it's not mutiny, Marcus,' Justin scoffed. 'Don't be so dramatic.'

'You don't know who he's got in his corner on the board,' Marcus warned. 'You could end up shooting yourself in the foot, Justin.'

'Look, they need to know what's going on. The board got us into this, they took a punt. Granted, it was an emergency. The place was on fire, and they called in a top-gun fireman, but he shouldn't be running the joint now. I looked into his HR file – he's a management consultant, a fucking number-cruncher. He doesn't even have any background in advertising. It's like having the leader of the country sending out troops when he's never served in the armed forces.'

'Jesus, Justin, that is such a load of crap,' said Mel.

'Why?'

'I don't have a problem with a leader who hasn't served in the army, I have a problem with him if he won't take advice from those who have. That's the problem here – the MD won't delegate or seek advice or confer with anyone.'

Charlie cleared his throat. 'He does have a point, though . . . maybe.'

Everyone at the table turned to look at him.

'The MD, what he said today, it does make sense.'

'What are you talking about, Charlie?' Justin said, clearly unimpressed.

He took a deep breath and sat forward, leaning his elbows on the table. 'After I left his office this afternoon, I did a bit of research. The MD questioned whether concept advertising actually works. Turns out it might not.'

All eyes were still on him. None of them looked the least bit convinced.

'There was a big campaign in the US a few years back to introduce a new airline,' Charlie went on, gathering steam. 'Television and radio, magazines, billboards, full saturation. But they never showed a plane in any of the commercials. Even the name of the airline was unrelated – it had nothing to do with flying or travelling.'

'And?' Justin prompted him.

'It tanked,' Charlie said simply. 'The airline eventually had to fold.'

'You can't necessarily blame that on the advertising,' said Mel.

'Maybe not. But in all the focus groups and market research they conducted, people reportedly loved the ads, but product recognition was poor to nonexistent. The vast majority had no idea what was being advertised. Even if the airline failed for other reasons, they wasted a whole lot of money on a campaign that didn't work.'

There was silence around the table as everyone appeared to be mulling that idea over; drinks were sipped, one or two were drained, a cigarette was lit.

'So why are you suddenly pissing in the MD's pocket?' Justin said finally, glaring at Charlie.

'I'm just saying, we're having a knee-jerk reaction. Maybe we should think about what he actually said.'

'So what are we supposed to do?' said Justin. '"Big Kev"-style ads? Go back to the days of "*Where do you get it?*".'

'I don't think it has to be one or the other,' Charlie said plainly. 'Can't we do tasteful, witty, clever, beautiful even . . . and still make it clear what the ad's selling?'

Mel looked thoughtful. 'Hard to argue with that.'

'That's all the MD was asking for,' said Charlie.

'I'd still rather knock the arrogant son-of-a-bitch off his fucking perch,' Justin grizzled.

'Let's make that Plan B,' said Marcus. 'In the meantime, whose round is it?'

*

Gemma didn't want to stay long; the cigarette smoke was making her feel sick, as was the Coke Charlie had bought for her. She made her move when another round was called, and Charlie grabbed the excuse to go with her.

'I was surprised you took the MD's side in there with the lions,' said Gemma. 'After the way he treated you today . . .'

'He didn't treat me badly,' said Charlie. 'Besides, he came to see me afterwards, you know.'

'He did?'

'He wanted to apologise in case I thought he was criticising my work.'

'*He did?* No wonder you were so eager to jump to his defence tonight,' she muttered.

Charlie glanced sideways at her. 'We ended up having a good chat about the whole thing. He struck a chord, to be honest.'

'What do you mean?'

'I was really proud of the work I'd done on that ad. I was using a new program, trying out some new techniques. The morphing was seamless. From a technical point of view, I leaped a couple of tall buildings.'

'So why weren't you pissed off when the MD trashed it?'

'Because sometimes I get so lost in what I'm doing that I forget what it is that I'm actually doing.'

Gemma frowned at him.

'Sometimes I look at an ad when all the editing is done, and the voiceover is in place, and I realise my amazing achievement is going to sell toilet paper.'

'Everyone needs toilet paper, Charlie.'

'Yeah, they do. But maybe they don't need all the hours, the expertise, the money that it takes to create an ad to tell them that.'

'No,' said Gemma, 'they need it to convince them to buy a particular brand.'

'Is it really that important?'

'It is to the client.'

Charlie sighed a long, drawn-out sigh.

Gemma looked at him. 'Hold on a minute, I've heard that sigh before.'

'Oh?'

'In fact I've heard this whole spiel before. Creative angst mixed with social conscience – a deadly combination. But it always passes.'

'Maybe.' He shrugged. 'Or maybe it won't this time. Maybe I don't want it to.'

Balmain

'I guess there's a certain amount of comfort in knowing that at least the MD took what I said about Charlie on board,' said Gemma to Phoebe on the phone the following afternoon. 'Not that he acknowledged it.'

'Well, hang in there,' Phoebe said. 'What do I keep telling you?'

'Yes, I know, "make myself indispensable". Easier said when the boss is a control freak.'

'Nothing wrong with control freaks.'

'And you would say that.' Gemma heard a series of sharp knocks. 'Oh, that's someone at the door.'

'I have to go anyway,' said Phoebe. 'Talk to you later.'

Gemma hung up and hurried up the hall as the knocking persisted. 'Coming, coming.' She opened the door to an older couple. The woman looked apprehensive, the man looked unapproachable.

'Who are you?' he demanded.

Gemma blinked. 'I beg your pardon?' she said calmly.

Now he looked suspicious. 'I, uh, I don't know you, do I?'

'I don't think so. But then again, I don't know you either.'

'Then what are you doing here?'

This man had the manners of . . . someone without any manners. 'I live here,' Gemma returned coolly.

'But that can't be. My son . . . his family . . . our grandson, Noah Chapman, lives here, with his mother.'

Aah. 'That would be Helen Chapman you're referring to?'

His eyes narrowed. 'You're a friend of Helen's?'

'She's my landlady,' said Gemma.

They both looked as though they'd just been dealt a synchronised slap in the face.

'Are Helen and Noah Chapman still living here?' the man asked, his patience obviously wearing as thin as his questionable manners.

'Of course they are. In fact I'm sure they'll be back any minute. It's nearly Noah's bathtime, and you know how Helen is about routine. Would you like to come in and wait?'

They both checked their watches, glanced at each other and exchanged a telepathic message, the way long-married couples do.

'All right,' he relented, as though Gemma had begged them.

As they stepped through the door, she thrust her hand towards him. 'I'm Gemma, Gemma Atkinson.'

He shook her hand stiffly. 'Jim Chapman. My wife, Noreen.'

Noreen obviously had some difficulty speaking for herself, so it was lucky she had Jim to do it for her.

'Well, come on through,' said Gemma, walking ahead into the front room. 'Take a seat.'

They sat side by side on the couch, and Gemma dropped into an armchair opposite. They looked awkward, to put it mildly. Excruciated would be closer to the truth, if you could say excruciated. Gemma wasn't sure.

'She's probably out visiting her mother,' Mr Chapman said after a while.

'I guess,' Gemma nodded, although she had no idea. Helen didn't report her whereabouts to her. She hadn't even known Helen had a mother. Well, she'd assumed she had a mother at some stage of her life, but Helen had not been inclined to offer up a lot of information thus far.

'So, when did you move in?' he asked.

'Just a few weeks ago.'

'Have you known Helen long?'

Gemma frowned. 'Um, no, just the few weeks. I answered an ad online.'

'She advertised? Never mentioned a word,' he muttered, glancing at his wife and shaking his head. She shook her head along with him.

Gemma didn't think she could stand much more of this. 'Would you like a cup of tea?' she asked.

'Yes, thank you.' He glanced at his wife and she took the cue.

'Jim takes his tea strong, with a splash of milk and one and a half sugars. I have it weaker, medium really, so you might want to pour mine first, and I have more milk but only the one sugar.'

Bugger. People who gave such specific directions for their caffeinated beverages took the whole thing a little too seriously for Gemma's liking. She preferred people who said 'however it comes'. They were more her type. But at least it gave her an excuse to get out of there.

'Coming right up,' she said brightly, jumping to her feet and heading for the kitchen.

*

Helen pushed the front door open and held it back for Noah to go through ahead of her. He jumped up the step and then ran into the hall. A second later she heard his delighted cry.

'Nanna! Pop-peee!'

Helen's heart plummeted into her stomach. What could this be about? Because it was always *about* something. They were forever giving her stern lectures, 'advising', generally butting their noses in where they weren't wanted. David had always known how to deal with them – he'd had so many years of disregarding and generally disappointing his parents he'd become quite adept at handling them. Helen was not so practised at it. She'd never been good with conflict. With her erratic outbursts and flares of temper, her mother had railroaded right over her daughter her whole life, so Helen had tended to follow her father's lead, which wasn't to lead at all, but to cower, generally.

Now David's parents thought they had some God-given right to tell her what to do, particularly with regards to Noah. Maybe it was about time Helen stood up to them, even just a little. She straightened her shoulders and took a deep breath before she walked the few steps down the hall to the front room.

'Helen, here you are,' Jim said, with less enthusiasm than the words suggested. They both stood, and there proceeded a perfunctory exchange of pecks on the cheek and stilted embraces.

'Have you been visiting your mother?' he said, taking his seat again.

Helen nodded. She really didn't want to talk about it though. Today had not been a good day. Usually the sight of Noah was enough to cheer up Marion, but she hadn't wanted either of them there today. She'd become agitated at first, and then plain belligerent. Helen hated Noah seeing her like that; it frightened him and, she had to admit, it frightened her as well. If it was the start of further decline, it could be a signal that the end was getting closer. Helen knew she should be relieved, or at least accepting. Marion had no quality of life. She spent most of her time vacillating between bafflement, distress and depression. Sometimes Helen felt, on a day like today, that the woman in her mother's room, on her mother's bed, was not her mother at all anymore. But whoever she was, Helen wasn't ready to let go of her right now. Surely there was only so much loss she could be expected to bear at one time.

'How's the old girl getting along?' asked Jim, as though she were a horse out to pasture.

'The same,' Helen said as she sat in the armchair opposite. Noah was wedged between his grandparents, and she noticed he was sucking a Chupa Chup. This close to dinner. They hadn't asked Helen if that was all right, they never asked. And they wondered why she didn't want Noah to stay on his own with them for any length of time.

Jim crossed his arms in front of his chest and looked squarely at Helen. 'We met your boarder,' he announced.

Bam. 'Oh?' Of course, how else could they have got inside the house?

'You didn't mention you were getting in a boarder,' Jim said.

Helen took a breath. 'Well, I didn't see any need to, um, to worry you with it.'

'So you admit that a stranger coming to live with our grandson is something of a concern,' he said, as though he'd made a particularly astute move in a game of chess.

'Gemma's not a stranger anymore,' said Helen, shrugging innocently.

'Still, do you think it's wise –'

'Look, Jim,' Helen interrupted as politely as she could manage, 'I discussed it with Tony and this was the best option we could come up with to alleviate some of the financial burden I'm carrying at the present time.'

She was being purposely garrulous so Noah couldn't follow what she was saying. Though in truth his attention appeared to be pretty well fixed on the Chupa Chup.

'Why don't you just go back to work?' Jim said flatly.

Not again. Helen didn't think she could stand another round of this. 'Well, that can't be what you came here to talk about, because you didn't even know I'd taken a boarder till you got here,' she said, playing her own chess move. 'So, what are you doing here?'

Jim looked a bit affronted, but just then Gemma came through the door carrying a tray. Helen jumped to her feet and crossed the room to meet her.

'Thanks so much, Gemma.' Helen took the tray from her. It was set with a teapot, the good china, a sugar bowl and milk jug, even a small plate of shortbread. Gemma had read Helen's in-laws like a book. Helen looked her in the eye across the tray. 'This is lovely. I appreciate it, really.'

'My pleasure,' said Gemma, smiling with relief, Helen noticed. 'Nice to meet you, Jim, Noreen,' she said from where she stood. 'Well, I'll leave you to it.'

And before anyone could protest or invite her to join them, she'd disappeared. It hadn't taken her long to get their measure, Helen realised. She set the tray down on the coffee table and proceeded to make the tea to their precise and exacting standards. She finally poured herself a cup and sat back down on the armchair, just as Noreen was passing the plate of shortbread to Noah.

'No, please, Noreen, he's still sucking on that Chupa Chup you gave him.'

Noreen recoiled like a child who'd been scolded, replacing the plate back on the table.

'Actually, Helen, there is something we came to discuss,' said Jim, sitting his cup back in its saucer. 'But I think it's best if . . .' He paused, clearing his throat meaningfully and cocking his head towards Noah. 'It might be best if N-O-A-H –'

'That's my name!' Noah jumped up, almost knocking Noreen's cup from her hand.

'What a clever boy you are,' said Jim, ruffling his grandson's hair. 'I bet you have to get up early in the morning to fool you, Noah Chapman.'

'Huh?' He frowned.

'Noah, why don't you go find Gemma?' said Helen.

'She's just being in her room.'

'Noah,' Helen said, a little more firmly.

He got to his feet and sighed dramatically. 'Oh-kay.'

'Thank you, sweetheart.'

*

Gemma was lying back on her bed, staring at the ceiling, when Noah poked his head around the door.

'Hello there,' she said.

He didn't move.

'Do you want to come in?'

Noah pushed the door open a little and sidled into the room. He stood looking at her, sucking doggedly on a lollipop.

'Is there something you wanted, Noah?'

He shook his head, before extracting the Chupa Chup from his mouth with a loud pop. 'Mummy said I hadda come find you.'

'Oh, does she want me for something?' Gemma hoisted herself up on her elbows.

He shook his head again. 'They just want me to go away.'

'No,' Gemma scoffed.

'Yes.' He nodded emphatically. 'They're gunna talk 'bout Daddy and they always make me go away when they talk 'bout Daddy.'

Gemma looked at him. 'Well, you can hang out here with me, if you want.'

He screwed up his nose, considering her invitation. 'What are you doing?'

She smiled. 'Come up here and I'll show you.' She patted the bed beside her.

'What is it?'

'It's up there, on the ceiling,' she said, cocking her head.

Noah looked up. 'I can't see nuffink.'

'You have to look from here.'

He lodged the Chupa Chup in his mouth and clambered up onto the bed, settling himself on his back beside Gemma.

'What is it?' he garbled with his mouth full.

'Can't you see it?'

'What?'

'I can't believe you can't see it,' Gemma said, pointing her finger. 'It's right there.'

'Where?'

'There.' She kept pointing at a distinct brownish splodge on the ceiling.

Noah removed the Chupa Chup with a slurp. 'What is it?'

'It's a hippo, of course.'

Noah screwed up his face. 'It's not a hippo.'

'Sure it is. It's wading through the water, see, that's that wiggly line. And there's a little bird resting on its nose. Look, it's so cute.'

She glanced across at Noah and she couldn't work out from his expression whether he pitied her or thought she was crazy. Probably both.

'My mummy said you gotta baby in your tummy,' he said, obviously deciding a change of topic was warranted.

'Your mummy's right.'

'It must be very very little 'cause you haven't gotta fat tummy.'

'Give it time,' sighed Gemma.

'Mummy said your tummy's gunna get really really big –' Noah spread his arms wide to show he meant business '– blown up like a balloon, and then the baby will come out your bagina.'

Gemma turned her head sharply to look at him.

'Mummy said it hurts really bad.'

'Thanks for reminding me.'

Gemma watched Noah take a contemplative suck of his lollipop.

'Why doesn't the baby come out now while it's small and tiny, then it won't hurt?' he asked.

'Because God's obviously a man,' said Gemma.

Noah shook his head. 'My mummy said there isn't any God.'

'She's probably right.' At least Gemma hoped so. If there was a God, he certainly didn't think much of her, so Gemma wasn't looking forward to meeting him. She'd never had much luck with authority figures anyway.

'So why doesn't your baby get bornded right now?' Noah asked, returning to his original question.

'Well, the baby can't even breathe properly yet. Its lungs have to develop.'

'You breave wif your lungs,' Noah said authoritatively.

'That's right,' said Gemma. 'So the baby needs to stay inside till its lungs are ready to breathe for themselves, and till all its body parts are ready, till it's fully cooked.'

Noah grinned a big wide grin. 'It's not getting cooked,' he said, shaking his head and giggling. 'It's growing and devepoling.'

Gemma giggled along with him. 'No, it's cooking. Like a cake. In fact, I'm going to call it Muffin if it's a girl.'

Noah positively shrieked with delight. 'What if it's a boy? What are you gunna call it if it's a boy?'

Gemma was struck dumb by the idea. The little person growing and 'devepoling' inside her might be a boy, with a penis, and an excessive flatulence gland, and all the other things that make up a boy . . . snails and puppy dogs' tails, what have you. It didn't feel right somehow. And worse, what if he ended up just like his father? That did not even bear contemplating.

'What are you gunna call it if it's a boy, Gemma?' Noah repeated, his eyes bright with anticipation of the hilarity to come.

Gemma rolled on her side to face him. 'I might call him Chupa Chup!' she said.

Noah dissolved into giggles as Gemma proceeded to list all the names she might call a baby boy – Jelly Bean, French Fry, Whizz Fizz . . .

Gradually they became aware of raised voices out in the hall, followed by the sound of the door, if not exactly slamming, then certainly closing forcefully. After a short delay they heard Helen call out for Noah.

'We're in here,' Gemma called back. 'In my room.'

Helen appeared at the door, her eyes glassy, her cheeks stained pink.

'Are you okay?' Gemma asked.

'Of course,' she said. 'Come on, Noah. You've bothered Gemma long enough.'

'He hasn't bothered me at all. We were having a nice chat, weren't we, Noah?'

He nodded, giggling again. 'Gemma's gunna call her baby Jelly Bean, Mummy.'

'Oh,' Helen said vaguely, not really listening as she scooped Noah up off the bed and set him on his feet.

'What happened?' Gemma persisted.

Helen stirred. 'Nothing. They just, um . . .' She hesitated. She didn't know if she felt all that comfortable talking about this. She barely knew Gemma. But then again, they were living together now, and Gemma would be sharing a pretty significant event with them soon enough. Helen swallowed. 'Noah, go and get ready for your bath.'

He pouted. 'Why do I always haffa go away?'

'You don't.'

'Yes, I do.'

Helen sighed, crouching down to his level. She should be honest. She and David always said they'd be honest with Noah about everything. 'The reason I don't want you to hear what I have to say is because I'm really cross with your nanna and pop, but they're really good to you, and they love you very much, so I don't want you to feel angry with them just because I'm angry with them.'

'I won't, I promise,' he pleaded, joining his hands as though in prayer.

Helen sighed. 'Well, it's not such a big deal, Noah. They just want to get a plaque for Daddy –'

'What's a plaque?'

'Um, well, it's like a flat piece of wood, or maybe metal, and it would have Daddy's name engraved on it, written on it, and the day he was born and the day he died.'

'Why?'

'Well, it would be like a sign, to say where Daddy's ashes are.'

'But we're taking Daddy's ashes to a special place, aren't we, Mummy?'

'That's right, at least that's the plan,' she said. 'Because that's what Daddy wanted. But Nanna and Pop think it would be better if his ashes were scattered in a rose garden at the cemetery, where a whole lot of other people's ashes are scattered, conforming to their idea of what is right and proper, not your daddy's wishes, scattering his ashes in a place he'd never even been –'

'Can I watch TV, Mummy?' Noah interrupted, his eyes glazing over. Obviously that was a little more information than he strictly needed.

Helen straightened up. 'Okay, you can watch TV for a little while. You should be in the bath. And only channel two,' she called after him as he scampered from the room.

Gemma was sitting up now, a couple of pillows propped behind her. She patted the bed. 'Sit.'

'No, it's okay, I don't want to bother you . . .'

What was with her incessant fear of bothering people?

'What did you say to them in the end?' Gemma prompted. 'About the plaque.'

Helen took a breath. 'I said if you want a plaque, get a plaque, but I don't know where you're going to put it because David's ashes are going to be scattered according to his wishes.'

'Good for you.'

'Except, I don't know,' she sighed. 'They carried on about how foolish it was, the whole idea. He must have watched too many trashy Hollywood movies, they said. Which only goes to show how little they knew him. David couldn't stand trashy Hollywood movies.' Helen perched one knee on the edge of the bed. 'The thing is, to be perfectly honest, I don't know for certain how much it mattered to David where his ashes ended up. He'd only ever said it casually, when we used to go to this place. It's in the Royal National Park, down south. He used to camp there as a child, when he was in the scouts. Every time we went back there he used to get nostalgic, and sentimental, and say this was where he wanted his ashes scattered. But I don't know if he really meant it. You don't seriously make plans for the disposal of your ashes when you're only thirty-five.' Helen paused. 'But I just know he wouldn't want his final resting place to be an urn in a cemetery, or scattered on a rose bush, with a silly plaque. He just wouldn't.'

'Then don't let it be,' said Gemma.

'But Jim wanted to know where they're supposed to go to remember him, which I guess is a fair point,' Helen admitted. 'But I said there was a lot more chance of remembering him at a place that was special to him than in a cemetery.'

'I agree.' Gemma drew her knees up, hugging them to her chest. 'My Nanna Lola died when I was a girl,' she said quietly. 'Twelve turning thirteen, you know – that age. I missed her so much. I felt like she was the only person in the family who understood me. Anyway, she was buried in a lawn cemetery, with a nice plaque, all very neat. We went to pay her a visit a few times, but it never felt like she was there. But when we'd go to see Grandad, I used to go out into the backyard. She loved gardening, she was always out there, surrounded by her plants, under her beautiful old jacaranda tree. She used to say that she matched her hair colour to that jacaranda.' Gemma smiled, remembering. 'And I'd sit on one of the low branches of the tree, and I knew she was right there with me.'

'Is the tree still there?' asked Helen.

'I think so, I hope so,' said Gemma. 'But Grandad passed away too, and the house was sold. Still, whenever I drive around the north shore when the jacarandas are in bloom, I always think of her.'

Helen smiled faintly.

'You should do what you think David would have wanted,' said Gemma. 'After all, you knew him better than anyone.'

Helen almost winced. Did she? She wasn't even sure about that anymore. She did know this much – David would have stood up to his father. He was always at loggerheads with Jim. They both held such strong opinions, polar opposites, but just as stubborn about them. A lot more alike than either of them would care to admit. Helen would never have stood up to Jim herself, but she had to do it for David.

Bailey's

Gemma put down the phone, smiling, as the MD appeared around the corner. 'Good morning,' she chirped.

He looked a little taken aback. 'Morning.'

'That was Joanne's mum on the phone. Jo had the babies yesterday – a boy and a girl, Luke and Leia.'

'You're kidding me?' he said, pausing at her desk.

Gemma shook her head. 'Wouldn't have picked her for a *Star Wars* nut, but there you go. Looks can be deceiving. So, I'll organise flowers?'

He frowned. 'Is that the done thing?'

'What do you mean? Of course it's the done thing.'

'Even though she got the job on false pretenses and only worked here for four months and now she's no longer an employee?'

'Nice to hear you don't hold grudges,' said Gemma.

'Pardon?'

'Nothing,' she said airily. 'So, I'll arrange for flowers to be delivered to the hospital, with all best wishes from Bailey's ...' Gemma paused, pretending to concentrate on her computer screen. 'And how about I make an appointment for you for a haircut while I'm at it?' she added.

'What was that?' he said, leaning slightly over her desk.

'I just thought it was due . . . and uh, well,' she said, trying feebly to hang onto her ill-timed chutzpah, 'you see, MD, I consider it part of my job to anticipate your needs, and so, the thing is, I know a good hairdresser, a very good, stylish hairdresser . . . and you, well, you obviously don't.'

Gemma dared to glance up at him then and she saw his face had darkened, indicating either anger or embarrassment. Whichever, neither was good.

'Here in Sydney, I mean,' she added quickly. 'I'm sure you had someone in Melbourne. I was only saying that I could put you onto a good hairdresser nearby . . . convenient, you know . . .'

Too late – he was walking away. He paused at the door of his office to look back at her. 'I'll be the one to decide when I need a haircut, thanks all the same.'

'Right you are!' she said brightly as he disappeared into his office, closing the door firmly behind him. She dropped her head on the desk. Gemma, Gemma, Gemma, when will you learn to keep your big mouth . . .

At five forty-five, Gemma decided to call it a day. The MD had left late morning and not returned; according to his schedule, he would still be in a meeting on the other side of the city. There was nothing more for her to do. As she went to shut down her computer, she heard the ubiquitous ping as an email was delivered. It was from the MD.

Please book haircut for Friday 4pm.

Balmain

'Mum was asking about you again,' said Phoebe. 'Or should I say, interrogating.'

Gemma sat down opposite her at the kitchen table. Friday afternoons had become a regular thing, Phoebe coming over for a drink – wine for her, juice for Gemma.

'You didn't tell her anything, did you?' she asked.

'No, but –'

'Phee,' Gemma warned, 'you promised.'

'And you promised that once you had a job and a place to live you'd tell them yourself.'

Gemma sighed dramatically. 'I just don't think I can face it, Phee. Not yet.'

'So when are you going to tell them? Are you going to call from the hospital when you've had the baby and say "Surprise!"?'

'Tempting . . .'

Phoebe groaned. 'I hate this, Gem. I don't like lying to them. Just pick up the phone, you don't have to see them if you really don't want to. But Mum's going to be so hurt if you don't tell her about the baby soon, and she'll have every right to be.'

'It's not just about the baby,' said Gemma. 'Can you imagine how she'll carry on once she hears that Luke did a runner? "He was no good, I knew it all along,"' she mimicked. '"Just another one of your hopeless loser boyfriends . . ."'

'So? It's the truth, isn't it?'

'Yeah, but I don't need to hear it from her.'

Phoebe dropped her head onto the table.

'Phee, okay, okay, maybe I deserve it. I know I pushed the boundaries a lot when I was growing up . . .'

'Pushed the boundaries? You knocked the boundaries down and trampled right over them.'

'Whatever. The problem is, Mum and Dad still see me as the same rebellious kid they have to keep rescuing. I haven't grown up in their eyes at all. Even when I had a good job they didn't really believe I was going to stick at it.'

'And they were right.'

'Yeah, well, no wonder I finally walked out of Bailey's, seeing it was exactly what they were waiting for me to do.'

'Oh, so you're saying it's their fault you left?'

'No,' said Gemma, frustrated. 'They're just like the parents who keep telling the kid up in the tree, "You're going to fall, you're going to fall," and he does, because that's the picture they've put in his head. Whereas if they said, "Climb down safely, you can do it," then he probably would.'

'Come on, Gem,' Phoebe exclaimed. 'Maybe you do need to grow up.'

Gemma blinked at her.

'I mean, listen to yourself, you still react to them like a child. If you want to be treated like an adult, you need to take responsibility for your own decisions.'

'That's exactly what I'm trying to do now. I have decisions to make and I don't need their interference while I sort out what I'm going to do.'

'What are you talking about exactly?' Phoebe asked, frowning at her.

Gemma hadn't told Phoebe giving up the baby was an option, because she knew she'd freak. Just as her parents would. They wouldn't allow it, not over their dead bodies, their grandchild would not be brought up by a stranger . . . blah, blah, blah. That was why Gemma couldn't talk to them yet. She'd lose control, it wouldn't be her decision anymore, and it was hard enough as it was.

Just then they heard the front door slam. Gemma checked her watch. Saved by bathtime.

A minute later Helen appeared in the doorway to the kitchen, obviously rattled. Her cheeks were pink, her eyes fiery, and she seemed to be out of breath. 'You're not going to believe what just happened.'

'What?' the sisters chorused.

'Oh, hello Phoebe.'

'What won't we believe?' Gemma prompted her. She was guessing the in-laws had something to do with it. They usually did. Helen could not so much as talk to them on the phone without getting into a flap.

'Um, I'd better get Noah in the bath,' she said vaguely, glancing back up the hall.

'Don't pat a dog with a wagging tail,' said Gemma.

'Pardon?'

'He's content, leave him be. It's Friday night – routines are allowed to lapse on a Friday night.'

Helen stared at her across the table. She was right, they used to have toasted cheese sandwiches on Friday nights, growing up. In front of the telly. They were allowed to stay up longer – it was the start of the weekend. She remembered it was fun. When had she become so rigid?

'Would you like a glass of wine?' asked Phoebe, waving the bottle.

'Of course she would,' Gemma said, jumping up to get a glass.

Helen sat down at the table, the glass was placed before her and Phoebe poured the wine.

'To Fridays,' said Gemma, holding up her glass of juice. They all raised their glasses and then watched as Helen took a sizeable gulp from hers.

'So,' Gemma urged, 'tell us . . .?'

'Oh,' Helen stirred, the colour beginning to deepen in her cheeks again. 'One of the fathers at preschool,' she began slowly. 'I can still hardly believe the audacity . . .'

'Go on,' Gemma said, wide-eyed. This sounded intriguing, and it didn't appear to have anything to do with the in-laws.

Helen cleared her throat. 'When I went to pick up Noah from preschool, one of the fathers . . . well, there's no other way to put it.' She paused for effect. 'He asked me out.' She looked across the table at both of the women, her indignation plain.

'I don't understand,' said Gemma, because she didn't understand. Had she missed something? Blacked out for a second?

'You and me both,' Helen said, confounding her further.

'So, he asked you out on a date?' said Gemma, attempting to clarify.

'Yes, that's exactly what he did. He tried to play it down, suggesting we go for coffee one morning after we drop the kids off. But he was asking me out.'

Gemma was still struggling to understand the problem. 'He's single?'

'Yes, of course. But that's not really the point though, is it?'

Apparently not. 'So, what's he like?'

'What do you mean?' Helen frowned.

'Is he good-looking?'

'I don't know.'

'What do you mean, you don't know?' said Gemma. 'Does he wear a mask?'

'I don't care what he looks like,' Helen insisted. 'He could be . . . I don't know –'

'Chris Hemsworth?' Phoebe suggested, sighing.

'Fine, he could be Chris whoever, it wouldn't make any difference.'

Phoebe and Gemma looked at her as though she had completely lost her mind.

'Come on,' said Gemma, 'are you telling me if the God of Thunder asked you –'

'Don't you get it, Gemma?' Helen interrupted her. 'He has no right to ask me out. It was completely inappropriate. I'm a married woman.'

Gemma and Phoebe were staring at her. Helen recognised that look. They thought she was crazy.

'You're just trying to say that it's too soon,' Phoebe said helpfully. 'That you're not ready yet . . .'

'Because you do realise,' added Gemma, in a tone Helen had often heard used at the nursing home, 'you're not married anymore.'

'But I am. I'm still the same person, nothing happened to me. I'm still David's wife.'

Helen looked earnestly at Gemma and Phoebe, while they looked gobsmacked back at her.

'Look, I'm not crazy,' said Helen. 'Think about it. If something happened to Noah, I'd still consider myself his mother, forever. If something happened to either of you, you'd still consider yourself sisters, wouldn't you? You may not have a sister anymore, but you'd still *be* a sister.' She paused as they contemplated that. 'It's the same for me. I may not have a husband anymore, but I'm still a wife. I didn't choose to be a widow, I don't feel like a widow.' She sniffed. Tears were nudging their way into her eyes.

They sat in silence for a minute. Gemma could see the logic, kind of, but it didn't stop it from being absurd.

'But, don't you think you have to . . . move on, eventually?' Phoebe suggested carefully.

'Why?' Helen sniffed again.

'Well, lots of reasons –'

'Sex for one,' said Gemma. 'You do want to have sex again in your lifetime, don't you?'

Now it was Helen's turn to look gobsmacked. 'I'd better go and run Noah's bath,' she mumbled as she got up from the table and left the room before either of them had the presence of mind to stop her.

Phoebe was glaring at Gemma across the table.

'What?' Gemma said innocently. 'I was only stating the obvious.'

'To you maybe,' said Phoebe. 'Gem, the woman couldn't cope with the idea of having coffee with another man, let alone sex.'

'Well, maybe she needs to be snapped out of it. It's not normal.'

'It's not normal that her husband was run over by a bus. Give the poor woman a break. I don't know how I'd handle it if anything like that happened to Cam.'

Gemma found herself daydreaming about Cameron being run over by a bus, which was a strangely satisfying thing to dwell on. She glanced at Phoebe, who was eyeing her suspiciously. Quickly, a diversion.

'So, do you think my belly looks big in this?' she asked, standing up and pulling her blouse taut over her stomach. 'Can you tell I'm pregnant?'

Phoebe tilted her head, considering her sister's midsection. 'Well, I'm not sure,' she shrugged, 'I know you're pregnant, so that probably affects my perspective.'

Gemma's jaw dropped. 'So you're saying that there is something to see?' She looked down at herself, aghast. 'I thought the MD was giving me a funny look the other day.'

'You're imagining things,' Phoebe scoffed. 'He probably just thinks you've put on weight.'

'Thank you. That makes me feel so much better.'

'What does it matter to you? You're going to get a lot bigger soon enough. Have you worked out what you're going to do yet, once you can't hide it anymore?'

Of course she hadn't. No lightning bolt had struck out of the blue. No magician had waved a magic wand to fix everything. 'Something'll come up,' she said offhandedly.

Phoebe gave her another withering look from across the table.

'You know, Phee, there's really no reason for me to get in touch with Mum and Dad when I get all the disapproval I can handle from you.'

Brookhaven

'I haven't seen you around for a while, Helen.'

She was sitting in the office of Dr Chris Taylor, one of the small team of visiting medical officers at Brookhaven, and her mother's personal physician since she'd moved there. Marion liked him; she tended to be drawn to men who had at least a vague likeness to Tony. And Dr Chris had the requisite height and hair colour, and he was around the same age as well. Which made him young for a geriatrician.

'Well, this is Mum's regular six-month evaluation,' said Helen, a little defensively. 'I would have seen you six months ago.'

'Sure.' He nodded. 'I was just commenting I hadn't seen you around lately.'

'I'm still visiting regularly, I might have missed a day or two a few months ago –'

'Helen,' he interrupted, his voice kind, 'it wasn't an accusation, just an observation. I've probably missed you in the corridors, that's all I'm saying.'

She nodded, pulling her cardigan around herself and crossing her arms in front of her chest. 'So, anyway, the evaluation?'

'Right, well.' He opened Marion's file. 'As you're probably aware, there's been some significant deterioration in the past couple of months.'

'Significant?'

'Well, it's significant insofar as the symptoms your mother's beginning to exhibit are generally classified as severe.'

'Such as?' Helen said in a small voice.

Chris hesitated, watching her closely. 'You know all this, Helen.'

'Could you just go through it, please,' she said, avoiding his gaze.

He sighed, though not with impatience. 'Okay. Loss of speech, loss of appetite and associated weight loss, loss of bladder and bowel control.' He paused, allowing Helen to take it in. 'These symptoms are only now starting to present, and they're still intermittent, but they do signal the beginning of further decline, as I'm sure you're aware. My biggest concern at the moment is Marion's loss of motivation – she's just not interested in anything. Probably the single most important element in keeping Alzheimer's patients healthy is to keep them active and engaged. But unfortunately your mother's hallucinations and paranoia are becoming distressing for her, and we're going to have to think about anti-psychotics. The newer medications have fewer side-effects but they still cause drowsiness, which leads to lethargy and further lack of motivation.'

'And depression,' added Helen, 'which is how it all started.'

'What do you mean?'

'You know her history, Chris. She was depressed after the death of my father, she never got over it.'

'And you know as well as I do, Helen, that Alzheimer's is a degenerative illness that damages the connections between brain cells, causing the brain cells to die eventually. That's not caused by depression.'

'Couldn't it be a trigger?'

'There's no evidence to support that. In fact, it's more likely that her depression was an early symptom of Alzheimer's.'

Which Helen should have picked up.

'Are you all right, Helen?' Chris asked suddenly. Invasively.

'Pardon?'

He leaned forward. 'This can't have been an easy time for you, since the loss of your husband.'

Why did everyone have to know that? Why was it everybody's business?

'Are you seeing anyone?'

Helen was startled. 'What . . . I'm sorry?'

'Are you seeing a counsellor?'

She breathed out. For a minute there she thought he meant . . . 'I have seen a grief counsellor a couple of times.'

'Is that helping?'

Helping what? she wanted to say. She wanted to say a lot of things, like *It's none of your business, Dr Chris.* But Helen had never been able to say things like that, least of all to someone with 'Dr' in front of his name.

So she just nodded. 'Yes, thanks, it's been helpful. So, I was wondering,' she went on, changing tack, 'are there any new treatments worth considering? Anything experimental even?'

He took a second to catch up with her. 'Oh.' He shook his head regretfully. 'They start off with promising ideas that largely turn out to have little or no benefit. It's frustrating, dealing with the brain, like trying to get a computer to function when the hard drive's damaged. The most success they're having is with mild cognitive impairment in the early stages. Early intervention is as important as ever.'

Go ahead, rub it in.

'That's not going to help my mother though, is it?'

Chris looked at her directly. 'No, it isn't. So we have to get her interested, find things for her to do that engage the part of her mind that is still functioning. Boredom is her greatest enemy right now.'

*

Gemma was bored. Helen was out somewhere with Noah, they'd left before she was even out of bed. It was Saturday, a day off, but Gemma didn't know what to do with her days off anymore, except sleep. And she didn't seem to need as much sleep as she had earlier in her pregnancy. She'd said as much to Helen one day, offhand, and Helen had explained about the glowing middle months of pregnancy, of peak energy levels and optimum health. Which was all well and good, but what was she supposed to do with all this glowing good health? She had phoned Phee, but they were going hiking in the Ku-ring-gai Chase National Park and Gemma was certain she'd rather be bored to oblivion than go hiking in the Ku-ring-gai Chase National Park with Cameron and Phoebe in their undoubtedly coordinated hiking outfits.

So she tried texting Charlie, twice, but he was either ignoring her or he was still asleep. It was after ten, but it was a Saturday, and he wasn't in the peak performance months of pregnancy, so he was probably enjoying a lie-in, considering the hours he kept. Charlie was typical of his breed. There was something a little vampirish about computer nerds.

She did think about getting in touch with some of her old friends, though it would certainly be too early in the morning for any of them just yet either. Gemma hadn't made contact since just after she returned to Sydney. She'd called Caz and Rach and Johnno while she was still in Brisbane to see if they'd heard from Luke, but they claimed they hadn't. She called them again when she got to Phoebe's place, and Caz gave her Tim's number – Tim being the friend who'd brought Luke to the party where they first met. Tim never answered his phone, and though Gemma left messages, he didn't get back to her. It had crossed her mind that Tim knew something and was avoiding her, but on the other hand, if Tim was anything like Caz or Rach or Johnno, or any of her old friends – or herself for that matter – promptly answering messages was probably not one of his strengths. So after a while Gemma had stopped calling.

The clock ticked over the hour and Gemma remained bored. She did a load of washing, remembering to place her bras in a drawstring laundry bag in the washing machine, and afterwards to hang her work blouses carefully on hangers under the back awning in the shade. Though the garment labels recommended this, Gemma had never bothered to do it before. Boredom obviously had the potential to make a person obsessive-compulsive. She had to find something to do. She wandered around the house restlessly till she found herself pacing up and down the back room, her eyes constantly drawn to the door, the locked door behind the ugly occasional table, with the ugly vase and the outrageously ugly plastic blooms. Gemma walked over and rattled the doorknob, as she had done a dozen times before. It was still locked, of course, barricaded, quite possibly even painted shut. There was a clear, unspoken directive to stay out.

But Gemma was bored.

She started looking around for the key to the door. Not that she was planning to use it necessarily, she just thought she'd see if there was a key. There had to be one somewhere, surely? She tried the drawer in the ugly table; it had its own little key that turned easily to unlock the tiny drawer to reveal a couple of yellowing notepads, a pencil and two packs of playing cards, but no key. Gemma turned her back to the pesky door and surveyed the room. Positioned at intervals around the walls were various bow-fronted cabinets, some with leadlight doors and side panels, chock full of china and crystal ornaments, small animals mostly, but miniature clocks, shoes and assorted cars and carriages also featured prominently. One cabinet had porcelain figurines of little girls and brides and nuns, Lladro and the like. Hideously expensive stuff. Gemma had never understood the appeal, but each to his own. Another held a display of Bakelite pieces, useful things like hairbrushes and mirrors and boxes, that had sadly not been put to the use for which they were intended for years, decades more like. Her mother would have salivated over such a collection; she had a passion for Bakelite, which was yet another thing that Gemma didn't understand about her.

After she had scanned each cabinet, searching under, behind or inside every objet d'art therein, Gemma was still keyless. But that only made the challenge all the more irresistible.

She went through the house, checking all the doors for keys and trying them one by one on the mystery door, to no avail. Somewhere in the house, Gemma was sure she'd seen a plain steel ring with four or five large old-style keys looped through it, hanging from a hook. She could picture it in her mind's eye now, high up, beside an architrave. But where? She checked the kitchen, beside the back door. Then she had a thought. She hurried outside to the laundry and poked her head around the doorway. Paydirt. Gemma unhooked the key ring and dashed back into the house, almost running through to the back room. There were four keys altogether. The first one didn't even fit into the keyhole; the next one seemed to fit but it wouldn't turn. Nor would the next. Nor would the fourth and final key. Damn. Gemma couldn't believe one of these keys wouldn't fit the door, so much so that she tried each one again.

They still didn't fit, not surprisingly. Gemma sagged back against the wall, defeated. She was out of ideas and out of keys. What the hell was in there? She knocked her fist on the wall a couple of times. She wondered how big the room was, whether it had any windows. Gemma went through the kitchen and out the back door again. She stepped slowly backwards into the yard, peering up at the windows, shielding her eyes from the sun rising above the gable of the roof. The back wall of the house continued probably another three metres past the last window, which Gemma recalled butted up to the perpendicular wall inside. The corner of the house was close to the boundary, but it left a path wide enough for Gemma to walk up the side. She spotted a door at the same time as she walked straight into a giant sticky spiderweb and promptly screamed. Nothing gave Gemma the willies more than spiders. She painstakingly removed every last strand she could find, shaking her head and brushing off her clothes repeatedly. Eventually satisfied there was nothing crawling through her hair or inside her clothing, Gemma proceeded to the door, still clutching the ring of keys. There were more spiderwebs across the door; she brushed them away with a twig. It was a panelled timber door, with no handle on the outside, just a weathered brass oval base plate framing the keyhole. Gemma tried one key, but it was no good. Undaunted, she inserted the second key into the lock. It was a snug fit. She took a breath and slowly turned the key. Her heart missed a beat as it moved around a half-circle and clicked. The door remained where it was, so Gemma gave it a light push. It didn't give, it appeared to be stuck. She squared her shoulder up towards the door and pushed with all her might.

The door flung open and Gemma landed on the floor inside. She sneezed as dust flew about her, as though staging a wild protest at the intrusion of light into the room. She quickly got back up onto her feet and looked around. Dust was still whirling about in the shaft of light, and Gemma sneezed again. The air in here was musty, with a distinctly chemical aftertaste. As her eyes slowly adjusted, Gemma could make out the door on the opposite wall, leading to the back room, but there was no light coming from behind it. It must be sealed tight. There was a window covered by a roller blind on the outer wall next to the door she'd come through.

Gemma picked her way between boxes and other unidentifiable mounds on the floor and pulled on the blind. It shot up with a jolt, but the window appeared to be painted black. Gemma reached her hand out gingerly to touch the glass, peering closer. Why on earth would someone paint the only window in the room black? She turned the latch on top of the sash and tried to lift it, but it was stuck fast, possibly even nailed down.

She looked around the room. In the dim light she could make out a couple of bulky wardrobes, similar in style to the one in her room. A bench ran the length of one wall, with a long shelf at head height above it. The room was cluttered with boxes of various sizes and shapes, old trunks, luggage and odd pieces of furniture – a pair of chairs stacked on top of each other, what looked like the parts of a baby's cot propped against a wall, and a very ornate, ugly old standard lamp with a wonky shade.

Gemma sneezed again, triggering a fit of sneezing that finally ended half a minute later with her eyes itching and her head buzzing. She sniffed loudly and rubbed her eyes, contemplating the door on the opposite wall. There was a sturdy barrel bolt at chest height. Gemma wondered if that was what had been holding the door in place all along. She walked over and tried to open it. It was a bit of an effort – she had to lean hard against the door to slide it across. As the bolt passed through the nib on the door frame, Gemma took her weight off the door and it almost popped open a little, allowing a slender blade of light into the room. But the bottom of the door seemed to be wedged hard into the carpet. Gemma wrapped her fingers around the side of the door and reefed it back, scraping the bottom edge across the carpet. There was the back of the ugly occasional table, the ugly vase and the ugly plastic flowers. And there was Helen's face, frowning at her.

'What are you doing?'

'Umm . . .' Gemma hoped something slightly more intelligent would come out of her mouth soon.

Helen was glaring at her, her expression grim. She slowly folded her arms in front of her, waiting for an explanation.

'I just wanted to see what was behind the door,' Gemma offered lamely.

'Well, now that you have, would you please close it up and leave it as you found it,' Helen ordered as she turned to walk away.

'Hold on,' Gemma stopped her, dragging the table out of the way.

Helen turned back again to look at her.

'Why is it all closed up? What's the point?' asked Gemma. 'There's a whole room you could be using, instead of filling it with junk.'

'Who said it was junk?'

'Oh, sorry, I didn't mean –'

'It's a storage area,' Helen said curtly.

'But it's a good-size room. Surely it could be put to better use?'

'I have all the rooms I need. I even had one spare to rent out to you, remember?'

'Well, I could always use another.'

Helen frowned at her.

'For the baby,' Gemma added.

Helen looked horrified. 'Why would you want to put a baby in there? You can't do that, you just can't.'

'Why not?'

Helen looked flummoxed. 'It's just, well, it's dark and dingy . . .'

Gemma walked back inside the room. 'It's not so bad with some light in it. And if you stripped the black paint off that window . . . Why on earth was the window painted black anyway?'

Helen had come to lean against the doorjamb. 'It was used as a darkroom.'

'Oh, right,' Gemma nodded. 'Who was the photographer?'

'My father,' said Helen. 'He wasn't a professional or anything, it was just a hobby.'

'Well that explains the chemical smell,' said Gemma. 'It certainly lingers.'

Helen took a couple of tentative steps further into the room, breathing in deeply. 'I'd forgotten that,' she said. 'Smells are so . . . nostalgic, aren't they?'

Gemma smiled. 'The last unconquered territory of advertising. They just can't get smell-o-vision right, but the theory is, if you could package a smell, you could sell just about anything.'

Helen sighed. 'It's nice to know some things can't be packaged for sale.' She looked around the room. 'I haven't stepped foot in here for years.' It had always given her the creeps, though it seemed pretty innocuous now. 'David used to store things away in here when we were finished with them, but I never came in here.'

'Mm, I noticed the cot,' said Gemma.

'Oh, that's right,' Helen said, stirring. 'You're welcome to it, if you want. There's quite a bit of baby gear in the cupboards too, I think . . . What am I saying? You probably want to buy new things for your baby.'

'Are you kidding me?' Gemma said. 'Beggars can't be choosers.'

Helen blinked at her.

'Not that I'm saying your stuff's only good for beggars . . . or that beggars don't deserve decent stuff . . . Oh, I don't really know what I'm saying, but you know what I mean,' she dismissed, opening up one of the wardrobes. 'Wow,' she murmured.

The hanging rack was crammed with mostly women's clothes, as far as Gemma could make out. There were lots of shiny, lustrous fabrics in royal blue, purple, green, red; she even glimpsed some silver and gold, and bright florals, polka dots, stripes. Gemma carefully moved aside the hangers. 'This stuff's all vintage.'

'It used to be called old or second-hand,' Helen remarked.

'Call it whatever you like, there's some gorgeous stuff in here.' Gemma drew out one hanger, and then another, holding the frocks up for inspection. Because 'frock' was the only word for them. One was elegant and striking in black and cream trim, very Audrey Hepburn, while the other was a rich flowered pattern on cotton voile.

'Were these your mother's?' Gemma asked, not waiting for an answer. 'You should be wearing some of these, not leaving them locked away in storage.' She held the floral dress up in front of Helen. 'Look at that, like it was made for you. Are you very like your mother?'

Helen was staring at her, unresponsive.

'I guess you could always sell it all off,' Gemma rattled on. 'Stuff like this would get snapped up on eBay.'

Helen suddenly roused, snatching the dresses from Gemma. 'Look, could you just leave it all alone, please?' she said tightly.

'I'll go through and find the baby clothes for you later. I think it's best if you just shut up the room again, if you don't mind.'

And with that she marched out and up the hall to her bedroom. She flung the dresses onto the bed and sat down heavily, feeling sad, and exposed, and confused. She should never have gone inside the room, it was easier not to have to think about it, to dredge it all up again.

She stared down at the dresses. Her mother had worn the black and cream dress at Tony's christening. Helen remembered it from photographs. She'd looked so beautiful, her dark hair swept up under a cream hat, and wearing cream gloves. But mostly Helen remembered her beaming face, her eyes brimming with happiness.

And the flowered print – Helen remembered burying her face into the folds of the skirt, just as Noah liked to do. She could feel her mother's hand touching her head, comforting, reassuring.

Helen picked up the dress and stood, holding it in front of herself as she crossed to the mirror. A slight lump rose in her throat. She couldn't imagine ever wearing it, but it was a beautiful dress – it was a shame for it to be hidden away out there. She opened her wardrobe. It was packed tight, all of David's clothes were still hanging there, her nursing uniforms . . .

Her life suddenly felt overcrowded, suffocating, buried under the weight of too much sadness and grief.

She tossed the dress onto her bed and hurried out of the room, down the hall to the back room. The table was back in place in front of the door, which was sealed tight again.

'Gemma!' Helen called as she dragged the table out of the way. She banged on the door. 'Gemma!'

'I'm just about to lock up, okay?' came her muffled reply.

'No, don't,' Helen cried.

'What did you say?'

'Could you open this door again?'

There was a pause. 'Are you serious?'

'Yes, please Gemma, just open the door.'

Gemma sighed and went back to the door, leaning against it as before and sliding the barrel bolt open. She wrenched the door back again as it scraped across the carpet.

Helen was standing on the other side, her expression contrite. 'My father died when I was a teenager,' she said. 'Suddenly . . . unexpectedly. This is where my mother found him. Here, in this room.'

Gemma didn't know what to say. 'Oh, I'm sorry, I didn't know.'

'Of course you didn't, how could you? It's all right,' Helen said quietly. 'We didn't use the room at all after he died. All his things were left as they were. It's probably why the chemical smell is in everything.' She paused. 'After a while, my mother, well, she started wandering in here, and it used to upset her so much, she even got hysterical a few times. So I had to seal it off. Try to make it look like the room wasn't even here.'

Gemma was confused. How could her mother forget a room in her own house?

'She has Alzheimer's,' said Helen, anticipating the unspoken question.

Now Gemma was plain dumbfounded. This family was some kind of case study in tragedy. 'That's so . . . sad,' she said lamely.

Helen nodded slowly. 'Yes, it is. She's in an aged-care facility now. It's a good one.'

'That's where you go to visit her?'

'That's right, though sometimes I wonder why; she hardly knows me anymore.'

Gemma wished she could think of something else to say except, 'That's so sad.'

'But she is better off there,' said Helen, as though she still needed to convince herself. 'She had a few minor accidents while she was still here at home, she could have hurt herself, or someone else. I had to keep everything the same around the house. If I moved even one little ornament she got upset, disorientated.'

That explained a lot. 'When did she go to the home?' Gemma asked.

'The facility?' Helen said. 'About five years ago.'

'And you still haven't moved anything?'

'I guess I thought . . . or hoped she might be able to come back . . .'

Gemma was watching her. Helen had never opened up this much to her before. She seemed to have a habit of going so far and then suddenly snapping shut again. Gemma knew she had to tread carefully.

'She's not coming back, though, is she?'

Helen looked across at her with glassy eyes, and slowly shook her head.

'Do you think that maybe it might be time for a change?' Gemma continued in a quiet, careful tone. 'Clear some of the clutter away?' She winced. That might have come across a bit bluntly. Subtlety was not her strong suit. 'Not that I'm saying it's clutter,' she added quickly. 'If this is how you like things . . .'

Helen managed a faint smile. 'I know it's cluttered. I often think about clearing it all out, but look at this place. Where would I start, and where would it end? It's such a huge job.'

'I could help,' Gemma offered.

Helen frowned. 'Why would you want to do that?'

'I promise you, I've got nothing else better to do.'

'But I couldn't ask you –'

'You didn't,' Gemma interrupted her. 'By the way, where's Noah?'

'Oh, he's with his grandparents for the rest of the day. I had an appointment with my mother's doctor, thought I'd ask them to mind him for a couple of hours, get them off my back, and next thing I knew they've organised to take him out for the whole day.'

'They really rub you the wrong way, don't they?'

'You met them – can you blame me?'

'Maybe they're just having trouble dealing with the loss of their son . . .' That was particularly empathetic of her. Gemma hadn't known she had it in her.

But Helen was shaking her head. 'They never liked me, right from the start. I don't know why exactly. Maybe it was just the standard "No one's good enough for our son".'

'Well, I don't know what else it could be,' said Gemma. 'How could anyone not like you?'

Helen looked a little self-conscious.

'I'm not pissing in your pocket,' Gemma said quickly. 'I just mean, what's not to like? You're the most inoffensive person I've ever met.'

Helen was not sure if that was a compliment.

'So when will Noah be home?' Gemma asked.

'By dinnertime, they promised. They wanted to keep him overnight, but I managed to put my foot down about that at least.'

'Well, let's take your mind off it,' she said. 'We've got a few hours – why don't we get a start on cleaning this place out now?'

Some weeks later

They had got a start on it, right there and then, and they had barely stopped since. What a lot of stuff had been packed into the place, jammed, rammed and crammed fit to bust. Gemma found the whole process quite exhilarating, rewarding even. Helen needed her, she realised, or at least someone like her. Someone who was not overly attached to stuff, not sentimental in the least – a real 'out with the old and in with the new' kind of person. Gemma was that kind of person. Helen, on the other hand, was the kind of person her grandmother would have called a 'hoarder'.

Gemma's own parents were incorrigible hoarders, they had no choice – they had so much stuff, and there was no end in sight to their accumulating more and more, so they had to hoard it. When there was no more even remotely useful stuff for them to buy, they started buying stuff for no reason at all, and thus was the beginning of their obsessive collecting. Her dad collected fishing flies, though he didn't fish; wine that he dared not open, and guns that couldn't be fired. Her mother's collecting energies were focused on the Art Deco and Art Nouveau eras – lipstick cases, compacts and perfume bottles, anything Bakelite, and her most recent obsession: antique toast racks, of all the useless things.

Trish Atkinson couldn't throw out a thing, especially if it had the slightest sentimental value whatsoever. Their baby shoes had been mounted, first teeth and hair clippings saved; every finger painting or shoddy collage or toilet-roll sculpture they'd made as children had been labelled, dated and stored away in a system to rival the archives at the National Gallery. And that was not to mention every birthday card, school report, certificate, award, ribbon, medal. It went without saying that Gemma's siblings had much more substantial collections than she did, but it was nonetheless not surprising that her mother was horrified when Gemma celebrated finally ditching school by building a bonfire out of all of her school memorabilia and setting it alight. The fact that she nearly burned down the gazebo in the back garden at the same time paled in comparison with her act of destroying her memories, as far as her mother was concerned. Gemma had tried to insist that memories could not be destroyed by fire, only stuff could. Memories were in her head. Her mother thought that same head likely needed examining.

So Gemma had made it a personal credo never to get so attached to anything that she couldn't give it up, making her the ideal person to help Helen unclutter her house. She had suggested they start with the makeshift darkroom and toss out what was actually rubbish – and there was plenty of that. The old photography equipment was largely defunct, particularly the bottles and containers of various developing and setting solutions. Helen nearly had a stroke when Gemma went to toss it all in the bin. That could not possibly be environmentally sound, she argued. Consequently, she rang the council and inquired about appropriate disposal of toxic substances, boxed it all up and delivered it to a designated depot.

And on they ploughed. Gemma was a little bemused to find what must have been all of Helen's father's clothes in one of the wardrobes, right down to socks and underwear.

'Your mother mustn't have thrown out a thing after he died,' she remarked.

'I don't think she was up to it,' Helen said lamely, aware that she hadn't done any better, though she consoled herself it was still only months, not years, since David's death.

Gemma was relieved that Helen didn't seem especially attached to anything in her father's wardrobe, and it was all swiftly bundled into garbage bags and deposited into a charity collection bin. Boxes of ancient photographic journals and manuals were relegated to the recycling bin, under Helen's watchful eye, but she finally relented that the last few bits of flotsam really belonged nowhere else but in the garbage. When they got to the furniture and heavier items, Gemma called on Charlie for help.

'Why do you need my help?' he asked, though not unkindly, when she went to find him at work one Friday afternoon.

'Because there's a council clean-up next week, so if we get the stuff out on the footpath, we won't have to –'

'Council clean-up,' Charlie said wistfully, leaning back in his chair. 'I used to love that time of the year.'

Gemma nodded. 'I furnished my first flat from a council clean-up. Mum went off her head when she found out, wanted to get the place fumigated.'

'My mum finally put a ban on me,' said Charlie. 'I used to drag all this junk home, not that it was junk to me, of course. But then there was the incident with the rat's nest in an old armchair, and my scavenging career was over.'

'Well, this is your chance to revisit those halcyon days,' Gemma said, jotting their address on a notepad. 'So we'll see you tomorrow? I won't expect you before midday, I know how you like your beauty sleep.'

'Explain to me again why you need me?' asked Charlie, looking more than a tad sceptical.

'You're a man,' she said plainly, 'and men are good at lifting heavy stuff.'

'Aah, this is where feminism falls right on its pretty face, hey?'

'Charlie, I'm pregnant. Feminism comes to a screeching, grinding halt right at my swollen ankles.' She tore the page off the pad and slapped it into his hand. 'Tomorrow, midday, and bring your muscles with you.'

'You do realise any muscles I may have had once upon a time have atrophied from sitting at a desk all my working life?'

But Gemma had already left the room and was on the other side of the glass wall, out of earshot.

Charlie had showed up the next day, on time, chirpy and motivated, which made Gemma suspicious. She expected him to come and help, but he didn't have to act as though he enjoyed it.

Helen liked him at once, and Noah stuck to him like glue. Funny, Gemma had never thought of Charlie as the fatherly type, but watching him with Noah was more than a little disarming.

'So how's Project Get On Boss's Good Side coming along?' Charlie asked when they were out front stacking boxes and broken bits of furniture into a neat pile. It seemed that every time they went back into the house, the pile was picked over, rearranged, and significantly thinned out. Even the wonky lamp had been snapped up, Gemma hoped by some poor struggling uni student, not just a hoarder with questionable taste.

'The project is going very slowly. Tortuously, you might even say.'

'He hasn't promoted you to assistant managing director then?'

'Don't be a smart-arse,' Gemma returned. 'I get to go to meetings in his office, some of the time, but he hasn't asked me to anything else. I really want to sit in on some production meetings – it's the only way I can show him I have something to offer.'

'I don't think he's interested in what you have to offer, Gem, he just wants an assistant. You're going to have to come to terms with that sooner or later.'

She pulled a face. 'Well, for your information, I am actually coming to terms with that. Being PA to the managing director might be quite stimulating if I was actually allowed to assist occasionally.' She stood up from a crouching position, arching to stretch her back.

'Wow, look at you,' Charlie said, with what could only be described as a silly big grin on his face.

Gemma frowned at him. 'What?'

'Check out that baby bump.'

'*What?*' she virtually shrieked, looking frantically down at herself. 'Am I showing? Is it obvious?' She stretched her T-shirt down over her unmistakeable, if still relatively petite, pregnant belly. 'Shit. Where did that come from?'

'Well, Gem, when a man loves a woman . . .'

'Charlie!' she cried. 'What am I going to do?'

'You still haven't worked that out?'

She shook her head.

'Well, you'd better start thinking fast. You're not going to be able to hide that for much longer.'

'It's not this obvious in my office clothes, I'm sure. Jackets hide a multitude of sins. I've still got time.'

'Then what?'

Gemma looked at him helplessly. 'I don't know. Embezzle company funds and run off to Brazil? Wanna come?'

He smiled. 'You know, if you put as much energy into coming up with a solution about how to break it to the boss as you do trying to wangle your way into meetings, you might get yourself out of this mess.'

'Nothing's going to get me out of this mess,' she said glumly, patting her stomach.

Charlie folded his arms, watching her. 'Did I hear you say you might be using that old darkroom for the baby?'

Gemma nodded. 'Well, not as it is, I have to get that black paint off the window, paint the walls, something bright, happy. I was thinking yellow . . .' She looked over at Charlie and he had that big silly grin on his face again. 'What?'

'Well,' he said, 'that sounds like you're thinking about keeping said baby, then?'

'I guess.' Gemma straddled an old vinyl kitchen chair, leaning her elbows on the back. 'Sometimes I can see myself with a baby. I catch myself making plans around it, thinking of the future . . . then other times, I'm terrified.' She paused. 'I never pictured myself as a mother, Charlie. I don't know how I'm going to handle it.'

Charlie perched a little precariously on a broken chair, facing her. 'I can totally picture you as a mother.'

Gemma looked at him. 'You can?'

He nodded. 'Sure. A bit of an unconventional one, a little loose around the edges, but I think the kid's going to be lucky to have you as his mum.'

Gemma felt a rush of something warm across her chest. 'Thanks for that,' she said seriously. 'No one's said anything that positive to me yet.'

Charlie shrugged it off. 'Maybe that's because hardly anyone knows about it.'

No, that wasn't it. It wouldn't matter how many people knew, Charlie was one of the select few people in her life who truly 'got' her, and that was a gift. She was really going to need him around when the baby came.

'Hey, why don't you stay for dinner?' said Gemma. 'Helen won't mind, she'll love it. She'll be cooking some vegie mush, but we can always order pizza as well.'

But Charlie was shaking his head. 'Sorry, I have plans tonight.'

Charlie had plans? 'Oh, heavy date?'

He took a breath. 'Not so heavy.'

Charlie had a date? Gemma suddenly felt a wave of nausea. That was odd – was her morning sickness coming back?

'First date?' she asked.

'Nope.'

'Well is it the second, the third?'

'I'm not sure, I've lost count.'

'What?' Gemma said, feeling flustered. 'Well, that's not *a* date, that's dat*ing*. You're dating someone, Charlie.'

He nodded. 'Yeah, sounds about right.'

'Well, why didn't you tell me?'

Charlie shrugged. 'It hasn't come up.'

'Oh, come on. How many conversations have we had since I came back?'

'We mostly talk about you, Gem.'

'You could have interrupted me to tell me you had a girlfriend.' She was waiting for Charlie to interrupt her now and say he wouldn't exactly call her his girlfriend. But he didn't. 'So what's her name?'

'Poppy.'

'Poppy? How old is she?'

'Gemma,' he chided.

She bit her tongue. Any girl who appreciated Charlie's particular charms couldn't be all that bad. Was probably, in fact, pretty great.

Gemma took a deep breath. 'I'm really happy for you, Charlie,' she said, trying as hard as she could to make that sound genuine. She was happy for him, of course she was happy. For Charlie. She was just feeling sorry for herself. She hated being single, it felt unnatural. Gemma liked having a man around – that was how she felt most comfortable. In fact, she almost didn't feel real unless she was in a relationship. Maybe that was why she kept picking such losers. Anyone was better than being alone. She looked across at Charlie and all of a sudden she felt a rush of jealousy for this Poppy. She obviously knew how to pick them.

'Here they are, Mummy!' they heard Noah cry out from the front door.

'Break's over,' said Charlie, standing up and putting a hand out to help Gemma up.

Winter

The fiddly, fussy, countless ornaments that had driven Gemma to distraction from the first day were the last things to face the chop. Phoebe had come over for moral support, but Helen was hesitant, to say the least. She picked up one item at a time, ummed and ahhed and winced and bit her lip, recited a potted history of the particular piece, and then put it down again, finding tenuous reasons as to why she should hold onto it, or at the very least, defer making a decision till 'later'. Finally Gemma could stand it no longer and gave her a pad of stick-it flags. She suggested that Helen place one on each of the pieces she was sure she wanted to keep, and Gemma would follow behind and remove the unflagged pieces. She and Phoebe gave her a head start while they went to make tea, but when they returned, Gemma found shelves and shelves of ornaments with stick-it flags attached, like miniature lifesavers at a miniature surf carnival. This was going to be harder than she'd thought.

'What's the problem, Helen?'

'Is there a problem?' she asked guilelessly, crouched down in front of one of the cabinets.

'I can't see any ornaments that haven't been flagged.'

Helen stood up, frowning as she surveyed the cabinets. 'That can't be . . .' But it was. She bit her lip.

'Do you actually want to keep them all?' Phoebe asked kindly. 'Do you have some kind of sentimental attachment?'

'No, no, not me. They all belong to my mother. I'm just not sure what she'd like to keep.'

'Would she even know the difference anymore?' said Gemma, not quite managing to mask the frustration in her voice.

Helen looked a little nonplussed, as did Phoebe, who made one of her best disapproving faces at her sister.

'I'm sorry, was that insensitive?' said Gemma. Sensitivity had never been her strong suit either.

'Maybe you could pick out your mother's favourite pieces and take them to her, to decorate her room?' Phoebe suggested helpfully.

Helen tilted her head, considering. 'She liked the crystal, Dad gave her a few pieces over the years.'

'Great, let's pack up all the crystal so you can take it next time you visit her,' Gemma said before Helen could change her mind.

She wasn't convinced. 'What if she breaks it?'

'So?' Gemma shrugged. 'It's hers to break, isn't it?'

Helen nodded slowly. 'I suppose you're right.'

'What about the porcelain figures, or the Bakelite . . .' Gemma added, not wanting to lose the momentum.

'No, the Bakelite wasn't Mum's. It belonged to an aunt. Mum ended up with it when she died. No one else wanted it apparently and Mum didn't want to see it thrown out . . .'

God, the world was overrun with hoarders.

'It's funny,' Helen mused, 'she wasn't close to that aunt, she lived over in WA. Mum didn't even know her all that well.'

Gemma shook her head. 'Then what's the point of keeping a cabinet full of stuff she didn't like and had no sentimental attachment to? Imagine the number of times she must have dusted it all!' Gemma was gazing at the orderly display of dressing-table pieces and jewellery on one shelf, dining table accessories on the shelf below. 'I can understand her not wanting to throw it out, but why not sell it? Can you imagine if Mum saw this, Phee?'

'She'd think she'd died and gone to heaven.' Phoebe stopped suddenly, her eyes wide and round. 'Oh my God, I'm so sorry, Helen.'

'Now who's being insensitive?' Gemma muttered smugly.

'It's all right, really,' Helen assured her. 'You're allowed to say the words "death" or "dying" in front of me. It's worse if you try to avoid them.'

They both nodded, vowing internally never to say the words 'death' or 'dying' in front of her again.

'So your mother likes Bakelite?' Helen said.

Phoebe nodded. 'She collects it.'

'Take it then,' she said. 'If you think she'd like it.'

'No!' Gemma blurted. 'She's got enough of the stuff, and besides, you'd be surprised what you might be able to get for this. And those Lladro figurines. And you won't need all the glass display cabinets once you get rid of the stuff inside them . . .' Her voice faded out as she became lost in thought. 'You should have a garage sale.'

Helen looked a little taken aback. 'But I don't have a garage.'

'You don't actually need a garage to have a garage sale, Helen,' said Phoebe. 'You could set it all up in your front yard.'

Helen was frowning. 'That'd be a lot of work, wouldn't it? This isn't the kind of stuff you could just throw into boxes –'

'What if we make it a garage sale "by appointment only"?' Gemma suggested as the idea occurred to her. 'That'd make it sound exclusive. You'd probably get a lot of antique dealers, like they do at –' She stopped short. She had been about to say deceased estates.

'What were you going to say?' Helen prompted her.

'Oh, you know, the dealers always go to the auctions, that kind of thing,' Gemma said vaguely, making no sense at all. Best to push on and hope no one noticed. 'I'll write the ad, cataloguing everything. And we'll only include a phone number, no address. That way people will have to ring to make an appointment.'

'And you think they will?' asked Helen.

'Of course,' said Phoebe. 'Gemma's right, you don't want the usual garage sale crowd, you want to attract the collectors who know what this stuff's worth. I don't think you'll have any trouble moving all this.'

Helen was listening, contemplating. Opening up and clearing out that room had had an astonishing and unexpected effect on her.

She felt lighter somehow. It occurred to Helen that the shadow of her father's death had been hanging over this house, over their lives, for too long. The house had become a kind of monument to grief, and Helen was beginning to feel that if she didn't excavate through the layers, she'd become buried under them, and she'd never have the space to grieve for David.

However, her mother was still alive, barely cognisant, but alive. And still the legal owner of this house, and everything in it. Did Helen really have the right to go divvying up her belongings, like she had no say in it? But what would she say if given the chance? She wouldn't remember; she'd probably become agitated, certainly confused. To line up all this in front of her mother and ask her to choose would be unnecessarily confronting. At times like that Marion appeared to have some awareness that reality had slipped irrevocably from her grasp, and the pain and fear in her eyes were almost unbearable. Helen couldn't do that to her, and Gemma was right – she wouldn't know the difference anyway.

'So what do you think?' Gemma was saying.

She would need to run it by Tony, but Helen didn't imagine he'd have a problem with it, especially if she assured him he'd get half the proceeds. She met Gemma's gaze. 'Let's do it.'

Bailey's

Gemma was feeling restless. The MD was due back in the office any time now. He'd been away for the entire week and Gemma had had very little to keep her occupied apart from answering the phone and opening the mail. She felt as though she was little more than a glorified receptionist. An assistant was supposed to assist, but the MD didn't seem to need or want her help. She merely provided remote backup support so he could run his own show.

The phone rang and Gemma picked it up uninterestedly. 'Good afternoon, Bai–'

'Gemma it's me, Helen, Helen Chapman . . . that you live with –'

'I know who you are, Helen,' Gemma said, amused.

'Oh, okay,' she said with a nervous giggle. 'I just wanted to tell you something,' she whispered loudly. 'But I wasn't sure if it was a problem ringing you at work?'

'You don't have to whisper, Helen, no one can hear you this side. And I gave you my number here at work, remember? I told you it's okay to ring me if you ever need to.'

'Well, I probably didn't need to. Not strictly speaking, you know, it's not like it's an emergency or anything. I could have left it till you got home –'

'Helen, what is it?' Gemma interrupted.

'Sorry, sorry,' she said. 'Well, the thing is, I've been getting calls all morning! I've almost filled the schedule for the entire day.'

'That's great.' Gemma had known they'd get a good response to the ad they'd placed, but perhaps not this quickly. 'Are they mostly dealers?'

'There were a few dealers, though not everyone said. One man was quite upfront – he's a private collector, begged me not to let anyone touch the Bakelite before he gets a chance to see it. Said he'll be here first thing Saturday morning, and that he'll better anything that a dealer offers.'

'Sounds good . . . disturbing, but good,' said Gemma.

'You will be here on Saturday?' Helen asked tentatively.

'Of course.' Like she had anything better to do. Out of the corner of her eye she caught a glimpse of the MD making his way up the corridor. 'Oh, that's my boss coming. I have to go, Helen.'

'Okay, bye,' she blurted, hanging up in Gemma's ear.

Gemma got to her feet and adjusted her shirt and jacket, straining to hold her tummy in. 'Hi,' she said brightly as he came by her desk.

He stopped, looking at her with a mildly puzzled frown on his face. 'Afternoon.'

'Good afternoon to you as well,' she returned, smiling. She was glad she'd talked him into that haircut – it was a significant improvement. He wasn't half bad-looking, actually, if he'd just do something about his wardrobe . . . 'How was your flight?'

'Uneventful.' He narrowed his eyes, considering her. 'You look different. Have you had your hair cut or something?'

No, her face was just bloated, along with everything else. Bugger. Gemma took a breath to pull her stomach in tighter.

'I think I might have put on a bit of weight,' she replied lightly. 'Not used to sitting at a desk all day,' she added with a forced laugh.

He lifted one eyebrow. 'Well, I'll be in my office. Lots to catch up on.'

As he walked away, Gemma promptly followed, unbeknownst to him, she realised, when he went around his desk and appeared to get a surprise to see her standing on the other side. 'Can I help you?' he asked.

'That's what I want to know.'

He looked blankly at her.

'If I can help *you*?'

'Oh, no, not right at the moment,' he said, a little wary. 'Thanks.' He set his briefcase on the desk and began to empty it, effectively ignoring her.

Okay, what was wrong here was that they didn't have a relationship yet. A working relationship. She was just someone sitting at a desk, a conduit to the office when he wasn't here, a keeper of the gate when he was. She had to build up a rapport with him. Become a confidante, an advisor, a friend.

'So how was your trip?' she asked, as a friend would.

He glanced across at her. 'You're still here.'

Did he think she'd give up that easily? 'How was your trip?' Gemma repeated.

'You already asked me that,' he said, closing his briefcase and placing it on the floor beside his desk.

'I know,' said Gemma. 'But you didn't answer me.'

'I did, out at your desk. You already asked me and I told you it was uneventful, remember?' He sat down and turned on his computer.

'No,' Gemma persisted, leaning forward, propping her hands on the edge of the desk. 'I asked you how your flight was. Now I'm asking you about your trip. Was it successful? Did you achieve what you hoped to achieve? Did any problems come to light? Are you planning –'

'It was fine, okay?' he said brusquely, focusing on the computer screen.

She'd had just about enough of this. 'No, actually, it's not okay.'

He turned his head to glare up at her. 'I beg your pardon?'

Oops, shit. She might have gone too far.

'MD,' Gemma began, 'you hired me to be your assistant, but how am I supposed to assist you when I'm not included in anything you do?'

'That's my call,' he said. 'Not yours.'

Gemma released a loud sigh.

He sat back in his chair, meeting her eyes. 'Yes, I hired you to be my assistant, Gemma,' he said. 'And a good assistant wouldn't be hounding me to pay her attention. She would understand that after a week away, I'm tired, I have a lot of work to catch up on, and I might want to be left alone to do just that. I think I at least have the right to decide when and for what I need your assistance. If that doesn't suit you, then, as you said in your interview, you're welcome to leave of your own volition.'

*

'I should have known those words would come back to bite me on the bum,' Gemma grumbled.

She'd met Charlie in the lift on the way out and had been recounting the whole episode till they got to the ground floor and walked out of the building. They started down the street together. Gemma pulled her coat around her but it didn't quite meet. They were walking directly into a stiff wintry breeze, and she felt cold and uncomfortable and cranky.

'Maybe I should just quit.'

'Maybe.'

'But then what would I do, Charlie?' she said. 'I can't raise a child without an income, and I couldn't get another job now, at this late stage. Besides, I've burned too many bridges in the past, my résumé is like Swiss cheese there's so many holes in it, and if I leave this job without an explanation . . .' Gemma came to an abrupt halt, overwhelmed by her own predicament.

'So I guess you'd better stick it out then,' said Charlie.

'But I hate it,' she whined. 'It's so boring. And he's such a pig.'

'So leave.'

'*Char-lie!*'

'*Gem-ma!*' he returned. 'What do you want me to say? Okay, I get it – you can't stand your boss, you hate your job, but unfortunately you need it. You think you're the only person who's ever had to put up with a boss they didn't like, or a job they hated? People do it all the time.'

Gemma pouted. 'I didn't ever want to be one of those people.'

'Welcome to the real world, baby.'

She frowned at him. 'What's wrong with you?'

'Nothing,' said Charlie. 'It just gets a little frustrating after a while, this broken-record routine of yours, Gem. The MD's not the villain here, he made it crystal clear to you what he expected from the start. He was honest. Stop trying to find someone else to blame for the mess you're in. The fact is, you made a whopping omission to get a job you didn't really want. What did you think was going to happen? That it would all magically sort itself out?'

Gemma hated it when people made perfect sense like that. Charlie did it all the time, so did Phoebe. And Helen was developing an annoying tendency in that direction too.

'Yeah, well, it'll all be sorted soon enough,' said Gemma. 'I'm going to lose the job when I can't hide the pregnancy any longer.'

'Probably.'

'*Charlie!*'

'I'm just calling it like I see it, Gem,' he declared.

'Well, I wish you'd stop doing that.'

'So you want me to say everything's going to be all right? That when the MD finds out you're pregnant, he'll grant you paid leave, find a temporary replacement and welcome you back in a few months after he's set up a crèche for the baby?'

But Gemma had stopped listening halfway through. 'That's what I need, isn't it?' she said.

'What? A crèche?'

'A replacement. If I have someone all lined up to take over, then he can't complain –'

'He can if he wants to,' said Charlie. 'What if he doesn't like your replacement?'

Now Gemma was getting frustrated. 'Charlie, I'm just trying to come up with a solution here. You said I should stop expecting everything to sort itself out.'

'Okay, fair call. Where are you going to find this replacement?'

'I'll talk to Kelly in HR.'

'She can't do anything without his say-so, you realise.'

Charlie was right. 'I know. I could go to the temp agency I used to work for when I first came to Bailey's. Actually, I have a pretty good reputation with them. I'd forgotten about that.'

'Once again, you can't line up a temp to take your place, Gem, it all has to go through the proper channels.'

'I hate that expression,' she grumbled. They came to the intersection where they would have to part ways. 'Hey, do you want to go and get a drink? Something to eat?' she asked hopefully.

'Sorry, I can't,' said Charlie.

Gemma looked at him. 'You're seeing Poppy?'

He nodded. 'As a matter of fact . . .'

'When am I going to get to meet her?'

'Oh,' he said, considering it. 'I was thinking around the twelfth.'

'The twelfth of what?'

'Of never.'

She pulled a face. 'Do the lame jokes work with Popsicle?'

'Don't call her that.' The lights changed on the intersection. 'Ah, there's my cue, gotta run.'

She grabbed his arm. 'Oh, come on, Charlie, let me meet her.'

'Not going to happen, Gem.'

'Why not?'

'Because you'd chew her up and spit her out for breakfast.'

Gemma was indignant. 'What do you mean by that? I'm a nice person.'

'When you want to be.'

Gemma looked up at him. She hoped he could see the hurt in her eyes, she was trying very hard to make it obvious. Charlie sighed. The lights changed again and he drew Gemma away from the throng on the corner.

'Look,' he said, 'Poppy's a very sweet girl. She's not used to people like you.'

'What's that supposed to mean? If you're trying to offend me, Charlie, you've succeeded. In fact, look over your shoulder, you crossed that line back on the twelfth of never.'

'I wasn't trying to offend you, Gem,' he said. 'Hey, Gemma? Look at me . . .?'

But she couldn't look at him. She was trying to blink back these bloody tears that were welling up in her eyes. Damn, damn, damn, she had no control of her bodily functions anymore. She was always leaking from some place or other.

She felt Charlie's hand under her chin, lifting it so she had to look at him. 'Gemma,' he chided. 'You're not –'

'No, I'm not.' She sniffed, shrugging him off and wiping her eyes. 'It's just the pregnancy, okay? It happens for no reason at all.'

'Okay,' he said, watching her doubtfully.

'Your light's green,' said Gemma, pointing back to the intersection.

'It's all right, I can wait –'

'Go,' she insisted. 'I'm going to miss my bus anyway.' She took a couple of steps away from him.

He stood where he was, still watching her.

'Bye, Charlie. Have a good night,' she said as she turned and headed down the street away from him. Alone.

Balmain

Gemma was dreaming she was a teenage girl again. Lying asleep in her bedroom, gradually coming to consciousness to the sound of her parents' voices. Often they were talking about her – if either of them knew what time she'd got in the previous night, if they suspected she'd been drinking, how they should handle it this time, should they bring it up, or should they just let it go, seeing as she had actually come home, after all.

Gemma's favourite tactic was to pretend to be sick. Actually, she didn't have to pretend all that often. Her parents could never bring themselves to punish her when she was sick, even if it was self-inflicted. In fact, they usually started to fuss over her, mixing up Berocca, making coffee, preparing a hangover breakfast if they were feeling particularly benevolent.

But her parents didn't seem to be talking about her this morning. Their voices were raised, polite, exaggerated . . . '*What a lovely home!*'

Gemma blinked a couple of times, bringing herself back to consciousness, back to the present. She stared up at the ceiling. There was the hippo, the little bird on its nose. She was in her bedroom in Balmain. So who did those voices belong to?

She dragged herself out of bed and wrapped her robe haphazardly around her as she stumbled out into the hall and wandered through the house towards the voices, like a child following the Pied Piper's tune. She couldn't still be dreaming, surely? She arrived at the entrance to the back room. There was Helen, in conversation with two figures whose backs were to Gemma, a man and a woman. But Gemma knew exactly who they were, and before she could stop herself she let out an involuntary gasp.

Helen looked up. 'Gemma?'

The two figures turned around and the man said, '*Gemma?*'

The woman just screamed. 'GEMMA!'

'Gem-ma,' the man repeated warmly, raising his arms towards her.

'Gemma?' said Helen again, clearly confused.

Just then Noah ran into the room from the kitchen, obviously startled by the commotion. 'Whata matta, Gemma?' he cried, his eyes wide, looking from face to face.

'It's all right, Noah,' said Helen, scooping him up onto her hip.

'Did Phee tip you off?' Gemma said once she'd composed herself.

'Phoebe knows you're back?' said the woman.

Now Gemma was mystified. If Phoebe didn't tell them, then . . . 'How did you find out where I was staying?'

'We didn't,' the woman said breathlessly. 'We came for the Bakelite.'

Shit. She should have known. Like bees to honey.

'We found this terrific site online that links collectors to auctions and sales in all localities,' the man said.

Damned internet had a lot to answer for.

'This is some coincidence,' he went on, his voice giddy with emotion. 'What are the chances?'

Seven hundred fucking billion to one, knowing Gemma's luck. But this had nothing to do with luck. Gemma should have known, should have realised. She should have left the damn Bakelite out of it.

'Gemma?' said Helen. She was still standing behind the man and the woman, who were gradually inching themselves closer to Gemma, preparing to pounce. Helen looked confounded, not surprisingly.

Gemma cleared her throat. 'Helen,' she began. The man and the woman turned around then to look at Helen. 'These are my parents, Gary and Trish Atkinson.'

They were already veering back towards Helen. Noah buried his face in her shoulder.

'Helen, it's so nice to meet you.'

'We haven't met you before now, have we?'

'I'm usually good with faces.'

'No you're not, Gary, but I don't remember you either, darling. Are you and Gemma old friends?'

'I'm pretty good with faces –'

Helen was trying to get a word in edgeways, but she didn't have a hope.

'You've never met Helen before,' Gemma said loudly to get their attention.

They both stopped, turning around to look at her again.

'What's going on, Gemstone?' her father asked, clearly bewildered, like everyone else in the room.

'What are you doing here? And is, um, is Luke around?' added Trish, glancing over Gemma's shoulder as though he might materialise behind her.

Gemma sighed. She wasn't going to get out of having the dreaded conversation. Unless . . .

'No, Luke isn't here,' she said flatly. 'I left him in Brisbane.' That was sort of the truth. It was the last place she'd seen him anyway.

'When did you come back to Sydney?' said Gary, a hurt waver in his voice.

Be vague. 'Oh, just a little while ago.'

'Why didn't you let us know?' Trish asked, the hurt in her voice gaining the sharp edge of accusation.

Gemma looked from her mother to her father to Helen. Helen looked from Gemma to her father to her mother, and back to Gemma again. Her parents looked at each other, then at Helen, then at Gemma.

Which meant everyone was looking at Gemma, waiting for an answer. A couple of loud knocks sounded from the front of the house. She breathed out.

'Oh, that's my next appointment,' said Helen, looking apologetic.

'You're going to have to go,' Gemma said to her parents.

They began to protest, as more knocks were heard, and Helen finally spoke over the top of them all.

'Gemma, just take them into the kitchen,' she said. 'Quickly.'

'Don't sell the Bakelite, dear,' Trish called as Helen hurried up the hall, Noah trailing behind her. He was clearly not about to hang back with the crazy people.

Gemma herded her parents into the kitchen and closed the door.

'So how do you know Helen?' Gary asked.

Gemma went to fill the kettle. 'She had a room for rent online.'

'There's no husband on the scene?' Trish asked.

She groaned inwardly. It didn't take her mother long to start making judgements. This would show her.

'Helen's husband died,' Gemma said, in a low voice.

They both looked aghast.

'She's so young. Was he a lot older than her?' Trish asked, already salivating over the details.

'I don't think it's appropriate to talk about that now, do you, Mum?' said Gemma, her eyes shifting towards the door and then back to them.

'Of course, you're right, darling,' Trish said, suitably chastened, but no doubt mentally making a note to find out the whole story at the soonest available opportunity.

'So you're renting a room here?' said Gary.

Gemma calmly plugged in the kettle and flicked it on. 'That's right.'

Wait for it . . . tick, tick . . .

'We have plenty of rooms at home, darling,' said Trish, her lip trembling ever so slightly. 'Empty rooms, just sitting there. But apparently you'd prefer to stay with a complete stranger, and give her your money, when you could stay with your own family, who love you, and who would never take a cent off you.'

'Mum, have you forgotten that I haven't lived at home since I was a teenager?' Gemma leaned back against the kitchen bench and her robe fell open.

'Oh . . . my . . . God,' Trish said slowly, for maximum dramatic impact. She was staring straight at Gemma's bump. The thin singlet she wore as a pyjama top barely reached her navel. Gemma grabbed the edges of her robe and wrapped it around herself again.

'What is it, Trish?' Gary said urgently. 'What's the matter?'

Trish reached for the table to steady herself. She was clearly going to wring every ounce of melodrama out of the situation. 'I think you'd better ask your daughter that,' she said ominously.

He looked at Gemma, completely perplexed. 'Gemstone?'

She sighed loudly. 'Okay, you had to find out sometime, so I guess this is it. Mum, Dad, I'm pregnant. And before you start –' she added, holding her hand up '– remember I'm a grown woman, I'm not a teenager. So don't talk to me like I'm a teenager, don't treat me like I'm a teenager.'

They were both staring at her, carefully contemplating their next words.

'It is Luke's?' her mother ventured after a while.

'Yes, it is.'

'But he's still in Brisbane?'

'I don't know where he is now.' Gemma was beginning to feel quite in charge of the situation. 'But I decided he wasn't good enough to be the father of my baby.' Which was entirely true. After he had walked out on her, she was absolutely convinced he wasn't good enough.

'Well, I could have told you that,' Trish tsked.

'I believe you did, Mum, a number of times.'

'I still don't understand why you didn't tell us you were here in Sydney,' she persisted. 'We're your family, Gemma, who else but family is going to help you through this?'

Gemma turned to get the cups. 'Like I said, I'm a grown woman, I can take care of myself.'

'Well, that's a matter of opinion,' said Trish. 'You don't have a great track record, let's face it, Gemma, and now with a baby on the way you're going to need us more than ever . . .' Her voice trailed off as Gemma turned around and folded her arms, giving her mother a baleful look.

'This is exactly why I haven't been in touch,' she said tetchily.

There was a pregnant pause, appropriately enough.

'She's right, Trish,' said Gary, resting his hand on his wife's shoulder. 'You know what the book said.'

Trish nodded sagely.

'What book?' asked Gemma.

'*Helicopter Parenting*,' said Trish.

'About parents who hover,' Gary added.

Good lord.

'The thing is, is this what you want, Gemstone?' he asked.

Gemma shrugged. 'I didn't exactly choose it, Dad.'

'But are you happy?'

How was she supposed to answer that? 'The jury's still out on that one too, I'm afraid.'

He looked a little bemused, but he came towards her and gave her a kiss on the cheek. 'Well, congratulations, Gemma.'

She felt a slight lump in her throat. That was the first time anyone had offered her congratulations.

'Thank you,' she said in a small voice.

'Am I at least allowed to ask after your health?' said Trish, still clinging to what remained of her righteous indignation. 'You look a little tired to me, Gemma.'

'I just got out of bed, Mum.'

'And what are you doing for money?'

'Working,' said Gemma, meeting her righteous indignation and raising it.

'Oh, Gemma,' Trish sighed. 'You can't be waitressing or working behind a bar in your condition –'

'I'm not. I'm back at Bailey's actually. Personal assistant to the managing director.'

Her mother had nothing to say to that, apparently.

'Well, that's great, love,' said Gary. 'Isn't that great, Trish?' he added, putting his arm around his wife and giving her a squeeze. 'They were prepared to take her back, pregnant and all.' He looked at Gemma. 'You must have done the right thing by them in the past.'

Gemma smiled weakly. There was a light knock and next thing Helen's head appeared around the door. 'Okay if I come in?'

'Of course it is,' said Gemma. 'It's your house, Helen. How's it going out there?'

'Really well,' she said. 'This man owns an antique place in Rozelle. He's putting together a list before he makes me an offer, so I thought I'd give him some space.'

'He's not interested in the Bakelite, is he?' said Trish urgently.

'I won't let anyone else have it,' Helen assured her. 'You were here first.'

'Well, I tell you what, young lady,' said Gary. 'I want you to carefully consider all offers for the Bakelite –'

'Gary!'

'Hear me out, Trish,' he said. 'You let us know the highest offer, and we'll top it.'

'That's really not necessary,' said Helen.

'Yes it is,' Gemma broke in. 'They can afford it.'

'So that's settled,' said Gary.

'And now we'd better get out of your way,' said Trish. 'Gemma, when are we going to see you?'

And so it begins. 'I'll give you a call.'

'Oh, no,' said Trish, 'if we leave it up to you, we'll be lucky to see our grandchild before he starts school.'

'Hey, Trish,' Gary said, smiling broadly. 'We're going to have another grandbaby.'

'Hmm,' she shook her head, 'and I don't look old enough to have one, let alone three!'

Gemma had been waiting for that.

'So, what night can you come over for dinner?' Trish persisted.

Gemma's shoulders sagged. 'I don't know, Mum, I get really tired after work.'

'So we'll make it lunch on Saturday, or Sunday.'

'Sunday lunch, now that sounds like a treat,' said Gary.

'Sunday it is then,' said Trish. 'I'll get on to Ben and Phoebe, and you must come too, Helen.'

'Pardon?' Helen was taken aback. 'Oh, no I cou–'

'Of course you could!'

'Mum, don't drag poor Helen into this,' said Gemma. 'How's she supposed to say no now?'

Trish took hold of Helen's hand. 'Why would she want to say no to a lovely family Sunday lunch? And she's like family now, aren't you, Helen?'

Helen didn't know what to say.

'And of course you'll be bringing that darling little boy of yours. He looks to be about the same age as Emily, our granddaughter. They'll have a lovely time together.'

'Thank you,' said Helen. 'I'd better get back out there.'

'Of course, see you next week.'

Helen slipped out through the door again.

'Now, we'll have to get a move on,' said Trish. 'We're meeting Kath and Rod at the club. You remember the Williamses, Gemma?'

She shrugged vaguely.

'Of course you do,' said Trish, slipping her handbag over her shoulder. 'They had that lovely boy, Jonathan, he was around your age. Dad and I used to secretly harbour hopes for the two of you. But he'd have been too staid and sensible for you, I'm afraid.' Trish shook her head regretfully. 'Anyway, Jon ended up in investment banking, married a delightful woman, a banker as well. You should see the house they got for themselves . . .' She mimed fanning herself with one hand. 'Up in the Hills District. Nothing short of a mansion. And they've got two gorgeous little girls. And bright, you have no idea.'

Gemma's brain was going numb. 'Mum, you don't want to keep the Williamses waiting.'

Trish glanced at her watch. 'You're right, you're right. Come on, Gary. Is it okay for us to go back out through the house?'

'Of course,' said Gemma, already holding the door open for them. Whatever will get you out of here the fastest.

Helen appeared to be deep in negotiations with the antique man, so they made their way out barely noticed. At the front door her mother paused. 'Oh, and you must start making a list, Gemma. What do you have for the baby so far? What do you need?'

'Mu-um . . .'

'Don't "Mu-um" me, Gemma. I want to get some things for my grandchild. It's not a crime, and like you said, we can afford it.'

Touché. Her father leaned down to give her a kiss on the cheek and a little squeeze. 'We'll see you next week, Gemstone.'

And they were gone. Gemma stood leaning against the doorjamb, watching them hurry up the street. They'd have had to park quite a way away, she imagined. She stood there long after they had disappeared around the corner. Then she realised she was still in her pyjamas and went back inside, closing the door.

Sunday night

Helen was sitting on the floor of the back room, propped against a wall, nursing a glass of wine. Phoebe regularly brought a bottle with her when she visited, but she only ever had a glass or two and left the rest, so there always seemed to be an open bottle in the fridge these days. It was nice to have a glass in the evening, after Noah had gone to bed. Helen had missed that. She gazed around the room. It looked a lot bigger, not surprisingly, now that almost everything had been cleared out of it. Even the lounge suite was gone. Helen hadn't planned to sell it, but it had become such a feeding frenzy yesterday that offers were being made on anything and everything that wasn't nailed down. But in the end Helen decided she didn't mind. She'd never liked that lounge anyway. It was a big, heavy, musty old thing, and it wasn't even all that comfortable any more. One of the dealers had made an offer she couldn't refuse, and he had promptly come back this morning with a flat-top truck to take the lot before she changed her mind. He'd also bought two of the glass cabinets and a couple of side tables. The ornaments had been snapped up in the first hour or two, much to the irritation of the people who had appointments later in the day. Helen had had to pack up all the Bakelite and put it somewhere out of sight, before anyone else saw it and started to haggle with her.

Sitting here now, in the empty room, she was feeling a range of emotions, not all of them entirely comfortable. Sure, she felt uncluttered and free of the past, to some degree. But a part of her felt a little guilty as well, as though she'd finally given up on her mother.

Gemma wandered into the room and smiled when she saw Helen. 'What are you doing on the floor?'

'There's not exactly anywhere else to sit.'

'You have a point. Mind if I join you?'

'Not at all, pull up a patch.'

Gemma lowered herself down and leaned her back against the wall opposite to where Helen was sitting. 'So, you really cleaned up, eh?'

'In more ways than one,' Helen smiled.

'What are you going to do with all the loot? Apart from buy a new couch.'

'Mm, I guess I will have to buy a new one.' In an unexpectedly generous gesture, Tony had said he didn't want a share of any of the proceeds. He'd insisted, in fact. 'With the rest I'm really going to spoil myself – buy food, pay bills, keep the wolves at bay.'

Gemma watched Helen take a sip of her wine. 'Things are really that tight for you?'

She shrugged. 'We'll survive.'

'I suppose you'll have to go back to work soon?'

Helen looked at her.

'Sorry,' said Gemma, 'I was only thinking, if things are that tight . . .'

'I can't leave Noah right now.' Helen was trying not to sound curt. 'His dad's gone, he needs me around.'

Gemma nodded. 'Of course.'

'Besides, shiftwork is impossible with a small child, now I'm on my own.'

Gemma nodded again. 'Fair enough.'

'And maybe I've had enough of looking after people.' Helen didn't know where that came from, and why she was talking so much. Must be the wine.

'It's been hard with your mum?' Gemma ventured tentatively.

Helen shrugged. 'It's easier now that she's at Brookhaven. They're very good to her there. It's an excellent facility. It'd want to be,' she added, 'considering what they charge.'

Gemma was thinking. 'You know, maybe you're not charging me enough?' Helen went to interrupt but Gemma kept right on. 'You do realise that if you were to let me use that room, I'd pay you more, you know. I wouldn't expect to get it for nothing.'

Helen sighed. 'You're really stuck on that idea, aren't you?'

'I keep thinking it might get a bit cramped in one room when the baby comes,' said Gemma. 'It's not the baby so much, it's all the gear I'm worried about, cots and prams and the rest. I don't want to leave stuff lying all around the place.'

'This is your home too, Gemma. I don't want you to feel that you can't spread out further than your room.'

'Thanks, but . . .' She paused. 'There's a whole empty room now.'

Helen was nodding. It made sense, of course, especially as Gemma had no way of knowing . . .

'There's something I should tell you about that room,' said Helen.

'You already told me,' Gemma said. 'I know your father died in there, but it really doesn't bother me. I mean, considering the age of this house, Helen, I doubt he was the first person to die here. Besides, I don't really know that I believe in spirits and all that.'

'You don't believe in an afterlife?' Helen asked her.

Gemma was about to answer automatically with an unequivocal 'no', but for once her sensitivity kicked in first and she hesitated. The notion of an afterlife had to be incredibly reassuring to anyone who'd lost someone close to them, especially if they'd died suddenly and unexpectedly.

'You don't want to say, do you?' said Helen, sensing Gemma's hesitation. 'Don't worry about upsetting me, I'm just interested. I don't even know what I think about it, but when death comes this close, it certainly makes you think about it more.'

Gemma didn't doubt that. 'The thing is,' she said, 'who knows for sure? Who's ever come back to give us definitive proof? Maybe there is a high old time being had up there by everyone who's passed on. It's an appealing thought. But if that's the case, they're keeping it to themselves. And maybe that's the way it has to be. We'd all be killing ourselves to get there if we knew.'

Helen was gazing at her from across the room. 'My father killed himself.'

Gemma gasped. 'What?'

'That's how he died,' she went on, 'in the room. It wasn't messy or anything. He took pills.'

'Shit.' Gemma swallowed. 'I'm sorry, Helen, I didn't know.'

'I realise that. It's okay.'

Gemma tried to regain her composure. 'Did you ever find out why?'

Helen shook her head. 'He didn't leave a note or anything. I don't know if my mother knew more; she never said, she just fell apart. And we've never been able to put her back together again.'

'How old were you . . . when it happened?' asked Gemma.

'Fifteen.'

'What was he like?'

'He was a nice man, you know, amiable, but quiet,' said Helen. 'He adored Mum, that was obvious. But as the years went by he just kind of shut down. I sometimes wonder if life didn't quite measure up for him. He locked himself away in his darkroom, but we never saw much of what he did. He said it was just for his own amusement. But when you think about it, a darkroom is a perfect place to hide out. No one can come in without your permission, you have an excuse to stay in there, alone, as long as you want.'

'Do you think your father might have been depressed?' Gemma asked carefully. She didn't want to sound like she was prying.

'Doctors told us at the time that it was more than likely. If you look at the statistics, he had to be either depressed, or there was some other undiagnosed mental illness. But by his age there would have been symptoms long before then. Financial problems are the next most common reason, but my parents didn't have any. Not that they were rich, but they'd inherited this house from my mother's mother, they'd never had a mortgage, never had to worry about putting a roof over our heads. Dad had a public service job, reasonable wage, good conditions, security.'

So this place really was like the family museum. Or rather, mausoleum.

'So,' Gemma said after a while, 'you didn't say, do you believe in an afterlife?'

Helen became thoughtful. 'I don't know. I used to wonder, and then when David came along he was so rabidly against the idea of a god, I guess I was swayed. He'd done a lot of aid work overseas and he reckoned there couldn't be a god because he wouldn't let people suffer the way they did.'

'And what do you think now?' Gemma asked.

'It would be comforting to believe that David's still around somehow,' said Helen. 'That he's still part of the universe, that we'll see him again one day. But I just don't know.'

Gemma shifted a little. Her backside was getting numb sitting here on the floor.

'I remember an old movie I saw once,' she said. 'I think it was Cary Grant, one of those guys. His wife had died and his little girl was asking him if she was in heaven, or something like that. They were on a pier, or a boat, near water anyway. He scooped up some water in a jug, and he said our bodies were like the jug, and the water was like our spirit or our soul, whatever you want to call it. He tipped the water back into the river and said that's what happens when we die.' She paused. 'I always kind of liked that idea.'

Helen had been listening intently. 'I think I like it too,' she said quietly.

'Well,' said Gemma, 'if I don't get up off this floor soon, I'm afraid I'm not going to be able to get up at all.' She heaved herself up onto her knees, but as she became upright her head started to spin. She held onto the wall. 'Whoa.'

'Are you all right?' said Helen.

'I must have got up too quickly. I'll be right in a minute.'

'Does that happen often?'

'More often than it used to,' said Gemma. 'Is that a problem?'

'Not if your blood pressure's okay.'

'Oh, right.'

Helen was watching her. 'It is okay, isn't it?'

'I guess.' Gemma shrugged. 'How would I know?'

'Well, if your doctor hasn't said anything, I suppose you can assume it's normal, but I'm surprised he wouldn't say.'

Gemma had an odd expression on her face.

'When was your last visit?' Helen asked.

'Visit?'

'Antenatal visit. You'd still be on monthly visits, right?'

Gemma didn't know what to say.

'You are seeing a doctor, aren't you?' Helen said.

She looked sheepish. 'Well, I did go to a doctor when I fell pregnant. She gave me a referral to an obstetrician, but I didn't get around to seeing him before I left Brisbane.'

'And when you got to Sydney?'

'Slipped my mind.'

Helen was horrified. 'Are you telling me you haven't seen a doctor since your pregnancy was diagnosed, and now you're more than halfway through it?'

'Is that bad?'

'Well, it's not advisable,' Helen said, crawling across the floor towards her. She took hold of Gemma's wrist, consulting her watch as she checked her pulse. 'You need to keep a regular check on your blood pressure, Gemma, as well as the protein levels in your urine, to make sure you don't develop pre-eclampsia.'

'What's that?'

'Something you don't want to happen. What's your blood type?' Helen asked, releasing Gemma's wrist.

'I don't know.'

'Why not?'

'I'm not sure I've ever had a reason to find out.'

'Well, you do now. What if you're rhesus negative?'

'What if I am?'

Helen shook her head. 'Look, I'll call the hospital where I used to work tomorrow and book you into the clinic there. It'll take too long to get in to see an obstetrician privately. Do you have insurance?'

'No.'

'Then the public clinic it is. I know some of the midwives there, they're great. You have nothing to worry about.'

'I wasn't worried . . . before.'

'Gemma, you're not even booked into a hospital,' said Helen. 'Where did you think you were going to give birth?'

She looked plaintively at Helen. 'I thought you just showed up.'

'Well, they wouldn't turn you away, but it's not exactly recommended. I mean, do you even know your due date? You could go into labour too early and you wouldn't know it. And if you go too far over, there are a whole lot of other complications that can arise. Or what if you had something serious, like placenta praevia, for example?'

Gemma felt a little overwhelmed. 'You know, an awful lot of babies came into the world before there were doctors and hospitals.'

'Yes, and an awful lot of them died,' said Helen. 'The infant mortality rate is fewer than five in a thousand births in Australia. It's more than a hundred, and closer to two hundred, in some third world countries.'

'You know that off the top of your head?'

'Like I said, David used to work for aid agencies,' she said. 'He knew his statistics. And anyway, why would you want to take risks when the medical help is right there for the taking?'

'I did intend to see a doctor,' said Gemma, getting up on her feet now that her head wasn't spinning anymore, not from dizziness anyway. 'But between finding a place to live, and work . . .'

The truth was, she'd also been scared she'd find out something was wrong. Gemma and Luke had partied their way up the coast, drinking, smoking . . . and not just tobacco. She'd stopped it all the moment she suspected she was pregnant, but Gemma still carried around a nagging feeling of guilt. Ignorance was not necessarily bliss, but it was easier than knowing she'd caused harm to the peanut.

'I'll call the clinic tomorrow,' Helen repeated. 'See how soon they can fit you in.'

'Do they have after business hours appointments?' Gemma asked.

'I think you're going to have to take whatever you can get this time,' said Helen. 'Besides, they'll understand at work – surely they'd expect you to have the odd morning or afternoon off, given that you're pregnant?'

Gemma smiled weakly. 'Yeah, I'm sure they'll understand.'

Monday

'What kind of appointment?' the MD asked. He did not look impressed.

'It's personal,' said Gemma, hoping to stop this line of questioning. Men never liked to pry into secret women's business. He'd assume she was going for a pap smear or something else to do with 'down there' – which in truth it was – and Gemma was quite sure he wouldn't seek any more information.

'If it's personal, why is it scheduled during work hours?'

Gemma blinked. He was not so easy to put off. 'I didn't have a choice,' she said. 'Look, MD, I haven't so much as taken an hour off –'

'I wasn't aware that taking hours off through the middle of a normal working day was some kind of entitlement.'

Gemma had had him up to here. She should tell him to shove his stupid job. Except right now she had to focus on blinking back tears. Damn pregnancy hormones, like sodden little traitors giving away her position to the enemy.

The MD was watching her closely. 'Okay, just don't make a habit of it,' he said finally, looking back at the computer.

Sure thing. No problem at all.

Tuesday

Gemma rushed into the office just shy of eleven. She hadn't expected to be kept waiting so long. Nor had she expected the several blood tests, or the peeing in a cup, or the internal examination, or the Gestapo-style interrogation on everything from her family medical history and the state of her sex life to what she put in her mouth and, most disgustingly, what came out the other end. She had felt strangely disconnected from her body, as though her head were attached to a walking incubator. Gemma the person was quite secondary to Baby Atkinson, which at least would get her used to being treated as a second-class person from now on, she supposed.

She dumped her stuff beside the desk and turned on the computer as she reached across and pressed the button on the intercom.

'Yes,' came the MD's voice, a moment later.

'Just letting you know I'm in,' she said, trying to muster up some enthusiasm.

'It's about time.'

Her heart sank. She didn't really want to have to take any grief over this, it was hard enough already. She felt weird, jittery, even a little teary – again. More than anything she felt overwhelmed with the burden of responsibility. The baby wasn't even born yet and already she'd been labelled a bad mother. Or at least that's how some of the staff had made her feel, with their tsk-tsks every time she said 'I don't know' to one of their innumerable questions. They had even asked her if she was taking drugs – now, still, at this stage of her pregnancy. Just because she'd had no antenatal treatment, there wasn't a father in sight and she couldn't remember when she'd had her last period, they'd decided she was a junkie. Helen had assured her they had to ask everyone those questions, they weren't picking on her; they'd seen a whole lot worse than Gemma. Which strangely didn't console her at all.

Whatever. Today she had been confronted with the cold, hard, needle-sharp, hospital-grade-disinfectant reality of her condition. She had to start taking this whole thing seriously. And that was going to mean fessing up here at work, sooner rather than later. She was going to have to take more time off for an ultrasound next week, and who knew what else after that. She felt like Harrison Ford in *The Fugitive*, when Tommy Lee Jones was closing in on him and he was running out of time, except there was no one-armed man to pin the whole thing on.

'I have a stack of files here I'd like you to put away,' the MD was saying into the intercom.

'I'll be right in,' she replied.

Brookhaven

Helen walked through the door of her mother's room, carrying the box of crystal ornaments and a few other bits and pieces she'd saved for her.

'What have you got there?' Marion asked warily. 'I didn't order anything. I didn't order anything and you're not going to make me pay for it either.'

Helen set the box down on a chair. 'You're not out of bed yet, Mum. You really should get up – it's not good for you to stay in bed all day.'

'I want you to take that away,' she said, pointing at the box, as though Helen had not even spoken. 'I don't want it in my room. I don't know where it came from and I don't want it here.'

'Let me show you what's inside,' Helen said patiently, opening the box. She had carefully wrapped each piece in tissue paper, and she picked up one from the top, removing the paper to reveal a small crystal bird. It was a pretty piece, and Helen took it across to her mother to show her.

'Look at this one, Mum, I bet Dad gave it to you.' She held it out on the palm of her hand. 'What kind of bird do you think it is? A robin, or maybe a wren? What do you think, Mum?'

But Marion wouldn't even look at it.

'Okay, why don't I put it over here?' Helen crossed to the sparse bookshelf. Her mother used to have more of her belongings around, but she'd gradually given things away, or thrown them away, or said she didn't want them anymore. The room was beginning to look a little spartan.

'I said take it away,' Marion snapped. 'I don't want it in my room.'

Well, this was going well. Helen returned to the box and unwrapped another piece, an elephant this time. Her mother had collected elephants for a while, which was a rather ironic talisman, considering what elephants were renowned for.

'Look, Mum,' she said, bringing it closer. 'This must have been one of your favourites.'

Marion still refused to look. Helen pulled a chair closer to the bed and sat down. 'Come on, Mum, just look at it.' She paused, considering her mother. 'Tony gave you this one.' Helen had no idea if that was the truth, but it got her mother to turn her head and take a look at it.

'I don't like it, I don't want it here. Take it away.'

'But Mum, you used to love these.'

Marion stared at the glass elephant. 'Why would I love that . . . that thing?'

'You did, you used to collect –' Helen frowned. 'What are they called, Mum?'

'Oh, you know,' she said, frustrated. 'Everyone knows what they're called.' But Marion didn't any more.

'It's an elephant, Mum.' Helen stood up and took it over to the shelf. 'You used to love elephants.'

'Well, I don't anymore,' she retorted, and suddenly she was at Helen's side. 'I told you I don't want them.'

'But Mum –'

Marion snatched the bird and the elephant off the bookshelf and walked over to the box, tossing them back in. 'I don't want things here, they only come and steal them.'

'Who steals them?'

'They do.'

'Who are they, Mum?'

'The . . . others,' she said. 'They come and steal my things in the night, when I'm asleep. They won't come if I don't have anything, so I don't want anything here. Take them away.'

'Mum, no one's going to steal them.'

'Why don't you just listen to me, you stupid girl? You never listen. I said take them away, and you can go right along with them.'

So Helen closed the flaps on top of the box, picked it up and walked from the room, down the corridors and out of the building. She was heading for her car when she noticed a skip bin at the far side of the parking area. She hesitated for just a moment, before walking briskly over to it. She lifted the lid and rested the box on the edge for a second. Helen took a breath and let go; it fell to the bottom with a clang. Then she dropped the lid and walked away.

Sunday

'You didn't have to come, you know,' Gemma said as they drove across the Bridge on their way to lunch at her parents'.

'Yes, I did,' Helen said plainly. 'Your mother's phoned every other day this week to remind us. It'd be rude not to show up now.'

'That's how she guilts you into doing what she wants,' said Gemma. 'She's like, like a, what's that dog whose jaw locks when it latches onto something? Is it a pit bull? You have to beat it till it lets go. That's what my mother's like.'

Helen smiled, shaking her head, as she veered to the right to take the Military Road exit. 'Gemma, I have no idea what issues you have with your parents, and I'm sure they're valid, but on first meeting they don't seem that bad.'

'I could say the same thing about your in-laws.'

Helen glanced across at her. 'No you couldn't.'

'No, I suppose not,' Gemma relented. 'Look, of course my parents seem fine when you first meet them. They're like costume jewellery – all shiny and colourful and fun. But overdo it and it's tacky, and it always tarnishes eventually.'

Helen laughed lightly. 'You have a lot of analogies for them.'

'Okay, if you want it upfront, they suck as parents. They only wanted to make us all over in their image, only better, maybe. They wanted us to have everything they never had, be everything they never were.'

'That's what parents do. It's natural for them to want the best for their kids.'

'But it's always been what they thought was best,' Gemma tried to explain, 'not what I wanted. I never felt like they understood me, or that they even wanted to understand me. That would have been too confronting.'

'What do you mean?'

'Well, despite all their hype about loving us for ourselves, only wanting us to be happy . . . truth is, they wanted us to make them happy, fulfil their dreams, give them something to crow about to their friends. Ben and Phoebe did just that, but I feel like they don't even know who I really am, and they don't want to know.'

Helen was thoughtful. 'My mother doesn't know me at all.'

'Then you understand what I'm talking about.'

'No, I mean really, my mother doesn't know me. It's been months since I've seen even a glimmer of recognition from her.'

There was a pause. Gemma didn't know if she was supposed to say something. If she was, she didn't know what.

'She doesn't even seem to recognise Noah anymore,' Helen went on, 'and he was one of the only people who could still cheer her up.' She pulled up at a red light. 'You know, I used to get upset because Mum would pick on my clothes or my hair, or the way I did something, anything.' Nothing Helen did had ever seemed to be right. She'd often got the impression her very existence irritated her mother. 'I used to wish she'd just leave me alone, not notice every little thing. Now I wish she'd notice anything at all.'

Gemma had the feeling she'd just been subtly put in her place. 'So are you saying I should feel lucky that my parents notice me at all, even if it is only to criticise me?'

'No, I wasn't saying that,' she said calmly, and apparently without any further need to explain herself.

'Maybe it'd be a relief if they didn't recognise me,' Gemma grumbled. 'I don't feel like they know who I am anyway.'

Helen glanced at her before taking off with the traffic again.

'Sorry,' said Gemma, 'that wasn't very sensitive, was it?'

'I'm beginning to get that sensitivity's not your strong suit,' said Helen.

'You're not wrong there.'

*

Gemma directed Helen through Neutral Bay and into Mosman, and finally into the street where she'd grown up – the highly desirable location set among other quality homes, quiet and leafy, close to schools and shops. As they pulled up out front, the door flew open, and even from inside the car they could hear Trish call, 'They're here, everybody. Come on, they're here!'

'She must have been keeping watch,' said Gemma. 'Hold onto your hat, it's going to be a bumpy ride.'

The family converged on them with all the restraint of a tsunami as they attempted to make their way through the front door, with Trish providing a running commentary.

'This is our eldest, Ben, Gemma's big brother, there's just the two years between them, but he's virtually running the family company now –'

'Steady on, darl.'

'Shoosh, Gary, you know it's true. And here's Ben's wife, Leisa, and our little princess, Emily. Have you seen a prettier little thing in all your life? Going to be a heartbreaker, she is. I think you and Emily might be right about the same age, Jonah –'

'It's Noah, Mum.'

'And Jasper's running around somewhere, probably kicking that soccer ball outside, can't get him to stop since he was named Player of the Match yesterday. Of course it was no surprise to us, he was Most Valuable Player last year, in his very first season. He's just like his dad, Ben always excelled at sports, got that many trophies we had to have a display case made. Isn't that right, Ben? Where did Ben go? Is he on the phone again? Oh, and I believe you and Phoebe have already met, Helen, but have you met her husband, Cameron? I didn't think so. Cam and Phoebe are both lawyers, a real pair of high-achievers. Though they're dragging their feet a little in the baby race –'

'Mum.'

'– and this is my sister, Lyn, and her husband, Bob, and here's . . .'

Gemma had not expected half the extended family to be there as well but, true to form, her mother had gone overboard in her enthusiasm to drag her daughter back into the fold. Helen looked a little shell-shocked, not surprisingly, and poor little Noah had his head buried under his mother's jacket and was clearly not planning to emerge any time soon. The rabble formed a cordon around them, drawing them further inside, firing questions without waiting for answers, tossing one-liners about, laughing at in-jokes that were all hopelessly lost on Helen.

She was unprepared for the number of people, or for the sheer size of the house. It had obviously been added to over the years, with no expense spared, but unfortunately without a lot of imagination either. It pre-dated the McMansion era but was essentially the same animal. Big was good. Huge was better.

Helen realised a drink had been thrust into her hand, a flute of champagne with a strawberry wedged onto the rim. 'Oh, thanks, but um, I'm driving,' she said.

'One's not going to put you over the limit, love,' said Gary.

'Besides,' Trish chimed in, 'Gemma can't drink. Why don't you drive home, Gemma? Then Helen can drink all she likes.'

'It's fine, really,' Helen protested feebly.

'No, let me drive,' said Gemma. 'Drink up,' she said under her breath to Helen, 'you're going to need it.'

'I'm just going to steal Gemma away for a minute,' Trish was saying. 'I want to show you what I got for the baby. Gary, why don't you show Helen around?'

Gemma saw the look of uneasiness on Helen's face. 'No, Dad, we left the box of Bakelite in the car. Helen, give Dad your keys.'

Her mother let out a squeal of delight. 'Yes, yes, Gary, you go get the Bakelite.'

Helen smiled, passing Gary the keys.

'Okay, then,' said Trish. 'This way, girls.'

They trailed her down a short hall to the ground-floor guestroom and Trish flung back the door for Gemma to see. Parked in the middle of the room was an enormous jogging pram in gleaming chrome and bright aqua.

'I can't stand these things, Mum, they're hideous,' said Gemma. 'They're like the four-wheel drive of prams.'

Helen winced, but Trish was unfazed. 'Oh, don't be ridiculous, Gemma, what's your problem?'

'They're such a wank.'

'Now you're just being a snob,' said Trish. 'They're actually very practical. And durable, and they're ergonomically designed for both mother and baby. The fellow in the store told me –' She stopped short as she saw the look of disdain on Gemma's face.

'I kept the receipt,' said Trish, changing tack. 'If you don't like it you can exchange it for something that suits you better.'

Just then Leisa walked into the room. 'Oh, these are great!' she gushed, quickly checking for the logo. 'And this is *the* brand to have, Gemma. You know the best thing about them, don't you? You can kill two birds with one stone – take the baby for a walk and go for a jog yourself.'

Why the hell would she want to do that?

'And –' Leisa wasn't finished, 'I'll tell you something for nothing, Gemma, when they're little, you just don't get any "me" time. Once, I had to go ten weeks between waxings. I nearly went mad. I don't know how I would have got by without Sara.'

'Sara was a godsend,' Trish agreed.

'Who's Sara?' asked Gemma.

'Our au pair, little British girl, don't you remember her?' said Leisa. 'Though she wasn't exactly "little", she could have lost a few pounds. She wasn't much to look at either, plain as an arrowroot biscuit, but the kids didn't seem to mind, and she was fabulous with them. Her visa ran out last year or I would have kept her till Emily started school.'

But Leisa still wasn't finished.

'Though it's probably just as well, what with Jasper's school fees, and all his extracurricular activities, and now Emily's taking pre-music lessons and dance class. It's constant. I was only saying to my masseur the other day that if I didn't have a personal trainer, when would I ever get any exercise, let alone any "me" time? Don't you find, Helen?'

She had been mesmerised watching Leisa's perfectly painted fingernails flick and swoop to punctuate her every word. Leisa seemed to be waiting for some kind of response to her stream of babble, but Helen couldn't think of anything to say. Not a single thing.

'I think I'd better take Noah outside to find the other children,' she finally came out with. 'Before he gets stuck permanently,' she added in a lowered voice, patting Noah's head, still planted firmly under her jacket.

'Leisa,' said Gemma after Helen had left the room, 'how about a little sensitivity?'

'What?' She blinked. 'What's wrong?'

'It's not exactly appropriate to stand there in front of Helen, going on about private school fees and music lessons and personal trainers.' She rolled her eyes. 'Surely you worked out her circumstances are a little different from yours?'

'Oh, that's right,' said Leisa, nodding. 'She's recently widowed, isn't she? I forgot.'

Gemma turned to glare at Trish. 'Mum! You told Leisa? Why did you go and blab all of Helen's business?'

'I did no such thing.'

Gemma was gobsmacked at the barefaced audacity of her mother – caught red-handed and she still wouldn't admit it.

'I didn't "blab all of Helen's business", Gemma, because you didn't tell me any of it,' she said airily. 'The only thing I know is that she's terribly young to be a widow. Was it cancer?'

Gemma groaned.

Leisa clicked her fingers. 'It wasn't something controversial like AIDS, was it?'

'Oh for . . .' There was only one way to shut them up. 'It was a road accident, okay? And it was very tragic and she's not over it, so do not say a word,' Gemma hissed threateningly.

'Okay, okay, you don't have to make such a fuss,' said Trish.

'You have to promise.'

Trish sighed dramatically. 'I promise.'

'Leisa?'

'Of course I won't say anything,' she said defensively. 'Do you think I'm completely socially inept?'

Gemma decided not to answer that.

Trish checked her watch and shooed them out to the kitchen to help serve lunch. For the next ten minutes Gemma and Leisa and Phoebe and Aunts Lyn, Carol and Sue, along with adult cousins

Rachel and Lauren, wore a path from the kitchen to the dining room carrying platter after platter of salads, meats and antipasto, a range of hot dishes, baskets of bread and rolls, bottles of wine and jugs of softer alternatives. The vast table looked as though it might collapse from the weight of it all.

'Pass me your plate, Helen,' said Trish when they were all seated and serving themselves. 'You must have some of this baked ham, it's divine.'

Helen glanced at Gemma.

'Helen and Noah are vegetarians, Mum,' Gemma explained for her.

'Oh my God, Gemma, why didn't you tell me?' Trish cried frantically. 'Well, this is just awful, what on earth are you going to eat, Helen?'

Helen surveyed the feast in front of her. 'I'm sure we'll find something.'

Trish stood up, anxious. 'I wonder if I've got any salmon in the freezer, that wouldn't take long to grill up . . .'

'Mum, sit down,' said Gemma. 'Vegetarians don't eat fish either, but there's enough food to feed a small African country here.'

'Honestly, we'll be fine,' Helen said.

Trish sat down with a heavy sigh of resignation, and soon the rabble resumed. Helen tried to keep up, but she felt as though she were suffering from sensory overload. There was so much of everything. The food on the table vied for space and attention with assorted table decorations, and every platter, dish and receptacle was virtually a work of art in itself, but lost among the clutter. The room was the same: so many cushions on the sofas, you'd have to move some to sit down; enormous vases filled with enormous arrangements of flowers everywhere she looked; the light fittings were huge sculptural edifices, but if they didn't provide enough illumination, elaborate wall conches were set at frequent intervals around the room, dotted amongst ornately framed pictures, paintings, photographs, in groups, rows, or alone if they were too large. Helen knew her place had been cluttered, but this took it to a whole other level.

The guests were all overdone as well: overdressed, coiffed and bejewelled. Only the men were a little more toned down.

Gemma's father seemed like a nice man, if a little mild. Cameron was a surprise. Helen had expected Phoebe would be with someone more ... genuine, perhaps, but the word 'wanker' was invented for people like Cameron. Ben was handsome in a generic, department-store-catalogue way. Helen could see the family resemblance, but that's where it ended. He seemed aloof, not really engaged in the conversations around him. Perhaps that was because he was constantly interrupted by calls on his phone. Trish would give a shake of her head each time he took a call, but with a smug little smile as if to say 'that's how important my son is'.

'Ben, the world will keep revolving if you stop to have lunch,' she finally remarked, but he didn't respond, answering his phone as he got up from the table once again. 'Apparently, it might not!' She shrugged, looking around the table, beaming with parental pride.

Ben was not the only one who couldn't leave his phone alone, however. There was a constant stream of beeps and buzzes and ringtones. The teenaged cousins spent the whole time flicking and swiping their screens, but they weren't alone. At one point Helen looked bewildered around the table as every second person was either reading or typing.

Phoebe caught her eye and gave her a wink.

'Cam, I've been meaning to ask,' said Gary. 'You're one of the only people I know who actually uses the cross-city tunnel. Did you get stuck after that big accident the other morning?'

Cameron shook his head. 'I was already at work before it happened. Did you hear they couldn't get the ambulance through because of the road closures?'

'Okay, that's enough,' Trish broke in firmly. 'A little sensitivity, please?'

Gemma groaned. Helen looked confused. Then the penny dropped. Helen glanced around the table. Some obviously had no idea what Trish was referring to – including Gary, it appeared – but others averted their eyes as Helen looked around. This was excruciating.

'Excuse me,' she said quietly as she slid out from her chair and darted down the hall to find the bathroom.

'Well done, Mum,' said Gemma. She got up from the table and followed Helen. She knocked on the bathroom door. 'It's only me, Helen. Are you all right?'

'Uh-huh, I'll be out in a sec.'

Gemma sighed. 'Helen? Do you want to let me in?'

'Not really.'

'Please?'

There was a moment's pause before Helen opened the door. Gemma stepped inside and closed it again, leaning back against the door. Helen sat down on top of the toilet seat, dabbing the corner of her eye with a bit of scrunched-up toilet paper.

'I'm so sorry, Helen,' Gemma began.

'Why did you have to tell them?'

'I didn't,' she said, realising she sounded like her mother. 'I mean, I didn't give them any details, I just said he died in a road accident.'

'But why did you have to tell them anything at all?'

Gemma took a breath. 'When they came to the house, Mum asked if you had a husband. I told her he died, but that was all. Then today, she and Leisa were speculating all kinds of things, so I said it was a road accident to shut them up.'

'That worked well.' Helen grimaced. 'I feel like a freak.'

'No, Helen,' Gemma insisted. 'It's my family who are the freaks.'

Helen looked at her squarely. 'Every time people realise I'm a widow, they treat me like I'm the carrier of a disease they might catch.'

'I don't think that's what it is. I think they're just taken by surprise because they don't expect it in someone so young.'

'I'd just like to be anonymous sometimes, for no one to know anything about me,' Helen said wistfully. 'Then I feel guilty for thinking that, because I don't mean that I want David to be forgotten. I want to be able to talk about him, for Noah's sake especially. But the whole thing just makes people uncomfortable, and then they feel like they have to say all these clichés, and that cheapens it, cheapens his memory.' Helen sighed. 'I don't really want to talk about him to people who didn't know him.'

Gemma nodded. 'That's fair enough, Helen. Would you rather we go?'

'No, that'd be rude.'

'They're the ones being rude. Stop worrying so much about other people and look after yourself for a change. If you want to go, we'll go. Whatever you decide.'

Helen thought for a moment. 'Look, Noah's finally settled down and enjoying himself with the other children, it'd only make a bigger fuss if we left now. I don't mind staying, I just don't want to walk out there again.'

Gemma pulled out her phone. 'I have an idea.'

'What are you going to do?'

'I'll text Phee,' she said, already typing, 'tell her to keep the conversation going on something else when we walk back out.'

As they came out of the hall a hush descended on the table. Gemma caught Phoebe's eye and glared expectantly at her.

'So, Gemma,' she piped up, 'does your boss know about the baby yet?'

Gemma looked at Phoebe, mystified.

'What's that?' said Trish. 'Is she saying they don't know you're pregnant at work?'

'Sorry,' Phoebe mouthed, wincing.

They returned to their seats. At least Helen was out of the frying pan now. Gemma had been thrown into the fire instead.

'Gemma,' Trish persisted, 'why didn't you tell your boss you were pregnant?'

She cleared her throat. 'Because I wouldn't have got the job.'

'But won't he just turn around and sack you when he finds out?' asked Gary, concerned.

'I don't know,' said Gemma. 'I'm not sure what my rights are . . .'

'Cam?' Gary prompted.

Cameron advised corporations in the finance sector on employment contracts, and not only that, he loved nothing more than to be asked for his opinion. He sat back, crossing one leg over the other, waiting till he had everyone's attention.

'He certainly can't sack her for being pregnant, that would be discriminatory. But the fact remains she didn't disclose.' He looked at Gemma then. 'It depends largely on what's in your workplace agreement. I take it you did sign one?'

Gemma nodded. She hadn't read it that closely though.

'If it's a condition that affects your job performance,' Cameron went on, 'then he'd have a right to terminate your employment.'

'Well, it doesn't,' said Gemma. 'I'm performing my job perfectly well.'

'That may be for now. But the minute you go off to have that baby, it's affecting your work performance. Then he's got you.'

'What do you think she should do, Cam?' asked Gary.

'I think she should be upfront as soon as possible. Try to renegotiate her workplace agreement in line with her change in circumstances.'

'Will they let me do that?' asked Gemma.

Cameron shrugged. 'Depends what you can bring to the table.'

Bailey's

Monday came and went with no appropriate opening for Gemma to make her announcement, or even to mention she had to take Wednesday morning off for an ultrasound. Tuesday was the same. So Gemma did the only thing she could do. She took the cyber coward's way out and did it by email.

From: gatkinson@baileys.com.au
To: mdavenport@baileys.com.au
Subject: tomorrow morning

Unfortunately I'll be late to work tomorrow. I have another appointment in the morning. I'll be here as soon as possible afterwards.
Gemma

From: mdavenport@baileys.com.au
To: gatkinson@baileys.com.au
Subject: re: tomorrow morning

What is it this time?

From: gatkinson@baileys.com.au
To: mdavenport@baileys.com.au
Subject: re: tomorrow morning

Still personal

From: mdavenport@baileys.com.au
To: gatkinson@baileys.com.au
Subject: re: tomorrow morning

Still work time

From: gatkinson@baileys.com.au
To: mdavenport@baileys.com.au
Subject: re: tomorrow morning

Ongoing investigations

From: mdavenport@baileys.com.au
To: gatkinson@baileys.com.au
Subject: re: tomorrow morning

Legal, medical, taxes?

Gemma sighed. She supposed she had to tell him that much.

From: gatkinson@baileys.com.au
To: mdavenport@baileys.com.au
Subject: re: tomorrow morning

Medical

From: mdavenport@baileys.com.au
To: gatkinson@baileys.com.au
Subject: re: tomorrow morning

Are you all right?

There had been a pause before the last email arrived. Gemma wondered if the MD was actually being a tiny bit considerate. But that was unlikely. He was probably only trying to ascertain how much he was going to be inconvenienced.

From: gatkinson@baileys.com.au
To: mdavenport@baileys.com.au
Subject: re: tomorrow morning

I'm fine. Routine stuff. See you tomorrow.

Tomorrow

Gemma had planned to catch a bus to work straight after the ultrasound, maybe a taxi if it took too long. Helen had driven her to the hospital as she didn't want her to have to cope with public transport and a full bladder, but Gemma had shooed her away at the front entrance. It was too hard to get parking, she'd insisted. Helen must have better things to do with her time, she'd insisted. She would be fine, she'd insisted.

She shouldn't have been so insistent. She wasn't fine. She was a wreck. Emotionally, psychologically, even physically. Gemma had virtually looked into the eyes of her baby. She had seen the future, and she was terrified.

'What are you doing home?' asked Helen, coming into the hallway when she heard Gemma at the front door.

'I, um, I felt sick,' said Gemma. 'I must have had a bad reaction.'

'To an ultrasound?'

Gemma walked past her and straight into her room, dropped her bag on the floor and herself onto the bed. Helen came to the doorway.

'What's up? Is the baby all right?'

Gemma groaned, rolling over. 'Yes, the baby's all right. Isn't anyone ever going to ask me how I am anymore?'

Helen suppressed a smile and walked further into the room, folding her arms. 'Are you all right, Gemma?'

'Do I look like I'm all right? I've seen the baby.' She sat bolt upright. 'I mean, *I've actually seen my baby*! Is that even right?

It doesn't feel right. It feels like I've looked into the future or something, that I'm going to muck things up because I know too much now. If God had meant for us to see our babies while they were still inside, he would have put in a window, a peephole, something, don't you think?'

Helen was calmly waiting for her to take a breath. 'Or perhaps, if there is a god, he gave someone the inspiration to invent ultrasound technology.'

'Who asked him?' she grumbled.

'What exactly is the problem, Gemma?'

'The problem,' she said, exasperated, 'is that it looked really real. Like a real baby, you know? When you're there, and it's live action, and they're describing it . . .' She took a breath. Her eyes filled with tears. 'You can see it as clear as day. Whenever I've seen those ultrasound pictures before, the baby always looked like a blurred blob, I had no idea what I was even looking at. Now it's unmistakeable.' She reached over for her bag and rummaged through it, finally extracting a photo. She thrust it at Helen.

The baby was quite distinct – its head, body, there was even a little hand raised, as thought it was waving. Utrasound technology had come a long way since those early blurred images.

'How am I going to do this?' Gemma went on, her voice trembling. 'Why did I do this? I brought a human being into existence. What was I thinking?'

Helen went over and sat down beside her on the bed. 'It wasn't too late,' she said after a while. 'Was it?'

'Pardon?'

'The first day you came here, you told me that by the time you found out you were pregnant, it was too late to do anything about it.' She paused. 'But it wasn't, was it?'

Gemma stared at her, then slowly shook her head. 'I was just being a romantic nong. I thought it'd change Luke, make him settle down. I thought we'd be this awesome little family unit, that we'd be the coolest, most unconventional parents out, and we'd have this amazing child.'

'You must have really loved him,' said Helen, a little wistfully.

'Why do you say that?'

'Well, to be able to picture your whole future like that, you must have felt very strongly.'

Gemma sighed. 'I don't know. I think I was kidding myself. I mean, look what a no-hoper he turned out to be. He didn't even have the guts to face me, he just snuck off like some petty criminal.' She paused. 'The thing is, part of me is glad that he's not going to have anything to do with the baby. I don't want someone like him in her life. But I can't help thinking that, as low as he is, he didn't want me, so what does that say about me?'

'Gemma . . .'

A tear spilled onto her cheek. 'I'm bringing this poor kid into the world, and all she's got is this pathetic mother who couldn't even keep her useless father interested. What hope has she got?'

'There's always hope,' Helen said quietly. 'I have to believe that. I mean, I know they say kids without a father don't do as well, but –'

'Oh Helen, I'm sorry. I wasn't thinking about the way that came out. Your situation is completely different. Noah will be fine. He'll always know he had a father, and that he didn't leave him. And besides, you're an amazing mum.'

Helen looked unconvinced.

'You are, you've got the whole thing down pat. Bathtimes and bedtimes, and only watching the right kind of TV, eating the right kind of food. I'm going to be hopeless at all that. I've never been good at routines, and how am I supposed to discipline a kid if I don't have any discipline myself?'

'I think you're getting a little ahead of yourself, Gemma. You'll work it out as you go along, find your own patterns, your own routines. There's no rigid schedule you have to follow –'

'Oh damn.' Gemma remembered suddenly. 'Yes, there is.'

'What are you talking about?'

She stood up, clearly agitated. 'I'm supposed to be at work, but I was too freaked out.' She paced back and forth. 'I don't feel up to going into the city, but the MD's going to hit the roof.'

Helen was still sitting on the bed, watching her. 'You said you don't do much else but file and answer emails and keep his schedule up to date, is that right?'

'So?'

'Well, you could do a lot of that from here.'

'What do you mean?' Gemma stopped pacing.

'I take it you can access your emails from any computer?'

She nodded.

'Then you should be able to access his schedule as well. I mean, it must be live online, if you can both access it at any time.'

'Are you sure?'

'Let's find out.' Helen stood and walked out of the room and Gemma fell in behind. 'I used to be able to check my roster online,' Helen said over her shoulder, 'put in requests for leave, that kind of thing. Do you have a different password to get into your boss's schedule?'

'Yeah,' said Gemma.

Helen arrived at the computer desk in the back room and sat down. 'Why don't you bring a chair in from the kitchen?'

The computer had previously lived in Helen's room, but after the garage sale she'd decided it was better out here. She had to fill this room somehow. She still hadn't got around to buying a new sofa, or even looking, so they'd moved the TV into the front room for now, where there was at least somewhere to sit. Gemma returned with a chair and sat beside Helen.

'What do you usually do first thing?' Helen asked her.

'Check the emails,' she said.

'Okay, so I assume we go to the company's home page and enter your password in the staff portal?'

Gemma nodded, reciting Bailey's website address as Helen typed it in. She followed the links and keyed in Gemma's password, and moments later her inbox came up on the screen.

'You probably ought to let your boss know what you're doing,' Helen said, as Gemma started to scroll down her emails, scanning for anything important.

She sighed. 'I don't want to talk to the MD, he'll only get annoyed.'

Helen looked at her. 'You realise you wouldn't be having this problem if you'd told him you were pregnant in the first place.'

'You're right. I wouldn't be having this problem because I wouldn't be working for him,' Gemma returned. 'Don't you get it,

Helen? I never would have got the job in the first place, and maybe you think I shouldn't have got it by lying, but it sucks. The father can leave, stay, work, go hitchhiking around the world, he can do whatever the hell he likes. No one or nothing is going to stop him. Except his own conscience, but if he doesn't have one of those, then he's off scot-free.'

Helen had been listening calmly to Gemma's little rant. 'You're right,' she said when she was finished.

Gemma blinked. 'I am?'

Helen nodded. 'It isn't fair. Men have babies too, but they rarely suffer any of the consequences.'

'Not even stretchmarks,' Gemma grizzled.

Helen smiled. 'Well, if there's any way I can help . . .'

'Right now you can help me get into the MD's schedule,' said Gemma. 'If he happens to be in a meeting, I can get away with just emailing him.'

Using Gemma's second-tier password, they were able to access the MD's schedule and it suddenly appeared, in all its convoluted glory, filling the entire screen.

'See what I have to put up with?' said Gemma.

'It looks a lot like a hospital roster,' Helen said, scanning the columns and rows. 'There must be a key, I take it?'

'Yeah, if you scroll down further.'

'Oh, right,' she said, gazing at the screen. 'Okay, well, it seems pretty straightforward.'

'Are you kidding me?' Gemma said, dumbfounded.

'All the information's right here. Meetings out of the office are colour-coded green, internal are blue, the letter codes are P for production, F for finance, HR and so on, then the acronyms stand for different teams and sections, am I right?'

'Yeah,' Gemma said vaguely.

'So at the moment, according to this, he should be in an internal production meeting, with the Duttmar team, on . . . Level 12.'

Gemma was staring at her. 'That's amazing. It took me a week to figure it out, and I work there. How did you do that?'

'Like I said, it's just like a nursing roster,' Helen dismissed. 'So, seeing as he's in a meeting, you can be a coward and send him an email.'

Bailey's

Gemma had waded through as much work as possible online yesterday. Okay, there were files piled up and some mail to open when she got to the office, but she made a point of getting in earlier than usual to catch up on whatever she hadn't been able to do from home. She wanted it to seem as though she'd never been away, so that the MD would have nothing to complain about, at least not legitimately. She even beat him to work. Well, not officially – he had a seven o'clock breakfast meeting. But still, Gemma was at her desk and hard at it when he arrived at the office.

'You decided to show up in person today?' he remarked as he approached her desk.

'Like I do virtually every day,' Gemma returned through gritted teeth.

'Don't be so touchy, it was only a joke.'

She looked up at him dubiously.

'I'd like to discuss something with you, please, Gemma.'

She blinked. 'Now?'

'Yes, now.' He strode off into his office, leaving the door open. Gemma stared at the doorway. She couldn't see inside from this angle, she could only see the shaft of light coming from the windows inside. The big corner windows, taking up half the available wall space, floor to ceiling. Windows that looked over a sizeable slice of the city and the harbour. Windows that said, I am the most powerful person in the building and you should be bloody well impressed.

He was going to give her the sack. But he couldn't do that, could he? That's what Cameron had said. He wasn't allowed to dismiss her on the spot simply because she was pregnant. He could, however, have a case if she'd withheld pertinent information in her application or interview. Mind you, he'd never asked if she was pregnant. She did have a leg to stand on, even if it was a very shaky one.

Gemma stood and slowly approached the door as though she were walking the green mile. If only they got on better, had a bit of rapport, a sense of camaraderie, but it had just not happened. It wasn't her fault, Gemma was quite sure of that. She always got on well with people, she was a 'people person', wasn't she? And new situations were her particular forte. It was only when people got to know her a little better that she sometimes rubbed them the wrong way. Gemma knew she had a tendency to be a little flighty at times, restless, unreliable, but the MD had witnessed none of that. At least, not until just recently, and she wasn't being unreliable, she was actually being highly responsible, not that he knew that. But by the same token, a couple of days away from the office for medical reasons could not be considered unreasonable, surely? Her frankness was another attribute that wasn't always appreciated, she had to admit. Perhaps he'd never got over the haircut thing. But he really ought to. He looked a damn sight better than he had before.

When she finally stepped into the doorway, the MD looked up from his desk. 'Close the door behind you.'

This was exactly like going to the principal's office in high school. Only back then Gemma was usually hoping she was going to get expelled, or at least suspended. Suspension was cool. You got anywhere from three days to a number of weeks off school, depending on the misdemeanour. Her parents usually insisted that she accompany them to work, though that rarely lasted more than a day or two. She made sure of that. Their idea was to give her a taste of the real world, make her buckle down, realise how important school was. Hardly. It just made her more certain she was never going to get stuck in a boring, mindless job with a boss she didn't get along with.

So much for that plan. Gemma walked over to the MD's desk.

'Take a seat,' he said.

She did. He proceeded to make a bit of a production over removing his glasses and rubbing the bridge of his nose, and replacing his glasses again. Just get on with it, she groaned inwardly.

'Gemma,' he began.

She looked at him expectantly.

'I know you're having some . . . issues, to do with your health, and I know you said it's personal, but I think you're going to have to tell me what's going on.'

'Why?'

'Because it's affecting your work.' His tone was a lot calmer than she'd expected. Even a little kind, or perhaps that was wishful thinking.

'If this is serious,' he went on, 'if it's going to take you away from work more, then I think I have a right to be informed. I'm not threatening you, Gemma, I'm only trying to understand what we're up against. I think you should know that Bailey's only wants to be supportive . . . in the event . . . um, if further . . . well, whatever's ahead of you.'

That was unexpected. And a little weird.

'But I don't want to undermine your privacy either,' he added quickly. 'If you can promise me, right now, that there will be no more days off, or half-days, or cryptic emails about side-effects of treatment . . .' He took a breath. 'Anyway, if you can promise me that, then the matter ends here.'

Of course she couldn't promise him that. This was it. Tommy Lee Jones had her cornered on the rooftop. Or was it in the basement? It was always one or the other. Crooks either ran up or down, both pointless exercises. Why didn't they just run out? That was exactly what Gemma would do right now given half the chance.

'Gemma?' he prompted.

She looked up at him. She had no way out. This was it.

'I'm pregnant,' she heard herself say.

He must have heard it too, because he blinked a couple of times, and leaned forward, and appeared to have stopped breathing.

'Did you just say what I think you said?'

'How should I know?' said Gemma. 'I don't know what you're thinking. What I said was, "I'm pregnant." Is that what you got?'

This was really not the time to be a smart arse, but it was a reflex action. She was reverting to the sixteen year old in the principal's office, or worse, perhaps she'd never grown out of that.

This time the MD removed his glasses and tossed them on the desk in front of him. He used both hands to rub the bridge of his nose, then his eyes, then the rest of his face. Gemma was waiting for the explosion, but all he did was slump back in his chair and make a noise somewhere between a sigh and a chuckle. 'I feel like the guy in that movie, what was it called . . .?' He paused, straining to remember. '*Groundhog Day*,' he said finally.

'Bill Murray,' offered Gemma.

He nodded. 'That's him. I feel like Bill Murray in *Groundhog Day*.'

'I feel like Harrison Ford in *The Fugitive*,' said Gemma.

The MD looked at her, frowning.

'Never mind.'

He sat forward, picking up his glasses again. 'So, how far along are you?'

Here was the rub. All very well if Gemma had just found out she was pregnant. He could almost be amused, *Groundhog Day* and all that. Ha ha. Isn't life weird, huh? But she didn't know what his reaction was going to be once he found out she'd lied through her teeth to him.

'Oh, somewhere in the vicinity, around about, going on . . . twenty-four, five weeks, or so . . .'

She hoped putting it in weeks would take him longer to work it out. That's how desperate she'd become. She watched his face . . . the realisation dawning . . . the brows knitting together . . .

'Yes, okay, I knew when I took the job,' Gemma blurted, beating him to the punch. 'So I guess that makes me a bad person. Only I'm not. I needed to get a job before I started to show, because who in their right mind was going to hire a woman who was pregnant? But I didn't plan to get pregnant, nor did I plan for the father to run out on me. I can't run away; I'm stuck with it. So what else was I supposed to do? I still have to support myself, and now I have a child to support as well. Would it be better for me to go on government benefits? Maybe, I don't know. But how come I don't get a choice simply because the umbilical cord is attached to me? You were willing to support me if I was ill. Why not this? Why is a single pregnant woman treated like a drain on society? A pariah? I'm bringing a life into the world. Doesn't that deserve a little support? Some compassion even?'

Gemma realised she was virtually shouting. And at some stage she had got to her feet, and she was leaning over the MD's desk, shaking her fist.

'Are you finished?' he asked, looking up at her, a little amused, she suspected.

'You tell me,' she said, plonking back down in the chair again.

'What does that mean?'

'It means, if you're going to fire me, then go ahead and do it.'

'I don't think I need your permission.'

Gemma met his gaze. He didn't seem angry . . . though she couldn't really read his expression.

'Look,' he said finally, 'despite what you seem to think of me, I'm not unsympathetic to your situation, Gemma. But try to see it from my position. Even if you were to work right up to the moment your baby was born, you'd have to take some time off then. What am I supposed to do? I need an assistant full-time.'

Gemma wasn't sure she was hearing right, but it sounded like he was prepared to consider some kind of solution. She had to bring something to the table, like Cameron said.

'I'll take leave without pay,' she said quickly. 'Of course, it's only fair, and then someone can simply replace me for a couple of months. No cost to the company.'

He winced a little. 'It's not that simple, Gemma. I don't want to have to go through breaking someone else in –'

'You won't have to,' she interrupted, trying to ignore the horsy analogy. 'I'll train the replacement, thoroughly, over a couple of months, starting as soon as we find someone.'

'And how will that be no cost to the company?'

'I'll bear the cost!' she said, rather foolishly. The MD was looking at her like she was a bit of a fool as well. She had to keep it real.

'What I mean is . . .' What the hell did she mean? She couldn't bear the cost, though in truth, she was prepared to cut her hours.

She'd been saving money easily, having very little to spend it on these days, and she was building a nice little nest egg to self-fund her maternity leave, along with the paid parental leave the government provided. So she could easily cut her hours, share them with someone else. 'We could job-share.'

'Job-share?'

'Sure,' said Gemma, making it up as she went along. 'As my pregnancy gets to the end stages I'll appreciate cutting my hours, and my replacement can gradually take over more and more. You won't even notice, it'll be a seamless transition,' she said, warming to her idea. 'Then, when I go off to have the baby, she can step in full-time. And we'll reverse the whole process when I'm ready to come back to work.'

He was listening, but he was frowning as well. 'This is all very well in theory, Gemma. But where will you find someone flexible enough to be able to do that? Or do you already have someone in mind?'

She absolutely did. Right now in her mind's eye. She was perfect. Why hadn't Gemma thought of this before?

'I do,' she said. 'She's highly competent, computer literate, super-organised, she helped me set up working from home yesterday. And you won't believe this –' Gemma paused for effect '– she took one look at your schedule, and after a few seconds she could tell me exactly where you were, what you were doing and with whom.'

He still wasn't giving away much in his expression, but at least he was listening. 'What if she gets pregnant? It seems to be going around.'

'She won't get pregnant,' Gemma said firmly.

'You seem very certain of that.'

'I am,' she replied. 'She, um, she doesn't have a husband.'

'Neither do you.'

Good point. 'No, you don't understand, her husband died.'

'What?' He frowned. 'How old is this woman?'

'She's only a couple of years older than me.' Gemma saw the look in his eyes, the now familiar flash of sympathy mixed with curiosity, like an onlooker at a road accident. Gemma realised she was holding the trump card. And now was the time to play it.

'Her husband was only about the same age,' Gemma went on, 'till he got hit by a bus.'

The MD's jaw dropped in disbelief. 'Okay, now you're just making things up.'

'I'm not. It's the truth.' She met his eyes, she didn't blink, didn't flinch, she just slowly nodded her head.

He sighed loudly. 'Bloody hell.'

'I'm telling you, this woman is amazing,' said Gemma, going in for the kill. 'She's bringing up their little boy on her own now, he's only four, cutest kid.' She was watching his face, he was hanging onto her every word. 'Her mother's in a home, Alzheimer's, doesn't even recognise her own daughter, but still she goes to visit her a few times a week. There's no one else. Her brother's overseas, and her father passed away when she was only young.'

The MD was visibly affected. 'I don't know, this might be too much for her. It sounds like she's got enough on her plate.'

'But she really needs a job,' Gemma insisted. 'She's struggling to pay the nursing home fees because, naturally, she put her mother in the best possible facility and it costs her a fortune. She's a qualified nurse, but she can't do shiftwork anymore. She doesn't want to leave her little boy – he's already lost his father.'

'So why would she be prepared to leave him for this job?'

Gemma had no bloody idea. 'Well, it's not shiftwork, for one thing. But also this is where this arrangement is going to work like a charm.' She pushed on. 'She and I can be backup for one another. There'll always be someone to take over for the other one. It's a perfect situation.'

'I think that might be overstating things a little,' he said dryly.

'But think about it, MD, this is a very progressive step you'd be taking for the company. I'm sure some government department or other gives out awards for this kind of thing. Family-friendly initiatives. I'll look into it. And you can bet there's not a whole lot of that going on in this industry. You'll be a trailblazer, a pioneer. And you've always been a little worried about what the staff think of you. This will certainly put any doubts aside about just where your heart is.'

'Okay, okay, I think you're laying it on a bit thick now,' he said.

Gemma held her breath. 'So what do you say?'

He picked up his glasses, replaced them and looked directly at Gemma across the desk. 'Do I at least get to meet this super-woman before I decide?'

She hesitated. 'Of course you do.' As soon as she let Helen in on the plan. 'When do you want me to set it up?'

'As soon as possible.' He clicked on his mouse to bring up his schedule on the computer screen. 'Tomorrow's good.'

Gemma swallowed. 'Tomorrow?'

He nodded, staring at the screen. 'I want to know if this has any chance of working, or if I'm going to have to sack you and start all over again.' He glanced at her. 'Is that a problem?'

Problem? Was it a problem? Of course it wasn't a problem! It was a fucking crisis.

But she just said, 'No, no problem.'

'Okay, meetings all morning,' he murmured half to himself. 'One o'clock. Get her to come in at one, tomorrow.'

Gemma forced a smile and stood up. 'I'll let her know.' She turned and walked towards the door when the lead weight dropped right into the pit of her stomach. She spun around again.

'Oh, MD, you can't, um, at least, you won't, you weren't intending to bring up about her husband, were you?' she said frantically.

'What do you mean?'

'Well, when you meet her tomorrow,' said Gemma, 'you won't ask her about the accident, or refer to her as a widow, or anything, will you?'

He sat back in his chair, regarding Gemma dubiously. 'So you did make all that up.'

'No!' she insisted, walking quickly back to his desk. 'How could you think I'd make up something like that?'

He didn't look entirely convinced.

'It's just that she's very sensitive about it, surely you can understand that?' Gemma paused, thinking. 'Look, his name is, was, David Chapman. It happened about six months ago, I think, near Railway Square. There must be some reference to it online, in news archives. There was an inquest, I'm pretty sure she said.'

He still didn't respond.

'I promise you, I wouldn't make this up,' Gemma said earnestly. 'But she really doesn't like talking about it, and she can't handle people feeling sorry for her.'

The MD sighed deeply. 'Okay, I won't bring it up if she doesn't.'

*

'Phoebe, it's me.'

'Why are you whispering, Gem?'

'Can't explain, can't stay on long, just wanted to ask if you can come over tonight.'

'Tonight . . .?' she said vaguely. 'What for?'

'I need your help. I can't explain now, but it's really important. Just come, please, and back me up, whatever I say.'

'What are you talking about? Back you up to whom?'

'To Helen.'

'Oh, I don't know, Gemma, I don't want to get in the middle of something between you two.'

'It's not like that, this is a good thing. It's a win-win situation.'

'Oh really?' Phoebe said doubtfully.

'You have to believe me,' Gemma insisted. 'I like Helen, and more than that, I respect her. I wouldn't do anything that wasn't in her best interests, I promise you.'

She heard Phoebe sigh. She had her.

'Great, I'll see you at home. And bring a couple of suits, you know, your best interview suits? And shoes. Look, what the heck, just bring whole outfits.'

'Gemma!'

'Have to go, see you later.'

Balmain, that evening

Gemma bolted for the door when she heard the knock. 'I'll get it!'

She left Helen standing bemused at the kitchen sink. She'd been skittish all evening, prattling on about her job more positively than Helen had ever heard before, being overly attentive to Noah, checking the door what seemed like every five minutes. Something was going on, and Helen had a feeling she was about to find out what that something was.

Phoebe was standing on the porch, loaded down with garment bags, when Gemma opened the door. 'Quick!' Gemma hissed, grabbing her arm and dragging her inside. 'Before she sees you with all that.'

'What are you doing?'

Gemma didn't answer her until they were safely behind her bedroom door. She took the bags from Phoebe and laid them flat across her bed. 'Thanks for bringing all this, Phee.'

'Are you going to tell me what's going on?'

Gemma turned to her. 'I finally told the boss today that I'm pregnant.'

'Oh?' said Phoebe. 'How did that go?'

'Surprisingly not as bad as I expected,' she admitted. 'He's prepared to consider letting me job-share.'

'Wow, that is good. Really good. So what's all this about? Why did I have to bring all my suits? I didn't think they'd fit you anymore.'

'They're for Helen. All going to plan, she'll be the one sharing my job.'

Phoebe raised her eyebrows. 'I didn't realise she was looking for work.'

'Well, she wasn't . . . exactly . . .'

Phoebe folded her arms. 'Spill. What's going on?'

'Okay, here it is,' Gemma said. 'Helen's financial position is pretty shaky, from the little she's told me, but she doesn't want to go back to nursing because shiftwork's too hard with Noah. So when I got to talking with the MD today, and the idea of job-sharing came up, I immediately thought of her. She'd be perfect.'

'But she hasn't got any experience in this kind of work, has she?'

'Well, not in advertising per se. But she's really organised and efficient. She understands the MD's rostering system, she's more competent on a computer than I am. That's all she needs in this job. It'd be so good for her, Phee, get her out of the house and into the real world. She could start meeting people, rebuild her life.'

Phoebe nodded. 'Okay, I agree, it all sounds good. So why are we talking about it in here, out of earshot, like it's a conspiracy?'

Gemma sighed. 'I was hoping you'd back me up. I haven't told Helen yet.'

'Hold on,' said Phoebe. 'You put her up for a job without checking with her first?'

'I just threw her name in the ring. Nothing's set in stone. He has to interview her first.'

'So that's why you wanted me to bring the suits,' said Phoebe, putting the pieces together. 'But why the rush? This only happened today, didn't it?'

'Yeah, but the interview's tomorrow.'

Phoebe's eyes widened. 'She has an interview tomorrow for a job you haven't told her about?'

Gemma nodded lamely. 'It all happened so fast. I just mentioned I might know someone who could job-share, and before I knew it he was scheduling an interview. He said he wants to meet her as soon as possible.'

'Gemma, what if Helen's not interested?'

'Then I guess I'm screwed,' she said. 'But I'm getting used to that. In the meantime, can you please try to think positively and help me convince her this is a good thing?'

Phoebe winced. 'I don't know, Gem . . . I feel a little uncomfortable. I don't want to railroad the poor woman. Don't you think she's been through enough?'

'I'm not trying to railroad her,' said Gemma. 'I wouldn't do that. I genuinely believe this would be good for her.'

'And it just happens to be good for you too.'

'Yes, it is,' she said. 'It'll save my arse if it works out, but if you don't think this is a good opportunity for Helen, then fine, go home. Don't get involved.'

Phoebe considered her sister's piqued expression for a moment. 'Okay, I'll stay, but you're doing all the talking. I'm only here for moral support.'

Gemma looped her arm through Phoebe's. 'Good, I need as much of that as I can get.'

When they walked into the kitchen, Helen had just finished the washing-up.

'You didn't have to do that,' said Gemma. 'I would have finished it.'

'It's not a problem.' Helen leaned back against the sink. 'Hi Phoebe. How are you?'

'Fine, fine,' Phoebe said, a little awkwardly.

Helen looked from Gemma to Phoebe and back again. 'Is everything okay?'

'Fine,' they chorused, a little too eagerly.

She frowned. 'Um, would you like me to get out of your way . . .?'

'No!' Gemma blurted.

Helen looked at her. 'What's going on?'

'Um, well, the thing is,' said Gemma, searching for the right words, a way to begin. 'I know, let's have a drink, shall we?'

'A drink?' said Helen. 'I'm not sure if we've got anything.'

'Damn, I didn't bring anything either,' muttered Phoebe.

'Phee,' Gemma whined. 'You always bring something.'

'Yeah, well, I was distracted, because of the . . . other stuff I had to bring.'

'What other stuff?' asked Helen.

The sisters turned to look at her simultaneously.

'Maybe you should sit down,' said Gemma.

Helen hated hearing those words. Her heart dropped sickeningly, her whole chest heaving with the dread of whatever they had to tell her.

'Oh, no, Helen, don't get the wrong idea,' said Gemma, seeing the expression on her face. 'It's nothing bad. In fact, it's good, it's great. I have a very exciting proposal for you, which I think you're going to find hard to resist.'

*

Helen sat and listened while Gemma talked. She had worked it out down to the finest detail; since speaking to the MD she'd barely been able to think of anything else. The fact was, this was a tailor-made solution for both their predicaments. Helen could start off working one of the days that Noah was at preschool, and eventually both, and Gemma would be home to drop him off and collect him. Solved. After the baby was born, Gemma suspected she'd virtually be housebound, so it wasn't going to be any trouble to look after Noah as well on the days he wasn't at preschool. Then, as she felt ready to return to work, perhaps – and she had a good feeling about this – Helen would be prepared to mind the baby, for a fee, of course, on the days Gemma was at the office. Depending on how it all panned out, some kind of variation on such a roster could continue for as long as everyone was happy. Which she was quite sure they would be. It was a perfect, simple, obvious solution. As though it was meant to be.

'I can't do it,' Helen said flatly as soon as Gemma had finished her spiel.

Gemma blinked. 'What do you mean?'

She sighed, getting to her feet. 'I can't do it. Sorry.'

Gemma jumped up to stop her. 'No, wait, there's room for negotiation here, heaps of room! You can't just walk away, Helen,' she gasped.

'I'm only putting on the kettle,' she said calmly.

'I'll do it!' Gemma exclaimed, dashing across to the bench and snatching up the kettle.

'Fine,' said Helen, sitting down again.

Gemma walked to the sink and turned on the tap. 'What can I say to sweeten the pot?'

'Nothing, really. The pot's sweet enough. I just can't do it, sorry.'

Gemma was floored. She hadn't expected a flat refusal. She looked across at Phoebe and made a face at her.

Phoebe shrugged, but then sat up straight, focusing on Helen. 'Helen,' she began, 'why do you think you can't do it? I'm sure you're quite capable –'

'That's not the point,' she said. 'I just can't leave Noah, that's what it comes down to.'

'What, ever?' said Gemma as she flicked the kettle on and turned to look at Helen.

'I think what Gemma's trying to say,' said Phoebe, taking over in a more conciliatory tone, 'is that you're going to have to leave him sometime, isn't that right?'

Helen shrugged. 'I think it's still too soon.'

'Well, that's fair enough,' said Phoebe. Gemma glared at her from behind Helen. 'I can't even imagine how you must feel in your situation, and you have to do what you believe is right for you and Noah.'

Gemma was beginning to wish she'd never called Phoebe. So much for moral support.

'But putting that aside for the moment,' Phoebe went on, 'just say Noah was ready, do you think Gemma's idea is at least viable? Think about it: his routine would not be disrupted at all; the only difference is that it'd be Gemma taking him to preschool and back, instead of you. I'd imagine there may even be some room to move there, wouldn't you say, Gem? Perhaps Helen could start a little later, or finish a little earlier?'

'I'm sure something could be arranged,' Gemma said. This was good. Phoebe clearly knew how to manipulate a negotiation, it was the lawyer in her.

But Helen was a little flummoxed. 'Look, I just don't think Noah's ready.'

Gemma sat back down beside her. 'Don't you trust me with him?'

'Of course I do,' she said quickly to be polite. It wasn't that she didn't trust Gemma, it was that she didn't trust Noah out of her sight.

'Well, he'd be at preschool most of the time, and then he'd be in his own house, with me. He'd only be away from you for a couple of extra hours a week,' said Gemma, trying to emulate Phoebe's more dulcet tones, and resisting the urge to shake some sense into Helen. 'This would ease your financial situation, Helen, and it'd give you some excellent experience, if you really want to get away from nursing.'

They were making sense, of course they were making sense. So why did Helen feel as though she couldn't breathe?

'You could think of it as a trial,' Phoebe suggested. 'If it doesn't work out, if Noah doesn't cope, then you don't have to stick it out.'

'But what will Gemma do then?'

'Probably get the sack,' Gemma said. Phoebe frowned at her. 'Helen, I'd be no worse off than I am now if you don't give it a go. Why don't you just meet him, see how you like him –'

'You're always saying he's a pig.'

Bugger. 'No, not seriously,' she said. 'I meant it in an affectionate way, you know . . .'

Phoebe rolled her eyes.

'Look, I have to admit, he's being really decent about this,' Gemma persisted. 'He's not such a bad guy. In fact, come to think of it, you'd probably get on really well with him. A lot better than I do.'

Helen looked doubtfully at her. 'Why do you say that?'

'Well, he's a schedule freak, like you.'

'You think I'm a schedule freak?'

'Not at all,' Gemma corrected herself. 'You're organised, and efficient, which is totally appropriate for a mother of a young child. I'm taking notes, believe you me.'

Helen appeared placated, but still not convinced. 'There's one more thing,' she said carefully.

'What's that?'

She sighed, looking apologetically at Gemma. 'I just don't know if I can bring myself to work in advertising.'

'Oh? Why not?'

'Well . . .' She hesitated. 'No offence, but I hate advertising, I'm totally against it, I won't even watch commercial TV. As far as I'm concerned, advertising has helped create the blow-out in consumerism that's corrupting our society.'

She sounded just like Luke. And look what a pillar of society he'd turned out to be.

'That's a chicken and egg argument if I ever heard one,' said Gemma. 'I don't think you can say that advertising *creates* consumerism.'

'Maybe not, but it certainly lights the way,' said Helen.

'Okay,' Gemma said, thinking quickly. 'Maybe advertising is evil, but have you ever considered it might be a necessary evil? What do you think pays for the big fat *Sydney Morning Herald* you read every Saturday? Not all advertising is bad, Helen.'

'Just most of it.'

'Look.' Gemma realised she was not going to win that argument; she had to take a different slant. 'I should point out you'd hardly have anything to do with that side of things. I could be working in a doctor's surgery for all my day-to-day job has to do with advertising. I keep the MD's schedule up to date, answer his mail, file . . .'

'And you're always complaining it's boring.'

'Parts of it are boring, I'll admit. But it's a job, and a well-paid one for what it is. In a nice office, with clean toilets and good coffee. This is a golden opportunity to try it out, Helen, working hours that fit around Noah. I don't think you'll get another chance like this.'

She sat there staring across the table. 'You're right,' she said finally. 'I'd be a fool to turn you down without even considering it. I promise I'll give it some serious thought.'

Gemma and Phoebe exchanged a frantic glance.

'Well, would you mind thinking seriously fast?' Gemma said. 'The boss wants to meet you, asap.'

'Oh? How soon?'

She held her breath. 'Tomorrow. One o'clock.'

'Tomorrow?' Helen exclaimed. 'You've got to be kidding me? I'm not ready for this.'

'Don't worry, Phoebe brought over all her failsafe interview suits.'

'*Interview?*'

'Meeting,' she corrected herself. 'Just a meeting, where you get to . . . meet each other . . . It's not really an interview, as such.'

'I don't know . . .' Helen said, her voice wavering.

'Can I say something?' asked Phoebe.

'Please!' Gemma insisted.

Phoebe ignored her. 'Helen, I reckon it might be better if you don't have too much time to think about it. If you're anything like me, the more time you have, the more nervous you'll become, the more you'll doubt yourself. And really, you're only going to meet the man. You don't even know if you want this job, so that puts you in the driver's seat.'

Helen was listening thoughtfully.

'I hope what I'm about to say is not going to sound insensitive or disrespectful in any way,' Gemma said carefully.

'Uh-oh,' Phoebe murmured.

'I just think you'd probably understand the concept of seizing the moment better than anyone, Helen.' She paused, letting that idea sit with her for a moment. 'No one knows what tomorrow's going to bring, or next week, next month. This could be the best decision you ever make, or not. But if you don't try, at the very least it'll be a lost opportunity, a moment that you'll never get back.'

Helen sat there, lining up all the lost opportunities of their lives like tenpins. David had always meant to go back to uni so he could do the kind of work he'd dreamed of. Helen had never exactly planned to become a nurse, she'd just drifted into it, and that's where she'd stayed. She'd had a dream once of meeting up with Tony overseas, but that hadn't worked out, and the opportunity had passed her by.

She stared into the distance, watching as the tenpins were knocked down, one after the other.

Helen finally took a deep breath, looking from Phoebe to Gemma. 'Okay, let's go try on some of those suits.'

*

But none of them fitted. Gemma and Phoebe were aware Helen was a little shorter, which wouldn't have presented a problem on its own, but what neither of them had realised was that her figure was completely different. Helen always got around in trackpants and loose tops at home, and she never wore anything fitted, or even the least bit flattering. The fact was, she had a pretty good figure – narrower hips than either Gemma or Phoebe, so the skirts just sagged in the bum, but more bosom than the both of them put together, which, apart from making them highly envious, ruined the hang of any of the jackets. The shoulders bunched and the buttons strained across the bust. There was no escaping it – she looked like she was wearing someone else's clothes. Badly.

'Let's check out your wardrobe, Helen,' Gemma suggested eventually, but there was little solace to be had there either. They stood in front of her open wardrobe, pretending not to notice that half of it was filled with men's clothing. Helen's mother had held onto her father's clothes for nearly twenty years, so Gemma figured Helen probably hadn't even contemplated getting rid of her husband's clothes yet. It was sad, and not a little morbid, to see them hanging there.

As it turned out, Helen's nursing uniforms were the only things she owned that could be considered suitable work clothes, but they weren't exactly the look they were going for. Then something caught Gemma's eye.

'Hey, I remember this,' she said, pushing back some hangers to reveal the black and cream dress she'd found out in the old darkroom.

Phoebe stepped closer to have a look, lifting the hanger off the rail and holding the dress up to the light. 'This is gorgeous,' she gushed. 'It has to be vintage. Where did you get it, Helen?'

'It was my mother's. It's not vintage, it's just old.'

'It's so Audrey Hepburn,' said Phoebe as she held it against Helen. 'It looks like it would fit you.'

'I don't know . . .'

'It's stunning,' Gemma declared. 'You have to wear it. You'll knock his socks off.'

'Is that the idea?'

'Well, it can't hurt.'

'It might be a little bare up top for an interview,' Phoebe remarked. 'She doesn't want to give the wrong impression.'

Helen felt herself blushing. 'I think there was a jacket that went with it, I seem to remember . . .'

'I'll go and look,' Gemma called, already on her way out of the room.

Phoebe thrust the dress at Helen. 'I think I brought the perfect shoes with me,' she said, dashing out after her sister.

Helen stood there, looking into the mirror, holding the dress in front of her. She felt strange, as though she was going behind her mother's back. She remembered a party she'd been invited to, a long time ago, she was only sixteen or seventeen. It was after her father died, but before Marion's condition had become obvious. She was just moody and unpredictable all the time. The party was on the Chinese New Year and it was fancy dress. Her mother had an exquisite oriental sheath made of sage green embroidered silk. Marion hadn't worn it in years, she'd lost interest in dressing up. She used to love nothing more, which was why she had so many clothes – unusual for someone of their relatively modest means. But Marion had always been vain, and she'd loved being noticed. Her father didn't mind her spending money on clothes; he probably felt he had to indulge her, seeing as the house was her inheritance. Helen had known the dress would be perfect for the party, but when she asked her mother if she could wear it, Marion had flatly refused, mocking her in the process. 'Who do you think you are, Helen? You couldn't carry off a dress like that.'

Helen looked in the mirror, and her heart began to flutter uncomfortably in her chest. She never wore clothes like this. She didn't have anywhere to wear them.

Gemma burst back into the bedroom, holding the matching jacket aloft in victory, but she was suddenly stopped in her tracks. Phoebe had returned ahead of her, and she was standing back, admiring Helen, who'd changed into the dress. It fitted her as though it had been made for her. It was basic black but for a broad scooped neckline edged in a band of cream, a wide cream belt at the waist, and pointed cream cuffs on the hip pockets. But it was the cut that made it special: the dress hugged her figure, cinching right in at the waist and clinging to her hips.

'Wow,' Gemma said in a low voice. 'You've got the job.'

Helen was blushing. 'You don't think it's a bit much?'

'No!' they both assured her.

'Try on the jacket,' Gemma said. 'That'll make you look more businesslike.'

Helen took the jacket from her and slipped it on.

'What I don't understand,' Gemma went on, 'is why you get around in those loose trackies all the time when you've got a figure like that.'

'Don't.' She was blushing furiously now.

'Do you always blush when you're embarrassed?' asked Gemma.

'Or nervous,' said Helen, adjusting the jacket. 'And I've been known to throw up as well.'

'I'd try to keep that in check tomorrow, if I were you.'

'Oh, you think?'

'You're going to be fine,' Phoebe assured her. 'Take a look at yourself now, with the jacket on.'

Helen turned around to the mirror again. The cream jacket was simple, box style, cropped at the waist and caught with one large button at the neck. It did help to make her look a bit more businesslike, while at the same time covering up the red blotches on her chest.

'How are the shoes?' asked Phoebe. They were black sling-backs with pointed toes, and cream piping right around the mouth. They looked as though Helen had bought them to go with the dress, except they didn't have her size.

'They're a little roomy,' said Helen.

'They're only a half-size bigger than you normally wear,' Phoebe reminded her.

'I don't normally wear shoes like this,' she said.

'So you should keep them on tonight,' said Gemma. 'Get used to walking in them.'

'You look like a professional working woman,' Phoebe said approvingly.

'Except I'm not.' The anxiety was creeping into Helen's voice again. 'What am I going to say in the interview?'

'It's not an interview, remember?' said Phoebe. 'You're just meeting him.'

'Besides, we can work on what you're going to say,' said Gemma. 'And we'll update your résumé –'

'Résumé?' said Helen vaguely.

'You do have a résumé?'

'No, I don't,' she said. 'I've never needed one. When I applied to get into nursing, I filled out forms. I filled out more forms to get a placement, and I've been at the same hospital ever since. Different departments over the years, on internal transfer, which meant more forms.'

'No problem,' said Gemma. 'A résumé is like a marketing brochure, and I know a bit about them. We'll put something together that will make it look like your skills are tailor-made for the job.'

'I don't want you to make things up,' said Helen.

'I'm not going to,' Gemma assured her. 'I'm just going to be creative.'

Helen looked suspicious.

'Give me examples of what you have to do as a nurse – standard, everyday stuff.'

'Well, there's routine observations,' said Helen. 'You know, check temp, heart rate, respirations, blood pressure.'

'Completes routine tasks with accuracy and professionalism,' said Gemma, 'at all times maintaining a sensitive and appropriate level of client interaction.'

Helen just looked at her.

'Go on,' Gemma urged. 'What else?'

She shrugged. 'Give out meds . . .'

Gemma was thinking. She started to pace the floor. 'Observes schedules, interprets and implements written orders. Demonstrates attention to detail and accountability in the handling and administration of sensitive material.'

Helen shook her head in awe. 'Keep charts up to date?'

'Well, that's easy,' said Gemma. 'Accurate management of client records . . .'

'Write up reports for change of shift.'

'Too easy – highly developed written and verbal communication skills when reporting to colleagues at all levels.' Gemma sighed. 'Give me a challenge.'

Helen narrowed her eyes, thinking. Her mouth curved into a smile. 'Empty bedpans, wipe patients' backsides, clean up vomit and assorted bodily fluids . . . I could go on.'

Gemma looked squarely at her. 'Proven ability to multi-task across situations of an acutely personal nature requiring a high level of empathy and diplomacy. Displays focus and determination while maintaining order and regularity in the day-to-day functioning of the workplace. Nothing is a challenge too great.'

Phoebe gave her a clap.

'That's amazing,' said Helen. 'How did you do that?'

'Years of bullshitting,' Phoebe told her.

'I'm just talented, that's all,' Gemma retorted. 'And the thing is, so are you, Helen. Everything I just said is the truth. They're called transferable skills, and you're loaded with them. All we need to do is identify each skill and then describe it in a way that makes sense in this workplace.'

Helen was still looking a little doubtful.

'Why don't you get out of those clothes,' Gemma suggested, 'but keep the shoes on, don't forget, and we'll meet you out at the computer and write this baby up.'

Helen followed them out to the back room a short time later, back in her ubiquitous trackies, still wearing Phoebe's shoes.

'That's a good look.' Phoebe smiled.

Gemma was already sitting in front of the computer. 'I'm just looking up the bus timetable for you, Helen,' she said, studying the screen. 'You can take the 431 at 11.55, it gets you there a little early, but the one after might be pushing it –'

'I can't take the bus,' Helen said flatly.

'Why not?'

'I, um . . .' She hesitated. 'I just, I have to drive.'

'You don't want to drive,' said Gemma, turning around to look at her. 'You'll never get a park. Take the bus, it's virtually door to door.'

'I can't take the bus,' she repeated firmly.

Phoebe was the first to twig. 'She can't take the bus, Gem. Okay?' she said meaningfully.

Gemma finally got it. 'Oh, sure, well, that's fine. No worries, there's visitor parking down in the basement,' she went on, thinking aloud. 'I'll clear that with security in the morning – it shouldn't be a problem. Then you'll take the lift to the ground floor so Eddie can sign you in and give you a temporary pass. Then you'll come to me on the fifteenth floor. Does that all sound okay?'

Helen suddenly realised she was doing this for real. It wasn't just dress-ups and playing around. Doubt and uncertainty began to course through her veins, making her heart pump a little faster.

Gemma knew the look, she could almost smell the fear. She mustn't give Helen any room for hesitation, no space for dillydallying. She turned back to the computer. 'Okay, let's get on with it,' she said chirpily, opening a Word document. 'Résumé of Ms Helen Chapman . . .'

12.26 pm, the following day

The man at the boom gate was very nice and treated Helen as though she were a VIP or something. He glanced briefly at his clipboard before giving her a broad smile.

'Of course, Ms Chapman, you're expected. Welcome to Bailey's. If you'll just follow the signs to visitor parking around the first bend to your right, you can park wherever you like in that section. Have a really great afternoon,' he signed off cheerily.

She smiled and mouthed 'Thank you.' She meant to actually say the words, but her voice didn't seem to have any volume, and her throat was dry, and she was a little out of breath as well. She had to pull herself together. She hadn't been able to sleep till some very ungodly hour of the morning – she wasn't exactly sure what time it was because eventually she'd had to stop herself from watching the minutes tick over into hours, gobbling up half the night like some greedy nocturnal parasite.

Even worse were the hours after Gemma had left the house this morning and Helen had dropped Noah at preschool, when she was on her own with no one and nothing to distract her. She even tried Spray'n' Wiping, but it just didn't do it for her this time.

She was nervous, of course; that was normal before a job interview. But there was more to it, and it had been niggling away at her since last night. She felt as though she was going behind David's back. There was no way in the world he would have approved of her working in an advertising agency. Helen had her own reservations, but David would never have let her even consider it. And she wouldn't have, when he was alive. After Noah was born, she'd raised the idea of leaving nursing a couple of times. She was worn out looking after people, she still had her mother to worry about, and she wanted to have the energy to enjoy her own child. But David had talked her out of it. Nursing was a noble profession, he'd maintained, and she had a responsibility to use her training for the good of others.

Why had Helen been the one who had to be so responsible, so self-sacrificing, all the time? David had hardly been doing anything to save the world or serve humanity, stuck as he was in his paper-pushing job, with no ambition, or dreams, or even the will to do something different. At least she'd been having a go.

But advertising? That might be going too far, not only out of her comfort zone, but way out of her moral and ethical zone and into another stratosphere altogether. The sublime to the ridiculous, in fact.

Helen felt like a fraud, wearing someone else's clothes and someone else's shoes, pretending to be someone she wasn't even sure she wanted to be. She pulled into a parking space on a wonky angle, but she didn't care. She cut the engine. Why did she let herself get talked into this?

Well, why did you? David would have demanded to know.

She breathed out heavily. Because she had to start earning some money, she had no choice. But she was not ready or willing to leave Noah a minute more than she had to. If she got this job she'd only be away from him a couple more hours a week, at least for the meantime. Gemma was right, it was a tailor-made solution and she'd be foolish not to give it a try at least.

'So, David, that's why I let myself get talked into it,' said Helen out loud. 'No, I'll rephrase that – that's why I decided to do this.'

And now she was talking to herself. She took three deep, slow breaths, like she'd learned in yoga, ignoring the trickle of perspiration she could feel running down her back. No matter, the jacket would hide it. She glanced at the clock on the dashboard. 18.47. Fat lot of good that did her. It had been out for months now, since soon after the accident, when she'd left the headlights on overnight one time, running the battery down. Helen didn't know how to adjust the clock. She was quite sure she could figure it out, it was just that she'd never had to do it before. And she only ever thought about it when she was driving. And she always wore her watch anyway. But not today, because Gemma said her utilitarian nurse's watch would spoil the outfit. Anyway, Helen was almost certain she wasn't running late – she'd left home too early to be late – but she hated this limbo feeling of not knowing the time for sure. Should she stay sitting in the car for a while longer? Or get out and walk around a bit more in these shoes? Or go in early? Would that make her look desperate, when she wasn't desperate at all? She was just nervous. She'd never done this before . . . it was okay to be nervous . . . it didn't mean she was desperate . . .

Breathe.

And again.

Get a grip, she told herself. You're a grown woman, you can do this, you don't need David's approval, he's not even here. You have to look after yourself from now on.

The man up on the ground floor would no doubt be as kind as the man at the boom gate, and she could ask him what the time was. If it was still way too early, Helen was sure she could wait in the foyer for a while, or even call Gemma to see what she suggested.

Now that she had a plan, Helen stepped out of the car and straightened the dress, feeling the fabric lift away from the wet patch on her back. She reached in to get the jacket from where it was hanging behind the front seat, slipped it on, and then reached back in to pick up her handbag and the folder with her résumé. She locked the door of the car and started to walk carefully across the concrete floor towards the lift bay, just as she heard a ping and saw the lift doors glide open, coming to a stop with a clunk. A man stepped out. Without really thinking it through, Helen decided for some reason that it was imperative she catch that very lift, and so she began an awkward, hurried skitter across the carpark. The shoes seemed bigger today, probably because she was wearing stockings, so her foot lifted in and out of the sling-back, causing the heel of the shoe to make a sharp clacking sound against the polished concrete.

The man near the lift saw her approaching and he held back the door, raising his hand to signal there was no need to rush, just as Helen's foot went over on its side and she lurched forward, watching the folder and her handbag fly out in front of her in slow motion.

Somehow, she didn't fall. She was still upright, barely, her arms flailing about in front of her like she was a blind person in unfamiliar surroundings. The man was suddenly at her side, taking a firm grasp of her arm.

'Are you okay?' he was asking.

She couldn't find her voice, it must have fallen on the floor along with her handbag and . . . oh no. Oh shit. Her bag had flung open and all its contents were lying scattered across the floor. A lone coin was rolling along on its edge, picking up speed as it headed for freedom. It hit a seam in the concrete and bounced once before falling flat on its side, all its tiny hopes dashed. Helen wanted to cry. She also wanted to move, but she couldn't seem to manage it. She seemed to be stuck somehow.

'Hey, hey, you're trembling,' the man was saying. His voice was soothing, and very close to her ear, and then she realised the rest of him was very close as well. He had one arm already around her waist, and he was closing his other arm across in front of her, holding her firmly. 'It's okay, just breathe,' he said gently.

She did as he said; there didn't seem to be much else she could do right now. He was taking deep, steady breaths, and she found herself matching his rhythm, slowly calming down, leaning into him, breathing in unison.

'Feeling better?' the voice said, still close to her ear.

Helen turned her head to look at him. She wasn't trembling anymore, but she felt a little giddy. He had a kind face, such a kind face. Was everyone here so kind? It'd be nice to work here if they were.

'Oh, what's the time?' she said suddenly.

'Just after twelve thirty,' he said, releasing her, but still leaving one hand at her elbow. 'Do you think you're okay now?'

'Yes, yes, I'm sorry.'

'Don't be.'

Helen looked down. 'I seem to be stuck.'

The man was crouched on the floor before Helen could stop him.

'Ah, here's the problem,' he announced. She felt his hands around her ankle, sending an unexpected shiver up her stockinged leg. 'The heel of your shoe is caught in the grate.'

'Oh no, is it ruined?' she asked. 'They're not my shoes.'

'Try to lift your left foot out of the shoe,' he suggested. 'It might hurt, lean on my shoulder for support.'

Helen winced as she released her foot from the shoe, and though she hadn't planned to, she did lean one hand on his shoulder.

'Well, the shoe seems okay,' he said. 'Give them a wipe-over and you'll never know.' He was still crouched at her feet. 'Let me just check this ankle while I'm here.'

She felt his hands again, his fingers prodding gently but with an assured touch. 'Are you a doctor or something?' she asked.

'Once upon a time I nearly was. Didn't quite get there.'

'Oh . . . *Ow!*'

'Sorry.'

'It's okay.'

'You've probably strained your *peroneus tertius*,' he said. 'I don't think you should be walking on it if you can help it.'

'Well, I can't help it,' Helen sighed. 'I have an interview for a job.'

He jerked his head back to look at her. 'You do?'

'Yeah, what's the time now?'

He glanced at his watch. 'Twenty-five to one. You've got time,' he said. 'I think you'd better take the other shoe off, I wouldn't try walking just yet in those heels.'

Helen slipped her foot out of the other shoe as he stood up. 'Come and rest against the wall and catch your breath. I'll get your things.'

'No,' she protested. 'I've taken too much of your time already.'

He smiled at her, firmly taking her arm in his. 'How about we see if you can manage to walk first before you go dismissing me so lightly.'

Helen smiled weakly back at him as they started off towards the lift bay. So much for her great leap towards independence – she couldn't even make it across the carpark without needing assistance. She felt so hopeless. The pain was localised, but quite intense right at the spot where her ankle met her foot. She had no choice but to limp. She was going to look ridiculous walking into this interview.

'How does it feel?' he asked.

She winced. 'It hurts, but I think I can put my weight on it. Just.'

'You really should get some ice on it as soon as possible.'

'Can't –'

'Interview.' He nodded.

They made it to the wall near the lift and Helen leaned back against it while the man placed her shoes on the ground nearby.

'Now while you're standing there, very gently rotate your ankle, just to keep some movement in it,' he said. 'I'll get your things.'

She went to protest again but he was already walking away, waving an arm to dismiss her protestations. She watched as he picked up her scattered belongings, trying to remember if there had been any loose tampons rattling around in her bag, or anything else potentially embarrassing. He walked back over towards her, handing her the folder and her bag.

'You know what they say about women's handbags,' Helen said ruefully. 'Now you know all my secrets.'

'Does that mean you're going to have to kill me?'

She smiled. 'Thank you so much,' she said sincerely. 'You've gone way beyond the call of duty.'

'That sounds like a dismissal.'

'I just don't want to keep you from whatever it was you were on your way to doing.'

'Well, I was only sneaking off for a cigarette,' he said, taking a packet from his pocket and offering it to her. 'Might calm your nerves.'

She shook her head. 'I don't smoke.'

'Neither do I,' he said, putting a cigarette between his lips and lighting it.

She laughed. 'Well, you're doing a pretty good impression of it.'

'I mean, I have the odd cigarette, obviously,' he admitted, exhaling away from her. 'But I don't smoke every day.'

'But when you do, you stand in front of the airconditioning duct so your smoke gets recycled around the building.'

He looked at her sideways. 'You think the air is drawn in from the basement carpark, exhaust fumes and all?'

She blinked at him.

'I'm afraid this, in fact, is where the used air is expelled. I leave the comfort of my office for the sake of my coworkers to stand in a draughty, smelly garage, and have their second-hand carbon dioxide blown out at me. Please don't give me a hard time while I'm at it.'

'Sorry,' said Helen, duly chastened. 'So, you work here, for Bailey's?'

He nodded. 'I do.'

'What's it like?'

'It's all right. Depends where you work, I guess. Like anything.' He glanced down at her foot. 'Keep it moving,' he reminded her.

She gingerly rotated her ankle again. 'I don't know why I wore those stupid shoes in the first place.'

'Why did you?'

'Because I didn't have anything that would go with this dress, which is not technically mine either.'

'Are you wearing a stolen outfit?'

She smiled. 'No, the dress was my mother's. They tell me it's "vintage", but I feel a little silly, like I'm playing dress-ups in my mother's cast-offs.'

'Well, you don't look silly at all,' he said seriously, gazing at her. 'You look, um . . . well, you look great, for an interview, you know.'

She felt herself blushing. 'What's the time, please?'

'A few minutes after the last time you asked, which makes it almost twenty to.'

She shook her head. 'I left too early. Though I guess it was just as well – I needed time to injure myself and still make it limping to the interview.'

He grinned. 'There's nothing wrong with being early for an interview. Better than being late. Shows you're keen.'

'Or nervous, inexperienced, clueless,' she said. 'I don't know what I'm doing here.'

'Oh?'

'I was talked into this. Along with the dress, and the shoes.'

'You don't want the job?'

Helen shrugged. 'I don't know. Maybe. Yes. I need the money, and the hours are ideal . . .'

'I hear a "but" coming.'

She looked at him. 'Never mind.'

'What? What is it?'

'You work here. I'd rather not say.'

'Oh, come on, get it off your chest,' he said. 'You'll feel better in the interview.' He leaned his hand on the wall beside her head, smiling down at her.

Helen wasn't in the habit of sharing secrets with people she knew, let alone complete strangers. But there was something about his face . . . He would have made a good doctor, at least on appearances. He wasn't strikingly handsome, but he was certainly agreeable enough. People were wary of doctors who were too good-looking: men mistrusted them, and women felt self-conscious around them. It was all very well to have pin-up Dr McDreamys on your TV shows, but not in real life. His face was just right – you'd feel comfortable telling him the most intimate details, you could trust him with your kidney stones or your broken limb or your undiagnosed pain, and he would make it all better.

She suddenly realised he was waving his hand in front of her.

'Sorry,' he said, 'I don't know your name, and you drifted away for a second then.'

She blushed again. 'Sorry, it's Helen.'

'Well, Helen, you were saying . . .'

She smiled. 'No, I wasn't.'

'Aah, the girl can't be fooled that easily,' he said. 'Seriously, if you have any doubts about working here, maybe I can clear some of them up for you.'

She considered him, that face. She only had Gemma's take on the MD – it might be good to get another opinion before she fronted him in an interview. It couldn't hurt . . .

'Okay,' said Helen. 'But this is off the record, all right?'

'It doesn't leave this garage,' he said, holding a hand to his heart.

She took a breath. 'What do you think of the MD? That's who I'll be working for,' she said. 'I'm going to start job-sharing with Gemma, his assistant. Do you know her?'

He nodded. 'A little.'

'She rents a room in my house, and she's a little nutty, but she grows on you. Anyway, she was always complaining about him, said he was a pig to work for, but of course now that she wants me to share her job, suddenly she talks as though he's a great guy. I don't know what to believe.'

'Maybe you should split the difference?' he suggested. 'The reality is most likely somewhere in between.'

She nodded, thinking. 'You're probably right . . .'

'So is that all that was bothering you about working here?'

Helen glanced up at him. 'To be honest, you might take offence if I told you what else.'

'Nah, I'm pretty thick-skinned,' he assured her. 'Go on.'

'Well, the thing is . . .' She screwed up her face. 'I don't exactly approve of advertising. I try to avoid it as much as I can. I think it's intrusive, and misleading, and a symbol of everything that's wrong with our society.'

'Oh.'

'See, I knew you'd be offended.'

'I'm not offended,' he told her. 'I'm not at the coalface, I don't design or write or make the ads.'

'What do you do?' She frowned, realising she hadn't asked, and he hadn't said.

'Oh, admin mostly, general office stuff,' he dismissed. 'That's more or less what you'd be doing too, isn't it? You wouldn't have anything to do with making the ads or putting them out there.'

'That's what Gemma said. But isn't it wrong for me to work in an industry I feel morally opposed to? Kind of like a right-to-lifer working in an abortion clinic.'

He looked a little uncomfortable. 'Don't you think that's drawing a bit of a long bow?'

'You're right, I'm sorry. That was extreme. It's not the same thing at all.'

'If you're so against advertising, maybe you can have a little influence, working for the MD?'

Helen shook her head. 'I doubt it. The way Gemma tells it, he barely notices her. She just files and answers his mail.'

'Then in that case your morals are unlikely to be compromised.'

She leaned her head back against the wall, smiling at him. 'You're right. I'm making a fuss about nothing.'

'Don't get me wrong, I'm not saying your morals are nothing to fuss about. If Bailey's was dealing in weapons, or drugs, you'd be right to be morally outraged. But maybe you should take advertising for what it is.'

'But there is evidence that advertising can be harmful. They're saying that junk food advertising is at least partly responsible for the obesity epidemic, especially when it's aimed at kids. And the credit blow-out is all because people keep wanting more and more of what is thrust in their faces every day through advertising.'

'Advertising doesn't make people fat, or broke, or greedy, Helen,' he returned. 'Aren't you getting a little sick of this culture of blame we hide behind these days? Don't you think people need to take responsibility for their own choices, and stop passing the buck? Or in this case, stop shooting the messenger?'

Helen had to admit he had a point. Maybe it was not entirely convincing, but then again, perhaps it was enough for her to at least consider working here.

'Or maybe I should get off your case and let you make up your own mind?' he said, watching her.

She turned to look at him directly. 'No, not at all, you've actually given me some food for thought.'

'Then my work here is done.' He glanced at his watch. 'And you should probably start making your way up.' Before she realised what he was doing, he'd crouched down in front of her and she could feel his hands on her feet again, and the accompanying tingle.

'It's okay, you don't have to . . .'

But he was already gently slipping the shoe onto her injured foot. 'It's swollen up a little,' he said.

'Oh well, maybe the shoe will fit better,' she said wryly, taking the weight onto that foot as he went to help her with the other shoe. It was a little painful, and she had to lean on him again for support. When he stood up straight again he was right in front of her, their faces close.

'Thank you,' she said.

'My pleasure,' he replied, stepping back. 'Come on, I'm assuming you have to sign in at the ground floor?'

She nodded. 'I'll be right from here, you've done enough.'

'I'm going up anyway. Let me at least help you into the lift.' He held his arm out to her, and she took it gladly for the few steps into the elevator. He pressed G, the doors closed and the lift began its ascent.

'Good luck,' he said.

'Thanks,' said Helen. 'I might see you around, if I get the job.'

'More than likely.'

The lift had come to a stop again and the doors were opening. Helen stepped forward gingerly.

'Are you sure you're going to be okay?' he said.

'I'll be fine,' she said bravely. 'Thanks again.'

'You know, Helen, whatever happens . . .' He hesitated, he seemed to be searching for words. 'It'll be okay.'

She nodded faintly. She wasn't sure what he meant by that. But the doors were closing again, and then he was gone. She turned and limped across the floor. Her ankle was beginning to throb. This was a disaster. She was going to look like an idiot hobbling into the interview.

At the reception desk she gave her name to another jovial security man, and he issued her with a visitor pass to wear on a lanyard around her neck. He walked with her back to the lifts to show her how the card worked.

She stepped into the waiting lift, and the man slipped a card in and out of a slot on the panel just below the buttons. 'That's all there is to it, then you can access nearly all the floors.' He pressed number fifteen. 'I'll call up to Ms Atkinson and let her know you're on your way.'

'Thank you.'

When the lift doors opened on the fifteenth floor, Gemma was there waiting for her. Helen walked out, trying not to limp too obviously, but Gemma frowned at her.

'What's wrong with you?' she asked. 'The shoes can't be that uncomfortable, surely?'

Helen sighed. 'My heel got caught in a grate in the carpark and I twisted my ankle, and dropped all my stuff . . .'

Gemma winced. 'Are you okay? Was there anyone around to help you?'

'Yeah, there was, in fact,' she said. 'This really lovely man got me unstuck, and stayed with me till I was okay.'

Gemma took her arm to give her some support. 'The security guys are wonderful around here.'

'No, he wasn't security, he said he was in admin.'

'Oh? What was his name?'

What was his name? Did he say? He must have said when he asked for her name. Whatever, she obviously didn't remember it now. 'I don't know, I didn't catch it.'

Gemma shrugged. 'Well, the MD is waiting for you. He said to send you straight in as soon as you get here. Are you going to be all right?'

'What choice do I have?' said Helen. 'You don't think it's a bad omen, do you?'

'No,' Gemma said firmly, 'it's just bad luck. It was an accident, Helen, you of all people should know that sometimes accidents just happen.'

'Okay, you're right.'

'Besides, it might be a good omen.'

'How is that?'

'You met a cute guy from admin.'

Helen blushed, elbowing her as Gemma led her slowly down the hall past the executive offices and all the way around to the province of the managing director.

'This is it,' she announced. 'What do you think?'

Helen gazed at the clean minimalist space, the white walls adorned with postmodern artworks, the intimidating glass and steel desk where she would be working, perhaps. 'It's very . . .'

'It sure is,' Gemma said. 'They have an image to maintain. That's what it's all about, after all.'

Helen sighed. 'Great, and I'm going to look like the maiden aunt come to mind the shop.'

'Cut it out,' Gemma chided, walking around the desk. 'You look totally fabulous, the MD will be very impressed. I'm just going to buzz him now.' She held a button down on the phone and a moment later a slightly hollow 'Yes?' came over the intercom.

'Helen Chapman is here.'

'Send her in,' he said. 'On her own, please, Gemma,' he added in his best, 'he who must be obeyed' tone.

Gemma pulled a face at the phone. 'Of course, MD,' she said sweetly. She released the button and looked across at Helen. 'Will you be all right?'

Helen took a deep breath and nodded. 'Wish me luck.'

'I won't say break a leg,' Gemma said wryly. 'Let me walk you to the door at least –'

Helen shook her head. 'No, stand there and tell me if I look like a freak when I walk.'

She headed towards the door to the MD's office, taking slow, measured steps, trying not to wince as she took as much weight as she could handle on the affected ankle. As she reached the door she turned to look at Gemma, who gave her the thumbs-up. Helen smiled stoically and took a firm hold of the doorknob. After one more calming breath, she opened the door and stepped inside, closing it behind her. She looked across the vast office as the MD got to his feet. Helen blinked, and her heart lurched in her chest.

'What are you doing here?' she breathed.

He looked awkward. 'I didn't get the chance to introduce myself.'

She stared at him. She couldn't speak. It couldn't be. He couldn't be . . .

'I made up an icepack for you.'

'I'm going to be sick,' she blurted.

'Helen, it's okay –'

'No, really, I'm going to be sick,' she insisted, a little frantic now. 'It's what I do.'

'Okay,' he said coming towards her, 'there's a bathroom through here.'

She began to hobble in that direction as he made it to her side, taking hold of her arm.

'Don't!' she said, snatching it away.

'Helen,' he tried to placate her, 'you can barely walk. Take those shoes off at least.'

He was right. She kicked them off, dropped her bag and folder on the spot, and hopped straight for the door he'd indicated, closing it firmly behind her. She looked around, breathing hard. It was a pretty bloody palatial bathroom for an office. For that matter, who had a bathroom in their office anyway? The managing director of an advertising agency, that's who. Not some nice guy from admin.

Helen went and leaned over the toilet, but her nausea seemed to be subsiding. She still felt hot, clammy, breathless, embarrassed, mortified, betrayed, tricked and misled. What kind of a show was he running here? Pouncing on unsuspecting job applicants in the basement carpark and tricking them into giving up personal secrets?

Shit! She'd told him what Gemma had said about him. If he used his ill-gotten gains to threaten Gem, or worse, fire her, well, Helen was going to . . . well, she was going to do something. She'd take it to the union, if there was one in this industry. If not, she'd go to one of those shoddy current affairs shows and expose him. See how far his threats and deception got him then.

Helen closed the lid of the toilet and sat down on it. An overwhelming sense of disappointment was creeping up on her. For a brief moment she'd ventured out into the big wide world, where no one knew her circumstances, where no one would have to feel sorry for her, where she could stand on her own two feet . . . perhaps she hadn't managed that part so well, but . . .

She hadn't even wanted this job in the first place, and now she felt strangely sad that she wouldn't get the chance to work here, with all the happy security men, and the nice guy from admin. Or rather, the big fraud who ran the place. Gemma had been right about him all along. And now Helen had probably completely screwed things for her as well. A quick, sharp pain suddenly shot through her ankle, as if to remind her she also had that to deal with. Helen peered down at her foot. The swelling was quite obvious now. She really should put some ice on it as soon as possible, get it elevated, but first she had to get back down to the garage and drive herself home. And she wasn't exactly sure how she was going to manage that.

A light tap sounded on the door. 'Is everything all right?'

'Yes,' she said curtly. 'I'll be right out.' Helen stood up on one leg and hopped to the basin. She turned on the tap and splashed a little water on her face. There was a stack of cotton handtowels on a shelf to her right, and she took one, dabbing her face and hands dry before tossing it into a wicker basket under the bench. What a ludicrous waste of resources. Fair enough, at least he wasn't using paper, but who washed his precious handtowels? And pressed and folded them and put them back on the shelf? That kind of conspicuous opulence sickened Helen. It was just as well she wouldn't be working here. She wouldn't have been able to stomach it.

When she opened the door a moment later, the MD was standing with his hands in his pockets, looking out through the wall of glass across the city. He came to attention when she appeared, taking a few tentative steps towards her.

'Are you okay?' he asked, doing a pretty good job of sounding sincere. 'Were you sick?'

'No, it passed,' Helen said gruffly. 'Where are my things? Please.'

'Um, well, they're right over here,' he said, crossing to a sitting area on the other side of the office.

Helen followed, half hopping, half hobbling, towards a long, low, brown suede couch, the kind she'd seen in ads for European furniture that cost about the same as a small Korean car. It was flanked by two matching armchairs that sat like sentinels either end of an enormous glass and steel coffee table. Helen had only ever seen offices like this in the movies, where they were inhabited by business barons played by Alec Baldwin or Andy Garcia. She hadn't thought they existed in the real world.

Helen spotted her bag and folder on one of the armchairs, her shoes placed neatly together on the floor. On the coffee table was a tray with a jug of water and a glass, as well as a small bottle of soda water, and an ice bucket with what looked like a tea towel draped over its side.

'I thought you might need a glass of water,' he was saying. 'I didn't know if you'd prefer soda water if your stomach's upset. But I can get you some tea, whatever . . .'

Helen looked at him, frowning. 'Thank you, but I'm leaving now.'

'You can't,' he said. 'What about the interview?'

'You've got to be kidding me.'

'No, I'm not,' he said seriously.

'I think I'll pass all the same,' she said. 'I've had enough humiliation for one day.'

'Helen, stop,' he said. 'You need to get off that ankle for a while. I've got some ice here.' He gathered together the ends of the tea towel and lifted it out of the ice bucket.

'This is ridiculous,' she muttered.

'No, it's actually the sensible thing to do.'

'And I will do it, when I get home.'

'How are you going to make it home on that ankle?'

'That's not your problem.'

'It is, in fact. You injured yourself on the premises. I want to make sure you're okay before you leave.'

'I'm not going to sue you, if that's what you're worried about.'

'No, I'm worried about you,' he said loudly. Helen blinked. He took a breath. 'Are you always this stubborn?'

'I'm not stubborn,' she protested. 'No one's ever called me stubborn in my life.'

'Then prove it.'

The fact was, her ankle was killing her. The pressure was building painfully, it felt like it was about to burst. She had to get it elevated.

'Fine, if you insist.' She limped around the coffee table and sat down on the couch.

'Put your foot up here.' He patted the seat further along.

Helen raised her leg and swung it around to rest on the couch. He gently lifted her foot and propped a loose cushion underneath, then arranged the makeshift ice pack over the site of the swelling. 'Does that feel about right?'

She nodded. The relief was immediate, the pain recoiling at once on contact with the ice.

'Now, would you like plain water or soda?'

'Nothing, thanks,' she mumbled.

He shook his head and poured water into the glass anyway, before pulling the coffee table over closer so she could reach it. Then he sat back in an armchair, shifting it slightly so that he was facing her directly.

'There's no need to nursemaid me,' Helen said irritably. 'You can go back to your work. I won't make a sound, and I'll be out of your way in ten minutes. Fifteen, tops.'

'We might as well do the interview while you're sitting there.'

She glared at him. 'Why are you doing this? Haven't you had enough fun at my expense yet?'

He was clearly bewildered. 'I didn't find what happened to you funny, Helen, and I don't know what I did to give you that impression. I was only trying to help.'

He looked almost wounded. Helen felt bad. Of course he'd helped her, she'd thought he was lovely till she'd realised he'd hoodwinked her.

'Look, I am grateful, you were very kind, but . . .'

'But what?'

'You lied to me. You took advantage of the situation to get me to tell you things I never would have said if I'd known who you were. And you knew that.'

He nodded. 'Okay, I can understand how you might see it that way. But I didn't mean to take advantage, and I won't use anything you said against you.'

'Or Gemma? The things I told you that she said –'

'You don't think I'm aware that the staff say negative things about me behind my back? When you're in my position it's par for the course. I've whinged about bosses behind their backs, everybody does. People say things all the time they never expect to get back to the person. My ego's not so great that I'd penalise someone for it.'

Helen considered him, still guarded. 'So you're not going to sack Gemma?'

'Of course not.'

She wasn't convinced.

'I told you that anything you said would stay in the garage,' he said, placing a hand to his heart as he had earlier. 'You have my word.'

'I don't know if your word is worth all that much,' Helen said. 'You lied to me. You should have told me who you were.'

'I didn't know who *you* were until I was crouched on the floor at your feet,' he reminded her. 'Tell me how you would have handled it if I'd suddenly said, "Oh, hey, I'm the MD, by the way. I'll be doing your interview today."'

Helen imagined the scene. She probably would have thrown up all over him.

'You were shaken, and hurt,' he went on. 'I wasn't going to make it any worse for you.'

'Then you shouldn't have grilled me for information afterwards.'

'I didn't grill you –'

She looked at him dubiously. 'Come on, "Get it off your chest,"' she mimicked. '"You'll feel better."'

He sighed, sitting forward in his chair as he clasped his hands together. He met her eyes directly. 'Let me explain something to you, Helen. Ever since I started here, people have been lying to me, left, right and every place in between, keeping things from me, picking and choosing what they tell me. Gemma's a prime offender. I don't know if there's anyone I can trust around here. At best they just tell me what they think I want to hear, which isn't any good to me either. As soon as people know who I am, straightaway they start treating me differently. You don't know what that's like, Helen.'

Oh yes she did. She knew exactly what that was like.

'So I admit, I enjoyed being incognito for a while, hearing what you really had to say, instead of answers you were probably coached to say.'

How did he know that?

'But I wasn't lying in wait to snare you, Helen. Call it coincidence, or call it fate, but I think it just may have given us a golden opportunity to have an honest working relationship,' he said. 'And I can't tell you how invaluable that would be to me right now.'

She regarded him curiously. 'Despite the fact that you know I detest advertising?'

He shrugged. 'Well, you know what they say – Keep your friends close, but your enemies closer. Not that I consider you an enemy,' he added quickly. 'But I think you might bring an interesting perspective to the job. That's if you'll consider taking it.'

Helen's head was spinning. This was all getting a bit much. This whole scenario was nothing like she'd expected. The MD was far from being a pig, and he certainly wasn't coming across as some kind of evil captain of industry. Sure, the office was over the top, but Helen was beginning to feel rather naive, and very unworldly.

He was watching her closely. 'Do you need some time to think about it?'

She nodded. 'Maybe, yes.'

'Why don't you sleep on it over the weekend? See how you feel then.'

'Thanks . . .' Helen realised she still didn't know his name. 'I don't know what I'm supposed to call you,' she said tentatively.

'Everyone around here calls me MD.'

She hesitated. 'You meant it when you said you wanted me to be honest?'

He nodded. 'Absolutely.'

'Well, truth is, I'd feel a bit silly calling you MD.'

He sighed with obvious relief. 'Good, because I feel pretty silly being called MD. I promise you it wasn't my idea. Makes me feel like a position, not a person. Somehow I think that's the way they like it.' He stood up and held his hand out to her. 'Myles Davenport, but please call me Myles. It would be a welcome change to have someone around here call me by my name.'

Helen shook his hand a little shyly. 'Okay, Myles.'

He smiled. 'Good.' He released her hand and walked over to the main door, opening it. 'Gemma, could you come in here, please?' He waited by the door till she walked through. She looked surprised when she saw Helen reclining on the couch.

'Are you all right, Helen?'

Helen was nodding, but the MD answered the question for her.

'She's probably sprained her ankle. She won't be able to get home on her own, so I'd like you to go with her, please. Take a taxi voucher.'

'My car's down in the garage,' Helen piped up.

'Oh, fine then. Can you drive her car?' he asked Gemma.

'Can I?' Gemma asked Helen in turn.

'Sure, thanks, if you don't mind.'

Gemma turned back to look at the MD. 'So, will I come back to work afterwards?'

He was shaking his head. 'No, take the afternoon off. Besides, I guess you'll need someone to pick up your little boy later, Helen?'

'How do you know I have a little boy?'

Gemma flinched, but the MD didn't miss a beat.

'Gemma told me,' he said, matter-of-factly. 'You're available to work the days he's at preschool, right?'

Helen nodded. 'Right.'

Gemma could only assume the interview had gone well, but she'd like some confirmation. She caught Helen's eye, gesticulating wildly using only the features on her face, which was not an easy thing to do.

'Gemma,' the MD said, watching her, 'in case you're wondering, I've offered Helen the job, and she's going to think about it over the weekend.' He was at the end of the couch now, carefully lifting the ice pack off Helen's ankle. 'How does that feel?'

'A lot better,' she said. 'Thanks, Myles.'

What did she just call him? Helen was gingerly getting to her feet, with the attentive assistance of the MD. This was bizarre.

'Grab her bag and things there, will you, Gemma?' he ordered. 'You're not putting those shoes back on, okay, Helen?'

'Okay,' she relented with a sheepish smile.

And getting more bizarre by the minute. Gemma bent down to pick up the shoes, while the MD walked Helen across to the door.

'Have a good weekend, both of you,' he added as Gemma joined them. 'I'll talk to you soon, Helen. It was good meeting you.'

'You too, Myles,' she said.

'Support her arm,' he instructed Gemma. 'Don't let her take too much weight on that foot. And keep the ice on it when you get home.'

Gemma led her away, waiting till they were out of earshot. 'What the hell was all that about?'

'What do you mean?' Helen said guilelessly.

'Did you give him a blow-job in there or something?'

'Gemma!'

'Sorry, I've just never seen him act like that before.'

'I think you might have the wrong impression of him,' said Helen. 'He's really a very nice man.'

They were totally in Bizarro World now. 'I've been working for him for months and you meet him for ten minutes –'

'No, listen to me,' said Helen. 'He was the nice guy from admin down in the basement.'

'What?'

'Myles, he was the –'

'Why do you keep calling him that?' Gemma said.

'What?'

'Myles.'

'Because that's his name.'

'But no one calls him that.'

'Yes, and he doesn't like it,' Helen said. 'Amazing what you can learn in ten minutes.'

'Now you're going to get smug?' said Gemma. 'And what do you mean, he was the guy in the basement?'

'When I fell, he was the lovely man I told you about, who helped me.'

'But you said he was from admin?'

'That's what he told me, because he didn't want to startle me after my fall. Mind you, it threw me when I first walked into his office and realised it was him. I thought he was playing some kind of trick on me. But we sorted it out.'

Gemma had been listening with increasing bewilderment. 'So what's the problem?'

'There isn't a problem.'

'That's what I mean. You two obviously got along.'

'Yeah, we did . . . What are you getting at?'

'Why did you say you'd have to think about it when he offered you the job?'

'Oh, well, I guess I felt a little overwhelmed, and when I didn't answer him straightaway, he said I should take the weekend to sleep on it.'

They had arrived at the lift, and Gemma pressed the button. The doors opened immediately. 'So what do you think you're going to say?' she asked, helping Helen into the lift.

They turned to face the doors as they closed. 'I'll let you know after I've slept on it,' she answered blithely.

Balmain

'Well, it sounds like you two certainly got off on the right foot,' Phoebe declared, holding her glass up.

Helen had just taken a gulp of champagne and she must have laughed at precisely the wrong moment, as suddenly she was gasping for breath and Gemma was hitting her on the back and Phoebe was squealing, mostly with laughter, and finally Helen's airwaves were clear and she was able to breathe again. They both stopped to look at her.

'Are you all right?'

Helen nodded slowly, as her shoulders began to shake, and she burst into a fit of uncontrollable laughter. Phoebe soon joined her and they rolled around on the floor giggling like a pair of schoolgirls at a slumber party. Helen had still not got around to replacing the lounge suite, so Gemma had set up the back room when they got home, spreading a doona on the floor and propping Helen up with every pillow and cushion she could find in the house.

Gemma had spent the afternoon playing nurse, mother, cook, and whatever else was required. She hadn't stopped. No sooner had she got Helen settled, made her a cup of tea and something to eat, than she was out the door to pick up Noah. Then it was off to the supermarket with a list Helen had dictated to her before she left. When she got home again she put dinner on for Noah while she packed the groceries away, refreshed Helen's ice pack, put Noah in the bath, made Helen another cup of tea, got Noah out of the bath, dressed him in his pyjamas, and she was just serving up his dinner when Phoebe arrived. It was Friday, after all, but she was also desperate to find out how Helen had got on, and she'd bought champagne to celebrate or commiserate, either way. She and Helen had sat out in the back room, quaffing champagne, while Gemma put Noah to bed. When he was all tucked in, Gemma had finally joined them, exhausted to say the least.

'So, did you know about your MD being the other kind of MD in a past life?' Phoebe asked her.

'No way,' said Gemma. 'He's never so much as mentioned it before. I think he was pulling your leg, Helen.'

'Actually, he really was pulling my leg at the time,' said Helen, which sent her and Phoebe off into paroxysms of laughter all over again.

'Would you two please settle down?' said Gemma, trying to be stern. 'And, Phee, slow down on the champagne, Helen's not used to it.'

Phoebe looked up at her sister, laughing wearily. 'You are the last person who should be commenting on anybody's combustion of alcohol,' she declared.

That set them off again. Gemma groaned. It was going to be a long night. She'd never realised before how inane drunk people could be.

'Well, I think Myles the mystery medico might just have the hots for our Helen,' Phoebe announced when they had eventually calmed down.

Gemma was shaking her head. 'He's not the type.'

'What, is he gay?' Phoebe asked.

'No,' said Gemma. Then she frowned. 'I don't think he is. No, I'm sure he's not. The way he dresses he couldn't possibly be gay.'

'Then why couldn't he be attracted to Helen?' Phoebe said. 'If I was a guy, I'd be attracted to her.'

That caused another ripple of giggling to pass between the two women. Gemma rolled her eyes.

'I'm not saying he's not interested because he couldn't be attracted to Helen,' said Gemma. 'I'm saying he's not interested because he's all work, no play – you know the type.'

'Aah, maybe he just hasn't met the right woman yet.'

Helen blew a raspberry. 'Stop it. He was only being nice. Can't a guy be nice without having an ulterior motive?'

'No,' Gemma and Phoebe chorused at once.

Helen looked at them. 'Well, I'm glad I'm not as cynical as either of you two,' she said. 'But I agree with Gemma – he wasn't coming on to me, he was just being kind, that's all there was to it.' She sipped her champagne. 'And you know what the best part about it was? He didn't know who I was; he doesn't know anything about me. He wasn't being nice to me just because I'm a widow and, you know, because of the way David died.'

Now Gemma wished she could have a drink. Phoebe was watching her suspiciously.

'He said he liked being incognito for a while,' Helen went on, staring into space. 'I know exactly how he feels.'

'Well,' Gemma said, slapping her hands together. 'I've hung up my apron for the night, so I'm going to order pizza, because you two definitely need something in your stomachs before you drink another drop.'

*

'You told him she's a widow, didn't you?' said Phoebe, pulling on an old T-shirt Gemma had given her to wear to bed.

'Shhh!' Gemma rushed to the bedroom door to make sure it was closed. Phoebe was too drunk to make her own way home. Gemma could have put her in a taxi, but Cameron was away so there wasn't really any need for her to go home. Besides, she didn't think Phoebe should be on her own anyway. She had begun to get a little maudlin when Gemma had finally pulled the plug and called it a night.

'You told him the whole sorry story, didn't you?' Phoebe went on, using her hands to mime a bus hitting a person, with accompanying graphic sound effects.

Gemma winced. 'Phoebe, keep your voice down!' she whispered loudly, moving away from the door and taking a firm grip of her sister's shoulders as she sat her down on the bed. 'Yes, okay, I admit I told him everything. He was wavering, I had to keep him interested –'

260

'Don't worry,' Phoebe slurred. She was very drunk. 'It's a good story, I'd use it in a court of law in a shot.' She tried to click her fingers, but couldn't quite manage it.

'But don't tell Helen, okay?' said Gemma. 'He promised he wouldn't, he said he'd wait for her to bring it up herself.'

Phoebe started to nod in agreement. But her eyes were closed and her head kept rolling back too far.

'Come on,' said Gemma, holding her up. 'Get in under the covers.'

She helped Phoebe into bed and walked around to the other side, grateful to climb in and lie down. She felt bone-tired. It was the end of a long day at the end of a long week. Phoebe was quiet – hopefully she'd passed out. Gemma reached over to switch off the bedside lamp.

Phoebe stirred, moving over closer to snuggle into her side. 'Can I feel the baby move?' she asked plaintively.

Gemma sighed. 'Sure, it's a bit quiet at the moment, though.'

She felt Phoebe's hand slide across her tummy. 'Wow, you've really popped out.'

'Mm, I'm always bigger at night, but it has suddenly popped,' she said. 'It's funny, it's like as soon as I let the cat out of the bag and told the MD, the baby came out of hiding. Like it knew or something.'

She heard Phoebe sniff. 'That's so cute,' she whimpered. 'That's your own little baby in there that loves you already.'

Now she was crying for real. She broke into sobs. Gemma felt drained. She'd never had to tend to the needs of so many people in one day in all her life.

'Come on, Phee,' she soothed, putting her arm around her and patting her shoulder. 'You're drunk, go to sleep.' Gemma was beginning to feel sleep creeping up on her, and she was more than ready for it.

'I want to have a baby so bad,' Phoebe sobbed.

'I know,' Gemma shushed her, patting her shoulder again.

'I want it so bad it hurts, Gem.' She took a tremulous breath. 'My belly hurts, even my boobs hurt . . .' Suddenly she lifted herself up on one elbow and reached across Gemma to switch the lamp back on.

Gemma squinted, blinking rapidly. 'Phee, what are you doing?'

'Maybe I'm having a phantom pregnancy!' she gasped, her face close to Gemma's.

'No,' said Gemma, pushing her away and turning the lamp off again. 'Just a mental breakdown. Now, go to sleep.'

Phoebe snuggled into her sister again, one hand across her belly, when the baby started to move.

'Oh, my God,' Phoebe breathed. 'Did you feel that?'

Gemma decided not to engage in conversation with her. With any luck Phoebe might assume she was asleep.

'Gem, Gem, your baby's moving!'

She groaned. 'I know, Phee, don't you think I can feel it?'

'What's it feel like, Gem?' Phoebe said breathlessly. 'To have that little soul encased inside your own?'

Jesus. 'Sometimes it's bloody uncomfortable,' she said, trying to snap Phoebe out of it. 'Like if it sticks its foot in my ribs, or in my groin, or it leans on my bladder.'

'That's beautiful,' Phoebe said, dissolving into tears once more.

Gemma sighed heavily, reaching out to turn the lamp on again. 'Phee, if you want a baby this bad, you have to make Cameron understand how important it is to you. You have to talk about it.'

She began to wail now, loudly.

'Phee, quiet!' Gemma shushed her.

Phoebe sniffed. 'I can't talk about it with Cam.'

'Why not?'

'He put an embargo on any further discussion: I'm not even allowed to mention it.'

'Who died and made him supreme ruler of the universe? Besides, what's he going to do if you bring it up? Ground you?'

The sobs had subsided. 'He said he'd have a vasectomy,' she said in a quiet voice.

'What?' Gemma shifted to look at her properly. 'Are you serious?'

Phoebe nodded gravely. 'He said if I didn't shut up about it, he'd just go and have a vasectomy and that would be the end of it.'

'He can't do that.'

'Yes, he can,' Phoebe said squarely. 'He said as we're not having a baby for a few years, he doesn't want to talk about it constantly until then. What's the point in putting it off if all you do is talk about it? I suppose I take his point.'

'No, no,' Gemma insisted. 'Tell him to take his point and stick it where the sun doesn't shine. This is all about what *he* wants, Phee, he's not taking your feelings into account at all. The reason you can't stop talking about it is because it's so important to you. Doesn't he care about that? Hasn't he ever heard of compromise?'

'You can't compromise over a baby, Gem,' Phoebe said sleepily. 'It has to be something we both want, at the same time. I'm just going to have to wait till he's ready. I haven't got a choice.'

She yawned loudly and rolled over. A minute later Gemma heard her breathing settle into a rhythm, punctuated by soft little snores. She'd finally passed out. And now Gemma was wide awake. She decided she hated Cameron with the passion of a thousand fiery suns, or thereabouts. Where did he get off ordering her sister around like that? What gave him the absolute right of veto over her life?

Unfortunately, it appeared Phoebe had given it to him, on a platter, and there wasn't a thing Gemma could do about it. She turned over on her side, pulling the covers around her. The baby shifted as well, adjusting to the new position. Gemma gave her belly a pat.

At least there was one positive she'd gained out of all this. For the first time, single parenthood had never looked so good.

The morning after

Helen opened her eyes, just enough to allow a tiny slit of light in, but still it stung her pupils. Her head felt as though it was being slowly but inexorably compressed in a vice. Why had she drunk so much? She wasn't used to it, she hadn't drunk like that in years. She'd forgotten what a hangover even felt like, or she never would have kept drinking last night. But unfortunately, hangovers were a bit like childbirth: you'd never put yourself through it again if you could remember the pain.

She squinted over at the clock on her bedside table. 10.04. God! She had to get up. She had a momentary sensation of panic as she tried to work out what day it was, if Noah was supposed to be somewhere, if she was supposed to be somewhere. Her heart was pounding in her chest as she gradually realised that it was Saturday, it was all right, no one had to be anywhere.

She rolled onto her back and took a deep breath. Oh God, here it comes.

Helen threw the covers back and leaped out of bed, landing right on her bad foot. She yelped in pain. 'Bugger! Oh, bugger, bugger, bum, ouch, shit!' she babbled as she sat back on the bed, clutching her ankle. But her stomach was giving her no reprieve. She stood up again gingerly, taking the weight on her good foot. She wasn't going to manage hopping in her condition, so she hobbled as fast as she could out into the hall and around to the bathroom. She made it in the nick of time, almost falling on her knees in front of the toilet bowl.

Standing at the sink a few minutes later, Helen splashed cold water on her face and rinsed out her mouth. She felt slightly better, but her head was still pounding. She turned off the tap and patted her face dry with a towel. The house seemed awfully quiet. She hoped someone had got up to Noah . . .

Helen felt a pang of anxiety, laced with a heavy dose of guilt as she quickly checked his room, before limping her way to the back of the house.

'Hi Mummy!' Noah cried as she appeared in the doorway. 'Did you sleep good?'

Helen winced. 'Not so loud, sweetheart,' she said softly, holding a finger to her lips. 'Where's Gemma?'

'She's hanging a washing on a line, and then we're gunna play Jenga!' He threw his arms in the air and started running around in circles making a whooping sound.

'Noah, Noah,' she pleaded. 'Mummy's head's hurting.'

'I fought it was your foot?'

'Huh?'

'You hurted your foot last day, now you hurted your head this day,' he said, holding his arms out for emphasis. 'Whata hell's going on, Mum?'

Helen smiled despite herself. She didn't have the presence of mind to correct him on his language right now; besides, for all she knew he might have picked it up from her last night. She honestly had no idea.

They heard the back door, and then Gemma appeared in the entrance from the kitchen.

'Oh, you're up,' she said. 'How are you this morning?'

'Don't ask.'

Gemma couldn't help feeling smug. There had to be some payback for a) not being able to drink and b) putting up with people who did.

'Is Phoebe still in bed?' Helen asked her.

'Nooo,' said Gemma, shaking her head. 'My obsessive-compulsive sister was up at six thirty and out the door. She didn't have her running gear, so she had to get home before she turned into a pumpkin coach. There's something seriously wrong with her. Hey, how's your ankle, by the way?'

'All right till I jumped out of bed right onto it.'

'Ouch,' said Gemma. 'You'd better get it elevated again.'

'Gemma!' Noah called from the other side of the room. 'When are we gunna play Jenga?'

'Just let me get your mum some breakfast first –'

'Oh, you don't have to –'

'Yes, I do,' Gemma said firmly. 'You set it up, Noah Balboa. I'll be right out.'

They left Noah rolling around with laughter at the 'Balboa' tag. Small children and drunk people would laugh at anything, Gemma decided. 'Sit,' she ordered Helen. 'I'll get your ice pack.'

Helen did as she was told. She watched as Gemma filled the kettle and turned it on, before retrieving her ice pack from the freezer.

'I really want to thank you, Gemma,' she said sincerely. 'I don't know what I would have done yesterday without you.'

Gemma glanced at her, smiling. 'Don't forget, I was the one who sent you there in shoes that didn't fit you.'

'It's not just that,' said Helen. 'I know I seemed a bit oblivious yesterday, but I do realise how much you were doing, especially looking after Noah.'

'Well,' Gemma said, positioning the ice pack carefully on Helen's ankle, 'I am auditioning for a role.'

Helen frowned. 'What are you talking about? What role?'

'Taking over your job while you take over mine,' she reminded her.

'Oh.' Helen nodded.

'How am I doing?' she said, straightening up.

'Great, really, you're doing a great job,' said Helen. 'To be honest, I had my reservations –'

'You did?'

'Not about you,' Helen assured her, though if she was brutally honest, she had had reservations about Gemma being responsible for Noah. But she'd have reservations about anyone taking care of Noah.

'I was worried about how I'd feel leaving Noah,' she explained. 'But watching you, I realise you know him, you know his routines, the way I do things. You understand. It's a huge relief.' She smiled. 'But now that you've had a taste, how do you feel about it?'

Gemma leaned back against the bench. 'Oh, I was tired yesterday, I'll admit. But it was a good day. I felt useful.' Strangely enough, she really did. And responsible, and needed and trusted. It was a new experience, and not an unpleasant one. 'Besides, Noah's such a lovely kid, and I'm not just saying that,' she added quickly. 'I hope I get one just like him.'

The phone started to ring. 'I'll get it,' said Gemma, dashing from the room. She returned not half a minute later with the phone, passing it to Helen across the table. 'It's for you,' she sang, then mouthed emphatically, '*It's the MD.*'

Helen frowned. She couldn't understand her. 'Hello, Helen speaking.'

'Helen, how are you this morning?'

'Myles, hi,' she said, recognising the voice.

Gemma frowned. She didn't know how long it was going to take her to get used to 'Myles'.

'I just wanted to find out how your ankle's doing,' he was asking Helen.

She glanced across the table. Gemma was waving her arms, mouthing, 'What's he saying?'

Helen tried to shush her but she was persistent. So she mouthed the word 'ankle' but Gemma didn't seem to understand her. She sighed. 'Excuse me for a sec, please, Myles.' She covered the mouthpiece and held it away from herself, under the table.

'He's just asking after my ankle,' she whispered impatiently.

'Oh.'

Helen brought the phone back to her ear. 'Sorry about that,' she said. 'Anyway, it feels much better this morning, but it's still sore.'

'Are you resting it?'

He didn't need to know she'd just got out of bed. 'I've had it up all morning.'

'That's good. Keep icing it for another twenty-four hours, won't you?'

'Sure.'

'Ten minutes on, ten minutes off, ten minutes on again. Then after an hour or so, repeat the procedure over again.'

Helen was smiling. 'I don't know if you got around to reading my résumé, Myles, but I am a trained nurse.'

'Oh yes, that's right, then I'll leave you to it.' He paused. 'But, um, while I have you on the phone, I wanted to ask if you'd given my offer any more thought?'

'Oh,' said Helen. 'Well, um, yeah, sure, of course I've been thinking about it.'

Gemma opened her mouth in shock. 'He's asking you about the job?'

Helen pulled a face at her, dismissing her with a wave of the hand and turning her face away. But Gemma just ran around into her line of sight again.

'You should *so* ask him for a parking space.'

'*What?*'

'I didn't say anything,' said Myles.

Helen sighed. 'Sorry, Myles, would you mind holding on again? I'll be quick.'

'That's okay, take your time.'

She covered the phone again. 'What are you talking about, Gemma?'

'Ask him for a parking space.'

'What?'

'He's obviously keen to have you work there – the ball's in your court, Helen.'

'I'm not going to ask him for a parking space. I'm just an assistant.'

'How are you going to get to work?' Gemma said pointedly.

Helen blinked at her.

'I assume you're not going to take the bus, so where are you going to park your car?' she persisted. 'It'll cost you a fortune to put it into a parking station.'

Helen was frowning now, cradling the phone and biting her lip.

'Just ask him. What have you got to lose?' said Gemma.

She slowly moved the phone back to her ear, taking her hand away from the mouthpiece. 'Hi, sorry about that, Myles.'

'No problem,' he replied. 'So what do you think?'

Helen cleared her throat. 'Look, I am interested,' she began, Gemma nodding on the sidelines. 'Definitely . . . very interested. It's just, I have a bit of an issue actually getting to the office.'

'I'm not following you.'

'Well, you see, I think I'm going to have to drive . . .'

'Oh?'

'Yeah,' she said weakly.

Gemma was making motions with her hands to try to get her to spin it out.

'You live in Balmain, don't you?' Myles was asking. 'You can't go by public transport?'

'Aahmm . . .' Helen didn't want to be the widow whose husband had been hit by a bus. Not yet. 'Oh, never mind, it's nothing.'

'No, please, Helen,' he said kindly. 'Tell me what the problem is. I'm sure we can work something out.'

Gemma was still gesticulating wildly, so Helen turned towards the table, shielding her eyes so she couldn't see her. She took a breath. 'You see, Myles, the thing is, well, there is the ferry, but I'd have to catch a bus once I got to the other side, or else there's buses direct to the city, and I . . . I, um, you see, the thing is, I can't take the bus. It's, um, it's kind of like a . . . a phobia.'

That was so lame, but she couldn't think of anything else to say. There was silence down the line for a moment. He probably thought she was a crazy person.

'Well, then, I guess we'll have to arrange a parking space for you,' he said finally.

Helen swallowed. 'You will?'

'Sure,' he said. 'Just, ah, just keep it to yourself for now, okay?'

Helen smiled. 'Okay.'

'There is one condition though,' he said.

'Oh, sure, what is it?'

'You have to agree to take the job.'

Helen was still smiling. 'I suppose that's only fair.'

'Good.' He sounded pleased. 'Glad to have you aboard.'

'Thank you,' said Helen. 'Thanks for everything.'

'Not a problem. Anyway, I'd better let you go. Look after that ankle.'

Helen turned round after he hung up and Gemma was standing there almost bursting. 'Well? What did he say?'

'He's going to give me a parking space.'

'Wow,' Gemma declared, in shock. Then she roused herself. 'So that means you're taking the job?'

A smile formed slowly on Helen's face. 'It was a condition of the parking space,' she said as the phone in her hand rang again, startling her. She pressed to answer and held it to her ear.

'Hello?'

'Helen? It's Myles again.'

Her heart sank a little. Had he changed his mind? Come to his senses?

'Listen, I was wondering if you could make it in to the office one day next week?' he said. 'We might as well get the ball rolling.'

'Oh, but I don't think Gemma wants to finish up just yet.'

Gemma's eyes widened, staring at her.

'No, no,' he assured her. 'I was only thinking you should have a little orientation first, seeing as you're so unfamiliar with the industry and how it works.'

'Orientation?'

'Mm, you can meet people from all the departments, get a bit of an idea of what they do, how the place is run. You'll be paid for your time,' he added quickly. 'I think it's important, Helen. You haven't worked much outside a hospital, have you? And by the time Gemma leaves I'll really need you to be up to speed.'

'Oh, well, sure,' said Helen. 'What day would you want me to come in?'

'What works for you? I know you have your boy to consider.'

Helen was thinking. 'Is Thursday okay?'

'Thursday's good. See you then.'

Thursday

It was all arranged for Helen to drive on in as soon as she'd dropped Noah at preschool. The guard would direct her to where she could park from now on, and this time the man at reception would give her her own security pass. They might as well get all that out of the way, Myles had suggested.

'I'm not ready to leave work yet, you know,' Gemma said, a little curtly, when she'd delivered what seemed like the umpteenth message to Helen from the MD that week.

'I know,' said Helen. 'Actually, we should probably talk about that so we can make some plans. When did you want to start cutting your days down?'

'Well, to be perfectly frank, before all this I was prepared to keep going as long as I possibly could.'

'Okay, if that's what you want,' said Helen. 'It's all the same to me.'

But it wasn't all the same to Gemma. Her feet were swelling up more lately, and sometimes it felt almost impossible to get out of bed on a Friday morning. An extra day off would be ideal right now. It would give her time to start work on the baby's room, as well as get some rest over the weekend. She could start from next week if she wanted. So what was stopping her?

Gemma was well aware she was cutting off her nose to spite her face, but she couldn't help it. She was annoyed that the MD was fussing over Helen like she was something special. She hadn't even done anything yet, except trip over her own feet. Was that it? Did he like helpless women he could step in and look after? Seemed an odd requirement in an assistant.

'Maybe they just click,' said Charlie when she had complained to him over lunch. 'Some people just click better than others. You ought to know that, Gem.'

'I didn't think the MD was capable of clicking with anyone,' she grumbled.

'Well, looks like Helen's shot a hole in that theory,' he said. 'And it doesn't surprise me – she's such a sweet person.'

'And I'm not?'

Charlie paused, considering what he was about to say. 'Gemma, there are a lot of words I'd use to describe you, a lot of good words, but "sweet" wouldn't be one of them.'

Gemma was scowling at him.

'The words "green-eyed" and "monster" do come to mind, however.'

'What?' she shrilled. 'You think I'm jealous? Jealous of Helen? I'm not jealous of Helen, I love Helen, Helen is adorable. This is not about Helen. Oh you're not suggesting . . . ? Oh God, Charlie, I thought you knew me. Nothing could be further from the truth. I don't find him the slightest bit attractive –'

'That's not what I meant,' he said with a sly grin. 'Though I'll resist the temptation to suggest you're protesting too much.' Gemma opened her mouth to speak, but Charlie got in first. 'You're jealous because you've been bending over backwards to make an impression and Helen walked in –'

'Stumbled in, more like it.'

Charlie ignored her. '– and now she's made a huge impression without even trying. I can understand how that'd make you feel.'

'You can?'

'Of course, but you have to look on the bright side.'

'There's a bright side?'

'Yes, you're not going to lose your job,' he said, slowly and deliberately.

Gemma was suitably chastened.

'Jeez, Gem, you ought to feel lucky. Or at least relieved. This has worked out far better than you could have hoped, and a lot better than you planned.'

He was right, of course. So Gemma tried not to feel too annoyed when she had to move heaven and earth to postpone, reschedule or otherwise juggle the MD's appointments for Thursday. Eddie was cued to call up when Helen arrived at reception, and Gemma was to buzz the MD as soon as she heard. He strode out of his office not half a minute later, slipping on his jacket.

'Okay, you can get me on my mobile if you need me,' he said as he sailed past Gemma, barely looking at her.

She sighed, pushing her chair back and lifting her feet up onto the desk as soon as he was out of sight.

*

When Helen stepped out of the lift on the fifteenth floor, Myles was waiting for her this time.

'Oh, hello,' she said, her cheeks turning pink. 'I didn't expect –'

'Well, I figured you've already seen my office, and your workstation, so I thought we'd get on with the rest of the tour.'

She nodded. 'Sure.'

'How's the ankle?' he asked, glancing down at her foot.

'Still a little sore,' she admitted.

'I bet it is,' said Myles. 'So you tell me if you need to rest today, okay, any time?'

'I'll be fine. I wore sensible shoes today. I hope I'm dressed appropriately.'

'Of course,' he said, gazing down at her. 'You look quite, um . . . you look, well, you look very . . . appropriate.'

Helen had spent a large part of the past week sorting through all of her mother's clothes. The wardrobe was the last thing left in the old darkroom, mostly because of Helen's ambivalence. Gemma wouldn't let her even consider putting the contents in the charity bin, and in truth Helen didn't really want to. But neither did she want to sell the lot on eBay, as Gemma had suggested. Now she was glad she'd dithered; she'd salvaged some excellent day dresses and fully lined skirts that were perfect for the office. The blouses were mostly not worth keeping, their more delicate fabrics having deteriorated with age. And Helen wouldn't have been able to wear the number of evening frocks and formal outfits if she went to a ball every week for a year, which was obviously not on the cards. Still, she couldn't resist keeping a couple of dresses that she remembered fondly, including the green sheath. Helen insisted Gemma and Phoebe both have whatever took their fancy as well, before she packed up what was remaining and presented the lot at an upmarket vintage shop, where she received the gushing gratitude of the proprietor and a surprisingly generous amount for her trouble. Helen figured it was appropriate to use the proceeds to buy whatever else she needed for work, and so a couple of neutral business shirts later, along with a pair of near-flat court shoes and a classic leather handbag to replace her saggy Oxfam shoulder bag, Helen felt ready for the office. And oddly excited.

'So if you'll just come this way,' said Myles, taking her elbow and leading her out of the lift bay, 'this is the area where we hold most of our client meetings, certainly when it comes to the pitch.'

They went around a corner into a vast open space dominated by the biggest flat-screen television Helen had ever seen in her life. Three long leather sofas, similar to the one in Myles's office, only white, formed a U facing the screen. There was another oversized steel and glass coffee table in the centre of the U, but apart from that, the room was sparse, save for a glass shelf unit displaying what looked like various trophies and plaques.

Helen was dumbfounded. 'It's very . . .'

'It has to be,' said Myles. 'This is where the teams pitch their ideas to clients, where they make their presentations.' He walked over to a brushed steel panel on the wall. 'The controls for the blinds, lighting and so on are all located here,' he said as the lights flickered on and off and sleek white blinds shimmied halfway down the window and back up again. Myles pressed another button and part of what Helen had thought was merely a wall slid away silently to reveal a thoroughly stocked bar. 'It's all to impress the clients, to put them in the right frame of mind to accept the pitch.'

'Does it work?' Helen asked.

'Hard to say.' He shrugged. 'But it's come to be expected.'

Myles continued the tour, floor by floor, through all the various sections. Helen was glad to have a guide. Every floor looked the same to her – lots of white and lots of glass. Myles took her around to meet the account teams, while he gave her an overview of the structure of the company. He had a couple of the teams show her what they were currently working on, before taking her up to the creative section, where Helen was pleased and relieved to see a familiar face.

'Hi Charlie!' she said, smiling widely.

'Hey, Helen, how's it going?'

'You two know each other?' said Myles.

Helen nodded. 'Charlie's a friend of Gemma's.'

'Oh, I didn't realise that,' he said.

'So, Helen, what do you think of the place so far?' Charlie asked her.

'It's a little overwhelming,' she admitted.

'Is it?' Myles said, frowning. 'Have I been going too fast? Do you want to take a break? How's your ankle?'

Charlie was giving him an odd look.

'My ankle's fine,' Helen assured him.

'Maybe we should stop for lunch?'

'It's only eleven o'clock, Myles,' she said. 'I think I'd be overwhelmed no matter what. It's okay, let's push on.'

As the morning ticked over into the middle of the day, Helen grew increasingly apprehensive. Myles had consistently introduced her as his new personal assistant, which prompted more than a few surprised looks. Helen would have liked to explain that it was only part-time, and temporary, but Myles didn't really give her the chance. He barrelled along, showing her what seemed to be every minute aspect of the business, inside and out. Why did she need to know all of this to keep his schedule up to date and answer mail?

At one o'clock Myles clapped his hands together and announced it was time for lunch.

'Okay,' said Helen. 'So we'll meet back here in half an hour, or an hour, what would you prefer?'

He frowned. 'I'd prefer to take you to lunch.'

'I beg your pardon?'

'I'm taking you to lunch.'

'That's really not necessary, Myles,' said Helen, feeling flustered. 'It's very kind, but you're a busy man and I've taken up half your day as it is.'

He looked at her directly. 'I cleared the whole day, and I made reservations for lunch.'

Helen blinked. 'Why?'

'What do you mean?'

'I just don't understand why you're doing all this,' she said carefully. She didn't want to seem churlish, but at the same time she couldn't help feeling uncomfortable. 'I'm only relieving Gemma while she's on maternity leave.'

'There's a good deal more to it than that,' he said. 'I was under the impression you'll be job-sharing for quite some time, Helen, indefinitely perhaps.'

'Sure, but . . .' She didn't know what to say.

'Listen, I'm getting hungry,' said Myles. 'Can we continue this over some food?'

*

As they were now running late for their reservation, they caught a taxi down towards the Quay, stopping outside a tower building. A doorman showed them into the foyer, from where they caught a lift to the penthouse floor. Myles led her into the kind of restaurant Helen had only seen in magazines on her rare visits to the hairdressers. The big glossy expensive magazines. And this was a big, glossy expensive restaurant. Helen felt immediately self-conscious and totally out of place. She and David had rarely gone to restaurants. Even on special occasions David baulked at 'lining the pockets of overpaid celebrity cooks, while their underpaid underlings did all the work'.

'Everything okay?' Myles asked, noticing her expression as she studied the menu.

She looked up at him, a little dazed.

'The veal's good,' he suggested. 'Or it was last time I was here.'

'Oh, well, I'm sure it still is,' said Helen. 'But I'm a vegetarian.'

'Oh.' He hesitated. 'Well, the seafood's also good.'

Helen tried not to smile. 'Fish aren't vegetables.'

Myles looked across his menu at her. 'So you're one of those vegans?'

She shook her head. 'I eat dairy and eggs, just not the animals themselves.'

He seemed interested. 'Is it a moral or a health choice, or something else? That's if you don't mind me asking,' he added.

'No, I don't mind,' she said, but she wasn't sure how to answer. David had introduced her to vegetarianism. It hadn't been such a hardship. She'd never been a big meat-eater anyway, and after he moved in it was just easier to cook the one meal. However, she became more serious about it when she fell pregnant with Noah – if she was going to keep it up she had to do it properly, so she had to believe it was worth doing. What she discovered through her research about the way animals were raised for food was enough to make her hair stand on end, and more than enough to convince her. But Helen had never been one to force her views on anyone.

'I do have some ethical concerns about the way animals are treated,' she said finally.

'Such as?'

Helen gave him a faint smile. 'I don't think we should have this conversation over lunch.'

They ordered and the waiter took away their menus. Myles leaned forward on the table. 'Okay, back at the office I interrupted you. What were you saying?'

Helen gathered her thoughts. 'I guess it's just that I'm getting the impression this job might be a bigger deal than I was led to believe.'

'PA to the managing director is a big deal,' Myles said plainly. 'It's an important role with a lot of responsibility. I don't know who led you to believe otherwise.'

'Well, Gemma, of course,' said Helen. 'She made out she was little more than a glorified receptionist. She must have been playing it down so she wouldn't freak me out. But seriously, I'm worried I might be in a bit over my head.'

Myles considered her for a moment before he spoke. 'First of all, I wouldn't have offered you the job if I didn't think you could do it, Helen. That would be a waste of my time and yours. I'm confident you've got the skills, but not to put too fine a point on it, as I told you the other day, it's more important to me to have someone I can trust.'

'But you don't know me.'

'I know all I need to know,' he said, folding his arms. 'You have beliefs and conviction and ethics, and I admire that.'

'None of that sounds like essential criteria for a job in the advertising industry.'

Myles laughed. 'See what I mean? I like that, when you say what you think. I feel as though I can count on you to be honest with me.' He became thoughtful. 'In fact, I'd appreciate your input on something when we get back to the office.' He took out his phone. 'Would you excuse me for a second?'

Input? What kind of input could Helen possibly hope to contribute? She was definitely in over her head.

'Gemma, it's me,' Myles spoke into his phone. 'Could you reschedule my meeting with Josh Macklin? Tell him I'll come by his office in about an hour . . . Thanks.'

He turned off his phone as their meals arrived. 'How's the time going for you?' he asked. 'This meeting won't take long, and then HR need you to stop by and sign some papers – will that give you plenty of time to pick up your son?'

'Oh, sure, that's fine,' Helen said vaguely. He really was an incredibly thoughtful person. And he listened to her. Helen wasn't used to having her opinions treated with such respect. She honestly didn't know what Gemma's problem was.

Myles picked up his cutlery. 'How old is your little boy?'

'He's four.'

'Does he have a name?'

Helen smiled. 'Noah.'

'Very fitting for the son of an animal rights advocate.'

'I'm not exactly an advocate. I just don't eat them.'

He grinned. 'So do you have a picture of Noah?'

Helen was flummoxed. 'No, no, I don't. Not on me.' So much for honesty. Of course she had a picture, but it was of David and Noah together, and she wasn't about to show Myles that. Instead she focused on her roasted vegetable stack, which was looking rather precarious. She wasn't sure how to attack it.

'I hope I'm not being too personal,' Myles said carefully, 'and please say if it's none of my business . . .'

Helen looked across at him warily. She didn't want to lie again, after everything he'd said about honesty, but she wasn't necessarily ready to tell the truth, not the whole truth, anyway.

'I take it Noah's father's not around anymore?'

She couldn't have said it better herself.

'That's right,' she confirmed. 'So do you have any children, Myles?'

He took a moment to catch up with her, she'd sidestepped his question so swiftly. 'Oh, no, no kids. Never married.'

She nodded, managing to slice away some eggplant without causing a landslide.

'Not that I'm against it or anything,' he was quick to add. 'In fact, I came close to getting married, once. Very close.'

'Oh?' Helen raised an eyebrow. 'Almost a doctor, almost a husband, you've had a lot of near misses.'

'Mm.' He frowned. 'Never really thought about it that way before. I wonder if it's a pattern?'

Helen decided to steer the conversation clear of the personal and ask him about work instead. 'So how did an almost-doctor end up in advertising? It's quite a flip, isn't it?'

He nodded. 'I suppose it is. But when I decided to leave medicine, I knew I was going to need some kind of bridging qualification to get into the regular workforce. So I did an MBA, and afterwards I joined a firm of management consultants. With my background they tended to place me with pharmaceutical companies at first, but over time I gradually spread my wings, requested different projects, built up some broader experience, and here I am.'

'So you're not with the management consultants anymore?' asked Helen.

'No, I am. But I'm contracted to Bailey's. I was doing some work in their Melbourne office when things almost went belly-up here. They didn't have anyone groomed to take over at this level, so they asked me to step in and clean up the mess.'

'So you don't have a background in advertising at all?'

He shook his head. 'Don't need it really, not for what I have to do.'

Helen nodded faintly, moving her food around on the plate, the stack long since disintegrated. She felt incredibly naive; she had no idea of the workings of the corporate world, any more than she knew how to eat a vegetable stack without it collapsing.

'So what made you leave nursing, Helen?' Myles asked after a while.

She wasn't expecting that question. 'I'm sorry?'

'You said you were a nurse?'

'Oh, yeah, sure. I'm a nurse. Or I was a nurse.' She hadn't really thought about it like that. She wasn't sure you could ever stop being a nurse.

'So why did you leave?' Myles asked again.

Helen took a breath. 'It's difficult with a young child . . . the shiftwork.' She shrugged, as though that was all there was to it. 'You didn't say why you left medicine,' she said, hitting the ball right back to him.

Myles dropped his gaze, staring down at his plate for a long moment before answering quietly. 'I just wasn't cut out for it.'

The subject stayed firmly on Bailey's terrain after that, as Myles attempted to fill her in on the rest of its operations. He was very thorough. Helen was sure she wouldn't remember everything, and even more sure she didn't need to. So she just listened, and nodded at the appropriate times, and asked the occasional question. When they finished lunch they headed back to Bailey's and directly to Josh Macklin's office.

'This is Helen Chapman,' said Myles. 'My new PA, part-time at least,' he added, bowing his head slightly in deference to Helen.

'Nice to meet you,' Josh said, shaking her hand.

'Josh is in research,' Myles explained to Helen. 'He's responsible for identifying new trends, hopefully before anyone else does. So what have you got for me, Josh?'

'In-game advertising,' Josh announced portentously. 'It's the next big thing, and it's going to have to be integrated into every campaign targeting eighteen to thirty-four-year-old males from now on.'

'In-game, you mean video games?' Myles asked.

Josh nodded. 'Playstation and Xbox primarily, as well as online gaming. The demographic we're looking at here has a mean age of twenty-eight, and they're not watching TV anymore – as little as half an hour a night according to some estimates – but they are playing video games for hours every night. The market's increasing every year but it's been largely untapped till recently. The guys in in-game advertising claim it could be worth as much as two billion.'

'Well, they would,' Myles remarked.

'I suppose,' said Josh. 'The guy who came up with it is Australian actually. He noticed there were all these fake ads in the background on video games, and wondered why they couldn't be genuine ads for real products.'

'So you mean things like billboards and signage?' said Myles.

Josh nodded. 'And pizza boxes, TV screens, soft-drink cans, you name it. Anything that's branded.'

Helen's mind boggled.

'But what's really interesting,' Josh went on, 'is that the software will enable advertising to be downloaded into a game while someone's playing online. So for example, it can be made geographically specific. And it won't end there: there's no reason why local advertising can't be slotted into the background in films and TV shows.'

Because too much advertising was obviously never enough, Helen groaned silently.

'So what does this mean for us?' Myles asked Josh.

'The Australian guy sold out to Microsoft and, as usual, they have the market sewn up,' Josh said. 'Not that there isn't room to expand, at the rate it's continuing to grow. I reckon Charlie Lambert would love to get his teeth into something like this. Whatever, the teams have to be made aware that this is the future: ads will have to be designed to work within a game scenario. We're losing traditional markets – the bulk of the advertising dollar has always gone to TV, but millenials are turning off in droves. The challenge is going to be how to stay in their faces.'

*

'So, what do you think?' asked Myles after they had left Josh's office and started along the corridor.

'I'm sorry?' said Helen.

'What do you think about what Josh had to say in there?'

'Oh, I don't know anything about all that.'

'But I'm asking you what you think, Helen,' Myles persisted, pausing to look directly at her. 'What was your gut reaction to what he was saying?'

Helen took a breath. 'Honestly? I think it's terrible.'

'Go on.'

She sighed. 'Aren't kids bombarded with enough advertising as it is?'

'Didn't you hear what Josh said, Helen? This is eighteen to thirty-four year olds we're talking about. They're adults, they're big enough to look after themselves.'

'But do we really need more advertising?'

They arrived at the lift bay and Myles pressed the UP button. 'From a business point of view, of course we do,' he said wryly. 'But the ads were there already, remember, they're simply making them genuine.'

Doors opened behind them and they turned around and walked inside the lift.

'Then will it make any difference?' said Helen.

Myles looked curiously at her. 'What do you mean?' he said, slipping his security card in and out of the slot before pressing one of the buttons.

'Do you really think subliminal advertising works?' she asked. 'I've heard companies pay a fortune for product placement in movies, that kind of thing. But just because George Clooney wears a certain brand of watch, do you really think people are going to rush out and buy it? I wouldn't even notice it.'

'Me either,' Myles said. 'But we're not the ones they're trying to snag.'

'We're not?'

He shook his head. 'You and I are what's known in the business as "lost causes". There are certain people who wouldn't be swayed whatever the hook, so they don't even try to catch us. There are plenty of other fish in the ocean who'll swallow anything.'

Myles was a 'lost cause' and yet he headed up an advertising agency? Helen was bamboozled.

'What about the kids, sorry, the eighteen to thirty-fours playing the games?' she asked. 'They must have tuned out the ads in the background if they're all fake. What makes them think they're going to tune in again?'

Myles nodded thoughtfully. 'That's a good point.'

Helen felt a little twinge, like a tiny surge of pride. She'd actually made a valid point? 'You know the streetscapes you always see of New York, Tokyo, places like that?' She was on a roll now. With all the neon lights?'

'Sure. Times Square, Shinjuku . . .'

Helen realised Myles had probably seen them for real. 'I've only seen them in pictures,' she admitted, 'but can you honestly say people distinguish each single ad in that whole sea of neon? And even if they did, is it going to make them rush out and buy the thing anyway?'

'It's not as straightforward as that, Helen. It's all part of an attempt to constantly imprint the brand onto the mind of the consumer. They don't have to run off and buy the product on the spot, but next time they're looking, the brand that has most successfully imprinted is likely to be the one they choose.'

'But when there's so many, how can one stand out among the rest?'

'That's the sixty-four thousand dollar question,' he said. 'And why so much is spent on market research and focus groups in the hope of finding that elusive image that will attract the customer. In the meantime, if everyone else is doing it, you have to do it too. Maybe you don't stand out, but at least you exist.'

The lift had come to a stop and the doors opened. Myles stood in the way to hold them back. 'Well, this is where I leave you, Helen, we're back at HR.'

'Oh, right,' said Helen, looking around. She would have been hard-pressed to tell the difference from any other floor.

'It's been good getting to know you better today,' said Myles, with a sincerity that made Helen's cheeks go pink. 'I'd like you to tell Kelly that I want you to start as soon as possible. That's if you're okay with that?'

Helen stirred. 'Um, sure, but I don't think Gemma's ready to leave just yet.'

'Well, Gemma doesn't necessarily get to decide that.'

'Oh.'

'She won't be going anywhere for a while yet,' Myles reassured her, 'but we need to get things rolling. You'll be training for the first couple of weeks under Gemma's supervision, then you'll be job-sharing till she's ready to leave to have her baby.'

He was right, it was all happening.

'Organise it with Gemma, okay? Let me know what you come up with.'

*

Helen decided not to drop by and see Gemma on her way out. She'd save that conversation for later; she had a feeling it wasn't going to go down all that well.

So that meant she had a little time to spare before picking up Noah, and a good opportunity to call in and see her mother.

'Hello, Helen,' one of the staff greeted her as she passed by the nurses' station.

Helen paused. 'How is she today?'

'Good,' the nurse said with a nod. 'The new medication is keeping her much calmer.'

Helen proceeded along the corridors towards the wing that housed her mother's room. So Marion was going to live out the rest of her days partially sedated, to keep her 'calm'. Helen knew on an intellectual level that it was for her own good – she had been getting increasingly distressed about everything, paranoid, delusional. That was no way to live. But neither, she felt, was this, existing in a fog, the drugs like an emotional straitjacket.

Helen knocked on her mother's closed door and opened it, peering into the dim room. Marion was lying on the bed, staring at the TV, but the sound was so low she couldn't possibly be following the program. It was just colour and movement, keeping her distracted.

'Hello, Mum,' said Helen, trying to sound positive. 'How are you today?'

Marion's head turned slowly towards her, her eyes glazed. Helen felt her heart breaking. Even her sniping and abuse were better than this.

'It's so dark in here,' Helen said briskly, crossing to the television and flicking it off. She walked around to the window and opened the blind. 'Look at what a lovely day it is out there.' Then she had an idea. She checked her watch. 'Come on, let's go for a walk,' she said, turning around to look at her mother.

But Marion shook her head. 'I'm tired.'

'You're tired because you've been lying in bed all day,' Helen said, hoisting her up. Her hair was stuck to the back of her head and she smelled stale. She was obviously getting to the point where she couldn't be left to bathe herself. Helen wondered if the staff were aware, whether they had a plan, when they would step up her care.

At least today she could get her mother out in the fresh air for ten minutes. Marion compliantly stuck each arm into the sleeves of her robe as Helen held them out for her. She knelt down and slipped her outdoor scuffs on her feet, then looked up at her. 'Are you ready?'

'Where are we going?' Marion asked, her voice small.

'Just into the garden,' Helen said brightly. 'It's a beautiful day outside.'

'I'm very tired.'

'I know, we won't stay long.'

Helen led her mother into the prettiest part of the garden, though it was still a little bare yet, being late winter. Some azaleas were beginning to bloom, but the rest would have to wait for spring to arrive. They walked over to a garden bench and sat down. There was a little bite in the breeze, but the sun was warm, and the aspect delightful. But Marion's face was not really registering anything. She seemed to be struggling with just being, let alone taking in her surroundings. Helen reached over and took hold of her mother's hand, where it lay listlessly on her lap.

'I'm going to start a new job, Mum,' she said. 'So everything's going to be all right. You don't have to worry about the money, about anything.' She paused. 'It's a good job, too. Not exactly what I would have chosen myself, but I haven't really had a choice about much that's happened this year, so I'm thinking I'll just go with the flow for now. And my new boss, he seems really decent, kind. He's interested in my opinion; that's a new experience for me. He thinks I've got something to offer. I guess we'll see.'

She turned her head to look at her mother. 'It's lovely out here, isn't it?'

Marion sighed deeply. 'I'd like to go in now. I'm very tired.'

Helen deposited her mother back in her room, back in her bed, with the flickering TV set turned on again and the sound muted. She resolved to go back tomorrow, bathe her, wash her hair, get her into day clothes and out of that room. She felt agitated. She knew she wouldn't have as much time once she was working the two days Noah was at preschool. She always saw her mother on at least one of those days, if not both, especially as she'd been less inclined to bring Noah of late, particularly for long visits. Would she even have the time for long visits after she started work? And what about after Gemma had the baby . . .?

Helen left her mother and started along the labyrinthine corridors, lost in thought. What had she let herself in for? It was untenable, wasn't it? She hadn't really thought it through. It was a job that suited her and Noah, but allowed very little time for her mother. By the same token, if she didn't take the job, she wouldn't be able to afford to keep Marion here for much longer.

'Hello, Helen.'

She jumped, startled to see Dr Chris coming towards her.

'Finally we bump into each other!' he said warmly.

'Chris.' Helen nodded. 'When did you last review my mother's medication?'

He looked a little taken aback.

'I'm sorry,' she said. 'I didn't mean to jump at you like that, it's just that she's almost comatose in there. Surely there has to be a balance between calming her down and sedating her?'

'Of course,' he said. 'And it's a very difficult balance to strike. I'd think you'd be aware of that, Helen.'

She sighed. 'I just don't like seeing her like this.'

'Why don't you come back to my office. I'll make you a cup of coffee and we can talk about it.'

She shook her head. 'I can't, I'm late for Noah already. But I'll be in tomorrow.'

'I won't be.' He glanced around to make sure they were on their own, then he drew her aside close to the wall. 'Look, I'm sorry if I sound blunt, Helen,' he said in a lowered voice, 'but you should know things aren't going to get much better for your mother. That's what I've been trying to prepare you for.'

Helen felt an ache in the back of her throat. She swallowed. 'I just want her to be a little . . . happier?' she said in a small voice.

Chris considered her kindly. 'I'll look in on her this afternoon, and I'll have a word to the staff. See what we can do.'

She nodded faintly. 'Thank you.'

*

Late that night Helen sat up in bed, hugging David's pillow. He'd know what to do. He'd calmly review all the options, the pros and cons, and help her come to the right decision. But David wasn't here, and that was the reason she was in this mess.

Helen sighed. That wasn't fair, and feeling sorry for herself wouldn't get her anywhere either. She contemplated the phone she'd been holding in her hand for the past half an hour. Just do it. She scrolled for a number, tapped it, then held the phone to her ear, waiting till she heard a ringtone. It was a female voice that finally came onto the line.

'Oh, hello,' said Helen. 'Um, I was after Tony. Tony Zelinsky?'

'Yeah, sure. Can I ask who's calling?'

'Um, it's his sister, in Australia.'

'Oh, brilliant! Hold on . . . To*nyyy!!* It's Australia on the phone!'

Helen heard more calling and a door banging, someone running on stairs, by the sounds of it, the woman's excited voice repeating it was Australia, his sister calling from Australia, and finally Tony . . .

'Helen, is that you?'

'Yeah, it's me, Tony. Hi.'

'Is everything all right?'

'Yes –'

'Mum's okay?'

'Oh, yes –'

'Noah?'

'Yes,' Helen assured him. 'Everyone's okay.' He obviously expected a call from Australia to mean bad news.

'How are you, Hel? It's good to hear your voice.'

And that was all it took. Helen burst into loud sobs, taking both Tony and herself by surprise.

'Hel, what's the matter?' he said urgently. 'Are you sure everything's all right?'

'Yes, kind of,' she sobbed. 'No one's sick or hurt, don't worry, but Mum's getting worse all the time.' She took a tremulous breath. 'And I got a new job, so I can afford her fees, but now I won't be able to see her so much, and I don't know if it's the right thing, but I can't keep her there if I don't have a job, and then I thought maybe I should just bring her home and nurse her myself –'

'Helen,' Tony broke into her blubbering monologue. 'Try to calm down, Hel, I can't make out what you're saying.'

She took a couple of deep breaths.

'You got a job?' Tony prompted after giving her a minute.

'That's right.' She sniffed. 'Part-time, when Noah's at preschool.'

'Well, that's good, isn't it?' he said encouragingly. 'Is it in a hospital?'

'No, I'm not nursing. It's, um . . .' Helen realised she hadn't said this to anyone yet. 'Well, it's, um, personal assistant to the managing director of an advertising agency.'

'No kidding?' said Tony. 'That's not what I expected.'

'No . . .' Helen said uncertainly.

'Sounds great though, Hel. How did you land that?'

'My boarder . . . oh, I didn't tell you about her, did I? But I took your advice and got a boarder in. Her name's Gemma, and well, turns out she was pregnant, which was a bit of a surprise. But on the positive, she had this great job that she didn't want to lose, so she approached her boss about job-sharing, with me, and he agreed.'

'And so you're enjoying it?'

'I haven't actually started yet. But I've met the boss a couple of times now, he took me on a tour around the place today actually. He's very nice, and well, very encouraging.' Helen paused. 'He said I, um, well, he said that he thinks I've got a lot to offer.'

'Of course you do,' Tony said, with obvious pride in his voice. 'I'm so happy for you, Hel, this is going to be really good for you.'

She sniffed. 'There's a problem, though.'

'What's that?'

'Mum's getting worse lately. They have to keep her on medication to calm her down, but she's like a zombie. She has no life. If I take this job, I'm not going to be able to visit her very much, and, well, I've been wondering if the best solution isn't just to bring her home and nurse her myself.'

'No, Helen, absolutely not,' Tony said firmly. 'That's not the best solution at all.'

'But the more I think of it,' Helen persisted, 'I won't have the fees, and I'll get some government help – not just money; I can use respite care for a break. And she'll be in her own home. Doesn't she deserve that?'

'What makes you think she'll even know it anymore?' Tony said carefully. 'How often does she recognise you, Hel?'

She sighed. 'Not often.' Not at all.

'And how are you going to give Noah the attention he needs if you're looking after Mum full-time? And what about your boarder? You can't just toss her out when she's expecting a baby.'

Helen hadn't thought of that.

'Hel, you can't do it,' said Tony. 'Your heart's in the right place, it always is, but this is not possible. Take the job, throw yourself into it, see Mum when you can, but don't stress about it. And stop feeling so guilty. In fact, package up all that guilt and send it over here to me. I should be the one wearing it, not you.'

'Tony . . .'

'It's true, Hel, you've done your bit.' He hesitated. 'And look, I wasn't going to say anything until I was sure, but things have taken an interesting turn here, and I might be able to help out a lot more, sooner than I thought.'

'Oh, what's going on?'

'I still don't want to say too much,' said Tony. 'But I'll let you know as soon as I can. In the meantime, promise me you're going to take the job.'

'I will, I promise.'

'Good.' He sighed, satisfied. 'I'm glad you called,' he said. 'I feel like your big brother again.'

Helen smiled.

'Let me know how it goes, okay?'

'Okay. Thanks, Tony.'

'Love you, Hel.'

Balmain

'Why didn't you tell me you'd finished up work?' Trish exclaimed when Gemma opened the door to her mother, standing impatiently on the front porch in full 'ladies-who-lunch' regalia. 'I had to hear it from Phoebe, which seems to be the only way I ever find out any news about you these days. Do you ever listen to your phone messages? And what on earth is that get-up you're wearing, Gemma?' she frowned as she walked inside, past her daughter.

'Come on in, Mum,' she muttered, trailing Trish as she charged straight through the house to the back room.

'Goodness,' she remarked, surveying the still almost empty room. 'What happened out here?'

'Helen sold nearly everything that weekend you came,' said Gemma. 'She just hasn't had a chance to replace the lounge.'

'We have a sofa we're not using. I'll get your father to organise someone to bring it around.'

'Don't you think you ought to check with Helen first?'

'I'm just saying, until she gets something.' She shrugged. 'But of course I'll check with her. What's her number at work?'

'Hold your horses, Mum.' Gemma's head was spinning. 'What exactly are you doing here?'

'Well, now that you've finished work I thought I'd help you get ready for the baby. You must have tonnes to do.'

'I haven't finished work altogether,' Gemma corrected her. 'Helen and I have just started job-sharing – she works two days and

I'm still on three.' By the skin of her teeth. She was sure that if the MD had his way, she'd be out of there already. So Gemma intended to hang on as long as she could manage. She wanted to make sure she had a job to go back to.

'I know about the arrangement, I just didn't realise it was going to start straightaway,' Trish said.

'It wasn't meant to. But I trained Helen for a couple of days last week and she could do the job standing on her head. There was no point the two of us being there.'

'Indeed,' Trish declared. 'And this will give us more time to get ready for the baby. So run along and get changed, I'm taking you shopping.'

'What for?'

'Oh, silly,' she scoffed. 'To buy things for the baby, of course.'

'Mum, you already bought enough for the baby. For three babies.'

'Nonsense, there must be something you need.'

'There isn't.'

'Then there must be something you *want*!'

Gemma sighed. 'Mum, between what Helen's given me of Noah's and everything you've bought so far, I'm not going to want for a thing.'

Trish's eyes narrowed. 'What did Helen give you?'

'Don't start on about second-hand stuff,' Gemma warned.

'I wasn't going to,' Trish said airily. 'In fact, Leisa's kicking herself now that she got rid of her baby things. It was all Bugaboo and what have you, only the best. She did hold onto it for a while. She toyed with the idea of having another, but she decided she wouldn't get any "me" time at all with three.'

And wouldn't that be a tragedy of epic proportions.

'Now why won't you let me take you shopping?' Trish persisted.

'Because I'm starting work on the baby's room today,' said Gemma, changing tack.

'Oh!' Trish clapped her hands together in delight. 'Where is it? You have to show me.'

'All right.' Gemma shrugged. Here goes nothing. She walked across to the door into the darkroom, forcing it open. The bottom of the door still caught on the carpet; she was going to have to do something about that.

Trish followed her in tentatively, the horror gradually dawning on her face. 'Gemma, you can't seriously be considering putting a baby in here?'

'It's just a room, Mum. As soon as it's all cleaned up it'll be fine.'

'It's like a dungeon.' She sniffed, peering across the room. 'Is that window painted black?'

'It was used as a darkroom a long time ago,' Gemma explained. 'I'm sure I can get the paint off the window. I was going start on it today as a matter of fact.'

'At least that explains the way you're dressed,' said Trish. 'But you're not starting on anything until I get our painter out here to take a look.'

'No thanks, Mum, all the same,' Gemma said firmly. 'I want to do this myself.'

Trish planted one hand on her hip. 'Gemma, didn't you just say this room used to be a darkroom quite some time ago?'

She nodded. 'So?'

'Did they use lead-based paint on the window?'

Bam. 'Um, I'm not sure . . .'

'You can't be breathing in the dust and fumes trying to strip it away, Gemma – think of your unborn baby. And just look at that ceiling. It's probably lead paint as well, and it will have to be resurfaced. Look at the flaking, and the damp over in that corner. Do you have any idea what a huge job this is?'

'Yes,' Gemma lied. 'I'm not stupid, Mum. That's why I'm starting now. Why do you always think I'm so incompetent?'

Trish looked at her, unfazed. 'I don't think you're incompetent at all, Gemma. I just don't want you to risk hurting yourself. Can see yourself up on a ladder, in a couple of months, painting those cornices?'

Double bam.

'I thought as much.' Trish took her phone out of her handbag. 'I'll call Warren now and see when he can fit us in.'

Gemma trudged defeated out to the kitchen and put the kettle on while her mother launched into Project Takeover Gemma's Life. She may as well give up now. The fact that her mother was actually right this time would give her so much momentum she would be unstoppable.

Not five minutes later, Trish strode into the kitchen, jubilant. 'How's this for serendipity? Warren is working in Five Dock, would you believe? You'd hardly ever find him this side of the Bridge. It was meant to be. Anyway, he's coming over when he finishes up this afternoon.'

'What time will that be? I have to pick up Noah at four,' said Gemma.

'Never mind, I'll be here,' said Trish.

Gemma groaned inwardly. That meant . . .

'We have the whole day together!' Trish exclaimed. 'What shall we do? I know, why don't we go and pick out colours for the nursery? You know what I think would look great? Something sunny and bright, like yellow.'

Damn. Gemma had wanted yellow. Now she was going to have to change her mind. Maybe. 'Do you want a cup of tea?' she asked wearily.

'Thanks, darling.' Trish walked back to the doorway, looking across the back room. 'You know, Warren might as well do this room while he's at it,' she mused. 'Before we send the sofa over.'

'Mum, I don't know if Helen can afford that –'

'Oh, your father and I will cover it,' she said, waving her hand dismissively. 'It can be our present for the baby, or a house-warming gift, or both, whatever.'

Gemma looked directly at her mother. 'What if Helen doesn't feel comfortable accepting that?'

'What?' Trish turned to look at her. 'A can of paint and an extra half-day of labour? Oh please, Gemma, I'm sure she's not as bull-headed as you.'

'I'm not bull-headed,' Gemma tried to say in an even tone. It was a common error to be bull-headed about insisting you were not bull-headed.

Trish laughed lightly. 'Oh Gemma, of course you are. I should know. It takes one to know one.'

'What?'

'Where do you think you get it from? You're so much like me.'

That was too horrifying to even contemplate. 'I don't think so, Mum.'

'Of course you are,' she insisted cheerfully. 'I used to give my mother merry hell as well. When we were having all the trouble with you, she used to say, "What goes around comes around".'

Gemma was crestfallen. 'Nan wouldn't have said that. Nan and I got on great, she was the only one in the family who understood me.'

'Of course she did,' Trish said. 'She'd had practice! Now, how's that tea coming along? Perhaps we should leave it till we're out. We really have to get a move on if we're going to be back for Warren, and what time did you say you have to pick up Jonah?'

'Mum, please, his name is *Noah*.'

'Sorry, sorry,' Trish said, shaking her head. 'I try to remember "ark", but then I think of water, and "whale" ends up popping into my head. I hope you haven't picked out anything too weird for your baby, Gemma. I've had enough Shilohs and Suris and God help me, please promise me you're not naming your child after a piece of fruit. What is wrong with celebrities these days?'

Gemma looked sideways at her. 'Yeah, 'cause in your day they were so much more sensible, just ask Zowie Bowie and Moon Unit Zappa.'

Trish laughed again. 'You're right, dear oh dear. Still, I'm sure you appreciate that your father and I didn't give you weird names. Can you imagine that poor child having to introduce herself when she's an adult? Hi, I'm Apple, but people tell me I'm a real peach!' Trish laughed and laughed at her own joke, till she was dabbing at tears at the corners of her eyes.

Gemma watched her, bemused. 'Are you on drugs or something, Mum?'

'Just high on life, darling,' she said, slipping her arm through Gemma's. 'Why don't you go and get changed – into something nice, please dear – we'll have lunch while we're out.'

Bailey's

Helen had just sat through her sixth meeting of the day, and she felt as though her head was going to explode. Advertising was all colour and movement, gaudy and hyperactive, and it was loud. Why did it have to be so loud? And why was everyone always laughing all the time? They laughed when they drank soft drink, took a Panadol, washed the car. And they were always in groups. Why did these people always have so many people around them, laughing uproariously? What the hell was so funny?

She was just feeling cranky. She'd been bombarded all day with campaigns currently under development for a car, pasta, headache tablets, insurance and toilet paper, involving images of children, firefighters, soccer players, rap musicians and a duck, and Helen was hard-pressed to recall which image went with what product. It was nudging five thirty on a Friday afternoon and she just wanted to go home.

'Okay, everyone, I think we've covered enough for today,' Myles said finally, and Helen could feel that collective sigh of Friday afternoon relief. 'We'll catch up again on this next week, all right?'

Everyone immediately began to shuffle their papers together to a muffled chorus of, 'Thanks, MD. Have a good weekend, MD.'

When the room had cleared and Helen had got to her feet, Myles leaned back in his chair and clasped his hands behind his head. 'So what did you think, Helen?'

He asked her the same question after every meeting, and she was beginning to run out of answers.

'I think I don't care that much about toilet paper,' she said, gathering her notes and files together. When she looked up again, Myles was regarding her with an odd expression.

'I don't mean any disrespect,' Helen said, 'but I don't think anyone cares that much, surely?'

'Everyone has to buy toilet paper.'

'Yes, and we all know what you do with it, so let's stop pretending it's something it's not.'

'What do you mean?'

'Toilet paper isn't sexy, or sensuous, and it doesn't need to be silky. The fact that it's on a convenient roll and it's not the texture of newspaper, like our grandparents had to use, that makes it a luxury. But who decided it had to feel like silk? I wouldn't wipe my backside with silk even if I were a millionaire. That's plain ridiculous.'

Myles seemed slightly bemused. 'That's a good point.'

'Mm. They're still going to make the crappy ad.'

'I'd avoid calling a toilet paper ad "crappy" if I were you,' he said with a sly grin as he got to his feet. 'So, I'll take that as a no, you didn't like the ad?'

Helen shrugged. 'It wasn't as bad as that one the other day,' she said, 'with the useless male who couldn't turn on a washing machine. I hate that stereotype – it's demeaning, for men and for women.'

'But it tests well,' said Myles.

'With who, other useless blokes, I suppose?'

'No, actually, with women,' he said as they walked out of the room.

Helen looked up at him. 'I don't believe it.'

'It's true. They've tried using a competent man before, cleaning, doing washing . . . Women say it's not credible.'

'But how are attitudes going to change if there are no role models on our screens?'

'Advertising reflects society, Helen,' said Myles. 'It doesn't have to change it.'

'Well, it should try.' She frowned. 'You want to know what really annoys me about the whole thing?'

'I have a feeling you're going to tell me regardless.'

'Sorry,' said Helen. 'I'm ranting.'

'No, don't get me wrong, I like to hear what you have to say,' Myles assured her. 'So what is it that really annoys you?'

'It's the cost. I mean, I always knew there had to be a huge waste of money in marketing and advertising, but now that I see the actual figures . . .' Helen shook her head, cringing. 'I keep imagining how many schools could be built, how many Africans could be treated for HIV.'

Myles grinned. 'You really are in the wrong industry.'

'I really am.' She nodded, but she was smiling too.

As they arrived at the lift bay there was one waiting and they stepped straight in. Helen slipped her pass into the slot and pressed the button for the fifteenth floor as Myles leaned back against the opposite wall.

'Okay, if you had to sell that toilet paper, Helen, how would you go about it?'

She was too tired for this. 'I don't know.'

'Well,' he said, changing tack, 'why do you buy a particular brand?'

'You want to know what toilet paper I buy?'

'No, I want to know why you buy it.'

She stared at the ceiling, thinking aloud. 'I buy it because it's cheap but not nasty, it's two-ply because honestly, one-ply is false economy – you just use twice as much. And most importantly, I buy it because it's made from recycled paper. It's a crime to use anything else when you're only going to flush it down the toilet.'

The elevator came to a stop and the doors opened.

'That's not bad,' Myles said thoughtfully.

They walked in silence back to the office as Myles scribbled notes on a pad. As they came to her desk, Helen unloaded the stack of files and papers she'd accumulated throughout the afternoon. She'd have to sort it all and put it away before she left; she liked to leave things neat and organised for Gemma on Monday. Myles still had his head bent over his notepad, writing furiously, till finally he stopped and looked up, watching Helen as she cleared her desk.

'Listen, Helen,' he said, 'I'd really like to talk about this some more.'

'Talk about what?'

'This idea, getting to the heart of why people actually buy the things they do . . .'

Helen wasn't really listening. She'd moved to the filing cabinet, sorting files and popping them away.

'I know you probably want to get out of here,' he continued, 'so what if we do this over dinner?'

Helen stopped abruptly. 'I'm sorry?'

'I'd like to discuss this some more – we could do it over dinner if you like,' he repeated.

'Sorry, Myles, I have to get home to Noah.'

'But Gemma's there for him, isn't she?'

Helen pushed the drawer of the filing cabinet closed and leaned back against it. 'But I want to be there for him myself.'

He sighed. 'Of course you do. I'm sorry, I wasn't thinking.'

She eyed him dubiously. 'It's Friday night, Myles. You know what they say about all work and no play. You must have something better to do on a Friday night than work?'

He gave her a sheepish smile. 'I have a feeling that what I'm about to say is going to make me sound like a sad loser, but no, I don't have anything better to do. In my defence, remember I come from Melbourne. That's where my friends are, my family, or half of it. I came up here to work, and that's about all I do.'

Helen didn't know what to say, at least not without making him sound like a sad loser.

'But, as luck would have it,' he continued on a brighter note, 'I have plenty of that to keep me going.' He tapped the stack of files under his arm for emphasis. 'I'll let you go, Helen. Have a good weekend.'

She watched, frowning, as he walked towards his office. She thought about all the nights she'd spent alone before Gemma came to live with them. All the bottles of Spray'n' Wipe she'd gone through . . .

'Myles,' she said as he got to the door. He turned around. 'Would you like to come back and have dinner with us?'

He smiled, shaking his head. 'Oh no, it's come to this. The pity invite.'

'It's not pity,' she chided. 'It's Friday night. You can't work on a Friday night. Friday nights are for throwing away routines, and for toasted sandwiches in front of the telly.'

'You're inviting me over for toasted sandwiches in front of the telly? Is there anything good on tonight?'

Helen smiled. 'What do you say?'

Myles stood there, gazing across at her. Helen was beginning to feel a little self-conscious.

He finally broke the silence. 'Will I have to eat vegetarian?'

'Now you're getting picky?'

'It's just that I am a carnivore –'

'No, you're an omnivore, actually. But don't worry, you don't have to eat vegetarian . . .' Her face creased into a frown. 'But you will have to eat Gemma's cooking. It's her night.'

'That bad, huh?'

'Let's just say it's not one of her strengths.'

'I tell you what,' said Myles. 'Why don't you call Gemma and tell her she's got the night off, and we can pick up something on the way?'

'That is an excellent idea,' said Helen.

*

'Of all the stupid ideas,' Gemma growled as she walked back into the kitchen, where Phoebe was tucking into her Friday night bottle of wine. 'What the hell was she thinking?'

'What are you so worked up about?' Phoebe asked.

'That was Helen on the phone. She's bringing the friggin' MD home for dinner.'

'Goody!' said Phoebe, picking up her glass. 'I finally get to meet him.'

'You can have him,' Gemma said in disgust. 'What am I supposed to do? She knows we don't get on, she could have checked with me first.'

'You're forgetting something, sister.'

'What's that?'

'It's her house.'

Gemma pulled a face. 'So you're staying?' she asked Phoebe as she dropped back down in her chair.

'Is that all right?'

'Sure, you can be a buffer, then I won't have to talk to him.'

Phoebe had taken to staying late most Friday nights, but she had never referred to Cameron's vasectomy threat again; in fact, she never referred to Cameron much at all.

'What's Cameron up to?' Gemma asked her.

Phoebe shrugged. 'Um, I think he's in Melbourne, or Adelaide . . . God, it could be Brisbane. Anyway, he wasn't sure if he'd make the last flight, so, I'll see him when I see him.'

Gemma regarded her, frowning. 'Is everything all right, Phee?'

'Yeah,' she dismissed, taking a swig of her wine. 'We're having a bit of downtime, it happens after you've been married a while.'

Despite her devil-may-care attitude, Gemma knew there was more to it than Phoebe was letting on. But her sister was not in the habit of broadcasting her woes, especially if they looked like failures. Phoebe was not allowed to fail. She'd already shown too much of her hand that night when she'd stayed over, and Gemma had realised, even at the time, that her quick exit the next morning had had more to do with emotional avoidance than exercise addiction.

'So, do you reckon the MD –' Phoebe hesitated. 'What am I supposed to call him anyway?'

'Helen will do the introductions,' said Gemma, 'so I guess you'll be calling him Myles.'

'Why don't *you* call him Myles?'

Gemma screwed up her nose. 'It doesn't feel right. He's the MD.'

'You called the last MD Jonesy,' Phoebe reminded her.

'Chalk and cheese,' Gemma dismissed.

'So anyway . . .' Phoebe returned to her original point. 'What do you reckon about Myles and Helen?'

'Is there something I should be reckoning?'

'Well, he is coming over for dinner . . .'

'He probably wants to discuss work. He's beyond workaholic, that man, he's like a machine.'

Phoebe took another slug of her wine. 'I don't know . . .'

'Well, I do. Believe me, Superman and Lois Lane have more chance of getting it together.'

'Why do you say that?'

'He's married to his work, and she's still married to her dead husband.'

'Still?'

Gemma nodded. 'Do you remember when that dad from the preschool asked her out? Well, he pounced on me the first day I went to pick up Noah. He wanted to know what the story was with Helen, and we got to talking. He seemed like a really nice guy, and he's cute as well, so I gave him her number, and he called her up.'

'What happened?' said Phoebe.

'She freaked. She went on again with all that creepy stuff about still being David's wife.' Gemma sighed. 'It's so morbid. The guy's dead and buried . . . or cremated anyway.'

'Gemma?'

She jumped, turning around to see Noah standing bug-eyed in the doorway. How long had he been there? 'What's up, mate?'

'There's nuffink for me to watch.'

'There must be something.'

He shook his head. 'Only the news lady talking and talking and talking.'

Gemma knew there had to be a perfectly good episode of *The Simpsons* playing on another channel, but that was off limits. 'What about a DVD?'

He screwed up his face, thinking about it. 'Which one but?'

'Well, it depends on your mood, Noah. If you're after a classic road movie, *Finding Nemo* has all the ingredients, albeit underwater. But *Shrek* is the obvious choice if you're looking for old-fashioned romance, and a rather fabulous rendition of "I'm A Believer".'

Noah was looking blankly at her.

'But for my money, I think it's hard to go past *Toy Story*.'

He smiled a small, contained smile, and nodded his head in approval.

'Okay, I'll come and set it up for you,' said Gemma, getting to her feet.

He gave her a plaintive look. 'I'm hungry but, Gemma.'

'Well, Mummy's on her way home with dinner. Can you wait, or do you want a carrot?'

He threw his arms up in the air. 'Carrot!' he cried.

'I've never seen a kid get so excited about a carrot,' Phoebe remarked, watching him dance a little jig.

'Me neither,' Gemma agreed. 'But you've got to admit, she must be doing something right.'

Once Noah was happily tucking into his carrot and his movie, Gemma returned to the kitchen to find Phoebe peeking around the plastic curtain that sealed off the back room. 'How's Trish's grand project coming along?'

'Getting there,' said Gemma. 'I'd show you the baby's room, but we're not allowed to walk across the floorboards until they're sealed.'

The rooms had become rather a bigger project than was first imagined, but then again, making mountains out of molehills was one of Trish's specialties. As her mother got more carried away, Gemma got more uninterested. She simply couldn't summon the energy to argue with her; the pregnancy had made her lethargic or apathetic or something. Charlie said the term she was looking for was bovine, right before she slapped him.

'How did Mum talk Helen into letting her do all this?' asked Phoebe.

Gemma shook her head. 'Helen was an absolute pushover.'

She had been no match for the persuasive talents of their mother. Trish had got her aside and babbled on about making it her project, and as she was doing up the baby's room as a gift for her grandchild, it was economically insane – that's right, insane – not to do the back room at the same time. And the carpet really had to be ripped up and you wouldn't put forty-year-old blinds back on the windows, and they wouldn't hear of Helen paying a cent: she was putting a roof over their daughter's head, not to mention their grandchild's. And when it was all done, they had a lovely sofa and some side tables and she was pretty sure there was a nice timber bookcase that wasn't being used, and before she knew it Helen had been tongue-lashed into submission.

*

Myles shared the ride home with Helen. He didn't have his car with him anyway. He rarely drove to work, he explained to her. He lived in walking distance of the office, and if he had meetings anywhere in the CBD it was much more efficient to get around by taxi. He'd catch a taxi home tonight as well, he assured her. It was just as easy.

'So, this is it,' said Helen as they walked through the gate, laden with bags of food from what she had assured Myles was the best Thai in the area.

'It's charming,' he said.

'It's dark,' said Helen, walking up to the front door. 'Don't expect a lot. The house has been in my family for a long time, and it's pretty much in original condition. Apparently we don't possess the renovation gene.'

She pushed the key into the lock and opened the door, as she heard Noah cry out. 'Mummy!'

Next minute he came shooting out from the front room and propelled himself right at Helen, wrapping his arms around her hips.

'Hello, sweetheart,' Helen said warmly, leaning down to hug him with her free arm. The nicest part by far about working was coming home to greetings like this. The door closed behind them and Helen remembered Myles. She turned halfway around. 'Noah, there's someone I'd like you to meet.'

Noah lifted his head to look, but of course the moment he spotted the tall figure of a man, he buried his face under Helen's jacket.

'Hi there, Noah,' said Myles.

'He does this for a while,' Helen said. 'He'll get over it soon enough.'

Myles smiled at her, but Helen thought she detected a shadow of apprehension in his eyes. So the man at the helm could get nervous like anyone else when he was out of his comfort zone. Helen found that a little endearing.

'Well, come on through,' she said, towing Noah along with her. When she arrived at the doorway into the kitchen, Gemma was standing expectantly between the table and the bench, clearly not knowing what to do with herself. Was everyone going to be weird about this?

'Hi, Helen!' Phoebe said brightly. At least she seemed okay, helped no doubt by the half-bottle of wine she'd already consumed.

'Phoebe, this is Myles,' said Helen.

'Nice to meet you, Phoebe,' he said, reaching over the table to shake her outstretched hand.

'You're the MD,' she remarked.

'Please, call me Myles.'

'I will indeed,' she said. 'As long as you call me Phoebe. I'm Gemma's sister, by the way,' she added.

'Oh, I didn't realise . . .' he said, a little awkwardly, glancing at Gemma.

'Hi.' She gave him a nod as she leaned back against the bench. It didn't seem right to call him MD out of the office. But she couldn't call him Myles . . . there was something not right about that either. Like calling a teacher by his first name. No matter how familiar you may have become, there are some lines that just shouldn't be crossed.

'Hello, Gemma,' Myles said politely. He was on her turf now, and Gemma sensed a certain level of discomfort. 'Thanks for having me . . .'

She was about to say, *Helen's the one having you*, but there was no way that was going to come out right. So she just said, 'Thanks for bringing the food.'

He nodded. Then everyone just stood where they were, looking around while trying to avoid making eye contact with anyone else.

'Let's start, shall we?' Helen suggested finally. 'Before it gets cold.'

The bustle that followed – fetching plates and cutlery and napkins, serving up the food, finding more glasses and pouring the wine – helped to mask the awkwardness for a time, but it soon began to creep back in once they were all seated at the table eating. After a few polite questions about how everyone's day had been generally, the dreaded seven-minute lull fell upon them.

Thank goodness Phoebe was already lubricated.

'So, Myles,' she said, 'how's the whole job-sharing thing working out?'

'I think it's working out really well,' he replied. 'But you'd better ask these two.'

Helen glanced across at Gemma, but she was looking directly, and rather pointedly, straight back at her, obviously expecting her to go first.

'Well,' Helen began, 'I feel like I've dived in at the deep end. But I guess I'm enjoying the challenge.'

'You're doing great,' Myles assured her. He looked back at Phoebe. 'She's a natural.'

'At advertising?' Gemma blurted. 'She doesn't even like it.'

'I'm aware of that,' Myles said calmly. 'But a certain level of cynicism is not such a bad thing in this industry. What I meant was, Helen's a natural PA. She has excellent organisational and communication skills, and she's extremely efficient, which is great for me.'

Gemma felt like a thirteen year old again, listening to her mother read out Ben's and Phoebe's school reports at the dinner table.

Helen just felt self-conscious. She was trying to think of something to say to shift the focus. But Noah beat her to it.

'What dat man doing here, Mummy?' he said suddenly. He'd eventually detached himself from his mother, but he was sitting with his chair as close to hers as he could get it, peering surreptitiously at Myles for much of the time.

'That man's name is Myles, Noah,' said Helen. 'And he's our guest.'

'What's guest, Mummy?'

'A guest is someone who comes to visit . . .' She hesitated, realising she didn't have a whole lot of examples to draw on. 'Like Nanna and Pop.'

'And Phoebe!' Noah declared.

'Yay me!' Phoebe smiled at him from across the table, raising her glass.

'Yes, Phoebe is our guest, and she's our friend as well,' said Helen.

'Is dat man our friend, Mummy?'

Helen glanced at Myles. 'Of course he's our friend, Noah,' she said. 'So you have to stop calling him "that man".'

'You can call me Myles if you like, Noah,' he said, which made Noah shrink back behind his mother's shoulder. 'Your mummy and I work together,' he went on, 'and so does Gemma.'

Oh, someone remembered she was here. Whoop-de-do. Just then there was a knock on the door. 'I'll get it,' said Gemma, pushing herself up from the table. Anything to get the hell away from this excruciating scene.

As she sauntered through the house the knock sounded again, a little louder this time. 'Coming!' Gemma sang out, intrigued as to who could be calling at dinnertime on a Friday night, unannounced and uninvited. Helen didn't appear to have a wide social circle. Gemma only hoped it wasn't the dreary in-laws. Imagine throwing them into the mix in there, as if they weren't struggling enough as it was.

Gemma opened the door. 'Charlie!' she cried. 'What are you doing here?'

He gave her a weak smile. 'You've been hounding me to come over . . .'

'I have, absolutely,' she said, looking past him. 'Did you bring Poppy?'

He shook his head. 'She had something on,' he said vaguely. 'So I thought I'd take the opportunity –'

'Come on in.' Gemma grabbed his arm and drew him inside. 'I'm so glad you're here, you have no idea.'

Just then they heard voices, and a short burst of laughter. Charlie peered down the hall, frowning. 'You have company?'

'Kind of,' said Gemma. 'But it's only my sister, and you'll never guess who else.'

He looked blankly at her.

'The MD,' she said, her eyes wide.

'Oh? What's he doing here?'

'Helen invited him. It was a last-minute thing, as far as I can tell.'

'Maybe I should go . . .'

'No way, buddy,' said Gemma, linking her arm through his. 'I need an ally.'

'What does that mean?' he said warily.

'Nothing,' she dismissed, leading him firmly down the hall. 'I'm just happy you're here, Charlie . . . Look who it is, everyone,' she declared as they got to the kitchen doorway.

'Hi, Charlie,' said Helen, getting to her feet.

Myles stood as well and the two men nodded and shook hands. 'How are you, Charlie?'

'Fine, thanks . . . MD,' said Charlie.

'Have you met my sister, Phoebe?' said Gemma.

'I think so . . .' he said vaguely.

Phoebe nodded. 'At the Opera Bar, remember? On that freezing night in July last year.'

'That's right.' He smiled, remembering. 'We were all huddled around one of those outdoor heaters trying to keep out of the rain.'

'But it didn't slow the drinking down.' Phoebe winked at him.

'Take a seat, Charlie,' Helen offered. 'Have you eaten?'

'Oh, I've interrupted your dinner . . .'

Everyone tripped over their tongues in an attempt to assure Charlie he had not interrupted anything and besides there was more than enough food. As they all settled back down again, Gemma put a beer in front of him, remembering he wasn't much of a wine drinker.

'Where's Noah?' Charlie asked.

'Here I am,' he exclaimed, popping out from behind his mother.

'Hey, Noah, how's it going?' said Charlie, leaning over to high-five him, which Noah responded to enthusiastically. 'How are those crazy Wastelander dudes?'

'They's good.' He nodded, smiling broadly.

'Who's your favourite, Noah?' Myles asked. 'I like Damas best.'

Every head turned to look at him, but Myles remained focused on Noah, whose curiosity began to get the better of him.

'I don't haff him,' said Noah, his eyes widening. 'But I haff Yangus.'

'And what about Spargus and the Leaper Lizard?' Myles asked.

Noah's face lit up. 'No, but I haff Daxter and Krondor and Flut-Flut,' he exclaimed.

'You have Flut-Flut?' said Myles, impressed. 'Wow, can I see?'

Noah nodded furiously, making a dash for the door. As he went to go through, he looked back at Myles. 'Hey, you haffa come too, Myers.'

'Noah –' Helen went to protest but Myles caught her eye, shaking his head.

'It's fine.' He got up from the table. 'Excuse me, everyone, I have to go and meet Flut-Flut,' he said as Noah grabbed his hand and led him away.

The rest of them sat in silent bemusement for a moment till Gemma finally spoke. 'What the hell was that all about?'

'He sure knows his Wastelanders,' Charlie said.

'Does he have kids?' Phoebe asked.

'No,' said Helen.

'Are you sure?' said Gemma. 'I know he's not married, but –'

'He's never been married, and he doesn't have any children,' Helen said firmly. 'Though he came close once. To getting married, that is.'

'How do you know all this?' said Gemma.

'A little thing called rapport,' Charlie suggested.

Gemma pulled a face at him. 'Who asked you?'

'Look, we talk.' Helen shrugged. 'It's not that big a deal.'

'Then why did you ask him back tonight?' Gemma persisted, raising an accusing eyebrow.

'To be friendly,' she said. 'He doesn't know anyone in Sydney.'

'Except for a couple of hundred staff at Bailey's,' Gemma pointed out.

'Oh sure, and look at the way everyone treats him, like he's the school principal or something.'

'Well if he didn't walk around like he's got something stuck up his arse –'

'Gemma!' Helen jumped up and poked her head around the doorway to make sure Myles was out of earshot. 'Keep your voice down. The man's a guest in our house.'

'I didn't invite him,' Gemma said grumpily.

'Well, I like him,' Phoebe declared. 'And he's a lot better looking than you made out, Gem.'

'You reckon?' Gemma glanced around for confirmation.

Helen avoided eye contact so she couldn't be drawn on the subject, it would only incriminate her.

'Charlie?' Gemma prompted.

'What?'

'Do you reckon the MD's good-looking?'

'You know you can't ask a guy that,' he said.

'Well, he is,' said Phoebe. 'And he seems nice as well.'

'He is, he's very nice,' said Helen. 'He's one of the best bosses I've ever worked for. He's kind and fair, and incredibly supportive. And he's a lot more sensitive than you realise, Gemma. He knows the effect he has on people just because he's the boss, and he can't do anything about it. But he's completely approachable and very easy to get along –'

Helen stopped suddenly. She looked across the table at the three faces staring back at her. Gemma looked sceptical, Charlie looked mildly amused, and Phoebe looked as pleased as punch as she gave Helen a suggestive wink.

'I have to put Noah to bed,' Helen said quickly, leaving the kitchen, along with their conjectures.

When she walked into Noah's room Myles was sitting on the floor with rows of toy figures lined up around him.

'Do I haffa go to bed yet, Mummy?' Noah blurted the moment he saw her.

'You have to start getting ready at least, Noah,' she said.

'But I wanna play wif Myers.'

Myles started to get up. 'Hey, Noah, we can play another time.'

'But when?' he wanted to know, plaintively.

Myles glanced at Helen. 'Very soon,' she said. 'Now, you'd better start packing up, Noah.'

'I don't wanna, Mummy, I wanna play wif Myers.'

'Come on,' said Myles, still on his knees. 'I'll give you a hand. Let's see how fast we can put everything away.'

With a little giggling and shrieking the toys were packed up and Noah seemed placated for now.

'Start getting changed into your pyjamas, Noah,' said Helen. 'I'll be back in a sec to help you.'

'Bye, Noah,' said Myles. 'See you next time.'

'Promise?' he said, staring straight up at him.

Myles nodded, ruffling his hair affectionately. 'I promise.'

'Bye bye, Myers,' Noah said longingly as they left the room.

'Well, you certainly made an impression, *Myers*,' Helen smiled, out in the hall.

'Fine judge of character, your son,' said Myles. 'But really, he's a great kid, you must be really proud, Helen.'

'Thank you, I am,' she said. 'Anyhow, you deserve another drink. I'll see you back out there as soon as I get him to bed.'

Myles looked uneasy. 'Actually, Helen, I think I might head off.'

'Why?'

He hesitated. 'It's getting late . . .'

Helen folded her arms. 'I'm just putting my four year old to bed,' she said. 'It's not late, Myles. Where's your much-prized honesty now?'

He sighed heavily. 'I just make everyone uncomfortable.'

'That's not true,' Helen protested. 'Phoebe really likes you.'

'So you were talking about me?' said Myles.

She shrugged. 'Your name might have come up.'

He lifted an eyebrow. 'And what did Gemma have to say?'

Helen was trying to remember anything Gemma had said that she could share with him.

'It's okay, Helen,' Myles said eventually. 'Gemma and I have a . . . difficult relationship. She shouldn't have to feel uncomfortable in her own home.'

'Well, it's not her home,' said Helen, feeling herself getting annoyed, and feeling herself getting even more annoyed because she was getting annoyed. 'I mean, it is, but it's my home too, and I invited you, and you shouldn't feel you have to go because she's being rude.'

'Helen –'

'Just don't go yet,' she said. 'Wait till I'm finished with Noah. Please?'

'Okay,' he relented.

'See you in ten,' she said, slipping back into Noah's room.

When she rejoined them in the kitchen, things seemed marginally more relaxed, probably due to the increase in the collective consumption of alcohol. Phoebe had the floor, and the highest blood-alcohol level, and she was chewing Myles's ear about the vagaries of a career in corporate law. It was time to rescue him, Helen decided.

'Are you ready to go, Myles?' she said.

He looked up at her, a little confused. Helen realised that probably sounded like she was kicking him out.

'Myles and I are going for a walk,' she said, clarifying it for him. 'Is that all right with you, Gemma? Noah's all tucked up in bed, you won't hear from him again.' She walked around the table as she spoke, collecting a couple of glasses and an open bottle of wine.

Gemma looked a little stunned, but eventually she stirred. 'Oh, sure, no problem. You kids go and have fun.'

Helen stopped in the doorway, looking at Myles. 'Ready?'

He nodded, getting to his feet. 'Ah, thanks, thanks again for having me, Gemma. Good to see you, Charlie, nice to meet you, Phoebe.' He seemed to be ticking off a list. 'Have a good weekend, everyone.'

Silence fell around the table until they heard the front door open, and finally close again.

'Woohoo,' Phoebe exclaimed, refilling her glass. 'Looks like things are hotting up in the old town tonight. Do you think they're going for a pash?'

Gemma frowned in distaste at her sister. 'Who even says "pash" any more, Phoebe? You're not fourteen.'

Phoebe considered her sister through half-closed eyes. 'Do you think something really weird has gone on with us since you got pregnant?'

'What are you talking about?'

'Well, you've gone all resplect . . . respectabable . . . you know, boring, and I'm the one sculling wine and talking about pashing. Maybe your dark side had to vacate your body because of the baby, and it came into me.'

Charlie laughed, but Gemma rolled her eyes.

'Well, good luck to Helen and Myles,' said Charlie. 'Whatever they're getting up to.'

'They won't be getting up to anything,' Gemma insisted. 'You haven't heard the way Helen talks, Charlie – she says she's still married.'

'What? Didn't her husband get hit . . .'

Phoebe did a repeat performance of her mime of a bus hitting someone, again with accompanying repugnant sound effects.

Charlie watched her, grimacing. 'That's in really poor taste.'

'Blame my evil twin,' she said, cocking her head towards Gemma.

'What do you mean, she says she's still married?' Charlie said.

'That's how she talks about it,' Gemma tried to explain. 'He might be dead, but nothing happened to her, so she's still his wife.'

Charlie was thoughtful. 'She's probably just trying to describe how she feels.'

Gemma shook her head. 'She won't even consider going on a date. A perfectly nice man she met through Noah's preschool asked her out and she flatly refused.'

Charlie shrugged. 'Maybe she's just not ready.'

'Problem is,' said Gemma, 'it's only going to get harder. And in the meantime, her husband's never going to age, get a gut or lose his hair, she's never going to have another fight with him, he's never going to piss her off for leaving the seat up, whatever. He's going to be pretty stiff competition for any poor bloke who comes along.'

Phoebe was nodding. 'Just like James Dean,' she said profoundly.

'What?' Gemma frowned.

'James Dean is forever young, forever cool,' Phoebe explained. 'But if he hadn't died, for all we know he could have ended up like Marlon Brando – sad, fat and totally weird.'

Gemma was nodding. 'Marilyn Monroe died, tragic but beautiful.'

'Elizabeth Taylor lived on,' said Phoebe. 'Sad, fat and weird.'

'Princess Diana –'

'No, stop there,' said Charlie.

Phoebe and Gemma both looked at him.

'Not Princess Diana,' he said seriously. 'She would have been beautiful no matter how long she lived.'

Gemma grinned. 'Why Charlie, I didn't realise you were a Diana-phile.'

'I don't want to talk about it,' he said firmly. 'It disrespects her memory.'

Phoebe made a snorting sound. 'Please tell me you don't have a collection of plates and tea towels at home.'

'Anyway,' said Gemma, getting back to the point. 'Helen's not over her husband, and if she's wandering into the bushes with the MD and a bottle of wine, he would have every reason to expect . . . something to happen. She's leading him on.'

'You're not suggesting she's doing it on purpose?' Charlie said dubiously.

'Who knows?' Gemma said. 'I mean, ever since she tripped into Bailey's, I've been shafted. After I did her a favour getting her the job in the first place.'

'I thought she was the one doing *you* a favour?' Charlie reminded her.

'Whatever, she's certainly manipulating it to her advantage now.'

'Oh, come on, Gem, Helen's not like that,' said Phoebe. 'She couldn't manipulate her way out of a paper bag.'

'So you say, but honestly, I'm beginning to worry I won't get my job back after I have the baby. Then what am I going to do?'

'I don't think you should worry about that,' said Charlie. 'I agree with Phoebe – Helen wouldn't do that to you.'

'But Myles would,' said Gemma. 'You didn't hear the way he was going on about her before you got here, Charlie. He's obviously smitten, and he feels sorry for her losing her husband. That's a heady mix. When men start thinking with their dicks, everything else goes out the window.' She looked glum. 'I thought there were supposed to be rules about not fraternising in the workplace?'

'It's not the fifties, Gem,' said Phoebe. 'These days if you don't fraternise at work, where else are you going to do it?' She stopped for a minute to focus on pouring wine into her glass. 'Besides, if what you say is true and Helen's not ready, nothing's going to happen anyway.'

*

Helen and Myles walked at a leisurely pace through the narrow back streets down towards the water.

'How do you know so much about the Wastelanders?' Helen asked him. 'Do Bailey's handle the account or something?'

Myles shook his head. 'I have nephews.'

'Oh? How many?'

'Five all up.'

'Five?' Helen exclaimed. 'Any nieces?'

He smiled. 'No, all boys. Runs in the family – I was one of three boys as well.'

'Where do you come?'

'I'm the youngest, then there's Rupert, and Hugo's the eldest.'

Helen considered him. 'I hope you don't mind me saying . . .'

Myles looked down at her. 'Go ahead.'

'They're very fancy-pants names. Did you grow up with a silver spoon in your mouth, Mr Davenport?'

Myles laughed, shaking his head. 'More like plastic. We grew up in St Kilda. It was a rough place back then, especially if you had a "fancy-pants" name. Poor old Rupe got it the worst. And he had such a temper, he used to fly off at anyone who so much as looked at him sideways.'

Helen veered Myles to the left, down a set of steps that ran between the houses.

'My mother came from England,' Myles went on. 'I don't think she had fully acclimatised to Australia when she had us. She didn't realise that if she'd named us Mick, Bob and Pete we would have got off a lot easier.'

'Was your father English as well?'

Myles shook his head. 'They met when he was backpacking around Europe, fell madly in love, and my mother disgraced the family by running off to the colonies with a no-hoper, as far as they were concerned. They were very upper class, her father was an earl.'

'Fancy-pants after all?' Helen said.

'They never had anything to do with us. They disowned my mother, cut her off completely. But that was okay with her. She hated the whole class system and was glad to get away from it. She certainly didn't want her kids to have any part of it.'

They came to a tiny patch of green edging the harbour. It could barely be called a park, but the view was stunning, looking straight across the water to the city.

'What a great little spot,' said Myles.

'My brother and I used to come down here when we were kids. The ferry wharf's just a little further up,' said Helen, pointing it out for Myles. 'We'd go fishing, bring jam sandwiches and cordial in a flask . . .'

And they'd talk, Helen remembered, for hours on end. Tony was a great storyteller, and as they grew older he'd told her about all the places they were going to travel. He brought her down here for her first illicit taste of alcohol, and her first puff of a cigarette, both of which made her sick. They lay on the grass under the shade, poring over Lonely Planet guides, while he made his plans to travel through Asia, Europe and finally to London. Helen had only one year left at school and she was going to follow him, meet up wherever he'd made it to by then. She was already saving from her after-school job at the local supermarket.

'There's only the two of you?' Myles was asking.

Helen nodded. 'Tony, but he lives in England now.' She turned around. 'Do you want to sit for a while?'

'Sure.'

They walked over to a bench and sat down. Helen passed Myles the wineglasses, and he held them while she poured.

Myles held his glass up. 'What shall we drink to?'

Helen thought about it. 'Let's drink to your mother. She sounds pretty great.'

'She was,' he agreed, clinking his glass with Helen's.

'What about your father?' she asked.

He shrugged. 'I never knew him – he took off after I was born. Turns out Mum's family were right, he was a no-hoper. He drank too much, he couldn't hold down a job, he just wasn't up to the responsibility of a family. So my mother was left to bring us up on her own. No help, nothing from her family of course, and my father's family were all interstate. Besides, they liked to pretend we didn't exist so they didn't have to feel any responsibility either.'

'Bringing up three boys on her own, that couldn't have been easy.'

'No, but my mother was an amazing woman. She was incredibly resourceful, considering she'd had such a privileged upbringing. She took us to the library religiously, read to us until we were old enough to read ourselves, made sure we covered all the classics that they weren't teaching us at school. She took us to art galleries, museums, anything we could get into for free. She loved festivals, concerts in the park, experimental theatre, weird performance art. She encouraged us to be open to everything.'

Myles paused, remembering. 'In the school holidays she'd plan these excursions, pack us off with a picnic lunch to find an Aboriginal site on the outskirts of the city, or some other historical place that she'd researched.' He stared wistfully out across the water. 'She was insatiable. She had a wonderful mind that she never really got to use, at least not for a career of her own. She said we boys were her life's work, her greatest achievement.'

Helen was watching him. She hadn't failed to notice that he only referred to his mother in the past tense.

'Listen to me,' Myles said suddenly. 'I'm making her sound like some kind of saint, and making myself sound like a bit of a nancy boy.' He paused. 'A fancy-pants nancy boy even.'

Helen gave him a faint smile. 'What happened to her?' she asked carefully.

Myles took a breath. 'She died just after I was accepted into uni, once she knew I was all set with a scholarship. Hugo had already graduated, Rupe was up at the Conservatorium in Sydney. She collapsed the first time just as I finished my final school exams. Breast cancer. The doctors said it was so advanced they couldn't do anything, and Mum didn't want chemo to prolong her life; she knew that would only make her sicker for longer and we'd have to look after her. She must have been having symptoms for a long time, but she never complained, never stopped, and never did anything about it. She just wanted to see us through. She died eight weeks after she was diagnosed.'

'She really was a saint,' Helen said quietly.

Myles didn't respond, only stared out at the water.

'So was your mother's illness the reason you went into medicine?' Helen asked after a while.

He looked at her then. 'And the reason I quit. After she died, I did one semester of the arts/law degree I was enrolled in, but I wasn't committed anymore. I decided I had to do something to help people. I think I had ideas of saving everyone else's mother. But it was so hard, I couldn't handle it,' he said, shaking his head. 'You don't cure many people in medicine, you just treat them, make them comfortable. I suppose you'd know that. Anyway, I think I had some kind of minor breakdown. I went to Tasmania to stay with Hugo for a while – he has a property down there – took some time out to decide what I wanted to do.'

'And you came up with business management? That's quite a leap.'

'That was the point. I wanted to deal with problems that could be fixed. But it's never that simple. There are always people involved, and they get affected by the decisions you make, sometimes for the worse. I've tried to avoid that, find solutions that work for everybody, but the responsibility feels overwhelming at times.'

Helen sipped her wine, thinking. No wonder he went around with the weight of the world on his shoulders.

'Okay, that's my quota,' Myles said suddenly. 'You let me talk too much, Helen. You really need to yawn occasionally so I know when I'm boring you.'

She smiled. 'But you see, you weren't boring me.'

'Hmm,' he said doubtfully. 'So what about you? You said your brother's in England. Are your parents around?'

Helen hesitated. 'My father passed away, but my mother's still alive. She's in a nursing home, special care . . . she has Alzheimer's.'

Myles shifted on the bench so he was turned towards her. 'Oh, I'm sorry, Helen. That must be hard.'

She shrugged. 'It can be.'

'Does your mother recognise you anymore?'

Sometimes the truth hit Helen like a harsh blow. She swallowed. 'No, not so much these days.'

'That'd be the worst part, I imagine,' he said gently. 'Were you close?'

Helen had to think about how to answer that. 'You know, mothers and daughters have particular issues,' she began. 'I was going through my teens while she was going through depression after my father died. Eventually she was diagnosed with Alzheimer's, so I suppose we never got to work through some of those mother–daughter issues.' Helen frowned, shaking her head. 'Listen to me, babbling away, I don't know what I'm saying.'

'I think you're trying to say that you didn't get on so well with your mum,' said Myles. 'That's not a crime, Helen.'

'We're just different, I guess.' She shrugged. 'We look alike, but that's where the similarity ends. Mum was very . . . out there. She had to be the centre of attention all the time, needed constant affirmation that she was attractive and desirable. My dad obliged, till his demons got the better of him.'

'What do you mean?'

Helen felt a faint twist in her heart. She wasn't ready to tell Myles everything. 'Oh, he kind of withdrew in the years before he died . . . Anyway, Mum was very close to my brother, but when he went away, and my dad was gone, she lost it completely.'

'Alzheimer's is an actual physiological disease, though, isn't it?'

'Yes, you're right, it is. But just like your mother was able to hold on to see you through, I wonder if my mother didn't let go once she felt she'd lost everything.'

'She still had you.'

'Mm, that wasn't much comfort apparently.'

Life was full of perverse ironies, it occurred to Helen. It was almost cruel. There was Myles's mother, so full of life, living for her sons, enjoying every last moment with them. And there was her mother, her life stuck on pause while she pined for those who weren't around any more. And David's life had been snatched from him with no warning at all, and he'd had so little time with his son. What would have become of their relationship as Noah grew older? What if he'd made choices David didn't approve of, as David had with his father? She wondered if he would have been any more flexible than Jim, really.

'Tell me something positive,' Helen said suddenly.

'Pardon?'

'It's getting too depressing. Tell me something uplifting. Your brothers, are they happy? Well? Successful?'

He smiled. 'Yes to all three. Hugo's an artist, living a very idyllic life on his farm in Tasmania, with a wonderful partner and three terrific boys. And Rupe's settled down now, after a rough start. He was hit hard by Mum's death, went feral for a few years, dropped out of the Conservatorium, got into drugs –'

'I want to hear positive,' Helen reminded him.

Myles nodded. 'I'm getting to it. He had a son during that time, and they've managed to reconnect in the last few years. He's in a band that's doing all right, they play alternative, blues . . . I don't know what you call it, but they sound good. And he finally found a woman who can handle him. They had a little boy together last year.'

Helen held her glass up to Myles. 'Here's to your brothers.'

'To all our brothers,' said Myles, clinking her glass. 'How long has it been since you've seen . . . was it Tony?'

She thought about it. 'I think the last time would have been when Noah was born. It was a flying visit though. It's difficult in his line of work, it can be very unpredictable.'

'What does he do?'

'He originally went over to break into theatre directing.'

'Tough field.'

Helen nodded. 'He stage manages mostly, though he's been a director's assistant on a few productions.'

'And you never thought of going over to see him this whole time?'

'Sure I did,' she said. 'I was supposed to follow him over after I left school.'

'What happened?'

'I couldn't leave Mum,' Helen said simply. She drained her glass and held up the bottle. It was empty. 'I think that might be our cue to go back,' she announced.

As they walked through the streets back to her place, Helen realised she was relieved Myles hadn't raised the subject of Noah's father again. She'd find it a lot harder to lie to him now, though she couldn't help thinking it was a little odd as well, now that he'd actually met Noah. She supposed he'd got the hint the first time and he was respecting her privacy, and she did appreciate that. She liked the ease that had developed between them, she didn't want Myles to start looking at her differently, with pity in his eyes.

'Would you like to come in for coffee?' she asked as they approached her house.

Myles shook his head. 'Thanks, but I should really get going this time.'

'Are you sure? Don't you want to come in and call a taxi at least?'

He took his phone out of his pocket. 'No need. Besides, I'm sure I'll grab one easily up on the main road.' He stopped outside her gate and turned to face her. 'I had a really good time tonight, Helen. Thanks for inviting me.'

She felt his hand slip into hers, and she had a sudden, terrifying thought that he might try to kiss her. She dropped her eyes and took a quick step back, but he just gave her hand a gentle squeeze before releasing it. When she looked up again he was walking backwards away from her.

'Good night, Helen. See you next week.'

She watched him as he turned and walked up the street, and suppressed the small but nagging pang of something that could only be described as disappointment rising in her chest.

Monday

Myles arrived in the office about an hour after Gemma, though as usual he'd already been to two meetings.

He paused at her desk. 'Hi, Gemma, did you have a good weekend?'

Oh great, now he decides he wants to be friends.

'Yes, thanks,' she returned. 'Quiet, I get pretty tired these days.'

He nodded. 'Did you finish up late on Friday night?'

Gemma sighed. Could he *be* more transparent? He obviously only wanted to ask after Helen. 'Helen went almost straight to bed after she came back from your walk,' Gemma reported. And not that he was really interested, but – 'I was tired too, so Charlie was kind enough to escort my sister home. She was in need of supervision.'

Myles gave her a faint smile. 'Do you like living there?' he asked.

She thought for a moment. Of course she did. Whatever was going on with Helen now, she couldn't want for a better housemate. 'Yes, I like living there very much,' she said. 'Helen's been really good to me, and she's a very easy person to live with.'

'I can imagine.'

'Very private, mind you,' Gemma added.

'Yeah, I get that,' Myles said, perching on the edge of her desk. 'She still hasn't told me about her husband.'

'And you haven't said anything, I hope?'

He shook his head. 'I told you I'd wait for her to bring it up. I just wish she felt she could open up to me,' he said wistfully.

Dear God, Gemma groaned inwardly. Did she really have to sit here and listen to his lovestruck angst?

'The thing is, she's not over it,' Gemma said bluntly. 'Nowhere near.'

Myles looked at her directly. 'You don't think so?'

'I know so,' said Gemma. 'Believe me.'

He looked thoughtful as he stood up again. 'Oh, that's right, I wanted to ask you, Gemma, is it okay if Helen works on Wednesday instead of you?'

'Pardon?' she croaked.

'Just for this week,' he added. 'Though you might want to think about gradually reducing your days over the next few weeks – you haven't got long to go, have you? And you said you're getting tired.'

She was about to snap, *That's none of your business*, till she remembered that it was entirely his business. Bugger.

'May I ask what's happening on Wednesday?' Gemma resumed, trying to keep her cool.

'There's a meeting I want Helen to be part of. It doesn't concern you, it's a project I'm just getting up and running, and you'll be off on maternity leave. So I thought if Helen could work on Wednesday . . .'

'It's all right with me,' said Gemma, trying to sound offhand. 'But I don't know how Helen's going to feel about it. Noah's only in preschool on Thursday and Friday.'

'I realise that. But after you have the baby, you're going to be looking after Noah then, isn't that the arrangement?'

'Yes,' she admitted warily. The finer details had never really been ironed out, and lately Gemma had been growing increasingly worried about how on earth she was going to look after a new baby as well as a four year old. Noah was a good kid, easy, but she didn't think the baby was going to be so easy. She was well aware that women did it all the time, but they had experience by the time they had to juggle two. She might manage after a while, after she'd got used to the baby, but what would they do about Noah in the meantime? Gemma knew it had been her idea in the first place, but lately she was getting the feeling it was all going to blow up in her face.

'Gemma? Is everything all right?' Myles prompted, leaning over her desk to get her attention.

She stirred. 'Yep. Everything's under control. I'll let Helen know about Wednesday.'

'Sure, you two talk about it,' he said. 'But I'm about to give her a call now anyway – I have some things I want to go over with her. I'll let her know that it's okay with you.'

Wednesday

'I don't get it,' said Justin, raising his arm a little as he let the sheet of paper he was holding slide from his hand, free-falling back to the table.

Every account team leader had been called to the meeting this morning in the boardroom, but none of them had been told what it was about. Myles and Helen had been working on the proposal since Monday, tossing it back and forth over the phone and via email. Helen had needed persuading initially – this was getting a little too close to the coalface for comfort.

'You know how I feel about advertising, Myles,' she'd tried to tell him.

'But it was your idea, Helen.'

'Not intentionally,' she'd declared.

'That's what makes it so good,' he'd said, 'and why I want you in on it from the beginning.'

'I don't understand. Why do you even want to get involved at this level? You're the managing director.'

'My role is to improve the efficiency of the business, and this is one way I believe I can do that. Look, I'm not going to run any campaigns, I only want to get them thinking.'

They knew Justin would be the first person to object; they could have placed odds on it.

'What don't you get, Justin?' Myles asked.

'"I buy it because . . ."?' Justin almost sneered, though not quite, he was too shrewd for that. 'I don't get it.'

'What's not to get, Justin?' Myles restated, displaying admirable restraint, Helen felt. She'd never really taken to Justin. He was the type of ad exec that gave ad execs a bad name.

'You want to mount an entire campaign with the catch cry "I buy it because"?' said Justin. 'I hate to break it to you, MD, but it's been done before.'

'Not exactly like this.'

'Close enough,' he shot back. 'I don't get what the big deal is.'

Myles cleared his throat. 'I think you're all aware that for some time I've been less than delirious about some of the self-referential, arthouse stuff we've been churning out here at Bailey's. If you'll look through the notes provided in the folders in front of you –' Myles paused, waiting for everyone to catch up. He looked directly at Justin. 'Do you need Helen to help you find it, Justin?'

Justin sniffed, opening up his folder.

'If you turn over to page four,' Myles went on, 'you'll find listed some very interesting figures. These campaigns are not achieving what they set out to do. They are, simply put, not hitting the mark.'

'Excuse me, MD?'

'Yes, Deb?'

'You've blacklisted the Pearson campaign. You do realise it won the Silver World Medal in New York last year?'

'Precisely my point, Deb,' said Myles. 'Look at the stats for product recognition, product recall, sales on the back of the campaign. This was an ad that won arguably advertising's highest honour, but it was a failure in the marketplace.'

'The same could be said for a lot of films that fail at the box office, MD,' said Lewis, possibly one of the stupidest executives on staff. Helen marvelled at how he had got to where he was, and, even more, how he managed to stay there. 'I mean, they get critical acclaim, they get Academy Awards, but no one goes to see them. Doesn't mean they're not good films.'

'No it doesn't,' Myles said, his frustration beginning to show. 'But we're not in the film industry, Lewis, that's the whole thing. We're not in the business of making art, yet we're trying to sell stuff to people in an overcrowded marketplace by being obscure and clever and arty. It's not working. Concept advertising was a turn-of-the-century buzzword. Its time has passed. People are cynical and tired, and so overloaded with information they can't see straight. They don't trust anyone, not the government, not police or teachers or doctors, and certainly not people trying to sell them something from behind a smokescreen. I believe if we turn it around and talk straight, using their language, we might just have a chance of getting through to them.'

'I disagree,' said Justin.

No surprises there.

'Which part do you disagree with, Justin?'

'Your basic premise,' he said flatly. 'People don't want plain speaking. They don't care about the truth. What they want is to believe they're special, they deserve the best, because they're worth it. They want luxury, they want prestige brands. That's the direction all the international agencies are taking. Did you know you can even do a masters degree in luxury goods management in the UK?'

Myles had been waiting patiently for Justin to finish his spiel. 'That's all very enlightening, Justin, but it's only one side of the coin,' he said. 'Last week I asked Helen how she chooses toilet paper, for example.'

Every face at the table turned towards Helen, whose own face was like a hot pink beacon, she was sure, shining for all to see.

'Do you want to tell them what you told me, Helen?'

No, she didn't. Couldn't he see that?

Myles lifted an eyebrow, waiting.

Helen cleared her throat and sat forward in her chair. She took a deep breath. 'I said I buy it because it's cheap but not nasty . . .' She glanced down at the introductory sheet for the meeting, where Myles had reproduced her words, verbatim, from the week before. 'And I buy two-ply because one-ply is false economy – you just use twice as much. And, most importantly, I buy it because it's made from recycled paper; it's a crime to use anything else when you're only going to flush it down the toilet.'

Justin stifled a yawn.

'Helen also told me that she's not interested in having her toilet paper feeling like silk,' said Myles. 'But perhaps some people are, like the ones you were talking about, Justin, who want luxury. I don't know. I don't know what people really think, and I'd warrant you don't know either.'

'This is bullshit, MD,' said Justin, shaking his head. 'Of course we know what people think, what they want, what they're going to respond to. Don't you know what a focus group is for, what market researchers do?'

Helen noticed Myles's jaw clench. 'Yes, Justin, I know all about market research, and especially focus groups. And I know how they operate. People are brought into an artificial situation, they're often paid a fee, or at the very least given a nice lunch. Then words and phrases and images are presented to them in a highly contrived and very carefully controlled manner. There is a science to it, and I appreciate that it provides marketers with certain kinds of information. But you're not getting the way people really talk, what they really think when they're reaching for the product on the shelf at the supermarket. And, most importantly, what they might say about it at the dinner table that evening, or when they're having coffee with their girlfriends, or over the fence to a neighbour. Yet what is the best marketing tool by far?'

Myles paused, looking around the table. No one was willing to hazard a guess.

'Word of mouth,' he said simply. 'Everyone knows that until you get good word of mouth going, it doesn't matter how much money you throw at marketing, it won't matter a jot.'

'MD,' Julia broke in, leaning forward on the table, 'isn't there a risk that we'll just end up with something like those cringy ads with celebrities sitting around talking about headache tablets?'

Deb laughed. 'Yeah, which actor is it rolling around on the floor with his kid? Like he ever gets up in the middle of the night . . .'

'Okay,' said Myles. 'Stop for a sec and listen to what you're saying. Those ads are "cringy", Julia, because we don't believe them. And why don't we believe them? Because they're celebrities and they're falling over themselves to gush about the product.'

'So now you're suggesting that celebrity endorsement doesn't work?' Justin said, barely containing his contempt.

'Celebrity endorsement works fine when they act like celebrities, not when they pretend they're just like the rest of us.' Myles took a breath. 'I'd like to see honest endorsements from ordinary people who pay for the products out of an ordinary wage. Take Helen's toilet paper spiel. It's a straight list of facts that's meaningful to a consumer, but it isn't dry or scientific, nor does it make out that the brand of toilet paper has changed her life. It shows Helen is intelligent and thoughtful, and not easily duped. I would suggest that's how most consumers would like to be treated.'

He gave everyone some time to absorb that while he took a sip of water.

'So what do you want us to do, MD?' asked Julia.

'I would like you to go back and look closely at upcoming campaigns, not anything that's in development already, and see if there aren't some that would work with this approach. I realise this won't suit every product, and I'm also not suggesting it can't be done with some creativity, some wit, some flair. In fact, obviously, I'd encourage it. But I want "I buy it because" to be the philosophy that drives a series of campaigns in the coming months.'

Everyone was jotting notes while he spoke. Everyone except Justin.

'Okay,' said Myles, checking his watch. 'That's enough for today. I'd like each one of you to report back, most likely the same time next week, but Helen will confirm that. I want at least one suitable test case from each team.'

'What if we don't believe any of our accounts are suited to this particular approach?' said Justin.

'Well, Justin, if you don't think you're up to the task –'

'That's not what I said.'

'What you did say earlier, however, was that you already know what people are going to respond to,' said Myles. 'But if that's true, how come your last campaign failed spectacularly and you lost the account for the agency?' He paused, allowing Justin to feel the full weight of his rancour. 'I think if you look real hard, Justin, you might find something suitable. If not, then write me a detailed report on each and every one of your team's accounts, outlining your argument. And have it on my desk twenty-four hours before the meeting next week.'

Justin stormed rather petulantly from the room, while the others followed without the histrionics. When they were eventually alone, Myles looked across at Helen. He didn't need to ask the question.

'You sold it to me,' she said.

He smiled. 'I think I might have had you on side already.' He pushed back against his chair and stretched his arms out above his head, sighing loudly. Then he dropped his arms again and looked at Helen. 'Come on, I'm taking you to lunch. We've earned it.'

He got to his feet and began gathering up the papers in front of him. After a while he glanced over at Helen. She hadn't moved; she appeared to be deep in thought.

'What's wrong?' he asked.

She stirred, looking at him. 'Oh, sorry. It was just, well, it was about lunch.'

He frowned. 'You're not going to argue with me, are you? I've had enough arguing for one day.'

'No,' said Helen. 'I was just going to suggest . . .'

'What?'

'Well, can we go somewhere a bit less . . . you know . . .?'

Myles was looking at her, intrigued.

'I always feel so intimidated in those swanky restaurants,' she tried to explain. 'I mean, the food's gorgeous, everything's gorgeous, but I just feel like I shouldn't be there. Couldn't we maybe get a sandwich down at the Quay, sit in the sun?'

He smiled broadly. 'I can't think of anything I'd rather do.'

A week later

'What do you want for lunch, Noah?' Gemma called from the kitchen as she peered into the refrigerator. She had an inexplicable hankering for McDonald's, which she would have loved to put down to serious cravings as an excuse to take Noah there for lunch, but Helen would never fall for it, and besides, there was no McDonald's in Balmain. Naturally.

Gemma felt bone tired, and it was barely noon. So much for the glowing middle months of pregnancy; they had been rather short-lived. Now she had sporadic indigestion, a feckless bladder, and other indiscriminate aches and pains, all serving to make a sound night's sleep almost impossible. Sometimes Gemma felt as though she and the baby were fighting it out for domination of her body, and the baby was winning.

But that wasn't the only competition going on. Every woman she met who had ever given birth felt duty-bound to disclose the worst of their experiences: nasty ailments, gruesome labours, and the dark, awful epoch of baby's first few months of life. 'You think it's hard now, just wait until . . .' was their favourite refrain. Gemma frequently had the urge to tell them to shut the fuck up. But that would never do. Pregnant women were supposed to be serene and Madonna-like. Not so much the all-singing, all-dancing, weirdly never-ageing Madonna, but the sitting-dreamily-in-a-white-flowing-caftan-listening-to-Mozart Madonna.

'Wait till you get to the last few weeks,' Trish had confided only this morning. 'You'll barely be able to walk if you end up anywhere near as big as I was.'

Her mother had already been and gone. Perhaps that was why Gemma was feeling sapped. Trish had so much energy she sucked the life out of any room she walked into. She had arranged to meet the blind and curtain man here at eight thirty, but at that time of the morning Gemma could no sooner focus on styles and colours than fly to the moon. So Trish took over, no surprise. She got on the phone to Helen and fast-talked her into whatever it was she wanted in the first place, and the deal was done. The blind and curtain man went on his way, and so did Trish. She'd been running late for coffee with Wendy Whatsit, before whizzing up to the most divine little place in Newport where she'd seen a darling lamp in this month's edition of *Belle* that would be utterly perfect for the baby's room, and then she had to fly back for lunch at Meredith McWhosit's, making sure she left in time for her hairdresser's appointment before dinner out with Mr and Mrs Who-the-Hell-Cared-Anymore? Gemma never ceased to be amazed that one woman could be so busy for so long with so little.

'Noah?' Gemma called again, the tail-end of his name morphing into a giant yawn. She was going to have to take a nap after lunch. If she curled up on the couch and put a DVD on for Noah, that would not be considered leaving the child unattended, would it? She was not sure Helen would approve, but then again, Helen was not here. Helen was slowly but surely stealing her job away. Myles had suggested that she might as well keep Wednesdays up now that she'd started, make it a nice gradual transition. Hmph, more like a coup by stealth.

Just then the baby gave her a sharp kick in the ribs. 'Ow, what was that for?' She winced. 'Don't tell me you're on her side too?'

Gemma heard a knock on the door at the same time as Noah appeared wide-eyed in the doorway.

'Gemma, Gemma!' he cried. 'Sum'n's atta door, you haffa hurry!'

'All right, Noah,' she said. He was always so urgent whenever someone was at the door. Gemma ambled through the house to the front hall as Noah scampered around her like an excited puppy, ducking in behind her just as she reached the door, and peeking around as she opened it.

'Nanna! Poppeeee!' he squealed with delight before Gemma's brain had even registered who they were. Oh great. She wasn't going to have to entertain them until Helen got home, surely? That wasn't in the agreement.

'Gemma,' Jim said sternly. 'Nice to see you again,' he added, like it was no such thing.

Gemma said 'Hello' vaguely, distracted by the fact that in less than thirty seconds, Noreen had managed to slip Noah a lolly. She had a touch of the Artful Dodger about her. Helen was not going to like it one bit.

'Is Helen about?' Jim said, peering past Gemma down the hall.

'I'm afraid you're out of luck,' she said with feigned regret. 'Helen's not here, and she won't be back till close to six.' So go away.

'Then who's looking after Noah?' he demanded.

Gemma glared back at him. 'I am. Helen and I have started job-sharing. I look after Noah while she's at work.'

Noreen managed to tear her attention away from Noah, and both she and Jim were staring at Gemma, gobsmacked.

'She's gone back to work?' said Jim. 'Since when?'

Great. Helen hadn't told them anything. What was Gemma supposed to say to them?

'Look it's only been a few weeks. Helen's been so busy, she probably just hasn't had a chance to call you.'

'We were talking to her only last week.'

'Oh?'

'Look, do you mind if we come in for a minute?' said Jim.

She did, but Gemma was pretty sure he was only asking rhetorically. She stepped back and allowed him to charge past, with Noreen in his wake, and Noah toddling along behind.

'What's going on here?' Jim wanted to know, confronted with the plastic curtain across the doorway into the back room. Trish had insisted it was kept in place till the rooms were all finished. She had grandiose notions of a ceremonial unveiling, Gemma suspected.

'We're just painting,' she explained, 'refinishing the floors, that kind of thing.'

He swept the plastic aside and peered in. 'How can she afford this?'

That was certainly none of his business. 'Look, what did you want to see Helen about? Maybe I can give her a message?'

He turned abruptly, allowing the plastic sheet to drop back into place. 'Well, we've got a lot more to talk about now than we did when we knocked on the door.'

Noreen stood at his side, her head bobbing in agreement.

Gemma groaned. 'Look, what do you want from me? I don't know why Helen didn't tell you she was working, or refinishing the floors, or whatever else you need to know about her business.'

Jim's eyes narrowed; he knew what she was implying.

'So you're a nurse as well?' he said.

'No way,' said Gemma.

'But you said you were job-sharing?'

'We are. Together we're the PA for the managing director of an advertising agency.'

'What on earth is she doing that for when she's trained as a nurse?' Jim asked gruffly.

Gemma shrugged. 'It was a good opportunity. We share hours, share childminding. At least, we will after I have a child to share.' That didn't come out right.

'But we can look after Noah,' Noreen said, her voice wavering.

'I don't understand why she wouldn't ask us,' said Jim, clearly irritated. 'We've offered dozens of times.'

Gemma decided it wasn't her place to tell them why Helen wouldn't ask them.

'She's only been working the days Noah's at preschool,' she said. 'There's been no need to ask for your help.'

'Noah's not at preschool today,' Noreen observed, with breathtaking acuity.

'This is only the second Wednesday Helen's worked,' said Gemma.

'So what's going to happen when you have your baby?' asked Jim. 'Is she going to work full-time then?'

Gemma sighed. This had gone on long enough. 'Look, I think this is a discussion you need to have with Helen. Sorry, but I was just about to make Noah his lunch.'

'We were going to see about taking him out to lunch,' said Jim.

'That's right,' said Noreen.

Gemma shrugged. 'Sorry. Perhaps you can set that up with Helen for another time.'

Jim frowned. 'He's our grandchild. Are you saying we can't take him out to lunch?'

'No, that's not what I'm saying,' Gemma said calmly. 'But you have to run it by Helen first.'

'Okay, do you have her number at work?' he said.

'I don't think that's appropriate. The boss doesn't like us taking personal calls during office hours.'

Jim was positively scowling at her. Helen was going to owe her big time for this. But right now she just wanted to get them out of here.

'Okay, so I'll tell Helen you came by,' Gemma said as she started to usher them back up the hall. 'And I'll make sure she gives you a call. Noah, give your nanna and pop a big hug goodbye.'

Bailey's

Myles walked briskly out of his office, pausing at Helen's desk.

'I'll be across town till after two. Call me if you need anything.'

Helen looked up at him. 'I'm sorry, didn't you get me to schedule the meeting with the team leaders for eleven, which is –' she consulted her watch '– less than fifteen minutes away?'

'Yeah, but you can take that meeting,' he said matter-of-factly.

Helen shot up from her chair. 'What did you say?'

'You take the meeting, Helen,' he repeated calmly. 'Report to me when I get back.'

She was gobsmacked. 'I can't take the meeting. How do you take a meeting, anyway? I don't even know how to do that.'

'Of course you do,' he said. 'How many meetings have you sat in with me?'

'I take notes, Myles. I don't take meetings.'

'Helen,' he leaned the edge of his briefcase on her desk, 'do you think I'd leave you with this if I didn't think you could handle it?'

She blinked, looking at him fearfully. 'What if *I* don't think I can handle it?'

'Did you draw up an agenda for the meeting?'

Helen nodded.

'Then you already know how to run it. Just follow the agenda, get everyone to report on what they came up with, and let them air any concerns or questions or ideas they have.'

'Air their concerns?' she said. 'You have to be kidding, Myles. None of them liked the idea. And I don't think any of them like me either.'

'I find that hard to believe,' he said. 'But anyway, none of them like me and I get by.'

'That's supposed to reassure me?'

'Helen,' said Myles, 'I'm not asking you to make any decisions, or even to deal with any problems that come up. Don't you realise they're less likely to raise issues with you than me? This way, they should stick to reporting their findings and a bit of discussion, rather than haggling with me. Trust me, this is the best way to go about it.'

It seemed Helen had little choice, because Myles was walking away.

'See you after two,' he called as he disappeared around the corner.

2.15 pm

'Well, look at that,' Myles said, walking up to Helen's desk, 'you're still in one piece.'

She glanced at him sideways. 'Okay, you were right, you threw me to the lions but they showed mercy. Or pity, I'm not sure which. Of course it helped that Justin wasn't there.'

'He didn't show?'

Helen shook her head. 'He sent one of his lackeys instead. Alyssa. She barely said boo the whole time.'

He smiled. 'Have you been to lunch?'

'No, I got caught up –'

'Have you eaten?' he persisted.

'I had a biscuit with my coffee . . .' She shrugged.

'I thought as much,' he said, producing a paper bag and dropping it on the desk in front of her. 'I picked it up from the restaurant.'

Helen just stared at the bag. She didn't know what to say.

'It's okay,' he said, offhand, 'it is vegetarian. Come into my office while you eat and you can fill me in on the meeting.'

Helen followed him in a moment later after she'd gathered up the reports submitted at the meeting, along with her lunch. Myles indicated a chair on the other side of his desk for her to sit in.

'Oh, you'll need a fork, I guess,' he said, ducking over to the wall unit that housed a virtual kitchen behind its sleek maple veneer panels. With the bathroom and a couch big enough to sleep on,

Myles could quite comfortably live here, which Helen suspected he almost did.

'Do you want something to drink while I'm here?' he was asking.

'No . . . thanks,' said Helen.

He came back to the desk and passed her the fork.

'Thank you,' she said. 'Really, thanks for this, Myles, you didn't have to.'

He waved dismissively as he took his seat opposite her. 'So, what have you got for me?'

Helen cleared her throat, opening a folder. 'Okay, well, I'll start with Dan –'

'Hold on, Helen,' said Myles. 'I don't need you to read every report out for me. I could do that myself. You'll save me a lot of time if you just tell me what you think.'

She looked at him expectantly. 'Think about what?'

'Which campaign will work best with this treatment,' he said simply.

Helen frowned. 'I have no idea, Myles. You said I didn't have to make any decisions.'

'I'm only asking for an opinion, Helen.'

She slumped in her chair. 'Oh Myles, I don't know.'

'I bet you do,' he said. 'Come on, what was your gut reaction?'

'I really think you're asking the wrong person. You have some idea that I'm an "everyman", or everywoman, I guess, but I'm not, really, I'm not at all. If anything, I'm just the opposite.'

He was listening to her, bemused.

'Did you know,' she went on, 'that every time I decide I like a particular brand of something, or even a flavour, or a type or a new line of some already established brand, they discontinue it?'

'Every time?'

'Nine times out of ten.'

'That much, eh?'

Helen suspected Myles wasn't taking her seriously. 'I'm telling you, I'm like a marketer's black spot. You'd be better off asking me what was going to fail rather than what was going to work.'

Myles sat forward in his chair. 'You should start eating before your food gets cold.'

'Oh, right,' she said, tearing open the paper bag.

'You know, Helen, people say what you just said all the time in focus groups.'

'What do you mean?'

'A significant number report that all their favourites keep being discontinued,' he explained. 'So you're not so out of the ordinary, after all, Helen.'

She popped a forkful of what looked like a very yummy frittata into her mouth. Helen loved frittata.

'The thing is,' Myles went on, 'companies are always looking for new ways to attract customers, and one way is through brand proliferation. They develop new ranges and styles and flavours all the time, at a much faster rate than ever before, so it'd almost be unusual if some product you liked hadn't been discontinued in the past few years. It took Coca-Cola more than sixty years to offer any alternatives other than Diet Coke, and only a couple of years to bring out half-a-dozen "new" flavours and diet variants.'

Helen swallowed down a mouthful.

'How is it?' Myles asked.

'Mm, very good. Thanks.'

'You're welcome,' he said, watching her closely. 'You know, Helen, you don't seem to have a lot of confidence in your own opinions. Have you always been like that?'

She stopped abruptly with another forkful on its way to her mouth. 'I . . . I don't know . . . I didn't think . . . Don't I?'

He smiled. 'It's not a criticism, just something I've noticed.'

But it felt like criticism. Helen wasn't completely comfortable being scrutinised like this. That's why she usually kept her opinions to herself. Myles was the one who was always trying to drag them out of her. She put the fork down again.

'I seem to remember you saying that I held very strong opinions about certain things,' said Helen. 'Vegetarianism, advertising . . .'

'I said you had strong values and ethics,' said Myles, 'and you do. You're very clear about your beliefs, almost to the point of sounding rehearsed.'

'They're not rehearsed,' she insisted. 'Just because I may have been influenced by people along the way doesn't mean they're not my opinions.'

'I'm not saying that,' he said. 'It's just when I ask you for an opinion off the top of your head it seems to throw you.'

'It doesn't throw me,' Helen returned, becoming quite defensive now. 'But is it such a bad thing to take time to think things through? Not to start sprouting an opinion before you've formed one?'

'Of course, you're right.' He seemed to be retreating all of a sudden. 'I apologise, Helen.'

'Why are you apologising?' she said, flustered.

'I've upset you –'

'You haven't upset me.'

'No, I have, and I'm sorry. I obviously struck a nerve.'

'You haven't struck a nerve!' Helen cried.

Their eyes locked across the desk. It was obvious to both of them that of course he'd struck a nerve.

'Sorry,' she said quietly.

'Don't be sorry, Helen,' said Myles. 'I want you to say what's on your mind. That's all I was getting at.' He paused. 'I'd like you to feel comfortable telling me anything. It won't make me feel any differently towards you.'

Helen's heart was beating rapidly. What did that mean? What did he want to know? And how did he feel towards her? No, strike that last question. She didn't want to go there.

Balmain

'So, what are you doing?'

'Working, Gem,' Charlie said pointedly.

She sighed into the phone. 'I'm bored.'

'Mm . . .'

Gemma could hear the clicking of a keyboard. 'You're not even listening to me, Charlie.'

'Sorry,' he said, and the clicking stopped. 'What's up?'

'Nothing, absolutely nothing. Nothing's up, nothing's happening. I'm bored and I'm lonely and I'm sick of myself.'

'Why don't you go for a walk or something?'

That would do nothing to relieve the loneliness. 'Never mind,' she sighed loudly. 'Anyway, I'm interrupting your work . . .'

'No, Gem, it's fine, really. What do you want to talk about?'

'It's okay, Charlie, thanks, but I'll talk to you later.' And she hung up.

*

Gemma picked up the remote and muted the TV. That was a knock at the door; she thought she'd heard something. She dragged herself up off the couch in the front room as she heard the knock again.

'Coming,' she called as she struggled up the hall. She was actually waddling. This was too depressing. She'd noticed heavily pregnant women waddling like overfed ducks and had vowed she was never going to look like that. As though she had a choice in the matter.

Gemma opened the front door. 'Charlie, what are you doing here?' she exclaimed. 'Shouldn't you be at work?'

He shrugged. 'You sounded so miserable on the phone, I wanted to make sure you were okay.'

Gemma's heart melted. 'That's so sweet. You really are a good friend, aren't you, Charlie?'

'And don't you forget it.'

She smiled. 'Well, come on in, it's an exclusive club.'

He followed her into the front room. 'What are you watching?' he said, looking at the TV screen.

'I don't know, some bad American talk show I stumbled across. They're discussing the secrets of happy couples,' she said, picking up the remote and turning it off. 'I don't want to watch it anymore, it's too depressing. '

'Happy couples depress you?'

'Absolutely,' she said, plonking down on the couch. 'Oh, sorry, do you want a drink or something?'

'No, no, I'm good,' said Charlie, taking one of the armchairs opposite her. 'So why do happy couples depress you, Gem?'

'Why do you reckon? I'm never going to be part of one, Charlie. I have to get used to the idea I'll be on my own for the rest of my life.'

'That's a little pessimistic, don't you think?'

'Not from where I'm sitting.'

'Give yourself some time, Gem. After you've had the baby, and you've got your figure back . . .'

She looked across at Charlie, who was grinning widely. 'Oh, thanks, kick me when I'm down.'

'I'm just trying to cheer you up.'

'You're doing a lousy job of it.'

'Okay,' he said sincerely, 'tell me why you're so down.'

'Let me count the ways . . .' Gemma shifted in the chair, wincing. 'For one thing, I can't get comfortable. Do you mind? I'm going to have to go and lie down.'

'Do you want me to go?'

'No, please, come in and sit with me?' she said, hauling herself up. 'Unless you have somewhere you have to be?'

'I don't have to be anywhere.'

'Why don't you have to be at work?' she asked over her shoulder as he followed her into her bedroom.

'We finished a big job yesterday. I've been working day and night for a week, so I figure I can take an afternoon off.'

Gemma climbed onto the bed, lying down on her side. 'I suppose you'd rather be doing something else on an afternoon off than sitting around here with me, moping. Will Poppy mind?'

'Poppy's at work,' he dismissed.

She patted the bed beside her. 'Come on, it's safe, I won't jump you.'

Charlie considered her dubiously before planting himself at the end of the bed, facing her. 'So what's up?'

Gemma let out a deep sigh. 'Do you think I'm a total waste of space as a human being, Charlie?'

He looked a little stunned. 'What?'

'Do you think I'm a –'

'No, don't repeat it,' he said. 'Why would you say something like that, Gem? That's a terrible way to talk about yourself.'

She looked at him directly. 'I've had a lot of time to think lately, Charlie, and I've had to ask myself, how many glaringly obvious signs do I need to hit me in the head and give me a wake-up call before I start facing a few home truths?'

He frowned. 'I think I just got lost in that metaphor maze.'

'My life has been made up of one bad decision after another. And for my pièce de résistance I left a great job – screwing the only chance I'd ever had of a career in the process – to follow a total loser, a man destined to abandon his unborn child. The lowest of the low, you could even say.' She paused for effect. 'So what does that say about me, Charlie?'

'That you're a little blind, I guess.'

'You're letting me off too lightly,' said Gemma. 'You know, when I do a stocktake of the men in my past, it amounts to the greatest bunch of losers and dickheads and straight-out bastards you'd ever come across. I've always said I'm a magnet for them. But maybe I only end up with guys like that because I'm tarred with the same brush. I'm one of their kind, so that's why they're attracted to me.'

Charlie sighed. 'You're really determined to feel sorry for yourself, aren't you, Gem?'

'Well, do you blame me? Look at how I've ended up. I spend half the week in a job where the boss barely tolerates me and is obviously counting the days till I'm out of there. The other half of the week I sit around here on my own.' She paused. 'Truth is, I'm lonely, Charlie. I used to think I had a lot of friends, but they were all losers too. I don't want to hang around people like that now that I'm going to have a baby.'

'You've moved on, Gem,' he said. 'And you're in a transition stage right now. Wait till you have the baby – you can start going to mothers' groups and stuff like that. You'll meet people in the same boat.'

'But what if they don't like me, Charlie?'

'Why wouldn't they like you?'

'This is what I was getting at before, facing some home truths,' said Gemma. 'Maybe I'm just not very likeable.'

'Okay, Gem, you're bordering on pathetic now,' said Charlie.

'It's the truth,' she insisted. 'You don't even like me enough to introduce me to your girlfriend.'

'That's not because I don't like you –'

'No, it's because I'm not "sweet", because I'd chew her up and spit her out. I don't think I'm a very nice person.' Tears were filling her eyes. 'I didn't mean to turn out like this, Charlie.'

'Gem . . .' Charlie swivelled around to lie back on the bed beside her. He drew his arm around her as she shifted, resting her head on his shoulder.

'Why can't I find someone like you, Charlie?' She sniffed. 'Someone who's decent, and kind, and good.'

'You don't go for decent guys, Gem. You go for the bad boys, the dangerous ones.'

'Not anymore,' she declared. 'I can't risk it. I have to think about the baby now. Do you know the statistics of men abusing the children of their partners? It's horrifying. No, the kind of guy I attract is not someone I want around my child.'

'Gem, did you ever think you attract that kind of guy because you don't think you deserve any better?'

She looked up at him. 'Is that what you think?'

'I don't know,' he said. 'I'm just a computer nerd – what do I know? Touchy-feely is not really my area. But it can't be good for you to be so down on yourself, especially with a baby on the way.'

'You know what worries me the most, Charlie?' Gemma said quietly, patting her stomach. 'What if she doesn't like me?'

'Of course she'll like you,' he chided. 'You're her mum, she'll love you.'

'That's not guaranteed,' she said. 'What about when she grows into a teenager, and we fight, which we will. I won't have a partner to stick up for me. You know, to say, "Don't talk to your mother like that!"' Gemma affected a deep voice. 'I've always thought it would be nice to have someone defend you like that.'

'You could always try to find Luke.'

She frowned at him. 'Why would I want to do that?'

He shrugged. 'He is the father.'

'He's the sperm donor. The best thing he ever did for me was to clear off and stay out of my life.'

'What if the baby wants to find him when she grows up?'

'Good luck with that,' said Gemma. 'She'll have to look under a lot of rocks.'

They lay there in silence for a while, staring up at the ceiling.

'I've got a better idea. I'll just send her round to you when she plays up,' said Gemma. 'You'll defend me, won't you, Charlie?'

'Oh, she'll just say, "You can't tell me what to do,"' he said in a high-pitched voice, '"you're not my father."'

Gemma laughed lazily. She realised the black cloud had begun to lift a little. 'Thanks for coming over, Charlie,' she said. 'Leaving work and everything.'

'Not a problem.' He glanced at her. 'Actually, I was going to tell you, I might be leaving for good.'

'Leaving Bailey's?' Gemma propped herself up on one elbow and looked down at him. 'Why, what happened?'

'I've been headhunted.'

'Really?' she said, her eyes wide. 'Another agency?'

'No, a film production company.'

'Feature films?'

He nodded, unable to keep a chuffed smile off his face. 'The MD put a good word in for me, actually. He has contacts in the industry.'

'Really?' Gemma was a little surprised. 'How does you leaving serve Bailey's interests?'

'It doesn't. But me staying when I'm unhappy doesn't do anyone any good either.'

'Oh, sure, of course, you're right.' She'd just been momentarily thrown by the MD's random act of kindness. 'Wow, it's so great, Charlie. Are you going to take it?'

'I'm thinking about it. You know I haven't been all that happy in advertising for a while now . . .'

'I know that, so what's stopping you?'

'Well,' he said, clasping his hands behind his head, 'after they made the offer I started looking into it, and I think I might prefer to work for myself. Then I'd really get to do what I want. Besides, if it works out, I know this really great production assistant who might come on board down the track. You know, maybe when her baby's a little older . . .'

Gemma took a moment to twig, then her jaw dropped all the way to the mattress. 'Do you really mean it, Charlie?'

'Well, I can't promise anything,' he said. 'But you'd be the first person I'd ask, if it came to that.'

'Really?' she said, inordinately touched by his faith in her. 'You'd want me?'

'Absolutely. We work great together, Gem. I've never worked so well with anyone else. I'd definitely want you on board, that's if you're interested.'

'Interested?' Gemma's head started buzzing. She'd have a career again, an amazing career, working alongside Charlie. It was like winning Lotto and the Melbourne Cup on the same day. 'I want to know everything, you have to tell me everything,' she said. 'I know, stay for dinner! Phoebe will be over later – we can celebrate.'

'Nothing's definite, Gemma,' Charlie reminded her.

'I realise that,' she said. 'But it's so exciting, can't we just be excited for a while? Why don't you call Poppy and ask her to join us? I'd really like to meet her, Charlie, and I promise I'll behave myself.'

He didn't respond, and he was avoiding eye contact, staring up at the ceiling.

'Charlie?' Gemma prompted, giving him a nudge.

He finally looked at her. 'We're on a break.'

She frowned. 'For how long?'

'It's kind of . . . permanent, I guess you could say.'

'Charlie!' She propped herself right up to sitting. 'Why didn't you tell me?'

'I am telling you.'

'But when did it happen? Are you all right? What's wrong with her? How could she dump you?'

'What makes you think she dumped me?'

Gemma blinked. 'You mean you did it?'

'Why is that so hard to believe?'

She thought about it. 'I just can't imagine you dumping anyone, Charlie. You're too nice.'

'I was nice about it.'

'Wow,' said Gemma, dropping onto her back again. 'So what was the problem?'

He shrugged. 'It just wasn't going anywhere.'

'And you wanted it to?'

'Well, no, or I wouldn't have broken up with her.'

Gemma frowned. 'I'm confused.'

'Don't worry about it. Let's just say it wasn't meant to be.'

She turned her head on her pillow, watching him.

'What?' he said after a while, glancing at her.

'So are you going to stay for dinner?'

'I suppose that means I'm cooking it?'

'No,' she said. 'I'll cook.'

'Not if I'm staying, you won't.'

She grinned, staring back up at the ceiling. 'So, what do you think of my hippo?' she asked after a while.

There was a moment's pause before he answered. 'You mean the one with the bird on its nose?'

For some reason that made her heart jump, and the baby started tumble-turning in response. She reached across and took Charlie's hand.

'What are you doing?' he said nervously.

She placed his hand on her belly and he looked over at her as the baby jigged around under his touch. He smiled, then he looked back up at the ceiling. And so did Gemma, feeling unusually contented. At least she had one good friend. Maybe that was all anyone needed.

Spring

Helen walked in the door just on seven. She didn't like coming home this late, but work had been frantic, and she still wasn't finished for the day. She was going to have to write up some schedules later, but they could wait until after Noah was in bed. And preferably when Gemma wasn't around. It seemed to annoy her whenever Helen did any work from home, or if Myles rang. She'd snoop around, wanting to know what it was about. And if Helen mentioned anything about a meeting, that would really set her off. So Helen had made her own personal policy not to talk shop with Gemma, no matter how much she goaded. She didn't want to upset her this far along in her pregnancy.

They must be out in the kitchen because Noah didn't come running as he usually did. Helen kicked her shoes off into her bedroom and dropped her bag. She slipped her jacket off on her way through the front room and tossed it on an armchair, too tired to care about hanging it up for the moment. When she appeared in the kitchen doorway, Noah's face lit up and he jumped out of his seat and scurried around to give her a hug.

Helen hugged him back, ruffling his hair. 'Hi,' she said to Gemma as she pulled a chair out and sat down, scooping Noah onto her lap. 'You shouldn't be doing dinner tonight.'

Gemma turned around from the kitchen bench. 'I didn't. This is one of yours. I just thought I'd better heat it up when it started to get late.'

'Sorry,' Helen said lamely, reluctant to offer any excuse. She'd taken to cooking meals on her days off and freezing them, partly due to Gemma's lack of culinary prowess, but also because she was too tired to cook most evenings, and she wanted to spend the little time she had then with Noah.

'Someone from Brookhaven called today,' Gemma said as she served up dinner.

'Oh, was it urgent?' said Helen, guilt and anxiety joining forces to mount a coordinated assault on her.

'No, they didn't say it was,' she said offhand. 'They just left a message for you to call back.'

Helen hoped there wasn't a problem. She hadn't been to Brookhaven for a few weeks. She'd been working too late to fit in a visit on her way home, and she never had enough time in the mornings to pop in before work. She had taken Noah a couple of times on her days off, but he'd been uneasy around his increasingly vacant grandmother so Helen was loath to push it. She mustn't forget to phone before heading out on location tomorrow.

They'd been shooting footage in a supermarket in Edgecliff but they felt they weren't getting a good cross-section of the population. They needed to hear from middle Australia – they needed to venture further into the suburbs. They settled on the Sutherland Shire and Helen had located two stores in the same chain and had made all the necessary arrangements with the management. The test case they'd selected was an established brand of washing powder, part of an extensive line of household cleaning products. It was being relaunched with new packaging, and Myles felt that if they made a presentation to the client on just this one product, they might get him to seriously consider doing an entire 'I buy it because . . .' campaign.

They were working with the team responsible for the account, thankfully not Justin's. They had brainstormed the best way to get to the 'man on the street' and decided, after initial trial runs, to go direct to the supermarket, to the very site of the purchase. They needed to find out what was going through the mind of the consumer as they reached for the item on the shelf. So they were going to ask them.

At first they were upfront: the interviewer approached shoppers, sporting a clipboard and ID with the camera operator in plain view. There had been some interesting responses. People either brushed by, shaking their heads and muttering, 'Not today, thanks.' Or they were tongue-tied and starstruck, and just plain useless. Or there were the show-offs, who thought their opinions were worthy of ten or more minutes of film, or who believed they were hilarious and took it as an opportunity to try out their best material. Whatever, they were hardly getting the inner motivations of people as they reached for their soap powder. So then they tried a hidden camera, involving a whole new set of logistics, revised permission from the supermarket management and release forms for the unsuspecting shoppers to sign after the filming to allow them to use the footage. Most wouldn't sign, some even expecting a ludicrous upfront payment for their newfound celebrity. It was difficult to explain that this was only preliminary shooting that was unlikely to be used in any finished advertisements.

The most successful strategy had come when they decided to use actors striking up conversations with real shoppers, caught on hidden cameras. The team devised a number of scenarios: the hapless bloke who'd lost his shopping list and couldn't remember what brand they usually bought; the young woman who'd just moved out of home; the harried housewife dissatisfied with brands she'd tried lately. They still had the issue of obtaining releases, but by and large the team felt they were beginning to get some worthwhile material. And so they were off to conquer the suburbs tomorrow.

Helen's role throughout all this had been as a kind of executive producer, at least that was how Myles described it. She didn't have to actually do the thing, she just had to help get it done. She'd been responsible for liaising with the supermarkets, and then with their own legal department to arrange the appropriate permissions and releases. Myles only attended the occasional progress meeting; the rest of the time he relied on Helen to keep him briefed. Her nursing training was actually standing her in good stead – she was used to documenting absolutely everything, which meant if she couldn't answer Myles's questions off the top of her head, she could quickly put her hand on the information. He was impressed, and he told her so, frequently.

Helen couldn't deny she was enjoying the challenge, being treated with respect, having authority . . . the whole thing was quite a buzz. And apart from the occasional feeling that David was tut-tutting over her shoulder, on the whole she felt comfortable with the straightforward approach of this campaign.

The only downside was that she missed Noah, not too badly yet, but she knew the time was coming when she'd be expected to work every day, and that was going to be tough. The morning rush hour and a quick story before bed did not seem nearly enough, though Helen knew that was by and large all the time the majority of men got to have with their kids. How did they cope, she wondered. How did they ever manage to develop meaningful relationships in so little time? And it wasn't just men. Helen was well aware that more and more women were in the same boat, and she was not sure it was one she wanted to board.

'So, what kept you at work?' Gemma asked as Helen sat down to eat.

She shrugged. 'Oh, you know, the usual.'

Gemma looked at her. 'Filing and answering the phone doesn't tend to keep me late.'

Helen sighed inwardly. Just change the subject. 'So what did you two get up to today?'

As Noah proceeded to prattle on, Helen avoided eye contact with Gemma, but she could feel the tension nevertheless. Perhaps one good thing would come of her taking over full-time – Gemma would be right away from Bailey's with a new focus and her own set of challenges. That had to be better for everyone.

Monday

Gemma couldn't understand why she was still feeling so tired. She'd had Thursday and Friday largely to herself, as usual, and she'd spent almost the entire weekend in a horizontal position. Phoebe had come over on Friday night, but she was a bit of a drag these days, ever since she'd talked Gemma into letting her be her support person during labour. Gemma was beginning to think that had been a mistake. Phoebe was acting like a coach before a big game. She had taken to scouring the birth manuals and marking passages to read out loud to Gemma, and then quizzing her on them later. This week her obsession was the benefits of perineum massage. Gemma said she could barely reach her perineum let alone massage it. So Phoebe had offered to do it for her, and that was right about when Gemma had told her to go home.

Then Charlie had turned up on Saturday afternoon to try to talk her into going out to see a film, but he couldn't budge her. As there was no beating her, he'd ended up joining her, and they'd both lolled around for hours watching Noah's DVDs because Gemma couldn't cope with anything more mentally taxing.

But all the rest seemed to have done little for Gemma's energy levels, probably because she wasn't getting more than a couple of hours' sleep at a time with the baby using her bladder for kick-boxing practice. She'd had to drag herself through most of the day today, and she was really beginning to wonder if she could make it into the office again tomorrow. She should just throw in the towel, take her leave and be done with it.

'So why don't you?' Charlie had asked when she'd brought it up between *Finding Dory* and *Inside Out*. 'I'm getting a little worried about you, Gem.'

'Well I'm just worried that the longer I'm away, the less likely I'll be to get my job back.'

'Gemma, we've already been over this. Helen won't do that to you.'

'How can you be so sure?' said Gemma. 'Everyone seems to have the idea that Helen's so sweet and innocent, but who really knows what she's thinking?'

'Then ask her!' Charlie declared. 'And while you're at it, ask the MD as well.'

'Ask him what?'

'Ask him if you're going to have a job to go back to after the baby,' he said simply.

'I can't just come out with it like that.'

'Why not?' said Charlie. 'I get the idea he'd much rather people were straight with him, you know. You should talk to him, get some of this out in the open. Might put your mind at rest, and then you can stop cutting off your nose to spite your face and finish up at work.'

But Gemma was not so sure. She slumped forward on her desk, resting her chin on her hands. She was sure she could go to sleep right now, just like this . . . she closed her eyes . . .

'Gemma?'

She jumped. Myles was standing over her desk, frowning down at her. She hadn't even heard him coming.

'Are you okay?' he asked. 'You don't look so good.'

'I'm fine,' she said, sitting up straight and giving her hair a flick.

He considered her for a moment longer. 'Are you sure?'

'Yes, I'm sure,' Gemma insisted through barely gritted teeth. 'Do you need something, MD?'

'Um, no . . . well, yes, actually,' he said. 'I was just wondering how much longer you intend to keep working?'

Here it was, finally. 'Why do you ask?'

'Well, Helen's well and truly settled into the position now, in fact she even does a bit of work Mondays and Tuesdays from home. There's no reason for you to soldier on, Gemma.'

'I'm fine, really,' she said curtly. 'I can manage.'

Myles stood his briefcase on her desk and leaned on it. 'The thing is, you mustn't have much longer to go. When are you due?'

She dropped her eyes. 'I'm not exactly sure.'

'Haven't you had an ultrasound?'

'Yes,' she said, 'but they're not a hundred per cent accurate.'

'I thought they were pretty close.'

'Oh, so when you had your baby, that was your experience, was it?' Gemma said petulantly. She glanced up at him and he was staring curiously at her. 'Look, I had no idea of my dates,' she said, 'so they work it out from the baby's measurements, and obviously babies come in all shapes and sizes. So the best they can do is an estimate.'

'So what's the estimate?' Myles persisted.

'A few weeks still,' she said vaguely. 'So, there's no rush to get me out of the door just yet.'

There was a pause as the acid in her words ate a new hole in the ozone layer.

'What's the matter, Gemma?' said Myles.

She didn't appreciate his tone. It was too . . . considerate.

'I'm just not sure this is going to work out,' she said finally.

'What are you talking about?'

'This job-sharing arrangement.'

'I think it's working out fine,' he said. 'Better than fine, in fact.'

'For you, maybe.'

'I hate to pull rank, Gemma, but I think I hold the deciding vote.'

She couldn't exactly argue with that.

'Are you going to tell me what's bothering you?' Myles said, using that tone again.

How much time did he have? Her back was hurting, her feet were so swollen she couldn't fit into any of her shoes, she had a vague sensation of nausea all the time, she had constant heartburn, she was so tired she couldn't see straight, and her emotions had a life all their own, so that right now, if she attempted to actually answer him, she couldn't guarantee what was going to come out of her mouth.

'Gemma?'

Bugger it. Charlie said she ought to be straight with him, and what did she have to lose anyway?

'Okay, you want to know what's bothering me?' she cried. 'I'll tell you what's bothering me. In all the months I've worked for you, answering your mail and updating your schedule and filing your files, you've never asked me to one meeting or included me in any "projects", and then Helen waltzes in here and you give her the run of the place.'

'Okay, putting aside the gross exaggeration,' said Myles, 'you're right. And the reason for that is I haven't had the same level of trust with you that I have with Helen.'

'Whose fault is that?'

He shook his head. 'Helen didn't lie to me to get the job.'

'But you only found that out a couple of months ago. What about before that?'

'Gemma, I knew in the interview that you were lying to me.'

She blinked. 'You did?'

'Not about the pregnancy,' he said. 'But I'm not stupid, Gemma. You had a very impressive record at Bailey's before you jumped ship. I knew you didn't want to be my PA, you were just trying to find a way back in.'

'So why did you give me the job?'

'I thought since you knew the business so well, you might be quite an asset, if you did as you promised and really threw yourself into it.'

'Well, I tried to,' she said. 'You just wouldn't give me a chance.'

'That's not true, Gemma. You sulked your way through most days, grudgingly doing your work, making it quite clear that you felt it was beneath you. You never tried to build any trust or rapport.'

'I did too!'

'What, by telling me to get a haircut and pushing your way into meetings?'

Gemma could feel herself going red.

'You know what, Gemma? I think you probably have a huge amount to offer, if you just got over the attitude that everybody owes you. So your boyfriend left you in the lurch. Life is unfair sometimes, but it takes two people to get pregnant. Start taking some responsibility for your own actions instead of blaming everyone else. If you want things to change, then get off your backside and do something about it.'

*

The *ping* announcing the arrival of an email broke Gemma's reverie. The MD had long since gone into his office, and she had no idea how long she'd been sitting here, staring into space. Where did he get off saying those things to her, homing right in on her insecurities like that? Who did he think he was?

She turned to the computer and clicked on her inbox. The email was from Mel.

Meet us at DryDock at six. It's important.

Gemma sighed, hitting reply.

Sorry, can't make it tonight.

Not more than a minute passed before the phone rang. Gemma picked up the receiver. 'Mr Davenport's office.'

'Gemma, it's Mel.'

'Oh, hi.'

'You have to come down to DryDock.'

'Mel, I'm exhausted –'

'It won't take long, but it's important. You're going to want to be there for this.'

'What's it about?'

'It's about your friend, Helen.'

*

Gemma walked wearily through the front door as Helen backed out of Noah's room, switching off the light.

'Hi, you're late,' Helen said in a hushed voice, pausing to examine her more closely. 'You look terrible, Gemma. Are you feeling all right?'

Gemma was about sick of hearing that. 'We have to talk,' she said squarely.

Helen nodded, trailing Gemma as she walked determinedly out to the kitchen.

'I served you up some dinner,' said Helen, crossing to the bench and picking up a foil-covered plate. 'Do you want me to heat it up for you?'

'I'm not hungry,' Gemma said grimly, pulling out a chair to sit down.

Helen turned to look at her. 'You should eat, Gemma. Or did you go out for dinner? Is that why you're late?'

'I met some of the staff after work,' she said.

'That's nice.'

'Why didn't you tell me about the campaign you've been working on, Helen?'

She shrugged. 'I did, I'm sure I've mentioned it.'

'Yeah, sure you've *mentioned* it,' said Gemma. 'Like it was no big deal.'

'It's not that big a deal, Gemma. It's just an idea Myles had –'

'I heard it was your idea.'

Helen shook her head. 'It was something I said to Myles, quite offhand, about toilet paper of all things, and he ran with it. He wanted to develop the idea of having real people talk honestly about why they choose the products they do.'

Gemma folded her arms. 'And he thinks that's never been done before?'

'No,' Helen groaned. 'Look, we had to go through all this with the teams, Gemma.'

'Yeah, well I had to hear it from the angry mob.'

'What are you talking about?'

'Down at DryDock tonight. Everyone was there and they're really pissed off about what's going on, Helen.'

She frowned. 'What do they think's going on?'

'Oh, just that some nobody without any advertising experience whatsoever has managed to bend the MD's ear with lame ideas and he's letting her run her own campaign.'

Helen's eyes narrowed. 'Who said this?'

'I told you, a whole contingent from the office met down at DryDock. Justin Moncrieff was the spokesman.'

'Why am I not surprised?' Helen leaned back against the bench and shook her head. 'He's so arrogant, that man. He shot down everything Myles said, he didn't listen, he didn't want to be open to new ideas. He actually didn't want any part of it, so I don't know why he's complaining. Were there any other team leaders there? I bet Julia Russo wasn't.'

'No, she wasn't there,' Gemma admitted. 'But Lewis –'

'Oh, come on, Gemma,' Helen said. 'Lewis is a complete idiot. He's an embarrassment. I don't understand why they keep him on staff.'

'His uncle's on the board.'

'Well, that explains that. You know, Myles actually has quite a lot of respect around the place, especially from people who don't listen to hearsay.'

'Look, there were about a dozen people there, all right?' said Gemma. 'And they're all really pissed off, Helen. They reckon this "I buy it because" idea is lame, and the MD shouldn't be dictating how the teams run their campaigns.'

'It's not like that,' she said. 'You're only getting their side.'

'Yeah, well, that's because you never told me anything about it.'

'And that's because you get miffed every time I do tell you anything that goes on at work,' Helen retorted, tired of this. 'If I say I've sat in a meeting, I have to listen to you complain for ten minutes because you never get to sit in on meetings. So I stopped telling you. It's not my fault the MD asks me to do this stuff. I don't know why he does.'

Because he trusted her so much, supposedly. That was his story anyway. Gemma hadn't believed one bit of his bluster today. He was making excuses, and she was going to out him.

'Everyone thinks it's because you're sleeping together,' she said bluntly.

'What?' Helen exclaimed. 'I hope you set them straight.'

She shrugged. 'How am I supposed to know what you get up to 24/7?'

'Gemma,' Helen said, clearly upset, 'you know perfectly well we're not sleeping together. I thought you were my friend.'

'And I thought you were mine,' Gemma threw back at her. 'You needn't get all wounded with me, Helen. I had to talk you into even considering this job in the first place, and now you're taking over. You don't know the first thing about advertising, you shouldn't be using the circumstances to get influence over the MD.'

'What does that even mean? What circumstances?'

Gemma shook her head. 'I can't believe you're so naive, Helen.'

'Please don't patronise me, Gemma. I'm not naive, and I'm not stupid. Just because you don't get along with the MD, you suspect there has to be something between us because I do. You've been implying it ever since the day we met, and frankly it's insulting.'

'How is it insulting?'

'It's insulting to suggest that Myles could only be interested in what I have to say because he's attracted to me,' she said, becoming shrill. 'That that could be the only reason he hired me.'

'It wasn't the only reason he hired you. There was a much bigger hook than that.'

'What are you talking about?'

'He knows about David,' Gemma said coolly. 'He's known from the start.'

Helen couldn't speak.

'When I was trying to talk him into the job-sharing idea, he wasn't convinced, until I mentioned you'd lost your husband . . .'

She could feel tears pricking behind her eyes. 'I asked you not to tell anyone about that, Gemma.'

'I didn't plan to, it just came out,' she said. 'That's why I asked him not to say anything to you. I knew you'd run a mile if you realised he knew.'

Helen crossed her arms in front of herself, breathing hard. 'How very manipulative of you.'

Gemma met her gaze. She hadn't done anything wrong, it was an accident, the way it had come out. And it was time Helen was made aware of exactly who was taking advantage of the situation. Myles had said if she wanted things to change, she should go ahead and change them. Okay, he'd asked for it.

'If you stop for a minute and think about it, Helen, I think you'll find Myles is the one doing the manipulating.'

Helen couldn't stand there any longer. She walked out of the kitchen and straight to her bedroom, closing the door behind her. She was trembling, tears filling her eyes. How could Myles have lied to her all this time? All his crap about honesty . . . it was a joke. Their friendship was a joke. The job was a joke.

And Helen was going to tell him what he could do with it. Right now, tonight, before she lost her nerve.

'Gemma,' she said a moment later, standing in the doorway to the kitchen. 'Noah's asleep, I just checked on him. Do you mind if I go out for a while?'

Gemma looked across the table at her. 'Where are you off to?'

'Does it matter?' she said. 'Look, I don't intend to be away long, Noah won't wake up, and I assume you're not going out –'

'It's fine, Helen, go ahead.'

'Thank you,' she said, and turned and walked away.

*

It didn't take long to drive into the city at this time on a Monday night. The roads were almost empty. Helen was even able to park the car out the front of the building. There was a different security man on the door, but he didn't blink when Helen presented her pass.

'Good evening, ma'am. Are you expecting to stay long in the building tonight?'

'No, I shouldn't be long at all,' said Helen.

'No worries, ma'am, take your time. We just like to be aware of the movements in and out of the building after hours.'

'Okay.' She nodded, walking to the elevator bay. Her heart started to pound harder in her chest as the lift made its ascent to the fifteenth floor and the doors slid open. Helen hesitated for a moment, before she stepped out and started tentatively along the corridor. She knew she was in the right, that this was what she had to do, but that didn't stop her from feeling rattled and upset. Really upset. So upset it hurt. She felt so humiliated, and worse, betrayed. She'd thought Myles had become a friend, and had been sure Gemma had. But they'd both been playing games with her, keeping secrets, abusing her trust. Helen felt naive and stupid, wondering how many times the two of them had talked about her in hushed tones, shaking their heads with pity.

As she went around the corner to her workstation, she saw that the door to Myles's office was open and the lights were on. She had assumed he'd still be here working; he'd told her many times that he never left much before ten. And to think she'd actually worried about him working so hard.

Helen took a deep breath and walked towards his office. She tapped lightly a couple of times on the door as she stepped inside. Myles wasn't at his desk, or over on the couch. Perhaps he was in the bathroom.

'Helen, what are you –'

The rest was drowned out by her scream as she nearly jumped out of her skin at the sound of Myles's voice right behind her.

'Hey, hey,' he said, turning her around. 'It's only me. I'm sorry, I didn't mean to frighten you . . . Helen? Are you okay?'

She couldn't stop shaking, and she could feel tears. The fright had obviously triggered an eruption – she felt like she was a volcano about to blow.

'Helen,' said Myles, his voice full of compassion as he drew her closer, 'what is it, what's wrong?'

But she couldn't speak. She could only sob big, tremulous sobs, while Myles held her close, gently stroking her back.

This was not the way it was supposed to go. She had to pull herself together, stop crying and find her rage again. But disengaging herself from Myles was proving difficult, like turning off the hot shower on a cold morning. She hadn't been held like this in so long, she'd almost forgotten the warm comfort of being folded in someone's arms.

Get a grip! Remember what he knows about you, imagine the pity he's feeling right this minute . . .

That did it. She shrugged him off, stepping back to put some distance between them.

'Are you okay?' he said, passing her a handkerchief, but she didn't take it, didn't dare meet his eyes, because she knew exactly how they were going to look. He had 'caring concern' down to a fine art in those velvety brown eyes of his.

How did she know his eyes were brown? Much less velvety.

'Helen,' he said, ducking his head to get into her line of vision, 'are you all right? Did something happen? Is Noah okay?'

That made a lump rise in her throat again, but she forced it down. She shook her head. 'It's nothing like that,' she managed to say, hearing him sigh with relief.

'Do you want to use the bathroom, splash some water on your face?'

She shook her head, wiping her eyes with her sleeves. God, it just occurred to her how she must look. She'd been home all day so she was wearing her housework clothes – old track pants and an ancient, frayed T-shirt, and an even older worn-out sweatshirt with bleach stains splattered across it. She looked like something the cat had dragged in.

'Um, I came straight from home,' Helen muttered, by way of explanation for her appearance.

'Yeah, I realise,' he dismissed. 'Why don't you take a seat? I'll get you a drink. Do you want water, or something stronger?'

'No . . . um, yes, okay,' she stammered.

'Something stronger?'

She nodded. 'Just a small one.'

As he went to get it Helen walked tentatively over to the sitting area. This was *really* not turning out the way she'd planned. Not that she'd had a plan, which was likely the problem. Okay, she had to get back in control. She looked at the couches, considering her options, before taking a seat in one of the armchairs. That would keep him at a distance. Distance was good. Distance was, in fact, essential. She would tell him that she knew he'd been lying to her, and that made their working relationship untenable. That's it, that's all she had to say, really. He certainly had no defence.

Myles walked over to her and handed her the drink, then he perched himself on the edge of the coffee table smack in front of her, gazing intently into her eyes. They were so close their knees were almost touching. Helen threw back one mouthful and swallowed. It was Scotch. She wasn't accustomed to drinking spirits, but it was very smooth – heinously expensive, no doubt. She took another mouthful and swallowed it down, feeling the warmth flood her chest.

'Better?' he asked.

She nodded.

'So what's going on, Helen?'

She looked briefly into his eyes. They were brown, and velvety, and they were gazing earnestly back into hers. Don't be swayed. He's a liar. Everything he's done for you was out of pity. Your relationship, such as it is, was founded on it. Helen put her glass on the table and stood abruptly. She couldn't be this close to him.

'What's the matter?' he said, swivelling around as she moved away.

'I have to stand while I say this.' She took a few steps back. Stay focused. Stick to the point. Keep it simple. That was the direction given to the supermarket actors. It had worked for them.

'Helen?' Myles was watching her expectantly. 'What did you want to say?'

'You've been lying to me,' she blurted.

'What? No, I haven't –'

'Don't make it worse, Myles,' she said, regaining her confidence. 'You have been lying to me – I have the facts.'

'Then please share them with me, because I have no idea what you're talking about.'

She took a breath. 'You've known about . . . what happened to my husband, the whole time.'

He sighed, but for some reason he didn't look guilty, or even contrite. 'That's what this is about,' he said, apparently relieved. 'Thank God it's finally out in the open.'

Helen was momentarily taken aback. 'Don't brush me off like that. This is serious.'

'I wouldn't brush you off, Helen. In fact, I wish you'd come to me sooner. I hated not being able to talk to you about it.'

This was confusing. He was double-talking her.

'Myles, you've been lying to me this whole time,' she restated.

'No, I haven't,' he insisted.

'You knew and you never said anything.'

'Because Gemma asked me not to. She told me without thinking, and then she said it really upset you to talk about it and that you were sensitive about being referred to as a widow. I promised not to bring it up unless you did.'

Helen was listening, but her head was beginning to hurt.

'I tried to give you openings a few times to talk about it,' Myles went on, 'but you always changed the subject. I figured Gemma was right. It obviously still upset you too much, so I didn't push it. But I never lied to you.'

Helen closed her eyes and shook her head. 'Stop it,' she said, before looking at him directly. 'How can you say you've been honest with me when you've known something so personal, so private . . . and I had no idea? You had no right to that information without my knowledge or consent, Myles. Maybe you got it by accident, but you should have told me that you knew. Especially once we got to know each other better.'

He was listening intently. 'You're right,' he said. 'I didn't think about it like that. I just didn't want to upset you. I apologise, Helen.'

He wasn't going to get out of it that easily. 'Well, fine,' she said, breathing hard. 'But you do realise I can't work for you any longer.'

'Why not?' He sprang to his feet. 'Helen, that's silly.'

'I'm not silly.'

'No you're not, that's not what I said. But there's no reason you can't work for me. I told you I was sorry, and I do understand how you must feel. Can't we get past this?'

'I don't see how,' she said curtly. 'You said you wanted me to take the job because you and I could be honest with each other, and that was the most important thing. Well, so much for that. You obviously only offered me the job because you felt sorry for me –'

'No, I didn't. Why do you assume that?'

'Come on, Myles,' Helen exclaimed. 'I had no experience, I sat with an ice pack on my ankle throughout the interview, after I'd slandered you and rubbished the entire industry.' She shook her head. 'God, you even gave me a car space. No wonder everyone's saying we're sleeping together.'

'What?'

'That's the rumour going around.'

'Well, it isn't true.'

'Don't you think I know that?' Helen said, flustered. She was getting a mental picture that was very distracting. 'And don't you see why I can't work here anymore? I'm a joke now, Myles.

Everyone thinks I'm getting special treatment, and the truth is I am, just not for the reason they're thinking.' There was that mental picture again!

'Look, I admit, Helen, maybe I was swayed when I heard your story to give you a chance,' said Myles. 'But you're not getting any special treatment. I genuinely value your input, and I genuinely enjoy working with you. That's the truth, and it has nothing to do with the fact you lost your husband.'

'I don't see how you can separate them.'

'Well, you certainly don't seem to have any trouble.'

Helen looked at him blankly. She detected an edge of frustration in his voice she hadn't heard before.

'That whole part of your life,' he went on, 'it's as though it's in a secret compartment no one's even allowed to know exists. Why can't you talk about it?'

'That's none of your business.'

'That's a cop-out, Helen. If you don't learn to talk about it, to live with it, you'll never come to terms with it. How can that be healthy, for you or for Noah?'

'So now you're presuming to tell me you know what's best for my son?'

'No, I'm not,' he said. 'But death is a fact of life, Helen. It's going to happen to everyone sooner or later. It's nothing to be ashamed of.'

'I'm not ashamed of my husband's death.'

'Then why won't you talk about it?' he said, raising his voice. 'What's the big secret?'

Helen glared at him. 'I talk about it.'

'You do?'

'Yes, I do. I talk about it all the time. I'm even seeing a counsellor.' She had seen a counsellor, a couple of times. But she'd stopped going because she didn't want to talk about it anymore.

'Oh, okay, I didn't realise –'

'Well, why would you?' she retorted. 'I don't talk about it at work, because . . . this is work. And you're my boss, Myles. Why would you think I'd want to talk about it with you?'

Myles looked as though she'd slapped him in the face. She was just being mean now, and she knew it. Apparently she had more of her mother in her than she'd realised. But this was the only way to handle things. It was all getting too close, too claustrophobic. Helen had always functioned best when she kept to herself. It was clearly time to take a step back, close the door, pull the blinds. Black out the windows, even.

'If you can't respect my privacy,' she went on, 'I don't see how I can work for you.'

'I can respect your privacy, Helen,' Myles said flatly. 'I've respected it all along. Isn't that what this is about in the first place?'

She had nothing to say to that.

'And I'll continue to respect your privacy,' he said in a level voice. 'But I'm still glad this came out. I've said from the start that I want us to be completely honest with each other.'

'Pity you didn't hold up your end of the bargain,' said Helen. 'Do you have any idea how it feels to suddenly find out that people you trusted have been lying to you all along?'

'Yeah, I do know how that feels, Helen,' he said seriously. 'I was mad as hell with my mother when I realised she hadn't told us she was sick. I was losing her, we had so little time left, but I couldn't get over the anger. Until I realised she was only doing it to protect us.'

Something snapped inside Helen then. 'Oh my God, I don't believe this.'

Myles frowned. 'What?'

'So you were only trying to "protect" me by not being honest with me, is that it, Myles?' she said. 'You couldn't save your own mother, or anyone else's mother, so you decided to take a stab at me, a poor wretched widow who landed right on your doorstep. You must have been rubbing your hands together when Gemma told you about me. But I'm not a project, Myles. I don't need you to save me or to protect me. I don't want your charity, or your pity . . . or your job.'

Helen walked out of the office without another word. There was nothing more to say anyway. She felt raw and exposed and excruciatingly vulnerable. When people can see your wounds it's so much easier for them to hurt you. Better to cover them up.

She didn't want to be like this, but she didn't know any other way. She was racked with guilt that she still had a life, a life that was moving on and branching out and going in directions it never would have if David hadn't . . . but how could she even think like that? Let alone talk about it. Helen had the feeling that if she were to start talking about it, any of it, then all of it might come tumbling out, and she might say something she wouldn't be able to live with.

*

Helen unlocked the front door and crept inside. The house was in total darkness; there wasn't even light coming from under Gemma's door. She walked quietly into Noah's room and over to his bed. He was sleeping soundly, the covers kicked askew. Helen straightened them, pulling them up snugly over his shoulders. She stroked his hair from his face. So peaceful, so beautiful. She'd always loved to watch him sleep. She and David used to creep in sometimes after they were sure he was asleep, just to stare at him. Helen felt tears welling again. She lifted the covers back and climbed in beside her little son, curling herself around him, waiting for sleep to overcome her so she wouldn't have to feel anything for a while.

*

'Helen! Helen, are you there?'

She jumped, startled. She was still lying beside Noah. She must have fallen asleep. She heard a warbled cry and then 'Helen' again.

It was Gemma. Helen slipped off the bed, careful not to disturb Noah, and hurried out into the hall, switching on the light. Gemma was standing in the doorway of Helen's room, gripping the architraves.

'Gemma, what is it?'

She turned around. 'Oh, thank God, I thought you weren't back yet.'

'What's going on? Are you having contractions?'

'I don't know,' she said fearfully. 'It's not stopping and starting pain, it's kind of . . . dragging, I guess.'

'Is it like a bearing-down sensation?' Helen asked her.

369

'Maybe, yeah.' She grimaced a little. 'It actually feels like I have to go to the toilet, really bad.'

That wasn't good. 'Come on, let's get you back to your bed –'

'I can't.' She winced. 'It's soaked.'

'Did your waters break?'

'I was wondering if that's what it was.'

'Okay,' Helen said calmly. 'Go and lie on my bed instead. I'm just going to call for an ambulance.'

'Don't leave me,' she blurted, grasping hold of her hand.

'I'm not going to leave you, Gemma. Come on, I'll help you onto the bed first.' Helen led her further into the room, but she could barely walk. Helen had a feeling this baby was on its way, sooner rather than later. She hauled the doona off the bed and helped Gemma to lie back, propping pillows around her for support. Gemma groaned, and Helen could hear the pain in her voice.

'I'm going to dash out quickly and get the phone,' she said. 'I'll be right back, don't worry.'

Helen ran out to the kitchen, turning on lights on the way, and grabbed the phone, racing back to the room as she dialled triple 0. 'Ambulance,' she said clearly when prompted.

Gemma was writhing about on the bed. 'I'm going to be sick,' she wailed, as Helen heard the operator come onto the line. She could only watch helplessly as Gemma threw up all over a pillow.

'Hi, I have a woman here who's about to give birth –'

'I can't have the baby here!' Gemma shrieked.

'Shh, Gemma, it's going to be all right. They're going to send an ambulance right away, aren't you?' Helen said into the phone.

'As soon as you give me the address.'

She rattled off her address as she dashed into the bathroom and grabbed a couple of facewashers, dousing them under the running tap.

'Now I'm going to stay on the line with you and talk you through,' the operator was saying as Helen hurried back to the bedroom.

'I don't think that'll be necessary.' She dragged the vomit-soaked pillow off the bed. 'I'm a nurse.' She leaned over Gemma to wipe her face down with the wet cloth.

'Oh, that's great. What's your name?'

'Helen Chapman.'

'Okay, Helen, the call has gone out: there should be an ambulance there in five to eight minutes. How far apart are the contractions coming?'

'I think we might have passed that stage. Her waters broke while she was sleeping. When she got up she felt like bearing down, and it looks like she might be going into shock as well,' she said, noticing Gemma's legs had begun to shake.

'It's coming on fast,' said the operator. 'Is she full-term?'

'Close enough.'

'Do you know if the head's crowning?'

'I haven't been able to check yet.'

'Okay, I'll stay on the line, Helen, but put the phone down somewhere close. I'll be here if you need me. My name's Liz, by the way.'

Helen raced around to the other side of the bed and placed the phone on the bedside table.

'What's happening?' Gemma wailed.

'You're going to have a baby,' Helen said calmly as she lifted Gemma's nightie up and over her belly. 'I'm just taking your pants off, Gem.'

'Why are you doing that?'

'So your baby doesn't come out wearing your undies on his head,' said Helen. 'It's not a good look.'

Gemma suddenly howled. 'Shit! It hurts!'

'What did you expect? Now stick your feet up here on my shoulders,' she said, taking hold of Gemma's ankles and doing it for her.

'I didn't ask for this, you know,' Gemma whimpered.

'You took the risk every time you had sex.'

She glared at Helen. 'You're going to give me a safe-sex talk now?'

'It's a bit late for that – your baby's on its way.'

'Oh fuck!' Gemma cried. 'Can't you stop it?'

Helen shook her head. Nothing's going to stop it now.'

'This can't be happening!' Gemma was frantic. 'I can't have the baby here – I have to get to a hospital. I have to have drugs!'

'Gemma, millions of babies are born all over the world nowhere near a hospital –'

'Yeah, and you said they all die.'

'I did not say that,' she chided.

But Gemma wasn't listening anymore. She let out a deep, shuddering bellow, which sounded not unlike a cow mooing, it occurred to Helen.

'Gem, we have to get you back up the bed a little,' said Helen. 'Can you use the post to push against with your foot?'

It was mostly Helen heaving and hoeing to get Gemma into a better position, but at least now she could see what was going on. Or coming out, rather. There, plain as day, was the bulging crescent of the baby's head, pushing through into the world. Helen snatched the phone up.

'Hi, Liz, the baby's head is definitely crowning,' she said. 'How far away is that ambulance?'

'They're saying three minutes, if you can get her to breathe through it –'

They were interrupted by a piercing scream as Gemma hoicked herself up on her elbows. 'Helen, get this fucking thing out of here, *it's killing me!*'

'Gotta go,' Helen said, dropping the phone.

She'd never delivered a baby before, but she'd watched enough being delivered. They really did it themselves. Helen knew as long as the baby turned itself sideways after the head was out, the shoulders would be able to pass through okay, and the rest should all take care of itself. Nonetheless she said a silent prayer to a God she didn't believe in that the cord wasn't wrapped around the neck or the baby didn't come out blue, or any one of a number of complications that she would not dwell on right now. The ambulance would be here any minute – they could deal with any emergency. She looked up at Gemma's face; she was straining so hard her eyes looked as though they were going to pop right out of her head.

'Gemma,' she said loudly, getting her attention. 'Push towards me, don't strain, put some oomph behind it.'

She panted for a few moments, and then started to push again.

'Towards me, Gem, towards me.' Helen watched as the head began to emerge. 'That's great, you're doing great!' she said, slipping the perineum down over the baby's chin till the head was completely free. 'You did it! The head's all the way out!'

Gemma collapsed back flat on the bed. 'Is it a girl or a boy?'

'Can't tell yet.' Helen laughed, looking at the squashed, angry little face as the baby turned itself sideways, just like it was supposed to do. 'But I'm looking at a pretty gorgeous face, and a head full of black hair.'

Gemma laughed weakly, and then she was up on her elbows again, the resolve plain on her face. She gave one last tremendous push and all of a sudden the body slithered out, whole and pink and perfect. Helen scooped up the baby and popped it on Gemma's stomach as the lights of the ambulance flashed through the windows into the room. Gemma was lying flat on her back, laughing and crying and feeling for her baby. Helen glanced at the clock. 'It's 4.07, Gemma. Congratulations.'

'What's the date?' she asked.

'It's the fifth,' said Helen, a smile breaking on her lips. She took a breath. 'It's my birthday.'

Gemma looked at her, her eyes glassy. 'Helen, that's so great! You have the same birthday . . . Oh my God, I don't even know if I have a son or a daughter.' Her voice was drunk with joy and sheer relief.

Helen grabbed a couple of pillows that had drifted down the bed and propped them up behind Gemma. 'Here, look for yourself.'

Gemma gazed down at the beautiful, wriggling little alien lying on her tummy. She cradled one arm around the baby, her baby, and shifted slightly.

'She's a girl, Helen,' she said staring up at her as tears streamed down her face. 'I knew it all along.'

*

In the commotion that followed, Noah finally woke up and was dazed and delighted to see the brand-new baby, but, it had to be said, much more impressed to see a real ambulance, flashing lights and the whole bit. As they wheeled Gemma out on the stretcher, she reached out to grab hold of Helen's hand. 'You're coming with me to the hospital, aren't you?'

'I won't be far behind,' said Helen. 'I'll get cleaned up and I'll be in as soon as I can.'

'You promise?' she said, still grasping tight onto Helen's hand.

'Of course. And I'll call Phoebe straightaway.'

'And Charlie, you have to call Charlie. Call Charlie first.' Helen stood with Noah perched on her hip as the ambulance trundled off slowly up the street.

'Why isn't the ambalints going ee-aww, Mummy?' Noah wanted to know.

'Because it's not an emergency,' said Helen. 'Gemma and the baby are both fine, absolutely fine.'

Noah insisted he wasn't tired and he didn't need to go back to bed, but Helen talked him into just lying down while she got ready. He drifted off to sleep barely a few minutes later. She phoned Charlie and then Phoebe, waking them both, but it hardly mattered once she told them the news. It was quite a wonderful thing to be the bearer of good tidings. And she was glad to hear they both intended to make their way to the hospital directly – in fact, the way Charlie responded, she had a feeling he might beat the ambulance there. Helen would have to get out of her clothes and have a shower before she went anywhere, and she had to clean up the beds before that.

She started in Gemma's room, stripping off the sodden sheets and liner and putting it all through the hot cycle in the washing machine. Helen's bed did not get off so lightly. It was a mess, and Helen decided that the sheets would have to go. She fetched a garbage bag from the kitchen and bundled all the linen inside, even the mattress liner.

Down on the floor she noticed the vomit-soaked pillow. Helen knelt beside it. It was David's pillow, still in the same case, the one she'd never been able to change. Tears welled, spilling over her lashes and running down her cheeks as she pushed the pillow into the garbage bag, drawing the ties together tight. She sat there on the floor and sobbed and sobbed, aware of a huge weight lifting off her. A baby had been born here today, a new life had come into the world, right here, in Helen's bedroom. This house had been so choked with grief and death, but it was as though this new life, this one little baby girl, had cleared the air, scattering the ghosts in her wake.

Helen stood up and carried the bag out to the bin, the tears still flowing freely down her cheeks. But she didn't feel sad. She went back inside and straight into the bathroom, shedding her clothes. She stood under the shower for a long time, until there were no more tears, no more sobs rising in her chest. She felt calm. And strangely unburdened. Maybe she would have a happy birthday after all.

She padded back into the bedroom wrapped in a towel and opened the doors to the wardrobe. There were David's clothes, all still hanging there, undisturbed since the day he'd died. Helen reached out and touched the sleeve of a shirt. She really needed to do something about all of this. She should give Steven a call, see if he wanted anything of his brother's. Helen sighed deeply, closing the door on that side of the wardrobe. Soon. One thing at a time.

*

Charlie arrived at the hospital first, only to be told he wasn't allowed in to see Gemma because he wasn't immediate family. When a message was relayed to her that he was there but they couldn't let him in, she fumed, 'Excuse me, doesn't my partner count as immediate family?'

'What did you tell them?' Charlie said when he finally made it to her bedside. 'They were falling over themselves to apologise.'

'I just said you were my partner.' She grinned. 'So you'd better make out like one and come and give me a hug.'

He didn't have to be told twice. 'I'm so proud of you, Gem,' he said, hugging her, careful of the baby. 'You did it, you actually did it.'

Gemma smiled up at him as he drew back. 'So what do you think of her?'

Charlie shifted his gaze to the baby and a look came over his face that Gemma found quite disarming. 'Wow,' he breathed. 'She's so perfect . . . so tiny, but so perfect.'

And she was so perfect, Gemma could hardly believe how lucky she was. That for once in her life she had got something so right.

'Do you know, I'd never held a newborn baby before?' she said to Charlie.

'Neither have I,' he said.

'Do you want to have a go?'

'I don't know,' he said warily.

'She won't break,' Gemma assured him, passing the baby into his arms.

'Wow,' was all Charlie could manage, looking down at her in quiet awe.

'I can't believe I thought I could ever give her up.' She leaned her head on Charlie's shoulder, gazing at her daughter. 'I've only had her for a couple of hours and if anyone touched a hair on her head I think I could quite possibly kill them.'

'She looks just like you, Dad,' said a nurse as she breezed past the bed to open back the curtains.

'Oh, no, I'm not –'

But Gemma nudged him. 'That's what I reckon,' she chirped.

The nurse smiled, leaving them alone again.

'I don't know what she was on about,' said Charlie. 'She looks just like you.'

'She does? You're not just saying that?'

'No, she really does.'

Gemma gazed down at her baby girl. 'I'm not being vain or anything, Charlie, I was just so scared she'd be the image of her father. I didn't want to be constantly reminded.'

Phoebe arrived soon after, teary and breathless, and it took her approximately fifteen seconds to burst into heaving sobs as she held her newborn niece. Gemma knew this was more than just a particularly emotional response to the birth of her sister's baby, but now was not the time to explore those murky waters. Though if Cam came anywhere near her, Gemma would personally give him a vasectomy, with a rusty knife.

She was beginning to wonder what was taking Helen so long when her mother burst through the door of the hospital ward like a southerly gust, her dad trailing in her wake.

'Oh my God, where is she? Let me see her, where's my new granddaughter?'

Gemma blinked, her eyes adjusting to the vision splendid that was her mother. How had she got dressed and fully made up this early in the morning?

'Do I know you, young man?' Trish asked Charlie as she swooped on him and confiscated the baby.

'This is Charlie, Mum,' Gemma said. 'My best friend from work.'

'Well, if he's such a best friend, why haven't we been introduced to Charlie sooner?' Trish declared. 'It's nice to meet you, Charlie, and you have to come to dinner, soon. Oh, Gemma, look at that hair,' she cried. 'Gary, look at that hair, just like Gemma when she was born. Do you remember?'

He was leaning over Gemma to give her a kiss. 'Of course I remember. Prettiest baby I'd ever laid eyes on. Until her sister came along,' he added, winking at Phoebe. 'Then it was a tie.' He took hold of Gemma's hand.

She smiled at him, cocking her head towards the baby. 'Not bad, eh?'

'Not bad at all.'

'So does she have a name yet?' said Trish, before wincing a little. 'Now, I've been preparing myself, Gemma. I promised myself I wouldn't say a word if I didn't like it.'

Phoebe snorted. 'So she's going to know now, Mum, if you don't say anything.'

'Her name's Lola,' Gemma announced.

Trish's mouth dropped open, and for once she was speechless, although Gemma noticed her eyes had developed a glossy sheen.

'Well, isn't that nice, love?' said Gary. 'Naming her after your mum.'

'Yes, it's lovely,' Trish said huskily, clearing her throat. 'Your nanna would be so thrilled, darling,' she added, squeezing Gemma's hand. 'When did you decide that?'

'I've always planned to call my daughter after Nan.'

'I didn't know you'd always planned to have a daughter.'

'I didn't really.' Gemma smiled. 'I'm just lucky, I guess.'

Phoebe sniffed, pulling a tissue from the box on the bedside cabinet.

'Does she have a second name?' asked Trish. 'Or is that not the go these days?'

'I didn't have anything picked out,' Gemma admitted, 'until she was born. Now it has to be Helen.'

Trish smiled. 'That's a lovely gesture, dear, but I'm afraid they don't go together.'

'What?' Gemma and Phoebe looked at each other blankly.

'I bet you haven't said it out loud yet,' said Trish. 'Lola Helen. See, it doesn't sound right, does it? Too many l's. You're going to have to rethink that, darling. Helen will understand. It's simply uncoordinated.'

'Mum, it's not an outfit,' said Gemma, 'it's her name.'

'Then it's all the more important,' Trish insisted. 'It's not as though she can change it next season.'

Gemma shook her head. 'Mum, that's going to be her name and that's all there is to it. Helen delivered her, and I almost forgot, it's Helen's birthday today as well. What kind of amazing coincidence is that?'

'Thank God she was there, is all I can say,' Gary broke in. 'I hate to think what would have happened if she wasn't.'

'So do I,' said Gemma. 'Lola was in such a hurry, did you know my body actually went into shock –'

'Well, I'm sorry, dear,' Trish said with a forced laugh, shaking her head, 'but if you're looking for sympathy because you had a quick labour, you'd better tell someone who didn't go through eighteen hours like I did with Ben, and then you were not so much better at fifteen –'

'How do you manage it, Mum?' said Gemma, shaking her head, feigning admiration. 'I gave birth barely a few hours ago and we're already talking about *your* labours.'

'All right, all right,' Trish said blithely, gazing down at the baby in her arms. 'She'll do the same thing to you, Lola, just you wait. It's what mothers do.'

Gemma was a mother now. The enormity of it hit her like a tonne of nappies. Her life was never going to be the same. Though the way she felt right now, she could only imagine it would be nothing short of sublime.

'How are you feeling, Gemstone?' asked Gary.

'Fantastic,' said Gemma. 'Like I'm on a high. I don't even feel tired.'

'Well, you should get all the rest you can while you're in the hospital,' said Trish. 'It'll be a different story once you get home.'

'But I'm planning to go home tomorrow.'

'You can't do that!'

'Well, actually, I can, Mum.'

'No, the window coverings aren't up yet, but I am going to ring the man the minute we leave here and tell him to rush it, and then we have to move the furniture into the living room, and the cot's being delivered tomorrow.'

'Mum, I told you, Helen gave me a cot –'

'I know that. I sent it away to have it refurbished,' said Trish. 'Now you simply can't come home tomorrow. You have to give me three days at least, darling.'

Just then the door swung open and Noah barrelled in, his arms wrapped around a big bunch of pink flowers. Helen was following behind, and she was nearly bowled over in the rush as Gemma's parents and Phoebe all came at her at once.

'How can we ever thank you?'

'Happy Birthday!'

'Thank God you were there.'

'You're amazing, Helen.'

They all took a turn at hugging her, something Helen was not altogether used to. Only Charlie stood back. She smiled at him across Gary's shoulder, and he winked at her.

'Don't mob her, let the poor woman through,' Gemma called from the bed.

Gary released her and Helen went over to the bedside, smiling broadly. 'How are you feeling?' Her eyes drifted to the baby. Trish had promptly planted her back in Gemma's arms when Helen had appeared in the doorway. 'Oh, Gem, she's so beautiful,' said Helen, leaning down.

Then suddenly Gemma's arm hooked around her neck pulling her close. 'I don't know how I'm ever going to thank you, Helen. What would I have done without you?' she said tearfully.

Helen extricated herself so she could look at Gemma's face. 'It's okay, you would have done the same –'

'No, because I'm not a good person like you.'

'Gemma, it's all right,' Helen said kindly, squeezing her hand. 'In fact, it was an incredible experience. I'll never forget it as long as I live.'

Gemma sighed tremulously.

'Can I hold her?' Helen asked.

'Of course.' She passed the baby into Helen's arms. 'I'm naming her Lola.'

'After my mother,' Trish chimed in.

'Lola Helen,' Gemma added.

Helen blinked. 'You don't have to do that.'

'I want to. Lola will be thrilled to have your name when she's old enough to know you delivered her. And you share birthdays. It's perfect.'

'Thank you,' said Helen. 'I'm really touched.' And she was.

'Hey, everyone, do you think you could give us a minute?' said Gemma. 'I need to talk to Helen about something.'

'Of course, of course, I'm dying for a coffee anyway,' Trish declared. 'I don't suppose they'll have decent coffee here . . . though you never know, it is the inner city. Jo – Noah, would you like to come with me and Uncle Gary and we'll find the cafeteria?'

He considered her sceptically. 'My name's not Jo-Noah.'

Phoebe held her hand out to him. 'Of course it isn't, silly old Aunty Trish.'

'Did you have to throw in "old"?' said Trish as they filed out of the room.

'Yes, Mum, I did.'

Charlie was smiling widely as he approached the bed. 'I think I'll get going, Gem, leave you to your family.'

'No, Charlie,' she protested. 'Don't let them frighten you away.'

'They didn't,' he said. 'It's just that I have to get to work.'

Gemma pulled a face.

'I'll come back later.'

'Promise?'

'Promise.' He leaned down and kissed her warmly on the cheek. 'Congratulations, Gem. You're a star.' He started for the door. 'See you, Helen,' he said with a wave as he walked out.

'He's such a lovely guy,' said Helen.

'I know,' Gemma said wistfully.

Helen was watching her with a raised eyebrow, but Gemma had other things on her mind.

'First of all, I'll never be able to repay you for what you did last night, Helen, but I'd love you to be Lola's godmother.'

Helen considered her. 'I thought you didn't believe in God?'

'I don't, and I won't be having a christening,' she said sheepishly. 'But I still want you to be godmother, you know, de facto or in spirit, or whatever.'

Helen smiled down at Lola. 'I'd be honoured.'

'Thank you.' Gemma took a breath. 'And I wanted to say sorry for everything I said last night, you know, before . . .'

'It's okay.'

'No, don't do that, Helen,' she said seriously.

Helen looked at her. 'Do what?'

'Don't brush it off like that. I've been bloody awful to you lately, sniping about you, whinging . . .'

'You were about to have a baby,' said Helen. 'Your hormones have been all over the place. I didn't take it personally.'

'Don't make excuses for me. I got it into my head that you were going to steal my job out from under me, that I wouldn't have a job to go back to after the baby . . .'

Helen frowned. 'Why on earth would you think that?'

She sighed. 'Because I'm a bitch, obviously. A crazy one, from hell.'

'Gemma –'

'No, Helen, let me get this out. I've been a bitch, I really have, and I'm not proud of myself.' She paused. 'At times like this you have to do a bit of soul-searching, and the thing is, I've made a lot of mistakes in the past, and some really bad choices, and . . . look, I've just done a lot of stupid, reckless things. But I've got to get my act together. I can't make excuses anymore, I'm a mother now. I can't afford to screw this up.'

'You won't,' Helen said. 'You're going to be a wonderful mother, Gemma.'

'I don't know about that,' she said. 'I look at you, you're so conscious about every little thing, so organised and disciplined –'

'And rigid,' Helen declared. 'Honestly, sometimes I don't know how I got so rigid. Probably all those years looking after my mother. Everything had to be the same, day in, day out, the routines, stuff around the house.' She sighed. 'Gem, you're spontaneous and fun and you tackle life head-on. They're really wonderful traits to have as a parent. Don't sell yourself short.'

Gemma was tearing up again. 'You've been so good to me, Helen, from the day you took me in –'

'I didn't "take you in". You make it sound like you were a charity case. I needed a paying boarder as much as you needed a place to live. We helped each other out.'

'But –'

'No, you listen to me now, Gemma,' said Helen. 'You need to realise how much you've done for me too.'

'What have I done for you?' She looked surprised.

Helen thought about what she wanted to say. 'My life was . . . well, I wasn't in a good place before you came to live with us, Gemma. I was very . . . disconnected from the world. That wasn't any good for Noah. Or me. But since you came, well, my life's opened up and expanded. Noah's somewhere in the building with your family and I don't feel the slightest bit anxious. And . . .' she hesitated, 'well, you know, I've stretched myself in so many ways I didn't think possible.'

Gemma was watching her. 'So, have you seen the . . . um, Myles? That's where you were going last night, wasn't it?'

Helen nodded.

'Did you work things out with him?'

She looked sheepish. 'Not exactly. I think I told him I didn't want his job, or anything to do with him, right before I stormed out.'

'Oh.' Gemma bit her lip. 'Helen, if you really don't want to work at Bailey's anymore, don't feel obliged because of me.'

'No, it's not that,' she said. 'I just feel embarrassed now, the way everyone's been talking about me.' Her voice wavered. 'I'm mortified that they think I'm sleeping with Myles.'

'Oh no, Helen, I really am a bitch,' said Gemma, hitting her forehead. 'I should have told you last night, I absolutely insisted to everyone that you weren't sleeping with the MD. I got the shits with Justin for even suggesting it, and so did Mel and some of the other women, and we ended up having this big heated debate about sexual harassment, and I didn't know, but Justin's been sleeping with the perky little blonde on their team –'

'Alyssa?'

'Is that her name? Anyway, she got all upset, and ran off in tears, and Justin had to chase after her. It was all a bit of a drama.'

'So you did stand up for me?'

Gemma nodded.

'So you're not such a bitch after all?'

She smiled weakly. 'But there's something else I should have said a lot sooner, as well. I'm sorry, Helen, but I just don't know if I can manage Noah and the baby straightaway –'

'Of course you can't,' she said. 'I never expected you to.'

'Oh? You didn't?'

'No, I've been meaning to bring it up with you. I guess I was waiting till you decided to stop work, but then this little lady was so impatient.' She glanced down at Lola, smiling.

'So what are you going to do with Noah?'

Helen took a deep breath. 'I'm going to have to bite the bullet and ask David's parents to help.'

'Whoa.' Gemma was frowning. 'Are you sure you feel comfortable about that?'

'No,' Helen admitted, 'but I am sure it's the right thing to do.' She didn't want to hang onto her little bit of power any longer. It suddenly didn't seem to matter. If she could finally throw out David's pillow, maybe she was ready to let go of a lot more besides. 'Anyway, I know they'll be happy to help.'

Gemma nodded. 'So does that mean you are going to keep working at Bailey's for now?'

Helen took a deep breath. 'I suppose, that's if Myles still wants me . . . working for him,' she added quickly.

'Oh, I don't think there's any question about that.'

*

'What's this place, Mummy?' Noah asked as Helen pulled into the driveway of Bailey's underground carpark. She decided she had to settle this as soon as possible, so they'd driven directly into the city from the hospital.

'This is where Mummy works, Noah.'

'Wif Myers?'

He didn't miss a trick. 'Yes, with Myers. In fact,' she said, glancing at Noah in the rearview mirror, 'we're going up to see him right now.'

'Yay!' he cried, clapping his hands.

Helen parked the car and they caught the lift directly up to the fifteenth floor. But when they made their way to the office, Myles didn't appear to be around. Helen checked her watch – it was only going on eight thirty. She felt as though she'd been through a whole day already.

'Where is Myers, Mummy?'

'He mustn't be here yet,' said Helen. 'Let's find out where he is.'

They went back to her desk and Helen turned on the computer, lifting Noah up onto her lap. She kept him amused for a while, letting him click the mouse and showing him the colourful patchwork of Myles's schedule, while she worked out exactly where he was right now. He'd had a breakfast meeting in the building at seven thirty, but he had nothing scheduled after that until ten. He couldn't be far away.

'Hello, this is a surprise.'

Speak of the devil. Helen swivelled around in her chair and Noah jumped off her lap, running towards him.

'Myers, guess what!' he said breathlessly, his eyes wide.

'You tell me, Noah,' said Myles, crouching down to his level, with a fleeting glance towards Helen.

'Gemma had a baby on Mummy's bed and a ambalints came but it didn't ee-aww 'cause they're absootley fine!' he said emphatically, holding out his arms.

'Wow.' Myles looked over at Helen. 'Gemma had the baby?'

She nodded. 'On my bed. I delivered her.'

He looked a little stunned. 'When did all this happen?' he said, straightening up again.

'Around four this morning,' said Helen.

'And everything's all right? The baby's all right? Gemma?'

'She had a perfect, 3.4-kilo baby girl. Mother and daughter are both doing extremely well.'

Myles was watching her intently. 'How about you, how are you doing?'

'I'm fine.' She nodded. 'Actually, I'm good, really good.'

'It's Mummy's birfday, Myers!'

'Noah,' she chided.

'But I didn't haf her a present,' he said, his little face full of regret. Myles was smiling down at him.

'Well,' he said, 'we'd best send some flowers to Gemma and to your mummy, what do you think?'

Noah nodded enthusiastically. 'We already tooked some to Lola,' he said, rolling the l's around on his tongue.

'Is that the baby's name?'

'Yes, and Helen too.'

Myles looked at her for confirmation.

'Gemma thinks she owes me for delivering her.'

'I would think she does.'

Helen stood up. 'Have you got a minute, Myles?'

'Sure.'

'Noah,' said Helen, 'how about you come over and sit at my desk, and you can draw a picture while Mummy talks to Myles for a few minutes?'

He went to protest but Myles interrupted. 'Would you draw something for me, Noah?'

'But I don't know what.'

'Mm.' Myles thought about it. 'Can you draw me a picture of the new baby? I haven't seen her yet, so I don't know what she looks like.'

Noah screwed up his face. 'She looks like a baby,' he said. 'I know, I'll draw Lola going in the ambalints!'

'Perfect.'

Helen lifted Noah into her chair, and placed some paper in front of him, as well as every coloured marker she could find. 'Stay put, Noah,' she warned. 'We'll just be over there by the door.'

She followed Myles into his office but stood just inside the door, where she could still keep an eye on Noah. Myles left his briefcase on the desk and crossed back over to where she was standing, thrusting his hands in his pockets. He seemed apprehensive.

'So I wanted to let you know about Gemma,' Helen began. 'She obviously won't be in today.'

He nodded, a faint smile on his face. 'She really is okay?'

'Yeah, she's fine.'

'It's just I, um . . . well I gave her a bit of a hard time yesterday,' he said.

'Oh?'

'She didn't say anything?'

'No.'

'Yeah, well, we had . . . "words".'

'You two.' Helen shook her head. 'That might explain what set her off last night, why she blurted everything.'

Myles looked at her. 'I was about to call you, Helen, to apologise again –'

'No.' She stopped him. 'You don't have to apologise anymore, Myles. In fact, I came here to apologise to you. I got nasty last night, there was no call for that.'

'You were upset, Helen, with good reason.'

'That's not an excuse to be mean, and I was, and I'm sorry.' She took a breath. 'The thing is, you were right, I don't talk about my husband –'

'Helen, it's okay, you don't have to –'

'Myles, please, I want to say this.' She glanced across at Noah and lowered her voice. 'You know how he died, I presume?'

Myles nodded faintly.

'Whenever I have to tell people, it becomes this gruesome, sensational story. It's like David's a freak because he got hit by a bus. I don't want people to think of him that way . . . That's why I don't talk about him. One of the reasons anyway.'

'That's fair enough,' he said.

'When I started working here, I thought no one knew anything about me. It was such a relief not to be this tragic figure, not to make people feel uncomfortable all the time, not to wonder what they were saying about me behind my back.' She stared down at the carpet. 'It was such a shock when Gemma told me you knew all along. I felt . . . betrayed, I guess.'

'Helen,' said Myles, waiting till she met his eyes. 'I've never spoken to anyone about it. Gemma and I didn't even talk about it. I don't think of you as a tragic figure, nothing like it. I think you're brave, and, well, I think you're pretty amazing . . .' He paused. 'And you certainly don't make me feel uncomfortable. Quite the opposite. I haven't felt so comfortable with anyone in a long time.'

He was gazing down at her so earnestly, with those eyes.

'Like I said last night,' he went on, 'I admit, maybe I did give you special treatment at first. Of course your story affected me, I'd be pretty heartless if it didn't. But it wasn't pity, I didn't feel sorry for you, Helen, I just thought you deserved a break. You've more than proven yourself in this job, and I'd really like you to consider staying on. In fact, I think I'd be a little lost without you now.'

Helen wondered if he could hear her heart beating; it was so loud it was echoing in her ears.

'So what do you say?' he prompted after a moment.

She cleared her throat. 'Okay.' Then she remembered the logistics. 'But it might take a few days to sort something out. With Lola arriving a little earlier than expected, I haven't organised anything for Noah.'

'No problem, take your time,' Myles said. 'Work around Noah's preschool hours, or from home, whatever you can manage.'

Helen folded her arms, leaning back against the doorjamb and looking right at him. 'Are you giving me special treatment again?'

'So what if I am?' he returned, his face relaxing into a proper smile. 'They think we're sleeping together anyway, you might as well get some fringe benefits out of it.'

'It doesn't bother you?'

'Let them think whatever they like,' said Myles. 'They will anyway. Besides, they're probably just jealous.'

Helen grinned. 'What, because I get to sleep with the boss?'

'No, I meant the other way around.'

That just made her blush. Fortunately Noah ran over right then, waving a piece of paper.

'I finished, Myers,' he announced.

Myles crouched down and Noah handed him the picture. He studied it carefully. 'Well, that's a totally awesome ambulance, Noah. And Lola looks very cute.'

'She's not really,' he said. 'She's all squashed.'

'All right, young man,' Helen broke in. 'I think it's time for us to head home and let Myles get some work done.'

'Can I keep this, Noah?' Myles asked, still holding the picture.

He nodded. 'I drawed it for you.'

'Thank you very much.' He stood up.

'I'll let you know as soon as I've organised things,' Helen said as she walked across to her desk to pick up her handbag. When she turned around Myles was standing in front of her.

'I forgot something,' he said as he stooped to kiss her softly on the cheek. 'Happy Birthday, Helen.'

Noah was giggling. 'Myers gived you a kiss, Mummy!'

*

When Helen pulled into their street half an hour later, there wasn't a space out front so she had to park around the corner. She ambled back towards their house, not in any particular hurry, while Noah skipped and jumped and scampered ahead of her. She felt tired, but by the same token she felt strangely wired as well. She supposed that was likely to happen when you'd had a hand in bringing a new life into the world.

But she knew it also had to do with Myles. He was beginning to wear his heart fairly boldly on his sleeve, and Helen wasn't sure she was ready for that. She wasn't stupid – she'd felt the attraction. She'd kind of been pretending she hadn't though, so she wouldn't have to do anything about it. She didn't want to encourage it, that didn't seem right. On the other hand, deep down in her heart, where no one else could see, Helen realised she didn't exactly want to discourage Myles either. But she was a widow, there was a time and distance that had to be respected, surely? She had no idea what that was, though. In other cultures there seemed to be established customs, defined periods of mourning. There were no rules that Helen was aware of, so pretending it wasn't happening had seemed to her the best way to proceed.

She noticed Noah had come to an abrupt halt up ahead in front of their house, then he turned on his heel and bolted back to his mother.

'What's dat man doing at our house, Mummy?' he asked wide-eyed.

Helen looked ahead as a tall figure stepped down from the front porch. The sun was shining towards them, so she had to put her hand up to shield her eyes. She walked a little closer, and then came to an abrupt halt herself.

He smiled broadly. 'Hey, Hel. Surprise. Happy Birthday.'

'What's dat man, Mummy?' Noah said, tugging on her arm.

She looked down at Noah as tears filled her eyes. 'Well, Noah, that's your Uncle Tony.'

*

After a slightly tentative hug, Helen ushered Tony into the house. She was happy to see him, of course she was, but she couldn't help wondering what he was doing here. Was he going to suggest selling the house? Did he need money? What exactly was going on?

Tony was taken aback by the changes to the rear of the house, particularly as it was still bereft of furniture and window coverings. It was now a large open space, unrecognisable from its former self, the floorboards polished, the walls a warm white. But he was most unsettled by the fact that their father's old darkroom had been opened up again.

'I can still feel him here,' he murmured, almost to himself. 'He never found a way out.' He was hovering by the door, reluctant to go all the way inside. 'Your housemate, she doesn't mind putting a baby in there?'

'It wasn't her father who died here,' Helen pointed out. 'And it was a long time ago, Tony.'

'Feels like yesterday, being here again,' he sighed. Then he seemed to snap out of it. 'Especially when I look at you, Hel. You've barely changed. What's your secret?'

'Clean living,' she quipped.

'Mm, don't know if that's worth it.'

Helen filled him in on the events overnight and Tony was duly in awe of his little sister's capacity in a crisis. Noah was captivated, as he seemed to be with most men around his father's age. He basked in the attentions of an uncle he'd never known, which gave Helen the chance to sit back and observe the brother she wasn't sure she knew anymore.

He had aged again, which was always confronting for Helen. Only seeing him every few years meant she'd watched him age in leaps and bounds, and now he was coming to the brink of middle age, his dark hair peppered with grey at the temples, the creases around his eyes grown deeper. But he was still a handsome man, so like their father, though with more light in his eyes.

The excitement of the long morning finally caught up with Noah, and he started to nod off over lunch. He didn't even argue when Helen suggested a nap, but he extracted a solemn promise from Uncle Tony that he would still be here when he woke.

Helen put him to bed and walked back down the hall to the kitchen with a certain amount of trepidation – they wouldn't have Noah as a distraction now. As she stepped into the doorway, Tony looked up and gave her a cautious smile.

'Another cup of tea?' she said lightly.

He patted the table. 'Come and sit down, Helen, we have a lot to talk about.'

She pulled out a chair. 'So are you going to tell me what you're doing here?'

'I thought you'd never ask,' he said. 'We're touring a play here, they've transported the entire production. I was stage manager in London, but the make-up of the tour crew was only finalised a short time ago. They had to negotiate with the host company, give some jobs to the locals. That's why I didn't want to tell you till I knew for sure.'

'So how long will the play run?' she asked.

'It's booked for a three-month season here in Sydney, with room to extend to four. And then we'll be touring it to Melbourne.'

Helen was counting up the months in her head. 'So you'll be in the country for at least six months?' she said hopefully, already planning a trip to Melbourne in her mind.

'No, it'll be longer than that,' said Tony.

'Oh?'

He nodded. 'I'm not going back, Hel.'

She just stared at him. 'You mean you're . . .'

'Staying. I'm home for good, Helen.'

She was still having trouble taking it in. 'Why? Is anything wrong?'

Tony smiled sheepishly. 'Nothing's wrong. I just decided it was time to come home. Now that you're on your own, I didn't want to be so far away.'

Helen felt tears creeping into her eyes. Did he really feel responsible for her?

'I wasn't sure how you were going to feel about it,' he said, watching her.

'What do you mean?' She sniffed. 'Of course I'm happy, Tony, you're my only brother.'

'Pretty lousy one, nicking off to the other side of the world and leaving you with everything.'

'You had no way of knowing how bad it was going to get –'

'Stop it, Hel,' he said suddenly.

She blinked at him.

'Stop being so nice, Helen. You're always so nice. But you don't say what you're really thinking. That whole debacle over the house . . . I know you thought I was looking after my own interests, but that wasn't it, really. I was actually trying to look out for you, I just went about it the wrong way.'

'What do you mean?'

'Think about it from my perspective – I'm on the other side of the world, I didn't know anything about David. Maybe he was a great guy, but just after you met, you're putting Mum in a home and he's moving in. I would have liked to see you get out of this house, Hel, build your own life. It worried me. I wanted to make sure things were watertight legally so he couldn't rip you off.'

'Or you.'

'You want to know something, Helen?' Tony said plainly. 'I'd have signed the house over to you in a heartbeat. I always felt you deserved it. But I was wary when David came on the scene. You could have lost it all if there'd been any trouble between you.'

'He would never have done anything like that,' she said.

Tony was looking at her in an odd way. 'Look, this might not be the right time to say this, but things changed after you got together,' he said carefully. 'He seemed to take over. I couldn't get near you to talk about anything without David butting in. And to be honest, you changed as well, Helen, or our relationship changed. I thought we'd always be able to tell each other everything, but it felt like you didn't trust me anymore, and that really hurt.'

Helen remembered the hurt she'd felt too, the estrangement. David had kept insisting that Tony had left her to look after their mother, so he shouldn't have a say anymore. She'd begun to look at him in a different way, she knew she had. For the first time she regarded him as selfish, and she'd never felt that before. She'd always been glad he'd got away, there was no point both of them missing out, and Tony's dreams were a lot more coherent than hers had ever been.

'I'm sorry,' he said, shaking his head. 'I've said too much. I shouldn't just walk in here after all these years –'

'It's okay, Tony,' Helen said quietly. 'You're right, David could be a bit domineering. It's funny, he tried so hard to be different from his father, but he was getting more like him all the time. He really did believe he was doing the best for everyone, the right thing. David was a very principled man, but he did tend to take control.' She paused. 'The thing is, I let him. He might have been jerking the reins, but I handed them over in the first place. It was just so nice to have someone to lean on after all those years on my own. He was the stronger person, and I let him take over. But after a while I lost myself, I stopped thinking for myself . . .'

She looked up and Tony was watching her intently. 'Was everything all right, Hel, before . . . he . . .'

'Of course it was,' she dismissed. 'I don't know what I must sound like, speaking ill of the dead . . .'

'Helen, it's me, Tony, your brother. You can tell me anything. You always did.' He reached over and put his hand on hers. 'When you got into trouble at school, the boys you liked . . . You even told me when you got your first period, remember?'

Her eyes widened and she covered her face with her hands. 'Oh my God,' she said, peeking between her fingers. 'I did tell you that. Why did I tell you that?'

Tony was grinning at her. 'Because you couldn't talk to Mum about anything. She always gave you such a hard time, made you feel bad about yourself.'

Helen brought her hands down to the table again. 'She did, didn't she?'

He nodded. 'She was jealous of you, I reckon.'

'How do you figure that?'

'You reminded her of what she used to be, and she couldn't stand it,' he said. 'I never understood how you stuck it out all these years. Did she ever get any better, any kinder at least?'

A loud, insistent knock sounded at the front door.

'Expecting someone?' Tony asked as she got to her feet.

'Not that I know of.'

She walked up the hall as Noah wandered out of his bedroom, rubbing his eyes sleepily.

'Sum'n's at a door, Mummy,' he said, yawning.

Helen opened the door to a delivery man bearing a huge arrangement of flowers. And her heart missed a beat.

'Helen Chapman?' the man asked.

'Yes, thank you,' she said, taking them from him.

'Look at the normous flowers, Mummy!' Noah exclaimed, trailing her down the hall. Helen had to carry them with both hands, so she couldn't even look at the card till she put them down.

Tony let out a long low whistle as she went back into the kitchen and set them on the table. 'Who's the admirer?'

'Actually, Noah, these are from you,' Helen said as he clambered up to stand on a chair next to her. She showed him the card. 'See, "Happy Birthday, love from Noah and Myers."'

Noah was awestruck. 'Did I get them for your birfday, Mummy?' he said, his eyes wide.

'Yes, you did. Thank you, sweetheart, they're the most beautiful flowers I've ever had in my whole life.'

Noah was beaming as she kissed him on the cheek.

'Is Myers the department store?' said Tony, confused.

'No, sorry, it's *Myles* actually, that's just the way Noah pronounces it.' Helen was trying to sound offhand, but she didn't think she was fooling anyone. Her heart had been fluttering erratically since she'd opened the door and seen the flowers and realised exactly who had sent them. 'Myles is my boss, you know, I work for him, and we called in this morning to see him, at work, of course, because I had to tell him about the baby, because Gemma works for him too, you know, and Noah blurted it was my birthday and that he didn't have a present for me, and Myles said he'd send flowers, so really, this was for Noah's sake, not mine . . .'

She stopped suddenly, noticing the look of bemusement on Tony's face.

'So what's "Myers" like, Noah?' he asked. 'Is he a good guy? Is he good to your mum?'

'Tony, he's my boss, that's all there is to it.'

'He gave Mummy a kiss,' Noah said, giggling again at the memory of it.

'On the cheek,' Helen added quickly. 'An innocent birthday kiss on the cheek.'

'And fifty quid's worth of flowers,' added Tony, raising an eyebrow.

'It's rude to talk about the cost of a gift,' Helen said airily. Besides, she didn't want to think about that. David had never given her flowers – he thought they were an obscene waste of money, but also, he liked to point out, an indefensible misuse of resources. Flower farms relied on excessive amounts of water and pesticides to grow what was totally nonessential produce. Flowers didn't feed anyone, heal anyone, or in fact provide anything of benefit to the community at large, according to David. But he was the type of person who thought making donations to charity in your name was the best gift he could give. And it probably was – maybe just not on every occasion.

'So, you're staying for dinner, aren't you?' Helen asked Tony, changing the course of the conversation. She had a feeling that anything she added after this would go into the 'protests too much' category. 'What am I saying? You're staying, of course, you're staying, this is your home. You're going to stay here, aren't you, Tony?'

'Well, they put us up in a hotel for the first week or two,' he said. 'After that we get a living allowance. Crew usually move to serviced apartments.'

'Tony, you have to stay here,' she insisted. 'This is your home.'

'It seems like you've got a bit of a full house though, Helen.'

'No, there's plenty of room. Noah can share with me.'

'I don't want to put anyone out –'

'You're not. I'd be put out if you didn't stay.'

'Look, the hotel's already paid for,' said Tony. 'But afterwards, I'd really like that, Hel. And I'm definitely going to start helping out with Mum. How is she? Really?'

Helen leaned back against the kitchen bench. 'She's been stable for a couple of months now, but she hasn't recognised me or Noah for quite a while. The best I get is that she's more comfortable around me than other people, like I'm familiar to her, she knows I'm okay, I can be trusted.' Helen paused. 'I wonder how she'll react to seeing you again.'

Tony shook his head. 'I doubt she'll recognise me, Hel.'

'But she asks after you all the time.'

'That's a fragment of her memory stuck on rewind, that's all. She's not going to know me.'

*

And she didn't, much to Helen's surprise. They went to visit her the following day, and Marion actually seemed wary of him. When Helen tried to reassure her it was Tony, Marion merely insisted she had a son Tony, and he was a very successful theatre director living in London.

Tony seemed unfazed.

'Are you okay?' Helen asked him when they left Marion's room.

'Of course,' he said. 'I told you I didn't expect her to know me. I've read up about Alzheimer's, Hel. It's a lot easier to take it in from a distance, to be objective about it. You had to watch it happen, suffer along with her. You've been a victim of it too, Helen. I can't imagine how difficult it must have been for you sometimes, and yet you stayed.'

She shrugged. 'It was my choice, Tony.'

'Was it really, though?' He paused. 'I've never said this to you, Hel, but I realised what was happening to Mum and I bailed, I ran away from it. After Dad, it was all too much.'

'But you'd always planned to travel, Tony.'

'Sure, I know, and I'm okay with what I did. I reckon I was entitled to my own life. Except my freedom meant you were tied down. I'm hoping one day you'll be able to forgive me for that.'

Helen slipped her arm through his. 'There's nothing to forgive,' she said. 'I made choices too,' she added as they walked out of the building and into the sunshine.

She paused at the door of the car, looking across at him. 'What did you mean yesterday, Tony, when you said that Dad didn't find a way out?'

He rested his forearms on the roof of the car. 'I think he couldn't see a way out, so he locked himself up in his own world.'

'You think they were unhappy? I always thought Dad adored her.'

Tony shrugged. 'Yeah, and as long as he adored her things were fine. But when he needed her, I don't think she had anything to give.'

'Did Mum tell you that?'

'Of course not,' he said. 'These are just the observations of a restless adolescent. I think Dad had been unhappy for a long time and suicide was the only way out he could see. That's why I had to leave, that was my way out.'

But Helen had stayed. She'd stayed so long she'd forgotten there was any other way.

'I'm glad you came back, Tony.'

He smiled at her. 'So am I.'

Thursday

Gemma had had enough of the hospital after three days, and told her mother that, ready or not, she was going home on Friday. That put Trish into a spin, and she consequently mounted a military-style operation to finish the rooms to her own exacting standards. Helen was glad to have an excuse to escape, taking the opportunity to go into work while Noah was at preschool. She joined the team as they reviewed all the material that had been collected or compiled. Hours of footage had already been edited down to a series of sound bites, and Julia and Helen went through them and selected the best. They'd also mocked up posters and print ads, and over the course of the day they whittled everything down to what they hoped would amount to an effective pitch, and then ran it all by Myles. There was still work to be done: the mock-ups had to be reproduced to a professional standard, the selected film clips collated into a punchy presentation, not to mention a myriad of other details, large and small, that would need attending to. But they all agreed they would be ready to pitch it to the client Monday week. Julia was to go ahead and make the necessary arrangements.

'You will be here for the pitch?' Myles asked in the elevator on their way back to the office.

'Of course,' said Helen.

She had finally got around to calling Jim and Noreen. Noreen had answered the phone and immediately offered to get Jim when Helen announced herself.

'No, that's okay, Noreen, I can talk to you about this,' Helen had assured her.

Noreen had been a little circumspect at first, but soon warmed up as Helen got to her reason for calling. She laid out the whole scenario for her – that she didn't expect Gemma to cope with Noah and the new baby for some weeks, even months, and although Helen was able to work from home a little, and Tony had offered to help in whatever way he could, Helen would greatly appreciate it if they could see their way clear to minding Noah at least one day a week on a regular basis, perhaps even two sometimes.

Noreen had been beside herself, and the warmth of her gratitude went a long way to defrosting any chill that remained between them.

Helen and Myles arrived at her workstation and she dumped the load of files she'd brought from the meeting onto her desk.

'I was just going to make coffee,' said Myles. 'Do you want one?'

Helen checked her watch. 'Sorry, Myles, I'll have to get going to pick up Noah. I don't know where the day went. And you do remember I won't be in tomorrow?'

He nodded. 'The homecoming.'

She smiled thinking about it. 'You know, I was so worried about taking Gemma on as a boarder, when I found out she was pregnant. But it's going to be pretty great to have a baby in the house again.' She looked at Myles. 'You haven't met Lola yet, have you?'

He shook his head. 'Couldn't get to the hospital. I've been short an assistant all week,' he said wryly.

'Well, you should come to the house on the weekend, if you're free, that is . . . any time,' said Helen.

He looked uncomfortable. 'I, um . . . maybe . . .'

'What is it, Myles?'

'I don't know that Gemma would be all that pleased to see me.'

Helen groaned. 'What is it with you two?'

Now he looked sheepish. 'It's complicated . . .'

'What does that even mean?' she said, frustrated. 'I don't understand, Myles. Gemma is a little out there, but she's not a bad person.'

'I know that.'

'In fact, she's a terrific person. She's vibrant and funny and bright, and capable, very capable . . .'

'I know.'

'She'd be way better at all this stuff than me. I wouldn't even be here without her.'

'I realise –'

'So why haven't you given her the same opportunities you've given me?'

Myles didn't say anything. But the way he was looking at her, maybe that was just as well. She turned her attention to the stack of files, feeling flustered. 'I'd better do something about this before I go.'

'Leave it,' Myles said, placing his hand on top of hers, on top of the stack. 'I want you to hear this, Helen. I haven't said anything before because Gemma is your friend. But the fact is she lied to get the job, and, as you know, I'm pretty sensitive about people lying to me. Maybe I'm too sensitive, and maybe I have been too hard on her, I don't know. But in my defence, I did hire her in the first place, and I didn't sack her when I found out she'd also lied about being pregnant. And I was open to the job-sharing idea even before I met you.'

Helen's head shot up. What was that supposed to mean?

'That is,' he added quickly, 'on its own merits . . . before I knew how it was going to turn out . . . oh, Christ, Helen, you know what I'm talking about.'

She couldn't look at him now. She stared fixedly at his hand covering hers. She could feel it all the way up her arm, like an electric current.

'I really have to get going,' she blurted suddenly, slipping her hand out from under his.

'Helen . . .'

She ignored him, grabbed her handbag and walked briskly away from the workstation. 'See you next week,' she called, glancing back as she got to the corner. Myles was still standing there, watching her as she disappeared down the corridor.

Homecoming

'Maybe I should stay another day . . . or two.'

'I don't think they'll let you,' Helen murmured over her shoulder. She was crouched in front of the bedside cabinet, packing Gemma's things into an overnight bag. Gemma hadn't been ready when she'd arrived to pick her up, not that Helen was particularly surprised. She was all too aware how eminently capable babies were of throwing a spanner in the works, how the smallest thing became a major strategic exercise, how on some days putting a brush through your hair could be considered an achievement.

'But what if something happens to her?' Gemma asked in a small voice.

Helen turned to look at her as Gemma's eyes filled with tears. 'Gemma,' she said gently, straightening up, 'you're healthy and Lola's healthy. Nothing's going to happen –'

'How do you know that?' She sat stiffly on the side of the bed, cradling Lola in her arms. 'Did you know that sometimes babies just stop breathing, for no reason? I was watching her last night, I pulled the crib close to my bed and just watched her sleeping, for ages. Her breathing was weird, stopping and starting, and sometimes I couldn't even tell if she was breathing . . .'

Helen could still recall the palpable fear she'd experienced taking Noah home. David had reminded her she was a trained nurse. Problem was, being a nurse meant she knew everything that could go wrong.

'Gemma, you're going to feel so much better in your own bed, in your own place, and I'll be right there . . .'

'Not all the time, Helen, you can't be there all the time. Not that I'd expect you to be.'

'We'll work out something,' Helen tried to reassure her. 'Between me, and your mum, and Phee, and Charlie, we've got your back, Gemma, I promise.'

That just made Gemma want to cry. But everything made her want to cry today. When they'd brought her breakfast, when the midwife had done Lola's final check, when Charlie had phoned, as he had every morning. Gemma felt like one giant tear duct.

'I don't know what's wrong with me. I've been so happy until now, I've been on a high, and now I feel . . . sad, and I don't understand why I'm feeling sad, because I'm not sad, I'm happy, so happy, and I love Lola so much, so why am I feeling so sad?'

'It's just the baby blues,' said Helen. 'It's completely normal, everyone gets them.'

'Oh, I think Phoebe read me something about that the other day, but I was only half listening. Will they go away?'

'Of course they will,' said Helen. *Hopefully. Usually.* 'I promise you, you're going to feel better once you're home. Why don't you go and have a shower, and I'll pack up your things so we can get out of here.'

'But what about Lola?'

'I'll watch her.'

'But you're going to pack.'

'I promise, I can manage both . . . and Lola will be my priority,' she added quickly, seeing the angst on Gemma's face.

'What if she needs feeding?'

'I'll knock on the bathroom door and let you know.'

Gemma bit her lip. 'I haven't given her a bath yet.'

'That's okay, I'll give her a quick wash.'

'Will that be enough?'

'Enough for what?'

'For the trip home?'

'You know,' said Helen, 'I think she'll be fine.'

Helen eventually shooed her into the shower and told her to take her time. But that was impossible; Gemma was convinced every distant cry of a baby throughout the hospital was Lola. Someone had told her that a mother could distinguish her own baby's cry. Bullshit. Or maybe she was a hopeless mother. That was probably closer to the truth. She started to cry herself. Poor, precious, beautiful Lola had drawn the short straw, and landed a mother who couldn't even tell her cry from any Jane Doe.

Gemma came out of the bathroom, still dripping, certain by now that Lola was hysterical, imagining Helen had left her on the bed and gone to start packing the car. But Lola was sleeping soundly in her crib, all wrapped up snug in that way only nurses seemed to be able to do, and Helen had collected all of their flotsam and jetsam into various bags and lined them up neatly along the bed, ready to go. Gemma could feel tears welling again. She wanted to be like Helen – capable, competent, calm – instead of harried and hopeless.

'Gemma, you're all wet,' Helen said.

She looked down. Her robe was soaked through and she was making a puddle on the floor. She couldn't even look after herself, much less a tiny baby who was totally dependent on her.

'Look, I'll take a load down and bring the car around to the entrance,' said Helen, 'and that'll give you time to get dressed, okay?'

She made four trips to the car while Gemma managed to dry herself, more or less, and put on some clothes, rather haphazardly. Her hair was still dripping onto her shoulders when they finally walked out through the main entrance of the maternity wing. Gemma felt the tepid, non-conditioned air, the sun on her skin. And she froze. This was it – she was all alone. She was leaving the safety net, flying without a parachute. She knew she had people around her, but in reality, when all was said and done, Gemma was on her own. Lola was solely her responsibility. And that was terrifying.

She felt Helen's hand on her back, gently propelling her towards the car. 'Let's go home.'

*

Despite her mother's protestations, Gemma had insisted she wanted Helen to take her home from the hospital. Trish in turn had insisted she would wait at the house, and that she'd supply lunch. In truth, her favourite caterer supplied lunch, and when Gemma and Helen arrived home, the kitchen table was covered with platters of gourmet finger sandwiches, miniature rice paper rolls and tiny savoury tarts, along with some decadent-looking cakes and slices. There was enough to feed a small peace-keeping force, although there were only the four of them. Gemma was so happy that Phoebe had taken time off work to come, she wanted to cry.

'Okay, ladies,' said Trish, getting their attention. 'It's time for the unveiling.' She crossed to the doorway, and stripped away the plastic sheet with the flourish of a magician.

Gemma stepped tentatively into the room so that she got the full effect. It was a pleasant surprise. Trish had curtailed her tendency towards excess and gone with a less-is-more philosophy. The sofa was an elegant charcoal, a simple timber shelf-unit housed the few ornaments, keepsakes and photographs remaining after the big cull. There were matching end tables and a coffee table, and unfussy timber blinds adorned the windows.

Gemma was overwhelmed: it was all so beautiful. Life was beautiful. Her baby was beautiful. She was sure to screw it all up. She wanted to cry.

'I can't even believe it's the same room,' said Helen, who was only getting to see it finished for the first time as well. Trish had been like a guard at Guantanamo Bay the last couple of days. No one had been given a look-in. 'It's wonderful. I don't know how to thank you, Trish.'

But Trish shrugged it off. 'Now, this is your father's and my gift to you, Gemma,' she announced, swanning around the one new piece of furniture in the room, as though she was a game-show hostess. It was an overstuffed, sumptuous-looking day bed, covered in plain cream cotton canvas. 'So you can be comfortable when you feed the baby.'

'Oh, Mum,' Gemma protested feebly, her throat tight, 'you've already bought me enough gifts.'

'No, they were all for Lola,' Trish dismissed. 'Now, come and see the nursery – it's my pièce de résistance.'

Don't cry, don't cry.

Gemma walked into Lola's room and caught her breath. Her mother had not restrained herself quite so much here, but still it wasn't overdone. The transformation was amazing. The walls were a lovely light sherbet lemon and all the woodwork and the ceiling were glossy white. The cot had been 'refurbished' to look like new, also painted white and made up with pretty lemon and white linen. The old bench had been converted into a change area, with everything Gemma would need lining the shelves within arm's reach. There was a thick white shag-pile rug on the polished floor, a rocking chair, a simple white wardrobe and chest of drawers, while a matching white bookcase fitted neatly into the alcove of the outer door, effectively sealing it off.

Perhaps the best feature of the room, at least for anyone who had known it in its previous incarnation, was the bright, clear window, which, while it didn't provide much of a view, did allow light into every corner.

Gemma couldn't speak. She was still looking around, awestruck.

'Well, darling, what do you think?' Trish finally prompted her.

'I think it's absolutely beautiful, Mum,' she said, tears springing into her eyes as she turned to throw her arms around Trish's neck. 'Thank you so much, thank you for everything,' she sobbed. 'I'm sorry for all the shit I've put you through . . . If I can be half the mother you are . . .'

'Oh, dear, you've got them bad, haven't you?'

Gemma lifted her head. 'What?'

'The baby blues.'

'You know about them?'

'Of course. Everyone gets them, darling, you needn't think you're anything special.'

For once Gemma appreciated Trish's unique way of stating the facts.

'Come along then, enough waterworks. Let's open that champagne and wet the baby's head, shall we?'

Gemma glanced at Helen. 'Is it all right for me to have a drink?' she asked her.

'A glass won't hurt, just make sure you have some food with it.'

There was no shortage of that, and the women spent the next couple of hours eating and drinking and talking and laughing. Except for Phoebe, who had her head buried in another baby manual for much of the time, reading out tips and interesting facts at intervals, until Trish, after she'd downed a couple of champagnes, picked up the book from Phoebe's lap and tossed it across the room.

'Don't read too many books, darling,' she confided to Gemma. 'You've got to work some things out for yourself.'

'Such as?' Gemma said.

'Well, for example, you'll never read in a baby book about what to do when your fifteen month old smears the entire contents of her nappy throughout her cot during the course of an afternoon nap.'

Gemma's jaw dropped. 'Who did that?'

'You, of course,' said Trish. 'I thought you'd been asleep for an unusually long time. I kept coming close to the door to listen, but there wasn't a peep. Then finally you started to call out. When I opened the door, it was the smell that hit me first.'

Gemma and Phoebe squealed in horror, but Helen just laughed knowingly.

'You were standing holding the side of the cot,' Trish went on, 'covered in poo from head to foot. The sheets were covered in it, the bumper, the cot itself, all your little rattles and toys hanging off the sides, your teddies . . .'

'How can one little baby do so much poo?' Gemma asked, glancing down at her angelic infant daughter.

'Wait till Lola fills one of her suits,' said Helen, 'and you see it oozing up over the collar.'

Phoebe looked like she was going to pass out.

'I had to take everything outside and hose it all off,' said Trish. 'Including you. Ben joined in, he was only three, and you both had a lovely old time dancing naked under the sprinkler.'

'So I was always getting myself into the shit, even from that young,' Gemma said wryly.

'Not at all.' Trish shook her head. 'You were a darling little thing. Always happy, full of beans, and you were my best sleeper.'

Gemma could feel tears coming on again. Her mother had never said nice things like that about her before. Or maybe she had, and Gemma just hadn't been listening.

Trish continued to regale them with tales of their childhood antics. Apparently once he was out of nappies, Ben liked to expose himself as often as he could get away with it, while as a crawling baby, Phoebe developed a taste, if not a craving, for bugs and snails and anything gross, and Gary once had to stop her determined little fist on its way to her mouth clutching a crusty dog poo.

Throughout the afternoon Gemma remained ensconced on her day bed, like a queen, feeding the baby at intervals while everyone waited on her. Lola was a contented little thing, so far, Gemma had been pleased to discover. And so exceptionally beautiful, she had trouble tearing her eyes away from her at times. She was still mystified as to how she'd managed to create such an exquisite little being. She was just going to keep her head low and be grateful, and cross her fingers that nothing bad would ever happen to her her whole life.

As the afternoon wore on, Gemma began to fade, almost nodding off in what was an extraordinarily comfy day bed.

'Well, I think that might be the signal for us to take our leave, Phoebe,' Trish declared as she began to bustle around clearing plates and glasses.

'Leave that, Trish,' Helen tried to insist.

'It won't take us a minute to clear this out to the kitchen at least. Save you a dozen trips back and forth.'

'I don't know why I'm so tired,' said Gemma, stifling a yawn. 'Was it the alcohol, do you think, Helen?'

She smiled. 'I suppose a glass and a bit could hit you hard when you haven't touched the stuff in a while. But coming home from the hospital really takes it out of you, Gemma, you'd be surprised. You should have a nap after they leave. I'll watch Lola.'

Gemma had to be persuaded, but in the end she slept the full hour and a half till Lola started to fuss for a feed.

Helen brought her into Gemma's room. 'I have to pick up Noah from preschool.'

'Oh, okay,' Gemma said sleepily, sitting up in the bed. 'Right now?'

'No, it's okay, take a minute to wake yourself up,' she said, swaying Lola in her arms.

'How long will you be?' Gemma asked.

'Not long, the usual.'

She nodded faintly.

Helen was watching her. 'You probably won't be finished feeding her by the time I get back.'

Gemma couldn't answer, for fear she was going to cry again.

'You can come with me if you want, for the drive.'

A knock sounded at the door.

'I'll get it,' said Helen, ducking out again.

Gemma realised she felt overwhelmed by the idea of being alone in the house with Lola, even for twenty minutes. She had an inordinate fear that something would go wrong and she wouldn't know what to do. She knew she had to get over it. She knew she had to learn to cope on her own, but did she have to do it so soon?

There was a light tap on her bedroom door.

'It's okay, Helen, I'm decent.'

But it was Charlie who stepped through the doorway, cradling Lola in his arms. He smiled widely at Gemma and she promptly burst into tears.

He went over to the bed and sat beside her. 'Hey, what's the matter, Gem?'

'I'm just so happy to see you,' she sobbed.

'You have a funny way of showing it,' he said, grinning at her.

She sniffed. 'Oh, this is just the baby blues, apparently. I have no control over it, I'm just sad all the time, even when I'm happy. I am happy to see you, really, Charlie.'

'Me too.' He put his arm around her and Gemma leaned her head on his shoulder, gazing down at Lola.

'Can you stay for a while?'

'Sure, I'm not going anywhere, Gem.'

Sunday

Gemma was lying back in the bath, feeling completely relaxed and finally at peace. The blues had begun to disperse yesterday – she'd actually physically felt it.

She looked down at herself. Her breasts were enormous now that her milk had come in, and she still had a soft little pot belly. But Gemma had never been so proud of her body; it had produced a human life, and now it was sustaining that life. She didn't feel hopeless anymore, she felt necessary, important, *essential* even. She was a little in awe of herself. The gloom had lifted and life and all its possibilities stretched before her.

Gemma finally dragged herself out of the bath, and when she was dried and dressed, she opened the door as Helen was just tiptoeing away. She turned around.

'Hi! You look like a new woman,' Helen remarked.

'I feel so much better.' Gemma sighed with relief. 'How was dinner?'

Tony had arrived that afternoon to meet Gemma and the baby, eventually suggesting they go for a meal somewhere along Darling Street. Gemma didn't feel up to it, so Helen, Noah and Tony had gone off together, once Charlie had assured Helen he was happy to stay with Gemma. He'd been hanging around most of the weekend; Gemma had a feeling that had a lot to do with the lift in her spirits.

'It was lovely, thanks,' Helen said. 'Hey, have you seen this?' she said, stepping into Gemma's room. Charlie was curled up on the bed, with Lola sleeping peacefully in the protective arc of his arms. 'Isn't that gorgeous?'

'He sure is,' Gemma said dreamily.

Helen bid her goodnight, and Gemma crept softly into the room and around the side of her bed. She carefully picked up Lola and placed her in the newborn crib she was keeping in here for now – she couldn't cope with being too far away from her just yet. Lola squirmed a little and then went quiet again. Gemma turned and sat in the space where Lola had been, gazing down at Charlie. He looked very boyish when he was sleeping. She reached out and stroked the hair from his forehead. He was such a good friend, such a good man, and he was wonderful with Lola. She sat watching him, and the longer she watched him, the more she felt as though she'd never really seen him before.

She placed her hand on his shoulder and gave him a gentle nudge. He blinked a couple of times and then squinted up at her, staring at her from that surreal place between asleep and awake. Gemma had a sudden, overwhelming urge . . . What the hell. She leaned over and kissed him soundly on the lips, lingering long enough so he couldn't mistake her intention. She drew back to look at him and he opened his eyes slowly again, focusing on her. He didn't say anything for a while. Finally he rubbed his eyes and sat up.

'Gemma?' he said huskily.

'Yes, Charlie?'

'Did you just kiss me?'

'I might have.'

'Because I was just waking up, and I wasn't sure if I was dreaming, or if you really kissed me.'

'Do you dream about me often, Charlie?'

'Don't confuse the issue.'

'Okay, what were you saying?'

'That kiss,' he said, 'it seemed to me that it wasn't the kind of kiss you give a friend.'

'No, I wouldn't have called it a friendly kiss either.'

He sighed deeply. 'I don't know if that's such a good idea, Gem.'

'Well I think it's a wonderful idea,' she said. 'I don't know why I didn't think of it sooner.'

'I did,' he said, 'but that was a long time ago.'

'I know you did. But then you've always been smarter than me, Charlie.'

'But that's the thing, Gem, I don't know how smart this is right now. You've got some crazy hormone action going on and you could snap out of it in a few weeks, and then what? We end up ruining a beautiful friendship.'

'Charlie, I don't feel crazy right now,' said Gemma. 'I feel sane and lucid and like I'm seeing things clearly for the first time.'

'Gem –'

'I don't want to ruin a beautiful friendship either, I just want to take it to another level.'

He looked into her eyes, touching her cheek with the backs of his fingers. 'Let's just leave things as they are, Gem. It's safer that way.'

His voice sounded different. Was his voice different?

'I don't want to be safe.'

'I thought that's exactly what you wanted,' he reminded her. 'You said you didn't want to take any more risks.'

She'd never noticed his voice had such a sexy timbre. It was making her a little goosebumpy.

'Yeah, with losers, not with someone like you, Charlie. I can't believe I've never thought of this before. How often have I said I'll never find someone as good and as decent as you? And you've been right in front of me the whole time.'

'Yeah, exactly,' he said. 'Doesn't that tell you something?'

'What do you mean?'

'Never mind.' He sighed heavily and dropped his head, rubbing it vigorously so when he lifted it to look at her again, his hair was more ruffled than ever. 'Listen, you just got home from the hospital with a brand-new baby. I don't think you should be rushing into anything.'

'But –'

'Gem,' he said, 'like I told you before, I'm not going anywhere. Okay?'

Okay. So he wanted to take it slow, that's all he was saying. That meant he was definitely considering it. Gemma could live with that.

The Pitch

Helen had managed to work every day of the past week; with all hands on deck, Noah had been looked after and entertained the entire time. Charlie had even offered to pick him up from preschool on Thursday and Friday so she didn't have to rush home on those days either. Charlie had become a regular fixture around the place. He'd taken some long-standing leave to explore his options in film production, and Gemma had effectively hijacked him to help out with the baby. He didn't seem to mind.

So the presentation was as ready as it was ever going to be. They'd even had time for Julia to run through a full dress rehearsal on Friday afternoon, in front of Helen and the rest of the team. Myles had been in a meeting, but he was satisfied from Helen's feedback that they were ready to go.

Helen and Myles hadn't had a lot to do with each other all week, which was just as well – Helen needed to maintain focus, and that was becoming increasingly difficult when Myles was around. She found herself getting flustered, behaving quite out of character, dropping things and forgetting what she was about to say. And any time she caught his eye, he looked at her in a way that was more than a little disconcerting. She found it easier just to avoid him.

Now, after a quiet weekend catching up with Noah, and the housework, and the washing, Helen had to admit to a little excitement over the prospect of sitting in on the pitch. She had not even sat in on a client meeting before, let alone one she'd been so closely involved in.

'Wow,' Gemma said from her throne in the back room when Helen walked out, dressed ready for work. 'What's the occasion?'

Helen had decided to wear her mother's outfit again, the one she'd worn to the interview. She hadn't ventured into it since, only the jacket a few times, worried that the full ensemble was a bit much for everyday office wear. But she thought it might be okay for today.

'Oh, it's just the pitch for that campaign I've been helping out on,' Helen said, still a little reluctant to tell Gemma too much. She shouldn't have worried though, Gemma's mind was somewhere else altogether these days. Even now she was gazing down at Lola in her arms, barely giving Helen half her attention. She stirred, looking up.

'Well, you look great, go knock 'em dead,' she said.

'Will you be okay on your own?' Helen asked. Jim had already been to collect Noah, which had given her extra time to get ready.

'Your brother's still in there asleep, don't forget,' said Gemma.

Helen wasn't yet used to the fact that Tony was living with them, he'd only moved in over the weekend. And he would be keeping actors' hours – not expected at the theatre till late morning and most likely not home until after dinner. After the play actually started they wouldn't see much of him at all, so despite his initial protests, he was hardly going to get in the way.

'Besides,' Gemma was saying, 'Charlie will be here soon enough. We're going to hit the shops today.'

'You take it easy,' Helen warned. 'It's still only early days.'

'Don't worry, Charlie fusses over me like an old woman. He won't let me do anything, let alone overdo anything.'

They hadn't spoken about the Charlie factor, mostly because he was generally always in earshot. 'Is there something going on between you two?' asked Helen.

'I don't know,' said Gemma. 'Kind of, I'd like there to be, but I'm running into some opposition.'

'So you've actually broached the idea with him?'

'You could put it that way.'

Helen was confused.

'I kissed him,' she said.

'That's pretty direct. Did he kiss you back?'

'Not exactly, he was half-asleep at the time.'

Helen frowned. 'Was he aware that you'd kissed him?'

'Oh, sure. But he reckons it's not a good time to start something. He thinks it's just my crazy baby hormones, and that when the air clears, I'll dump him. He's so wary, and I don't want to be, but he makes me a little wary as well.' She paused. 'How did you know David was the one?'

'Pardon?' Helen said, flinching slightly.

'How did you know David was right for you?'

She shrugged, perching on the end of the day bed. She noticed one of Lola's tiny feet had poked out of her bunny rug, and reached over to cover it again.

'I don't know that I'm the best person to give advice on anyone's love life,' Helen said wryly.

'Why, you and David were happy, weren't you?'

'Of course,' she said. 'I just haven't had a lot of experience, that's all.'

Gemma lifted an eyebrow. 'Was there anyone before David?'

'Oh, sure. Years back. No one particularly earth-shattering though.'

'So, how did you know David was right for you?' Gemma repeated.

'I don't know, really. He was persistent, I gave in.'

'You gave in?'

'I guess I eventually believed that he really did want to be with me, and I accepted it.'

'So I just need to persist then?' said Gemma. 'Till Charlie's convinced that I'm serious.' She smiled down at Lola. 'That it's not just baby hormones.'

Helen watched them for a long moment before she roused herself. 'I'd better head off. Listen, the pitch is not till later this afternoon – I'm not sure what time I'll be home.'

'No problem,' said Gemma. 'Charlie and I will be here for Noah.'

During the drive into work, Helen couldn't get the conversation with Gemma out of her head. David had been persistent, certainly. But there hadn't been much in the way of romance – the omnipresence of a dementia-riddled mother had put a dampener on that. Or maybe she and David just weren't romantic types. Once upon a time Helen thought she might have been. She'd had crushes on boys at school, a few flings when she was training to be a nurse; she'd had her passionate moments. But where had it all gone? Helen feared she had turned into someone she'd never intended to become, and she wouldn't have become, had the circumstances of her life been different. What if her mother had been well? What if she'd gone overseas to join Tony after all?

But that was just pointless speculation. Everyone had to operate within the circumstances life threw at them. She was no different.

*

When Helen arrived at Bailey's she went directly to her workstation. Myles would be out of the office all morning, but she had a tonne of filing and correspondence to deal with after having been otherwise occupied for much of last week. It would be good to have a focus, fill in the time, take her mind off the butterflies that had curiously fluttered into her stomach. However, she couldn't resist firing off a quick email to Julia to make sure everything was set and to check if she needed anything. For the next few hours Helen became absorbed in her work. It wasn't the most exciting stuff, but she quite enjoyed the routine tasks – more the completing of them than the actual doing of them. It was very satisfying to have an empty in-tray, a clear desk, and every email answered or actioned appropriately.

It had just occurred to Helen that she hadn't heard back from Julia when Myles came around the corner. He smiled broadly as soon as he saw her.

'Hey, look at you,' he said. 'That was the dress you wore to the interview, wasn't it?'

Helen nodded, reaching for the jacket hanging over the back of her chair. She'd found it a bit warm for this time of the year, but she slipped it on now, aware that Myles was watching her.

'I'm remembering why I gave you the job,' he murmured.

She flicked her hair out from under the jacket. 'Keep it up and I'll go home and change.'

'No, no, don't do that. I'm very glad you went to the trouble to dress up, though they're not the same shoes, I hope?'

That made Helen smile, despite herself.

'Come into my office, would you, Helen?' he said. 'We need to talk.'

That sounded vaguely ominous. She grabbed a notebook and followed him. She stood on the other side of his desk, a little apprehensively, while he calmly unpacked his briefcase and closed it again, placing it on the floor beside him. He looked across at her. 'Sit, make yourself comfortable.'

'What's going on, Myles?'

He sat down, waiting for her to do the same. She lowered herself onto the edge of the chair behind her, looking expectantly at him across the desk.

'Julia has taken ill,' he began.

'Oh no –'

'It's not serious,' he assured her quickly. 'But she's in no state to deliver the pitch. She thinks she might have eaten a bad prawn at a barbecue yesterday.'

'Oh, that's awful,' said Helen, grimacing. 'What are we going to do? Should we postpone?'

'Oh no, that's not necessary.' Myles leaned forward in his chair and replaced his glasses as he began to shuffle the papers in front of him. 'You can handle it.'

Helen didn't quite catch that. 'I'm sorry?'

'You can handle the pitch.'

Her stomach did a sickening flip. 'No, I can't.'

'Yes, you can.'

'No, I can't.'

'Can too.'

'Can *not*.'

Myles looked at her over the top of his glasses. 'We could play this all day but it won't get us anywhere, Helen.'

'Exactly,' she said. 'I can't do it, and that's the end of it.'

'You know, I don't place a lot of stock in what you have to say in that regard.'

'What?'

'Helen,' said Myles, removing his glasses again to look at her directly. 'You've been saying "I can't do it" for months now, about almost every opportunity or challenge that's put in front of you.

And yet time and time again you prove yourself wrong. It appears you're a very poor judge of your own abilities, and therefore not really capable of making this decision. So I'm going to have to make it for you. I have complete faith that you can deliver the pitch, and, unlike you, I haven't been wrong yet.'

Helen was staring at him, gobsmacked. 'Myles,' she said, her voice quivering, 'you have to believe me . . . I really can't do this.'

He gave a sigh like a bemused teacher hearing that the dog had eaten her homework again. 'Helen, listen to the facts. You have been involved in this campaign from the very beginning. You've worked more closely with the team than I have –'

'Someone else in the team can do it!' she said suddenly. 'There, that's it. That's the answer.'

But Myles was shaking his head. 'No one else feels confident.'

'Well, neither do I.'

'But we've already established that you don't know what you're talking about.'

She frowned at him.

'At least in this respect,' he was quick to add. 'I've been down discussing it with the team and we looked at all the options. Everyone agreed you were the obvious choice.'

'But I'm not, Myles,' she said. 'I hate getting up in front of people –'

'There's nothing to it. You know what they say – you just have to imagine your audience naked.'

Helen groaned. 'I assure you, that's not going to help. You don't understand, I was never any good at public speaking at school.'

'How long ago was that?'

She raised an eyebrow. 'Well, thanks.'

'Sorry,' he said, holding up his hands. 'I didn't mean . . . oh, never mind.' He sat back in his chair, gazing steadily at her. 'I wish you'd believe in yourself more, Helen.'

She looked at him to see if he was teasing her, but the sincerity in his eyes was quite disarming.

'Six months ago,' Myles went on, 'would you have dreamed that you'd be handling a job like this? Not only handling it, but excelling at it?' He paused, weighing his words carefully. 'Twelve months ago,' he said quietly, 'could you ever have imagined that you'd find the strength to go on, let alone achieve everything you have?'

Helen felt a sudden pang in her heart. Twelve months ago she'd had no idea what was ahead of her, how much her life was about to change.

'You can do this, Helen,' Myles was saying. 'I know you can, but you won't know it until you give it a go.'

She went to speak but only a strangled croak came out. She cleared her throat. 'What if I screw up, Myles? And I don't mean fluffing a line, I mean hugely, disastrously, catastrophically screwing up.'

He appeared to be contemplating that seriously. 'Well, you know, I'm pretty sure that whatever happens, the world will keep revolving, and the sun will still rise tomorrow.'

She rolled her eyes. 'I'm serious, Myles.'

'So am I. What's the worst that could happen? Couldn't be any worse than anything you've been through already.'

'But –'

'Enough, Helen,' said Myles, getting to his feet. 'I'm the MD and I choose you. The buck stops with me if it doesn't work out. Are we agreed?'

She sighed heavily. 'I don't seem to have a choice.'

'So we are agreed,' he said cheerfully. 'Now, how about lunch?'

'I couldn't, I'll be sick.'

'You'll be sick come three o'clock if you haven't eaten anything,' he said, getting up and going round to her side of the desk. 'Come on, take your mind off it for a while.'

'I doubt that,' she grumbled, allowing him to lead her from the room. 'I might find out where Julia got her bad prawn.'

Myles looked at her. 'But you're a vegetarian, you don't eat them.'

'I could make an exception just this once.'

Three o'clock

Helen made one last-ditch attempt to get out of it as she and Myles made their way around to the presentation lounge. 'What if I throw up?' she hissed.

'Pardon?'

'What if I throw up?' she repeated, under her breath. 'It's what I do, you know, when I get nervous.'

'You're not going to throw up,' said Myles, unperturbed.

'How do you know?'

'Because I'm psychic.'

Helen looked at him sideways.

'No, really, I have psychic powers. Haven't I told you that already?' he said, deadpan. 'I thought I had.'

'Now you're being ridiculous.'

'You mark my words, because you'll be eating them later.'

'That doesn't even make sense.'

They had arrived at the lift bay and the doors were sliding open. The client might have been a giant of the cleaning products industry, but he was a rather weedy, insubstantial man in person. He came complete with a sidekick – together they resembled a live-action version of Burns and Smithers from *The Simpsons*. Helen had no intention of trying to imagine either of them naked. The fact that the client seemed rather innocuous did help her to feel a little less anxious, but on an anxiety scale of one to ten she was currently sitting on seventy-three, so it didn't make a whole lot of difference.

But a strange thing happened to Helen as soon as she took the floor, after everyone was introduced, seated and waiting for her to begin. She stepped outside herself, and the part remaining stepped into Julia's shoes, moving back and forth across the front of the room with ease and confidence, reciting the same words, the words Helen knew off by heart anyway, rattling off statistics, dropping the odd witty anecdote as she worked in tandem with the images on the screen. Helen watched herself, fascinated. She looked around the room. The rest of the team were hanging off her every word, smiling encouragingly whenever she made eye contact. The weedy man laughed here and there, making a rather gross catarrh sound in his throat. The rest of the time he listened intently, nodding now and then. The only thing putting her off in the entire room was Myles, the look in his eye. He'd better not be imagining her naked.

And then Helen realised she was done. The presentation was over. She slipped back inside herself in time for her closing line.

'So, to finish, Mr Booth, we believe that with this campaign on screens, in print and on billboards around the country, before long everyone will be talking about why they buy Bio-Jet.'

Helen was finally game to glance at Myles. He was smiling proudly at her, giving her a discreet thumbs-up.

'Well, young lady,' said Mr Booth, 'that was a very enjoyable little show you put on. I haven't met you before today, have I?'

'No, sir,' his faithful assistant chimed in before Helen had the chance to answer.

'I didn't think so,' Mr Booth said, nodding. 'Anyhow, no offence to you, my dear, but I hate the idea.'

Helen could only stare at him, gobsmacked.

'What are you saying exactly, Mr Booth?' Myles broke in.

He turned his head away to look at Myles. Which was just as well, because Helen thought she was going to pass out. She stepped closer to the lectern, leaning on it for support. This was bad. Clearly she'd completely botched the presentation. But she thought it had gone so well. Maybe she was delirious the whole time? She must have been. That whole out-of-body experience was obviously part of her delirium. God only knew what she'd really said.

'I'm saying I'm not fussed on it, Myles,' Mr Booth repeated. 'Didn't grab me at all. Thanks for making an effort, people,' he glanced around, 'but you know what I like? I like all that sciencey-techno stuff, enzymes blasting the stain molecules, wiping them out,' he said, making sound effects like a video game and then laughing to himself, while Smithers echoed his laughter. 'And those snippy little animations that clever young lad puts together, what's his name?'

'Charlie Lambert,' said Smithers.

'Ah, yes. Is Charlie around today?' he asked.

'No, he's on leave at the moment, Mr Booth,' Myles said.

'Pity. Okay, well anyway,' he said, standing up, so they all jumped to their feet as well. 'Call me again when you've got something along those lines. Stain-fighting enzymes,' he added, making another sound effect.

Myles escorted him and Smithers back out to the lift bay. Helen was still standing in the same spot, dumbfounded. 'I'm so fired,' she finally managed to say.

'No, no.' The team clustered around her, assuring her she'd done a great job it wasn't her fault stuck in a timewarpcrazyoldguy . . . but their words all ran into each other so Helen couldn't understand what they were saying anymore.

'I have to go,' she said, stumbling out of the room. She thought she might be sick. She wasn't sure, but she felt very strange. When she made it to Myles's office she burst through the door, shedding her jacket on the way to the bathroom. She leaned over the toilet for a few minutes, but nothing happened. She just felt flushed and a little spaced out. She wet one of the cloth handtowels at the basin and held it over her face. That felt better. Helen slid down onto the floor, onto the cool tiles.

She was still there when Myles knocked on the door a little while later. 'Helen, are you in there?'

A weak 'Mm' was all she could muster.

'Are you okay?'

'Mm.'

There was a pause for a moment.

'Can I come in?'

'Mm.'

Myles tried to push the door open but Helen was in the way. She shifted, sitting up with the towel still pressed to her head, as he opened the door right back.

He crouched down, concerned. 'Were you sick?'

She shook her head.

'Well, see, I told you you wouldn't be.'

Helen lifted the cloth off her forehead and looked at him squarely. 'Myles, you also said that I could do it, that you had every confidence in me.'

'I do,' he said. 'And you did.'

'And it tanked!' she cried.

'Not the presentation,' he said calmly. 'Just the idea.'

'Myles,' she groaned.

'It's true. Mr Booth said so himself – you put on a great show. He just didn't like the idea.'

'It was my idea as well.'

'No, you can't take the credit for that. It was my idea to take something you said and create a campaign. That's what tanked. You were great. So, can we get out of here now?' He straightened up again. 'It's a little cramped.'

Myles reached out his hand and Helen took it reluctantly, letting him help her up onto her feet. Out in the office he opened one of the built-in panels to the wet bar and took a bottle out of the fridge. 'Champagne?'

'You can't be serious?' said Helen.

'Why not? Don't you want to celebrate?'

'Myles, you do realise what actually happened back there?'

He glanced at her. 'No need to get patronising, Helen,' he said levelly, grabbing two glasses from the rack. 'Don't be a wet blanket. We've worked really hard for weeks on this. Ah! Don't!' He held up a finger to stop her as she went to protest again.

'As I was saying,' he continued, 'we worked really hard and put together a very impressive presentation, which you pitched perfectly. Come on, you must have felt it, Helen, you were fantastic.'

'But he didn't like it,' she said weakly.

'He didn't like the *idea*,' Myles repeated patiently.

'Why doesn't that bother you?'

'It does,' he said. 'Obviously I would have preferred that he liked it, but it doesn't wipe out all the good work we did. And it's not going to stop me opening this champagne.'

Helen released a defeated sigh as she trudged over to the couch and fell onto it, fully prone, while Myles proceeded to open the bottle and fill their glasses. He turned around to see her sprawled out on the couch.

'Well, look at you,' he said. 'Right back where we started.'

Helen rolled onto her side, propping her head on her hand and taking the glass Myles offered. He moved the coffee table out a little and sat himself down on the floor, resting his back against the couch near her.

Helen decided she couldn't really drink lying down like this, so she slid off the couch to join him. He smiled at her, holding his glass up. 'What are we going to drink to?'

'I can't think of a single thing,' she said. 'I can't believe you're not bothered about what happened.'

'Look, I'm not thrilled, Helen,' Myles admitted. 'I'm certainly not looking forward to the next time I have to face Justin,' he added with a wry grin.

'But all that work, all that effort, a whole campaign down the tubes.'

'Not a whole campaign, just a pitch. There's no guarantee a pitch will be successful. They often have to be reworked or even dumped altogether.'

'What about all that money? It seems like such a waste.'

'That may be, but it's par for the course,' said Myles. 'Don't forget, the idea could be adapted for other campaigns – it's not completely dead in the water yet. Besides, everybody would have learned something from the experience.'

Helen was looking at him dubiously.

'It's true. Like I learned that I don't know shit about advertising.'

She laughed then.

'You know, Helen, if we only attempted the things that were guaranteed to succeed, we wouldn't get very far.' He shifted to face her. 'What about you, huh? You didn't think you could do it,' he said, 'and you nailed it like a pro.'

Helen shrugged.

'I really didn't think you'd go through with it today.'

She looked up at him. 'You didn't give me a choice.'

'You always had a choice.'

'Now you tell me.'

He smiled. 'You know you're a pretty amazing woman, Helen. And I'm being serious, I'm not just flattering you,' he added, seeing her blush. 'You came into this job cold and look how well you've done. What do you think you'll do after this?'

'I'm sorry?' She frowned.

'Well, you're obviously not going to stay in advertising forever. But I reckon you could do pretty much anything you set your mind to. So what do you want to do, Helen?'

She thought about it. 'You know, I don't think anyone's ever asked me that before.'

'Then that's definitely what we should drink to,' he said, raising his glass. 'To you, Helen, and to your future, whatever you want it to be.'

Whatever she wanted it to be ... It was true – Helen could decide that now, reinvent herself. Perhaps she'd already started the process. She clinked her glass against his, and then drank the entire contents down in one go. She put the empty glass on the coffee table and wiped her mouth with the back of her hand.

Myles was just watching her. 'Okay, you're on. Let's get drunk.' He got up again to fetch the bottle. 'I reckon we're entitled after today.'

'No, Myles, I can't,' Helen protested. 'I have to get home for Noah, and I'm driving, so that's my limit.'

He turned around to look at her. 'Who has Noah today?'

'His grandparents.'

'Can't they keep him for the night?'

Helen shook her head. 'I don't really like him staying there overnight. Besides,' she checked her watch, 'they've probably already dropped him home.'

'So who's with him at home?'

'Gemma, and Charlie as well, most likely. And Tony later on. I told Gemma I wasn't sure what time I'd get home and she said it was all right, they'd be there.'

'Okay then,' Myles said, dropping back down on the floor beside her. 'So you don't have to leave so soon.'

'They'd still expect me by dinner, and I still have to drive,' Helen pointed out as he went to refill her glass.

'We'll see about that.' He put down the bottle and took his phone out of his pocket.

'What are you doing?'

He ignored her, pressing buttons on his phone and holding it to his ear. 'Charlie,' he said a moment later. 'It's Myles here, the MD . . . No, Helen's still here with me. Is Noah home yet?'

Myles covered the phone with his hand. 'They just dropped him off. He said there's no need to hurry.' He spoke into the phone again. 'Well, here's the thing, Charlie, Helen might not make it home till quite late. I'm going to take her out and get her drunk –'

'Myles!' she exclaimed.

'– so is Noah okay there with you guys?' He listened before covering the phone again. 'He says it's fine,' he told Helen. 'And that we should have a good night.'

'Can I talk to him, please?' she said archly.

Myles handed her the phone and proceeded to refill her glass.

'Hi, Charlie?' said Helen.

'Hey, Helen.'

She could hear the tone in his voice, see the knowing smile, the raised eyebrow. And wait till he told Gemma. 'Are you sure this isn't a problem?' she said. 'Were you planning to hang around there tonight? I'm not sure when Tony will get home.'

'Doesn't matter, I'll be here anyway,' said Charlie. 'Go out, have a good time, Helen.' There was that tone again.

'Thank you. Um, is Noah around, can I speak to him?'

'Sure, hold on. *Noah?* Your mum's on the phone.'

A few moments later Noah's voice came on the line. 'Hi, Mummy, guess what?'

'What, sweetheart?'

'Lola smileded at me! And Gemma said it was the first time!'

'Oh, that's wonderful, you must be her favourite,' said Helen, and Noah giggled in response. 'Listen sweetie, are you okay if I don't come home till later tonight? It might not be till after you're in bed.'

'That's okay, Mummy,' he chirped.

'Did you have a good time with Nan and Pop today?'

'Mummy, Charlie's calling me. I haffa go, we're making pancakes!'

'Oh, okay, darling, I'll see you later, though you probably won't see me till morning . . . Noah?' But she realised he'd already hung up. Helen lowered the phone, contemplating it.

'Is everything all right?' Myles asked.

'Great, apparently,' she said, handing him the phone. 'I don't think he's going to miss me at all.'

'And that bothers you?' he said, handing her the glass he'd refilled.

Helen shrugged. 'I don't know. You want them to be strong and independent, then when they are, you realise they don't need you anymore.'

'Helen, Noah's only four years old. I think he's going to need you for a while yet.'

'But it's the beginning of the end,' she said wistfully, sipping her champagne.

'I wouldn't have taken you for a "glass half-empty" kind of girl,' said Myles.

She looked at him sideways. 'Don't you think I have more reason than most people to expect the worst?'

'Maybe,' he shrugged, 'but then again, you also have more reason than most people to understand how short life is, to try to live every day to the full, like it could be your last.'

Helen snorted. 'That's so much bullshit.'

Myles looked at her. 'Helen, I've never heard you talk like that.'

'Then you'd better get used to it, drink loosens my tongue.'

He raised a sly eyebrow. 'There are so many lines I could say right now, but I'll restrain myself.'

'The thing is,' Helen went on, ignoring the innuendo, 'if it was your last day on earth and you knew it was, of course you'd do things differently. You wouldn't do the laundry and clean the bathroom, but someone would have to after you were gone. Those things still have to be done. Besides, I reckon anyone who knew they were going to die would give anything to have the rest of their lives just to do the ordinary day-to-day things.'

Myles nodded. 'Do you think your husband would have done anything different if he'd known?'

Helen looked at him. 'Well, I hope he wouldn't have stepped off that kerb.'

'Good point.'

'No, living each day as though it's your last is just a romantic notion,' she said, taking a long sip from her glass. 'And I'm not much of a romantic.'

'You're not?' Myles asked.

'No, apparently. Not that I have anything against it – it might be kind of nice, in fact. I just don't think I've ended up that way.' She turned to look at him. 'What about you?'

'I'm a hopeless romantic,' he said without hesitation. 'I think that's why I'm still single.'

'Poor Myles.' Helen smiled. 'But hold on, I seem to remember you saying you were nearly married once. What happened there?'

'I called it off.'

'You called it off, Mr Romance?'

'And there's that patronising tone again,' Myles said. 'Thought I'd just point it out, you might want to work on that.'

'So what happened?' Helen persisted, ignoring him.

'We'd been together a few years, living together for eighteen months,' he began. 'We met at management school. She was a real go-getter, very ambitious, and not only about her career – she had this whole life plan thing worked out.'

'Did "she" have a name?'

He looked sheepish. 'Michelle. So we dated, got serious, moved in together, and we'd started thinking about buying our own place, when Michelle pointed out that in her life plan she had "wedding" before "mutual real estate purchase". So I said okay.'

'You didn't propose, Mr Rom–' Helen pressed her lips together.

'I admit, I don't remember actually proposing, but next thing we were planning a wedding. It was like a military exercise, the whole thing turned into a nightmare, taking up all our time, costing a small fortune . . . I woke up one day and realised I couldn't go through with it.'

'So what did you do?'

'I knew I had to tell her, as soon as possible, before one more cent was spent or one more rose petal plucked or bead sewn or dove placed into captivity.'

'Wow, it was going to be one of those weddings.'

'Think over-the-top, and then exaggerate. It was a huge choreographed extravaganza designed to impress everyone. It didn't seem to have anything to do with our feelings for each other. And that's when I realised that my feelings were never going to live up to the hype of the wedding. It was all a lot of false advertising.'

'Weddings generally are, don't you think? Designed to numb you into a false sense of security. Happily ever after and all that,' Helen said wistfully.

'Did you have a big wedding?'

'God no, David would never have stood for that,' she said. 'We went to the registry. My mother couldn't have coped with anything more anyway, and Tony wasn't able to get back, so we really didn't have any reason to make a big shebang out of it. David's family were a bit miffed though, so we compromised by having drinks back at their place afterwards with a whole lot of relatives we didn't know.'

'Good times,' Myles said dryly.

Helen sighed, scoffing down half her glass.

'I'm sorry, that was really insensitive,' he said seriously.

'But also true,' she said. 'So what happened in the end? I take it Michelle must have been pretty pissed off if she was in the middle of organising a big wedding and you suddenly pulled the plug.'

Myles nodded. '"Pissed off" is putting it mildly. But when she calmed down and we talked it out, we both realised we weren't all that sure we wanted to be married to each other for the rest of our lives. We didn't hate each other, we just didn't really love each other that much.'

Helen had been listening intently, and she'd also emptied her glass. She went to reach for the bottle when Myles realised and picked it up first. She watched him refilling her glass. He'd rolled his sleeves back, so his forearms were exposed. They were strong forearms, she noted, very manly. She had a sudden urge to stroke the hair . . .

She picked up her glass and gulped down a couple of mouthfuls. 'So,' she said, trying not to look at his forearms, or think about his forearms for that matter, 'no one's caught your eye since Michelle?'

Myles opened his mouth to speak, but then he changed his mind. He just looked at her instead, with those bloody brown puppy-dog eyes of his.

'You know what, don't answer that,' said Helen, jumping up to her feet too quickly so she almost overbalanced, except that Myles reached up and grabbed her hip to steady her. And he was gazing up at her still, with those eyes, his hand firmly grasping her hip, apparently sending some kind of electrical charge through her body. What was it with his hands?

'Let's get out of here,' Helen declared, a little breathless.

'Where do you want to go?'

'Oh, somewhere loud, with music, and people. Lots of people.'

*

They caught a taxi out front and proceeded to drive around the city for the next forty minutes, looking for some action. The heat had brought a brief thunderstorm and rain, and the traffic snarled along, getting them nowhere in a hurry. The best they could find was a couple of quiet bars with piped jazz music playing in the background, though there was a piano player at one place they poked their heads into. Not exactly what Helen had in mind.

'What is wrong with this city?' she said, frustrated. 'All these years thinking I've been missing out on something and there's nothing going on anyway.'

'It is a Monday night,' Myles reminded her.

'So? Doesn't anyone like going out on a Monday night?'

'I do know a place that plays really good music . . .' Myles said tentatively. 'It's not far from here actually.'

'Oh?' said Helen. 'Well, what are we waiting for?'

'There won't be a lot of people around though.'

She shrugged. 'Beggars can't be choosers at this point.'

Myles gave the driver an address and they pulled up in front of what looked like a hotel. He paid the driver and they got out of the taxi. Helen looked up. 'What is this place?' she asked.

Myles glanced at her a little warily. 'It's where I live, actually.'

'Oh, it is, is it?' She put her hands on her hips, eyeing him suspiciously. 'You failed to mention that little detail before.'

'We don't have to stay, Helen,' he said solemnly. 'We could go to one of those bars, or back to the office, or we could always go to your place if you want.'

Helen considered the options. She didn't want to go anywhere they'd checked out already, and she certainly didn't want to go back to the office. She felt like kicking back a little, and she wouldn't be able to do that at home with Noah and the baby, not to mention Gemma and Charlie and now Tony looking on, making their innuendoes, pulling their silly faces and conjecturing till the cows came home. Helen just wanted to have some fun, without an audience. But she wasn't sure what Myles had in mind. Or how she felt about that.

She looked at him. 'Do you really have good music?'

He plucked his phone out of his pocket. 'A thousand songs.'

'What? Are we going to have to share headphones?'

He smiled. 'No, it syncs into my sound system.'

She hesitated, but became conscious of her stomach growling mildly. 'Do you have any food up there?'

Myles nodded. 'And running water and electricity and all the mod cons. We could go up and relax, have something to eat, listen to music . . . Or if you like, we could stand out here all night.'

He was right, this was silly. She was a grown adult, and she liked Myles. She liked being with him, she felt good around him. And she trusted him. Maybe she was being naive and unworldly, but there was no reason to assume that going up to his apartment had to lead to anything. Though just to be on the safe side . . .

'Okay, but let me make one thing clear,' said Helen. 'I'm not going to sleep with you.'

Myles feigned shock. 'Well, I'm glad we sorted that out. I didn't want you getting any ideas. I'm not that easy.'

Helen grinned, taking the arm he offered as they walked into the foyer. 'Is this a hotel? Do you live in a hotel, Myles?'

'It's a serviced apartment. My home away from home.'

'So you still have a place in Melbourne?' she asked as they stepped into the lift.

'Sure,' he said. 'I still live there, officially.'

'And here unofficially?'

'I guess you could say that.'

They arrived at his floor, and Myles led her along the corridor until they came to his apartment. Inside was a reasonably spacious living area with a sleek kitchen tucked behind a breakfast bar. It had that typical hotel look, everything ultra coordinated and a little soulless. But there was a pretty spectacular view to make up for it. Helen walked to the wall of glass that looked out over the city to the Domain, and on to the harbour towards the Heads.

'This is fantastic,' she said.

'Not bad, is it?' said Myles, a little wistfully. 'Though I can't say I'm here that much to enjoy it,' he added. 'Oh and just so you know, Helen, the bedroom's through there –'

'And why would I need to know that?' she said accusingly, turning around to face him.

'Because as I was about to say,' he went on, 'the bathroom's off the bedroom, if you need it.'

'Oh, okay. Good idea actually. Back in a tick.' Helen walked into a similarly hotel-style bedroom, dominated by a massive bed. The bathroom was on the lavish side as well, with a spa bath, double shower, double handbasin. It was all very shiny and clean, she was impressed to note.

'What would you like to drink?' asked Myles from the kitchen when she reappeared. 'I don't have any champagne, but I do have white wine, or red, or beer, or –'

'White will be fine, thanks,' Helen interrupted him. She'd best stay with the same colour at least. 'You're very neat,' she remarked as she walked over to the breakfast bar.

He shrugged. 'Not if I don't have to be. It's serviced, remember.'

She shook her head. 'Myles, can't you even make your own bed?'

'Yes, I can, in fact,' he said, passing her a glass of wine across the bench. 'But if I'm paying for someone else to do it, why should I?'

'Fair enough.' She took a sip of her wine, but then she felt her tummy rumbling again. She needed to put something in it before she made herself sick. 'Can I be rude and ask for something to eat?'

'I was just getting to that,' said Myles, turning around and opening the fridge door. 'What do you feel like?'

'What have you got?' she asked, going around into the kitchen to join him in front of the fridge.

He reached for a couple of pieces of wrapped cheese, as well as a nob of salami. 'Don't worry, I know you won't eat this.'

'That stuff'll kill you, you know,' she said with a grimace.

'But what a way to go.'

Helen scanned the contents of the fridge. There were several containers half filled with dips and olives, some stuffed vine leaves and other curious bits and pieces. It looked as though he'd raided a delicatessen. 'You're a grazer, aren't you?'

'What's that?' asked Myles as he laid the cheese out on a plate with crackers.

'You graze instead of eating a proper meal.'

'I eat proper meals, but usually in restaurants, on business,' said Myles. 'I don't get a chance to cook much here. I like to have stuff to snack on when I get in late.'

Helen had found a couple of fresh tomatoes and an onion. 'Do you have oil?'

'I do,' he said, passing her a bottle. 'What are you going to do with it?'

'I'll make us some bruschetta. Do you have any bread?'

'Yeah, I hope it's not stale though,' he said, opening a cupboard door. 'I always seem to be throwing out half-loaves.'

'No problem, I'll be toasting it anyway,' said Helen as he passed her a Vienna loaf. 'Perfect.' She made her way around the kitchen, collecting a chopping board, knives, a bowl and the toaster.

'What can I do?' asked Myles.

'Why don't you put on some of that music you promised?'

'What would you like to listen to?'

'What have you got?'

'Do you want me to run through the whole thousand?'

'Play something you like,' said Helen, chopping tomatoes.

Myles was over fiddling with the sound system. 'This could be risky, Helen. What if you don't like what I choose?'

'I'm sure it'll be fine.'

'I don't know,' he said doubtfully, 'you're bound to make assumptions about me depending on what I play.'

'What do you mean?' said Helen, glancing over at him.

'Well, take for example if I were to put on . . . I don't know, some boy band music.'

'You listen to boy bands?'

'No, I don't,' Myles said categorically. 'I want to make that clear, it was just for example's sake. I swear I don't have one song by a boy band on this playlist,' he added, holding a hand to his heart.

'Okay, because then I might have thought you were gay,' said Helen. 'Not that there's anything wrong with that.'

'This is exactly what I'm getting at,' said Myles. 'You'll make assumptions about me based on the song I put on first. It's a defining moment, Helen. So I want to make it clear right now that the song I'm about to play is not significant to me in any way. I like it well enough, but I could live without it. It wouldn't make it onto my list to take on a desert island, so don't read anything into it.'

Helen smiled, shaking her head. 'Just get on with it, would you, Myles?'

She didn't recognise the song that came on, but that was hardly surprising. Helen didn't really know any music from the last decade, or even further, she had to admit. She was a 'classic hits' girl, and deeply uncool, she suspected. But the music Myles had chosen was nice, easy to listen to without being bland, mellow without being soporific.

Helen passed the various plates of food over the bench to Myles, and he set them down on the coffee table. They soon found themselves sitting on the floor again, their backs against the sofa. Helen had discarded her jacket and shoes, and after another glass of wine she was feeling very relaxed, if not a little tipsy. But she didn't care. She felt comfortable with Myles. The only expectation he had of her was that she should say what was on her mind, be who she wanted to be. That was incredibly liberating, but also a little perplexing. Helen realised she wasn't sure enough of herself to actually be herself, if that made any sense.

'I think it's your turn to pick some music,' Myles said after a while.

Helen screwed up her face. 'I don't think I should.'

'Why not?'

'I don't have very good taste in music.'

'Who says?'

'Oh, David used to tease me about my penchant for bad eighties pop, and angsty teenage girl songs.'

Myles raised an eyebrow slightly. 'What kind of music did David like?'

'He was a Dylan man, big time.'

'And let me guess . . . Neil Young, Crosby, Stills and Nash, Joni Mitchell . . .'

'That's the stuff.' Helen nodded. 'He always said I was lucky I had him to educate me.'

Myles was watching her thoughtfully. 'Tell me something you liked before he "educated" you.'

'No, I'm too embarrassed.'

'Come on, I played my music for you.'

'Yeah, but you have good taste,' she said. 'I didn't recognise most of the songs, but they were kind of classy, and interesting.'

'Why, thank you.'

'You're welcome.'

They clinked glasses.

'Come on, one song,' Myles persisted, handing her the phone.

'I don't know how to work this,' she protested.

'It's easy,' he said, leaning over her shoulder. 'You just scroll down to the name of a band or a singer, and then select . . .'

Helen was peering at the tiny letters on the screen. They were beginning to swim in front of her eyes. 'Oh, Myles, you do it,' she said, thrusting it back at him.

'You still have to tell me what you want to hear.'

'You won't have the kind of stuff I like on there.'

'You never know. Try me.'

'Mm, well . . .' She hesitated, her head dipping close to his shoulder as she squinted at the screen. 'I used to love the Doobie Brothers.'

'There's nothing wrong with the Doobies,' said Myles, scrolling down the menu till he came to D.

'You do not have the Doobie Brothers,' she said.

'Do so.'

Helen smiled, dropping her head all the way onto his shoulder.

'And I bet I know which song's your favourite,' said Myles, scrolling and selecting so quick that she didn't catch it.

'But,' he went on, jumping to his feet, 'you're going to want to dance to this one.'

'No . . .' she protested. But then the music started. And he was right. She had to dance to it.

She put her hand out and Myles helped her up, drawing her close. It was probably a little upbeat for dancing arm in arm but Helen needed to hang onto him so she didn't fall over. At least till she got into the swing of it, then she found herself moving to the music independently, and singing . . . loudly. This was one of those songs that carried her away whenever she heard it, all the way back to her teens, when a song on the radio had the uncanny ability to express every deep, hidden feeling locked away in her heart. She'd still had her whole life ahead of her back then, anything had seemed possible. Just as well she hadn't been able to see too far into the future. Though it occurred to Helen that if she had caught a glimpse of this particular moment, perhaps she would have thought things were going to turn out all right after all.

Myles had taken hold of her hand again, drawing her back into his arms as the song began to fade. Helen leaned heavily against him, resting her head on his shoulder as another song started to play. She didn't recognise it, but it was lovely . . . lilting guitar, a man's tender, heartbroken voice.

Her face was close to his neck, he smelled good, all crisp and male. Helen was intensely aware of the feel of his body against hers as they swayed to the music. Urges that had long been suppressed, that she'd forcibly suppressed, were rising up inside her so that she started to feel giddy and a little breathless. All of her senses seemed heightened – the smell of him, the touch of him, the reality of him in her arms was becoming intoxicating. She nestled closer and he leaned his head against hers, his lips brushing her hair. Helen brought her hand up to touch his face and he covered it with his own, drawing it to his lips and kissing her palm. She lifted her head to look at him. They were both breathing hard. Helen moved first: she drew herself up taller, wrapping both arms around his neck, and brought her lips onto his. It was almost a shock at first. Actually, finally connecting, tasting his lips, kissing him. She was kissing another man.

She stopped suddenly, pulling back, her heart pounding, holding her hand to her mouth.

'What's the matter, Helen?' he asked gently.

'I, um . . . I don't know . . .'

'It's okay,' he said. 'Let's just pretend that didn't happen.'

'No, no,' she said in a daze. 'Unless . . . is that what you want?'

'No,' he said quickly. 'I mean, um, I want whatever you want, Helen, I just don't want you to think I planned this, trust me . . .'

'Of course I trust you, Myles,' she said. 'I was the one who started it.'

'Okay, but it doesn't have to go any further,' he assured her.

'Why not?' she asked, her heart beating fast. 'Don't you want to?'

'Oh Helen,' he breathed, resting his forehead against hers. 'I want to, you don't know how much, but maybe this isn't the right time, maybe it's too soon for you, maybe we should wait . . .'

'Maybe you should stop talking,' she said huskily, her lips hovering against his. Helen just wanted to do it, do it fast and hard and not talk, not say anything, not think. Especially not think.

But Myles still hesitated, drawing back to look at her. 'Are you sure this is what you want?' he said, searching her eyes.

'I'm sure, just don't talk.'

This time she kissed him hard, opening her mouth against his and pressing her body into him. She heard him moan deeply, and finally he wasn't holding back anymore. They were kissing almost ferociously now, their mouths tasting, biting, sucking, pleasuring. Helen wanted to feel his skin against hers. She fumbled to undo the buttons of his shirt as she felt his hands on the zipper at the back of her dress, his fingers sliding from her neck right down her spine, following the zipper as it opened. Helen knew she wasn't going to last much longer. She stepped back from him, slipping the dress off her shoulders and peeling it the rest of the way down, till it fell from her hips onto the floor. He was watching her, breathing heavily, as she stepped close again and opened his shirt, pressing herself against his chest, his warm skin, his heart beating against hers. His lips found hers again and he walked her backwards into the bedroom, taking the lead now, kissing her urgently. She could feel his hands tugging at the catch of her bra until it sprung open and he leaned back to look at her, his chest rising and falling, as Helen shrugged the bra off and tossed it aside.

'You're so beautiful,' he murmured, burying his head into her breasts as he lifted her up, and in one or two strides they were on the bed, writhing around, discarding what was left of their clothes until it was just them, skin to skin, nothing between them. Helen felt exhilarated, free, her sensations so charged she could barely stand it . . . but as Myles finally plunged deep inside her, she felt tears well up all of a sudden. She held them back, wrapping her legs around him and thrusting hard against him, driving all thoughts away as she forced herself to stay in the moment, to focus on the sensations only, until they finally engulfed her.

And then Myles came, surging into her with a cry, before collapsing against her, breathing hard. His lips found hers briefly, and he buried his face into the crook of her neck, catching his breath.

Helen could feel his body pulsating on top of her, inside her still. But she couldn't seem to catch her breath, and then her limbs began to shake uncontrollably as the lump rose up again, filling her chest with a choking pain as tears sprung into her eyes. She couldn't stop them now, they came like an avalanche, building to loud, wailing, gut-wrenching sobs as Myles gathered her up in his arms and held her close, pulling the bedclothes around them, soothing her gently, patiently. Gradually she grew calm, her limbs still, her breathing steady. She felt as though she was floating along with Myles, drifting with the tide. She imagined she could quite possibly stay like this forever.

'Helen.'

His voice, bringing her back into the room, back into the reality of lying here, in his bed, naked. She lurched up suddenly, turning away.

'Helen,' he said, sitting up behind her. 'What's wrong?'

'I have to get dressed,' she said, trying to cover herself with the sheet.

'Helen, don't. Please stay, it's going to be all right.'

'I have to put something on, Myles,' she insisted, her voice breaking.

'Okay, okay, no problem. Here,' he said, hopping off the bed to grab his discarded shirt and wrapping it around her. She pushed her arms into the sleeves and crossed it over in front of her, hugging herself, while Myles found his trousers and pulled them on. He sat down beside her again. 'Are you okay?'

She nodded, not looking at him, not daring to meet those eyes.

'Do you want to talk about it?'

She shook her head. What would she say?

He brought his arm around her and leaned his head against hers. 'I understand how you must be feeling –'

'No you don't,' she cried, breaking away from him and standing up. 'How can you understand what I'm feeling if I don't even understand it?'

He got to his feet, facing her. 'Helen, it doesn't matter. Whatever you're feeling, it's okay.'

'But it's not.' The ache in her throat was making it difficult to speak. 'I've never felt like this before, Myles, never had feelings like that,' she cried, pointing at the bed as though she were accusing it. 'I don't think I'm ready. I don't think I can handle this. I've never . . .'

'What?'

Helen took a breath. 'I've never had sex like that before in my life, Myles.'

He gazed steadily at her. 'Neither have I.'

She stared at him.

'Because I've never felt this way about anyone,' he went on. 'I love you, Helen. You must have known, must have felt it. I fell in love with you from the start, I think, a little. And it kept getting stronger every time I saw you, till I didn't know how I could hold myself back . . . But I did, and I waited. I waited for something from you, some sign, some indication that maybe you felt the same way, that you were ready. I probably shouldn't have brought you up here tonight, and I didn't mean for this to happen. But I'm not sorry it did.'

Helen was breathing hard. Her mouth was dry.

'Maybe the timing's wrong,' said Myles, 'or maybe you would have felt like this no matter how long you'd waited. Did you think of that, Helen? Maybe you just have to get through this.'

She swallowed. 'I don't know how.' Her voice was barely a whisper.

'Then let me show you,' he said, moving closer, so close she could feel the heat off his skin. 'Slowly, I think we should go very slowly.' Her shirt was hanging loose now, unbuttoned, and Myles slipped his hand inside, his fingers skating across the surface of her skin, making her quiver under his touch. Helen's heart started to pound again as he drew his arm around her, bringing her hard up against him. She looked up and he brought his mouth down onto hers in an overpowering, knee-weakening kiss, and Helen surrendered to it, her body melting into his. He led her back to lie on the bed. And then he made love to her, slowly, painstakingly, long into the night. Till she was completely and overwhelmingly spent, floating once more with him, drifting on the tide.

*

When Helen opened her eyes she could hear Myles breathing in a steady rhythm behind her. He was sound asleep. And suddenly she felt wide awake. It was still dark, she didn't know what time it was. Very carefully she raised herself and turned to look across Myles at the bedside clock. It was nearly four. God, she had to get home, what if Noah woke up and she wasn't there? Myles stirred, shifting onto his back as the arm that had been across her slid away and dropped onto the mattress beside him. Helen took the chance to slither quietly off the bed. He murmured, then rolled over onto his side, his back to her now. Helen gazed down at him, flashbacks from last night playing out in her head, bringing a rush of feelings – part of her wanted to climb back in beside him and press her body up against his and feel his lips on hers, his arms around her. The other part of her, the part filled with guilt and shame and confusion, just wanted to get out of here and not have to look into those eyes, not have to deal with this. That part appeared to have the upper hand at the moment.

Barely ten minutes later Helen was standing in front of the building, feeling dishevelled in yesterday's clothes and a bad case of bed-hair. Thank God there was no one around, because she might as well have been wearing a sign to announce she'd had sex. She peered up and down the street, dubious about her chances of getting a taxi at this time of the morning after a quiet Monday night in the city. She started to walk in the direction of the Quay, where she'd have more chance of finding a taxi, or even a ferry across to Balmain, though she had no idea what time they started up. When she finally arrived at the end of Macquarie Street, Helen was relieved to see three taxis waiting in the rank in front of the station.

It was a quick trip home at that time and it was still dark when she got out of the taxi, though first light was just starting to break in the sky. As noiselessly as possible, Helen slipped inside the house and closed the door with a single click, then crept down the hall to her room. But she stopped in the doorway, somehow afraid to go in. A strange, unsettling sensation came over her as she stared at the bed she once shared with David. She couldn't remember the last time they had made love. It could have been as much as weeks before he died, or longer – Helen just couldn't recall. She'd tried before now, but it was no good – she couldn't remember the actual occasion, any circumstances around it, anything that made it noteworthy. When she thought about sex with David it all blurred into sameness; there was nothing particularly memorable about it. They had it down pat, knew each other's moves, knew what was expected. Maybe that's what it was like for all married couples after a while. She would have remembered if she'd known it was to be the last time they would ever make love. But so many things would have been different if they'd known . . .

'Helen?'

She jumped, jerking around.

'Sorry,' Gemma said in a raised whisper.

'What are you doing up?' said Helen. 'Did I wake you?'

'No, Lola took care of that. I was just putting her down when I heard you come in.'

Helen just nodded.

'So, big night?' Gemma prompted.

'Ah, yeah, no, sort of . . . yes, it was.'

Gemma was frowning. 'Is everything okay, Helen?'

Helen could feel them coming on again, tears, spontaneous bloody tears always ready to rise up and betray her. She remembered the days after David died, how she couldn't cry. These days she couldn't seem to stop.

'Helen,' said Gemma, concerned, 'what's the matter, what happened?'

But Helen couldn't speak, she was trying too hard to keep the lump down in her throat, stem the tears. She pressed her fingers to her eyelids, holding them back.

'Come out here for a sec,' Gemma said quietly. She led her down the hall into the front room, away from the sleepers. 'What is it, Helen? What happened? Where have you been?'

'I was with Myles,' she sighed, wiping her eyes with her thumb.

Gemma looked at her expectantly. 'By "with Myles" I take it you mean . . .'

Helen nodded. 'We slept together,' she said gravely.

'Was it that bad?'

'No. Yes . . . no, it's not that, it's not him, it's me.' She took a breath. 'I drank too much, and I threw myself at him, like some kind of animal let out of a cage.'

Gemma shrugged. 'I wouldn't think that would bother most guys.'

Helen stared down at the floor.

'Sorry,' said Gemma. 'So what happened?'

'After . . . it was over, well, I freaked out.'

'Freaked out how?'

'Crying, wailing, general hysteria,' she said, staring blankly in front of her, reliving it.

'What did Myles do?'

Helen looked up. 'He just held me till I calmed down. And then he told me he loved me,' she croaked, her voice breaking again.

'Wow,' Gemma murmured. 'Though I can't say I'm surprised. I always said he was besotted with you from the start.' She looked at Helen, at the turmoil on her face. 'So how do you feel about him?'

'I don't know,' she said in a small voice. 'I'm confused, it just feels like . . . too much. Like it's not right somehow.'

Gemma was watching her helplessly.

Helen sighed. 'Sorry, I'm not making much sense. I'm just so tired. I think I'll try to grab a little sleep before Noah wakes up.'

'That's probably a good idea.'

Helen walked back into her bedroom, slipped out of her clothes, and pulled on a loose T-shirt. She climbed carefully onto the bed so as not to disturb Noah. He was curled into a ball, a tiny bump under the covers. Helen lay there, staring at the ceiling, but all she could see was Myles, feel the weight of his body on top of her, his lips and his tongue sliding across her skin. Her heart started to race and she felt hot, throwing the covers off. The sheer intensity of her feelings was overwhelming. Helen had never felt like this before. But it was all wrong. She couldn't get Myles out of her head, but she couldn't even remember making love to her own husband. David was becoming nothing more than a shadow from a former life; it was as though every touch from Myles were smudging him out of existence. How could she do that to him, how could she allow that to happen?

Daybreak

Helen stood on the side of the road holding Noah's hand firmly. She didn't know this place; there was nothing around her as far as the eye could see, just the tarmac of the road like a black ribbon unravelling through the desolate flat landscape, dusty and dry. She could see the bus in the distance, gradually approaching until it loomed larger and larger, coming to a stop right in front of them, the doors swinging open with a swoosh. Helen looked down at Noah and gave him a reassuring smile. They stepped up into the bus together.

'Myers!' Noah exclaimed.

Myles was driving the bus. He smiled at them, waiving the fare. They sat right up front, watching out the large windows as the bus picked up speed. Then she saw him, standing right in the middle of the road ahead. But Myles wasn't slowing down. She tried to call out to warn him, but she didn't have a voice. The bus kept going, getting closer, till she could see David's face.

Helen lurched upright, gasping for breath. Her legs were trembling as she stumbled out of bed and rushed to the bathroom, dropping to her knees and throwing up into the toilet. She leaned back against the tiled wall, catching her breath. She was still trembling, and she'd broken into a cold sweat. She felt unsteady as she got up onto her feet and turned on the shower. But standing under the stream of warm water, smoothing soap over her skin, Helen's mind drifted again to Myles, and last night, and her heart started to race. Oh, for crying out loud. She dropped the soap and turned off the hot tap. She had to pull herself together. She turned the cold water on hard and stood there until she was shivering.

*

'Is it Sat-day, Mummy?' Noah asked when he woke up, seeing her dressed in trackpants and a T-shirt. He was obviously getting accustomed to her working full-time.

'No, sweetie, it's only Tuesday. Mummy's going to stay home with you this week,' she said, trying to sound chipper. 'What would you like to do?'

'Can we wake Unka Tony up?'

'Not yet, we have to let him have a bit of a sleep-in.'

When Gemma got up with Lola soon after, she regarded Helen curiously. 'You're not going to work?'

'No, I'm not,' Helen said in a tone that did not invite further discussion.

'Aren't your in-laws lined up to have Noah today?'

'God, you're right,' she said. 'Thanks for reminding me.'

Helen called them right away, and though the disappointment was plain in Noreen's voice, she didn't push it. She simply said to call any time this week if she needed them. When she hung up the phone, Helen wandered out to the back room and leaned against the doorway, watching Noah playing with Lola. Not playing *with* so much – Lola wasn't really up to that. But Noah delighted in pulling faces and making silly noises, singing selections from his preschool repertoire with all the accompanying hand actions, shaking her toys and rattles. Any reaction from Lola, even though at this stage they were mostly involuntary ticks, was enough to keep him going. Helen wondered who would tire of it first.

Her phone began to ring, and she hurried up the hall and into her room. She fumbled for it in her handbag that she'd dropped on the floor last night.

'Hello.'

'Hi, Helen.'

Her heart leaped into her throat and stuck there.

'When did you leave?' said Myles. 'I was worried about you.'

'Sorry, I didn't mean to worry you,' she said. 'I just wanted to get back before Noah woke.'

'So why didn't you wake me? I would have driven you home.'

'You were sound asleep . . . I didn't want to disturb . . .' Her voice trailed away.

There was a pause. 'Is everything all right, Helen?'

'Sure.'

'So, I'll see you soon?'

'What?'

'At work.'

'Oh, I'm not coming into work today,' she said. 'I can't, sorry Myles, didn't I mention that?'

'No, you didn't,' he said, his voice flat.

'Oh, well, it's just after working so hard, I wanted to have some catch-up time with Noah. I thought you'd understand . . .'

'Of course I understand.' She heard him sigh. 'Helen, what's going on? Last night was . . . last night was amazing, Helen. What's happened in the last few hours? Talk to me.'

She stepped over and closed the door, breathing hard as she leaned back against it.

'Helen?' he prompted. 'Tell me what's wrong?'

'What's wrong is that I'm married,' she said finally.

'What?'

'Don't worry, I'm not crazy, I know he's dead. But the thing is, Myles, one day I had a husband, and the next I didn't. Nothing happened between us, we didn't have a fight, he didn't get sick, we didn't even say goodbye. I still feel like I'm married, or tied to him somehow.' She took a breath. 'And so now, after last night, I feel guilty, and ashamed . . .'

'Helen,' he chided gently, 'you have nothing to feel ashamed about.'

'But I do, Myles, and I don't know how to get past it.'

'You get past it by getting past it, Helen. And I'm not saying that'll be easy, but do you think we shouldn't even give this a chance because it might be hard? I think some things are worth it.' He paused. 'I think you're worth it. I guess you just have to work out if I am.'

'Myles –'

'No, I'm serious. You have to work out if I'm the guy you want to do this with. Because you're going to have to do it sometime, Helen.'

She didn't say anything. She didn't know what to say.

'Take your time,' he said tenderly. 'I'm not going to stop loving you. And I'm not going to give up.'

He hung up, and Helen flopped back onto the bed with a heavy sigh. But as soon as she was lying there, staring at the ceiling, she got the mental picture again of Myles, looming above her, lowering himself to kiss her . . .

She groaned, lifting herself up again. What had she turned into overnight? The genie was out of the bottle, and Helen didn't know how to put it back in. She took a deep breath and stood up; she had to keep busy, occupied. She walked to the door and opened it, just as Tony did the same from his room across the hall. He smiled sleepily when he saw her.

'Hey, Hel, what time did you get in last night?' he said, yawning.

'Oh, um, why do you ask?'

He considered her sceptically. 'Why are you being defensive?'

'I'm not being defensive. I got in . . . late, if you must know. It was late.'

He nodded, leaning against the doorjamb. 'Where'd you go?'

'Oh, um, out, just out . . . we wanted to listen to music.'

'"We" being –'

'People from work,' she said quickly.

He frowned. 'People? I thought you were with department-store guy.'

'Who?'

Tony was rubbing his eyes. 'Myers,' he said finally. 'You know, the guy who bought out an entire florist to wish you a happy birthday? Completely platonically, of course.'

Helen looked at him, shaking her head. 'You always were prone to exaggeration, Tony.'

'Who, me?'

'Unka Tony!' Noah had spotted him from down the hall and was running straight for him, giving Helen the chance to slip away and out to the kitchen, avoiding any further interrogation.

Wednesday

'She's been acting weird since yesterday,' Gemma told Charlie after she'd grabbed him aside and given him an abridged version of what had happened, at least the little she knew. 'She has these bursts of activity, running around the place with the Spray'n' Wipe bottle, then you come across her a little while later and she's sitting somewhere in a trance.'

Charlie had arrived to take her out to lunch, but Gemma didn't feel comfortable leaving Noah. 'He would have been better off going to his grandparents',' she said. 'Helen's so distracted, she barely notices him.'

'We can make some sandwiches and go to the park if you like,' he said. 'Then Noah can come with us.'

'You are too wonderful,' said Gemma, kissing him lightly on the lips.

'Yeah, yeah,' he dismissed.

Gemma checked that it was okay with Helen, or even if she cared to come too, but she only got monosyllabic answers. Yes, Noah could go with them; no, she didn't want to come along.

'So what do you think's going on with her?' Charlie said when they were sitting on a bench at the park, with Lola asleep in her pram beside them and Noah off to conquer the climbing frame. 'You said Myles told her he loved her, so what's the problem? Doesn't she feel the same way?'

'I don't think she knows what she feels,' said Gemma. 'I'm sure it has to do with her –' She put her hand to her mouth. 'I was going to call him "ex".' She winced. 'That doesn't sound right. Anyway, it has to do with her husband . . . who's no longer with us. I think Helen's still so torn up with grief and guilt she can't let go and move on.'

'I can understand that,' said Charlie. 'I mean, people go on loving after they've been dumped, abused, all kinds of horrible things. Helen's husband didn't abandon her on purpose or anything, he just died. Suddenly, without any warning. That's got to be hard to get over.'

'I realise that, but what's she going to do?' said Gemma. 'Wear black like a Greek widow and be alone for the rest of her life?'

He shrugged. 'You know, in India you can choose to burn along with your dead husband in the funeral pyre.'

'Oh, there's an idea,' said Gemma. 'I think it might be a little late for Helen to go with that option.'

'I'm only saying, it goes to show how deep grief can run.'

'I think it has more to do with the fact that widows don't have a life in India, so they might as well die along with their husbands.' Gemma sighed. 'But Helen's only young, and she could have a wonderful life with Myles.'

'I thought you didn't like him much.'

'It doesn't matter what I think of him. Besides, he's different around Helen. I think he really does love her.' Gemma leaned her head on Charlie's shoulder and tucked her arm into his. 'It'd be sad if she didn't give herself the chance to be loved again in her life.'

*

When they returned to the house a couple of hours later, Helen was lying out on the sofa in the back room. Just lying there, no television, no music playing, no book. She stirred as they came into the room, swinging her legs onto the floor and sitting up. Her face was all flushed and she seemed to be in a bit of a fugue.

'Are you all right, Helen?' Gemma asked her.

'Yeah, sure,' she said, clearing her throat. 'Um, there was a call for you, Gem, while you were out. I took down the number.' She slid a piece of paper across the coffee table towards her.

Gemma looked at it; it was a mobile number she didn't recognise. 'Did they leave a name?'

'Oh, no, he didn't say,' Helen said vaguely. 'Sorry, I suppose I should have asked.'

'*He?*' said Charlie, raising an eyebrow. 'Ooh, a gentleman caller?'

Gemma rolled her eyes. 'So I guess he wants me to call back?' she asked Helen, who nodded in reply. 'Okay, I'm officially intrigued.'

She slipped her phone out of the baby bag, picked up the piece of paper and walked out of the room, leaving Charlie holding the baby. He glanced at Helen and gave her an awkward smile. Helen felt as though she were suddenly made of glass and everyone could see right through her.

'So how was the park?' she asked, trying to sound normal.

Noah clambered up and straddled her lap, facing her. 'I climbed on a climbing fing and went on a slide and went on a swing, but Lola can't have a turn 'cause she's too little and tiny. And when we came home, Charlie put me on his shoulders, Mummy, like Daddy use to did!' Noah was staring wide-eyed at her, waiting for some kind of reaction. He held her face between his hands. 'Whata matta, Mummy? Why are you sad?'

But before she could answer him, Gemma walked back into the room, looking a little baffled. 'You're never going to guess who that was,' she said. 'In a million years you'd never guess.'

'So you better save us a lot of time and just tell us,' said Charlie.

'It was Luke.'

'*Luke* Luke?' he asked.

Gemma nodded. 'Father of Lola Luke.'

'What did he want?' Charlie asked.

'He wants to see her.'

'So what did you say?'

Gemma shrugged. 'I said yes, of course. He is her father – I suppose he has rights.'

'Didn't he forfeit those when he pissed off?' Charlie glanced across at Noah and winced. 'Sorry, Helen.'

'It's okay,' she said. 'Come on, Noah, let's get a drink, or something to eat.' She scooped him up with her as she got to her feet and headed for the kitchen, discreetly closing the door behind her.

'Is there something wrong, Charlie?' Gemma frowned.

'No, not at all,' he said, rocking the baby back and forth.

'You seem annoyed.'

'I'm not annoyed, why should I be annoyed? I don't have any reason to be annoyed. You can do what you want. It's your life, your baby.'

Gemma regarded him curiously. 'That's right,' she said, walking into the baby's room.

'That's right,' he echoed, following her. 'Just don't expect me to hang around to pick up the pieces when he screws you over again.'

'Charlie, what are you talking about?' Gemma took Lola out of his arms. 'He's only coming to see the baby.'

'You reckon that's all he wants? Just to see Lola and then he'll go away again?'

'You know what, to be honest, Charlie, I have no idea what he's got in mind. He wasn't exactly the easiest person to read when we were together.' Gemma lowered Lola gently down onto the changing bench and proceeded to unwrap her. 'I'm not that keen to have him involved in Lola's life, but there's not much I can do to stop him if he really wants to.'

'Of course there is.'

Gemma frowned at him.

'But you won't, will you?' Charlie said. 'You want to see him for yourself just as much, Gemma, admit it.'

'I suppose I would like to hear what he has to say for himself. I mean, I never got a reason, never had so much as a word from him. I think I'd like to know what happened, why he did what he did.'

'What if he tells you he's realised he was wrong and he's been trying to make his way back to you ever since?'

'I'll say he could have picked up a phone.'

Charlie just grunted.

'And I'll also say he can take a flying leap,' Gemma added. 'I'm not interested in him. You should know that better than anyone, Charlie.'

'Why is that?'

'Do I have to spell it out?' she groaned. 'Look, he's coming tomorrow at two, you can see for yourself.'

'I'm not going to be here.'

She turned around to look at him, keeping a hand on Lola's tummy. 'Why not?'

'I have no interest in being here. It's got nothing to do with me.'

'I'd really appreciate your support, Charlie.'

'Sorry,' he said. 'You know, Gemma, you no sooner get your life together than you have to find a way to ruin it. You're like a train wreck waiting to happen. And I'm not going to stand around and watch you crash and burn again.'

Gemma was staring at him, gobsmacked.

'I'll see you around,' he said, with a fleeting glance as he left the room.

Thursday

Gemma heard the knock on the door as she was pressing the studs around the crotch of Lola's all-in-one. She still hadn't mastered this. She always seemed to have one stud left over, and then she'd have to open them all and start over. Of course opening them all would often startle Lola, and sometimes make her cry, which would startle Gemma and make her rush, and she'd do up the studs all wrong again . . . and then she'd give up. What did it matter anyway? Lola wasn't about to be photographed for a fashion shoot. Gemma heard the knock again, more insistent this time. Maybe it was Charlie, come to apologise for his dummy-spit yesterday, and to tell her that he'd be here for her today after all.

She scooped up Lola and walked out through the back room to the hall. That would be significant, Charlie showing up now, it would mean something. Maybe he'd even admit that he had feelings for her, that they should give it a go . . . Gemma felt her heart racing and – oh, great, now her breasts were leaking. She'd forgotten to put her breast pads in, again, and she could feel the warm gush seeping through her armour-plated maternity bra and onto her T-shirt. Why was it that you never saw a woman with damp patches on her T-shirt on the covers of those mother and baby mags? No, they didn't want to publicise that particular indignity.

Gemma opened the door expectantly, in time to see the back of Myles walking down the porch steps. Would she be able to close the door again before he realised?

He turned around. Bugger.

'Gemma,' he said awkwardly. 'Sorry . . . I didn't mean to bother you . . . I was just looking for Helen.'

She'd never have guessed. 'She's not here.'

He nodded. 'Oh, right, okay . . .'

They both stood where they were, waiting to see if the other was going to say anything.

'So this is the baby . . . ?' Myles offered.

No, it's a sack of potatoes I'm taking to market.

Why was she always such a smart-arse around him? He was in love with her best friend. And more importantly, it was pretty obvious her best friend was in love with him. Gemma had to learn to restrain herself, be nice to him. For Helen's sake.

So she shifted Lola, holding her in her arms so Myles could see her properly. 'This is Lola.'

He stepped up onto the porch and bent to look at her. 'She's beautiful, Gemma. Really. Looks just like you. Congratulations.'

At least he was saying the right things. 'Thanks for the flowers.'

Myles glanced at her sheepishly. 'It's the done thing, apparently.'

She smiled then, despite herself.

'How's it going?' he asked.

'Swings and roundabouts,' she said, jiggling Lola as she started to squirm. 'But it's the best thing I've ever done.'

'Helen says you're a natural.'

'She does?'

He nodded. 'Listen, I should let you know that they've found a permanent MD and he'll be taking over soon. I've made sure the job-sharing arrangement will be maintained, at least until a team vacancy comes up.' He paused. 'I've put in a strong recommendation that you be given first consideration if one does.'

Gemma blinked. 'You didn't have to do that.'

'I think I did. I think I owe you that much.' He thrust his hands in his pockets. 'You caught me at a bad time, Gemma. I was still trying to clean up the mess at Bailey's – you have no idea how deep it went. I didn't have the time or the energy to nurture staff.'

'Until Helen came along . . .'

Myles looked embarrassed.

'Don't worry, I get it,' said Gemma. 'We can't help who we fall in love with.' She propped Lola against her shoulder again. 'To be fair, I wasn't honest with you, and I, um, well, I never apologised for that. And so, now I am.'

His face relaxed. There was even a hint of a smile in his eyes. 'Thanks for that, Gemma. It means a lot.' He breathed out. 'Well, I guess I'll leave you to it.'

Gemma nodded, watching him turn back down the steps. 'Oh . . . Myles?'

He turned around again.

'Helen was taking Noah to preschool,' she said, 'and then she was going to visit her mother.'

He was looking blankly at her.

'She's in a place called Brookhaven. I don't think it's very far from here.'

Gemma realised he wasn't taking the rather considerable hint she was attempting to give him.

'You know, the thing with Helen is that you're going to have to be persistent. It's what works with her, apparently.'

Bingo.

'Brookhaven, you said?'

'That's right.'

He smiled. 'Thanks Gemma, I appreciate it.'

*

Helen had dropped Noah at preschool and was on her way to visit her mother. She'd decided to get out of the house this morning before Tony was up and about. It was okay with Noah around; he was a buffer, commanding nearly all of Tony's attention, so they could mostly only manage small talk. But with Noah at preschool, Helen had the feeling Tony was going to start grilling her about 'department-store guy' and frankly she wasn't up to it.

It was bad enough with Gemma asking her how she was every five minutes. Helen didn't want to talk about it. She couldn't possibly put into words the chaos going on inside her head as she tried to work out what she felt for Myles, with the spectre of David lurking in her consciousness.

Helen drove into the carpark at Brookhaven and pulled directly into a space. She got out of the car, locked the door, and as she turned around Myles was standing at the back of the car, a few feet away.

'Myles, you gave me a fright,' said Helen, her heart racing at the sight of him, which probably had nothing to do with the fright.

'Sorry, I didn't mean to.'

'What are you doing here? How did you know where to find me?'

He took a couple of steps towards her. 'I dropped by your place. Gemma told me you were visiting your mum at Brookhaven. It wasn't that hard to find.'

Helen was staring at him, finding herself a little mesmerised.

'I'm sorry if I'm intruding . . . I just wanted to see you, Helen.'

She stirred. 'I don't think it's such a good idea, Myles.'

'Well, I disagree.'

'I'm sorry?'

'I disagree, and I'm part of this, so I have a say, don't I?' He didn't wait for an answer. 'I miss you, Helen. I miss seeing you at work, I miss talking to you. You swept me off my feet and now you've abandoned me. I didn't think you'd be the cruel type.'

Helen could see the glint in his eye. 'You said you were romantic, Myles, not melodramatic.'

'I also told you I wasn't going to give up,' he said, taking another step closer to her.

'This is not the time or the place, Myles. I'm here to visit my mother.'

'Can I come with you?'

She frowned. 'Why on earth would you want to do that?'

'She's your mother. I'd like to meet her.'

Helen put her hand on her hip, looking at him. 'You're intent on making this difficult, aren't you?'

'I'm intent on making it difficult for you to ignore me.'

She breathed out. 'Fine, you can meet her. It won't mean anything to her, so you won't be scoring any brownie points.'

He followed Helen into the main building and through the maze of corridors till they got to Marion's room. Helen went in first. 'Hello, Mum, how are you today?'

Marion turned her head to frown at her; she didn't seem cranky so much as curious. She glanced past Helen to Myles, who was hanging back near the door. And the frown began to fade from her face.

'Who's that?'

Myles came forward to stand beside Helen.

'This is Myles Davenport,' she said. 'He's a . . . friend of mine.'

'How do you do, Mrs Zelinsky,' said Myles.

'Oh, young man, you're very polite,' Marion said in her girlie voice. 'But you have to call me Marion.'

'If you insist,' he said.

'Sit down, sit down,' said Marion.

Myles glanced at Helen and she nodded, walking around to the other side of the bed. He pulled up a chair and sat down.

'So are you a doctor, Mr Davenport?' Marion asked.

'Now, Marion, it's only fair, you have to call me Myles.'

'Okay, Myles,' she said, almost blushing. 'So are you a doctor?'

'No, I'm not,' he said. 'I used to be, but I gave it up.'

'Why would you do that, a handsome young man like yourself?'

Helen had no idea what that had to do with being a doctor but it obviously made some kind of sense to Marion. She smiled faintly at Myles from across the bed.

'And tell me, are you married, Myles?' Marion was asking now.

'No, not yet,' he said.

'You know, I have a daughter you might like to meet.' Helen held her breath.

'I know your daughter, actually,' said Myles.

Marion looked surprised. 'You do? She doesn't get out much. I don't know why she's always hanging around the house.'

The staff had told Helen that Marion often talked about her, but she'd always thought they were just being kind. Her mother never recognised her, but perhaps she only knew the daughter that existed in the deep recesses of her mind, 'stuck on rewind' as Tony had put it.

'So tell me, what do you think of her?'

'I think she's very beautiful,' said Myles, glancing across at Helen.

'Well, you know,' Marion confided, 'people say she looks like me when I was her age.'

'I can certainly see the resemblance.'

'You should get to know her,' Marion said wistfully. 'She's a good girl.'

A single tear escaped from Helen's eye, running swiftly down her cheek.

'She's a wonderful girl,' Myles said, gazing straight at Helen. 'And you know what, Marion? I'm very much in love with her.'

'Well, I hope you get on and do something about it. She's not much of a go-getter, my Helen. Needs a bit of a push.'

*

Later, after they'd left her room and walked back through the corridors and out into the sunshine again, Myles turned to Helen. 'Looks like I have your mother's blessing.'

'She'll have forgotten by tomorrow,' said Helen. 'By this afternoon.'

'She seemed like a pretty wise woman to me.'

'Except she didn't know it was me sitting right beside her.' Helen glanced at him sideways. 'You know, I might get Alzheimer's one day. There's some evidence it's genetic.'

'You also might get hit by a bus.'

She turned abruptly to look at him.

'But I'm willing to take my chances,' Myles said, coming closer. 'I know you're scared, Helen, but I've also seen what you can do when you put your mind to it. Like your mum said, you just need a little push sometimes.'

Helen could feel her throat tightening. She did not want to go to pieces out here in the carpark, she had to keep it together. Or maybe fleeing was the best option. 'I have to get going –'

'Wait, Helen, there's another reason I wanted to see you today,' said Myles. 'I thought you should know they've chosen a permanent managing director to head up Bailey's. There's a board meeting tomorrow where he'll be introduced to key staff. Hand-over will take place across the next week or two. By the way, I've made sure you and Gemma will be kept on under the existing arrangement.'

But Helen wasn't listening anymore. 'So does this mean . . . you'll be going back to Melbourne?' she asked in a small voice.

'That all depends,' he said, looking at her steadily. 'Ball's in your court, Helen.'

She was just staring at him.

'I have to go,' he said. 'But I want to leave you with something to help you decide.'

Before Helen knew what he was doing he'd pulled her into his arms and was kissing her soundly, putting forward a pretty compelling argument. He eventually drew back enough to look in her eyes, still holding her close. 'Keep that in mind, okay?' he said softly, before releasing her.

She felt a little light-headed, watching him walk away towards his car. He turned to wave. 'I'll wait to hear from you then,' he called before he climbed into the driver's seat.

Helen was still standing, rooted to the spot, as he drove past her and out of the carpark.

*

She was still feeling a little light-headed when she pulled up in front of Jim and Noreen's about ten minutes later. She was going to ask them if they could pick up Noah from preschool and occupy him for a couple of hours. She'd promised Gemma she'd stick around for moral support when Luke came, and besides, Helen wanted to keep Noah out of the line of any potential fire.

Jim and Noreen's place was between Brookhaven and home, so Helen had decided it was just as easy to call in on her way through. But as she walked up the pristine concrete path, past the precision-clipped lawn towards the immaculate but austere facade of the house, her stomach began to churn uncomfortably. What if they could tell? What if she looked different? She'd slept with another man. She had made passionate love, the likes of which she'd never had with their son, with a man they'd never even clapped eyes on. She could imagine their horror, their disdain, their abject disapproval. She had visions of them tearing Noah away from his harlot of a mother, standing up in court declaring she was unfit . . .

Helen realised there was no way she could face them. She was about to turn on her heel when the front door opened and Noreen peered out through the flyscreen. 'Helen, is that you, dear?'

She cleared her throat. 'Oh, hi, Noreen, I wasn't sure if you were home . . .'

She glanced sideways at the gleaming twelve-year-old showroom-condition Ford sedan parked in the spotless driveway.

'What are you doing here, Helen?' said Noreen, a little anxiously. 'Is everything all right? Where's Noah?'

Helen took a breath. 'Noah's fine,' she assured her. 'Everything's fine, Noreen. I was just passing by, and I wanted to ask you a favour.'

Noreen fumbled with the lock on the flyscreen and finally opened the door. 'Well, come in, dear. I'll make you a nice cup of tea.'

'Oh, that's okay,' said Helen, walking towards her.

Helen saw her face drop. Of course, what did you do with visitors if you couldn't serve them a beverage of some description?

'I'd love a cup of tea, thanks, Noreen.'

She looked relieved.

'You have to remind me how you have it, Helen,' she said as she walked ahead out to the kitchen. 'I think it's been a while since I've made you a cup of tea.'

'Who's there, Noreen?' Jim's voice came from up the hall.

'Oh, I just have to let Dad know you're here,' she said breathlessly, hurrying out of the kitchen again to David's old room, where Jim had set up his study.

Moments later she reappeared, huddling behind Jim.

'Hello, Helen,' he said sternly. 'This is unexpected. Mum tells me everything's all right though?'

'Of course, I was just passing,' said Helen.

'I'll put that kettle on now,' Noreen said, still breathless as she trotted over to the other side of the kitchen.

'Take a seat,' said Jim, pulling a chair out from the kitchen table and sitting down himself.

'I was just saying to Noreen that I have a favour to ask you.'

Jim regarded her suspiciously. 'Go ahead.'

'I was wondering if you were able, if you're free that is, to pick up Noah from preschool this afternoon?'

Noreen had drifted over to listen, and she was smiling eagerly at the prospect.

'I, uh, I have to do something for a friend this afternoon,' said Helen, 'so it would be a big help to me if you could fill in some time with him, say a couple of hours? Take him to the park . . .'

'Maybe we could take him for an ice cream,' Noreen said hopefully.

Helen looked at her. 'Sure, take him wherever you like. He loves being with his nan and pop.'

She detected the slightest softening on Jim's face. 'You know we're always happy to help out, Helen, any time. Now, where's that cup of tea, Mum?'

'Oh,' Noreen said, flustered. 'I was just wondering which biscuits to put out, the Monte Carlos or the Scotch Fingers, or there's fruitcake . . .'

Helen tuned out as they discussed the relative merits of each choice, or rather as Jim laid them out and Noreen hung off his every word, waiting for him to give his final proclamation. He was like the king of his little dominion, but Noreen was hardly the queen. Helen felt a rush of sympathy for her, or perhaps it was empathy. They were not so unalike, her and Noreen. David hadn't been nearly as domineering as his father, they were a generation apart, but Helen had been too prepared to defer to his opinion, to let him make the decisions, to give him the run of her life.

Jim and Noreen were not bad people; they'd settled into their roles and never had a reason to change. But Helen had to wonder how Noreen would ever cope if Jim died first. And she found herself silently thankful that she was young enough to adapt, to change her life, find her feet. Even if she was still a little scared to see where they were going to take her.

Balmain

Luke had said he'd be there around two, but Gemma remembered his fairly loose relationship with time, and decided not to watch the clock. So when there was a knock on the door just after one, she was a little surprised. It turned out it was only Phoebe, however.

'I thought you might be Luke,' said Gemma when she opened the door.

'Sorry?' Phoebe said, confused.

'Luke's coming over later.'

'*Luke* Luke?' she said, stepping into the hall.

'The one and only,' Gemma replied, closing the door again.

Phoebe was staring at her, her mouth gaping. 'Whoa, when did all this happen?'

'Nothing's happened,' Gemma said calmly, making her way back down the hall, Phoebe trailing behind. 'He called yesterday and asked if he could see Lola.'

'How did he find you?'

'I got in touch with some of our old friends months ago. They passed on the number when he came back to Sydney.'

They walked into the back room and Gemma retired to her throne as usual, while Phoebe plonked herself on the sofa.

'So how do you feel about seeing him again?' Phoebe asked.

Gemma screwed up her face. 'I don't know.' She paused. 'I'm a little worried about what he's actually got in mind, if he suddenly wants to play happy families.'

Phoebe looked horrified. 'You wouldn't take him back, would you?'

'Give me a little credit. Doesn't anyone believe I've got a brain in my head? Even Charlie had a go at me about my life being a train wreck and not wanting to stand around and watch me do it again.'

'I know where he's coming from,' Phoebe muttered.

'What?'

'Come on, Gemma, you haven't exactly got the best track record.'

'The last thing I would do is take Luke back,' Gemma said firmly. 'I've done some pretty stupid things in the past, I realise, but I'm not a complete idiot.'

'No, you're not.'

'Anyway, I doubt very much that Luke's coming here to win me back. I just wish I knew what he was after.'

'Well, you're going to find out soon enough.' Phoebe kicked off her shoes and curled her legs up underneath her. 'It's quiet around here. Helen at work?'

'No, she was going to visit her mother, thank God.'

'Why do you say that?'

'She's been moping around the place for days. She hasn't been to work, she's barely shifted off the sofa, and when she does, she has these manic cleaning fits.'

'What's going on?' Phoebe said, concerned. 'Why isn't she going to work?'

Gemma considered her. 'I guess it's all right to tell you.'

'Tell me what?'

'Helen would tell you, that's if she wasn't in la-la land right now.'

'What's going on?' Phoebe repeated anxiously.

'Maybe I should wait and let her –'

'Just spit it out, would you, Gemma!'

'She slept with Myles.'

'Woohoo,' said Phoebe, wide-eyed. 'That's been coming for a while. So what's the problem?'

'Remember how she didn't think it was right to date anyone, how she still felt married?' said Gemma. 'I think that's getting to her, but she won't talk about it.'

'Poor thing,' Phoebe said wistfully.

'Actually, now that I think of it, she said she was going to be back before Luke gets here. I didn't want to be alone when he came, but now that you're here, maybe I should call her so she doesn't rush to get back.'

'Fine with me,' said Phoebe. 'I'm in no hurry.'

Gemma regarded her closely. It was midafternoon on a weekday and Phoebe was wearing jeans and a T-shirt. There was something wrong with this picture. 'And why is that, Phee?'

'Why is what?'

'Why aren't you in a hurry? What are you doing here and why aren't you at work?'

'I've got some news of my own,' Phoebe admitted sheepishly. 'But I'm thinking this might not be the best time – there seems to be enough going on around here as it is.'

'Well, you have to tell me now,' said Gemma. 'I won't be able to stand the suspense.'

'Okay.' Phoebe sat forward. 'I suppose you've picked up that I've been feeling a little broody since you had Lola?'

'A little?'

'All right, a lot,' she said. 'So, I had it out with Cam. I told him I wanted a baby, that I wasn't going to wait.'

'Good for you,' said Gemma. 'As if he was going to go ahead with that stupid vasectomy threat. So what happened?'

'He booked in for a vasectomy,' Phoebe said dryly.

'No!'

'So I said, you go ahead with it, Cameron. It's over. You can pack your bags.'

'Then what?'

'He packed his bags.'

'Oh Phee,' Gemma said plaintively. 'He actually left?'

'No, actually, in the end, I did,' she said. 'I never liked that apartment anyway.'

'You didn't?'

'Not really.'

Gemma was trying to take all this in. 'So where are you staying?'

Phoebe looked a little cagey. 'Don't get mad –'

'You didn't go home to Mum and Dad's?' Gemma groaned.

'Just till I find something,' Phoebe insisted.

'But aren't you worried Cameron might rip you off somehow, if he's the one staying in the apartment?'

Phoebe shook her head. 'We're both lawyers, don't forget. We drew up a pre-nup so watertight neither of us can sneeze without the other one blowing their nose.' She became wistful. 'I should've known then. Who needs a pre-nup if they really believe they're in it forever? I remember I said that to Cam at the time, and he said that was romantic claptrap.' She paused, staring off into space.

'When did this all happen, Phee?' said Gemma. 'Why didn't you tell me before now?'

'You'd just had a baby, Gem,' Phoebe reminded her. 'And what could you do anyway? The last few weeks have been tough, but I just had to get through them. I really fell apart at first, but now the good days are outweighing the bad. I didn't cry all day yesterday, and not so far today,' she said. 'It was coming for a long time, Gem, ever since he threatened the vasectomy I knew on some level it was over. I guess I chose to bring it to a head.'

'So what are you going to do now? Will you buy a place of your own with your share?'

'I don't know. Sydney real estate is so expensive, and I'm not sure I want to be tied down. Besides, I may have to live off the money for a while – I might even do a little travelling.'

Gemma was confused. 'I'm not following you.'

Phoebe heaved a big sigh. 'I put in my resignation at work.'

'You didn't!'

'I did.'

'What did Mum and Dad say?'

'Mum and Dad are just going to have to get over it,' said Phoebe. 'This is my life.'

'What's happened to you, Phee?' Gemma marvelled. 'You really have become the evil twin. And it's freaking me out.'

'Don't be freaked out. I'm okay, I really am. It's a little weird, actually. It's made me realise how much I was kidding myself before.'

They were interrupted by a knock on the door.

'Ooh, do you think that's him?' Phoebe gasped.

'Only one way to find out,' said Gemma, getting up. 'But we're going to return to this later,' she added.

This time it was Helen at the door.

'Sorry, I gave Tony my key,' she said when Gemma let her in. 'I keep forgetting to get another one cut.'

'No problem. You didn't need to hurry back as it turns out,' said Gemma as they started down the hall. 'Phoebe's here.'

'I don't mind,' said Helen. 'You moved the crib in here?' she said, noticing it in the corner of the front room as they passed through.

'Lola's asleep, so I thought I'd receive Luke in the front parlour,' Gemma said airily. 'I don't really want him snooping through the whole house. Not until I see what he's up to.'

'You don't have a whole lot of faith in this guy, do you?'

'Do you blame me?'

'Hi, Helen,' Phoebe said as they walked into the back room. She leaped up from the sofa and gave Helen a rather demonstrative hug. 'How are you? Is everything okay?'

'I take it Gemma's been filling you in?' Helen said wryly.

'It hasn't all been about you,' she said. 'In fact, it's hardly been about you at all because I don't even know what's going on with you.'

Helen didn't say anything.

'Anyway Phoebe's got much bigger news,' said Gemma.

'Oh?' said Helen as they all sat down again.

'Cam and I have separated,' said Phoebe.

Helen took a moment to compute. 'I'm so sorry, Phee,' she said, putting her hand on Phoebe's knee. 'That's awful. Are you all right?'

'It was pretty devastating at first,' she said. 'Until it occurred to me that I was never going to have a baby if I stayed with him. And it's more important for me to be with someone who wants the same things as I do. And I don't just mean a baby.'

'What else do you mean?' Helen asked.

'Everything. I finally realised how unhappy I've been. Things had been bad, really bad, for months, longer. People live in loveless marriages for the sake of the kids, but if we weren't even going to have kids, then what was the point? I was living this totally empty life, existing in a void, all style and no substance.'

'So you didn't love him anymore?' asked Gemma.

Phoebe sighed. 'I don't know, and I don't know whether Cam ever really loved me. I think he had a mental checklist of everything he wanted in a wife, and I filled it. He had a checklist for his whole life, really – the right kind of friends, the right apartment, career, wife, tick tick tick tick. So when I started going off the script, wanting something messy like a baby, he just wasn't prepared to go along with it.'

Gemma was strangely relieved to hear Phoebe talking like this. Not that she wanted her sister's marriage to end, but at least she wasn't such a bitch for never liking Cameron after all. He really was a king-size dickhead.

'Hey, Gem,' Phoebe went on, 'I know you've said this to me before, but I didn't listen, or I didn't want to hear it. But I've been working so hard all my life doing what other people wanted me to do, I've never worked out what I wanted. I'm shit-scared, but maybe now I'll get a chance to do that.'

'That's very brave, Phoebe,' Helen said quietly.

They both turned to look at her.

'Thanks, Helen. I don't know if I'm feeling all that brave right now.'

'But moving on,' said Helen. 'It's so hard, I don't know how people do it . . .' Her voice trailed off, and they waited to see if she'd say anything else, but she didn't.

'Come on, Helen,' said Gemma, 'you've moved on, you've done some amazing things.'

Helen looked over at her. 'Oh, sure, you're talking about work . . . and that . . .'

'Myles seems like a pretty great guy,' Phoebe said carefully.

'He is,' Helen agreed. 'He really is . . . it's just . . .' Her forehead creased in deep concentration. Finally she gave up. 'It's hard to explain.'

'You could give it a try,' said Gemma. 'We're not going anywhere.'

They were interrupted by another knock at the door.

'Or maybe I am.' She looked apologetically at Helen. 'Sorry, I have to get that.'

'Of course you do,' said Helen. 'Go ahead.'

Gemma got to her feet and took a deep breath. 'Wish me luck.'

'Just remember you're too good for him,' said Phoebe. 'And he's really bad for you.'

As Gemma walked up the hall to the front door, she realised she was nervous about seeing Luke in the flesh after so long. But when she opened the door, she got a shock. Her heart didn't jump or miss a beat or any of those callisthenics it was supposed to do at a time like this. In fact, looking at Luke now, Gemma honestly had to wonder what she'd ever seen in him. He was a scrawny, stringbean of a man, with straggly hair and an even stragglier goatee, in grubby jeans and a ripped T-shirt. Not that she cared about any of that, really. Though if he wanted to touch Lola he was going to have to wash those hands first.

'Hey, Gem, lookin' wicked, babe.'

God, had she really fallen for corn like that?

'Thanks, Luke, good to see you too. Come on in.' She stepped back and he walked inside, taking a good gawk around.

'Cool digs.'

'Yeah, well, I'm only boarding here,' she said, making her situation perfectly clear. 'The baby's just through here.' Gemma led the way into the front room and over to the crib. She stood aside and Luke walked closer, peering down at the baby.

'I named her Lola Helen,' Gemma went on. 'Lola after my grandmother – I don't know if you remember me talking about her? And Helen's my landlady. She ended up delivering her, right here in the house, she came so fast. She was 3.4 kilos born, but she's put on stacks of weight since then. The clinic sister is really pleased with her progress.' Gemma didn't know why she was talking so fast.

'She's awesome,' Luke said, nodding. 'Looks like you.'

'Do you think?'

He shrugged. 'Sure.'

He didn't seem inclined to touch her, much less hold her. Gemma was relieved, although she had expected a bit more than a passing interest. What was he doing here? She offered him a seat.

'So are you happy, babe?' said Luke, dropping into an armchair opposite her.

She really wanted to tell him to stop calling her that, but she didn't want to seem snippy.

'I am happy,' she said.

'You're glad you kept her then?' He cocked his head towards the crib.

'Of course.'

He nodded. He was getting to something. 'You know I would've been a really fucked dad.'

He wasn't going to get an argument out of her.

'I'm no good at settling down, never have been. I reckon it's better I leave you to it, Gem. You look like you're doing a real good job.'

'Thanks,' she said guardedly.

'So you don't have to worry, I won't bother you again. If you find yourself another bloke, let her call him Dad, tell her whatever you like.'

This was plain weird. Why go to the trouble of making contact to tell her he didn't want to have any contact? His total lack of contact had made that pretty obvious.

'So you really are happy you had the baby?' he persisted.

'Yes, Luke, I really am happy.'

'Then I'm happy I got to do that for you.'

Gemma looked at him. 'What do you want, Luke?'

He laughed, nodding, like she'd caught him out. 'Yeah, you're right, there is something,' he said. 'The thing is, I heard that the government gives you a handout for having a baby, like four grand, they said.'

Gemma didn't know where Luke was getting his information; the government had dropped the baby bonus years ago. But she was intrigued to see where he was going with this.

'So, I was thinking,' he went on, 'seeing as you wouldn't have had her without me, that maybe it's only fair that we, ah, split the prize money, you know?'

Gemma blinked. 'What?'

'Split it. My sperm, your egg, I reckon fifty-fifty's fair.'

'Are you serious?'

'Okay,' he relented. 'Can't say I didn't try. Fair enough, you gotta look after her, so I'll accept sixty-forty.'

Gemma was looking at him, dumbfounded, and then without warning there was an explosion in her chest and she burst out laughing. She couldn't stop. She laughed so much she started to cry, and every time she tried to speak, the laughter welled up again and she couldn't get the words out. Luke just sat there, looking bewildered. Gemma finally ran out of puff. She wiped her eyes, sniffing. 'Oh, Luke, thank you so much. You don't know what a gift you've given me.'

He was still frowning at her.

'Come here,' she said, standing up. 'There's something I want to show you.'

Luke followed her out of the room and up the hall to the front door.

'What is it, what do you want to show me, babe?' he said.

'The front door,' said Gemma, opening it. 'I'm showing you the door, Luke. Please never come anywhere near me again.'

He stared at her for a second, till the penny dropped, and then his expression became a little less amiable.

'Crazy bitch,' he muttered as he walked past her and out the door.

Gemma closed it behind him and turned to hear Lola stirring. She hurried back to the crib and scooped her up in her arms. 'Come on, Mummy's little cash cow,' she cooed, kissing Lola on the nose. 'Wait till the girls hear this.'

*

'You know what the worst part of the whole thing is?' said Gemma, after Helen and Phoebe had expressed first shock, then disbelief, then hilarity.

She was sitting cross-legged on the floor next to Lola, who was lying under a mobile, kicking her legs. 'The worst part is I was actually in love with him once.' Gemma shook her head. 'Or I thought I was.' She looked up at Phoebe and Helen, who were sharing the sofa. 'I just want to state for the record that you both have my permission to do an intervention if I ever turn up with another guy like that.'

'Luke had better be the last in what has been a very long line of losers and misfits,' said Phoebe. 'The guys she used to bring home,' she rolled her eyes at Helen, 'talk about dregs. They were the fish John West didn't even consider for rejection, not even for cat food, not even –'

'Okay, Phoebe, I think she's got the picture,' said Gemma. 'So tell me, what's my problem? Do I choose them or do they choose me?'

'I reckon you choose them,' Phoebe said, 'because you don't think you deserve any better.'

'Charlie said something like that.' Gemma wrinkled her brow, thinking. 'But I don't get it. I don't know whether I deserve better, but I'd certainly like to have better. Why would I intentionally choose someone who was no good for me?'

'Self-loathing,' Phoebe said bluntly. 'You've never thought you were good enough, because you didn't think Mum and Dad loved you as much as Ben or me. You are sporting the classic middle child – otherwise known as "chip on shoulder" – syndrome.'

'Are you thinking of writing a self-help book, Phee?'

'I get to watch Dr Phil now that I'm home in the daytime,' she said airily. 'He makes some interesting points, you know.'

'Maybe, but I still don't reckon I choose losers because I think Mum and Dad don't love me,' said Gemma. 'I've worked out that they do, in their own peculiar way.'

'Yeah, but this stuff is buried pretty deep, Gem,' said Phoebe. 'Even after we've rationalised it as adults, it's still there. And it's a classic defence mechanism against rejection to pick someone who can't really love you.'

Gemma was frowning. 'What do you mean?'

'You pick deadheads so you've got someone to blame when it all goes pear-shaped. I picked a robot who's probably incapable of love, so I can reassure myself now it's over that it wasn't because I'm not lovable.'

Helen winced, waiting for Phee to cast her X-ray vision on her.

'You've got it all worked out, haven't you, little sister?' said Gemma.

Phoebe shrugged. 'It's not rocket science. I mean, let's face it, how scary is the idea of someone getting really close, loving you, right deep down to your soul?'

Helen was just taking a sip of her tea and she coughed, spluttering it everywhere. She put her cup back on the coffee table and grabbed a tissue, mopping up the spills on her T-shirt as she cleared her throat. When she looked up, both Gemma and Phoebe were staring at her, clearly bemused.

'You right there, Helen?' Gemma drawled. 'Phoebe touch a nerve?'

'It just went down the wrong way,' Helen mumbled.

'Did Myles find you at Brookhaven today?' Gemma asked.

She nodded faintly.

'So, what happened?'

'He, um . . .' She cleared her throat again. 'Actually, he wanted to let me know they've found a permanent MD, so he'll be heading back to Melbourne. He's put in a good word for both of us though.'

'Hold on,' Gemma said. 'He's going back to Melbourne? He didn't say anything about that.'

'Well, it is where he lives.'

'What kind of game is he playing?' she cried. 'Just when I'd started to think he wasn't so bad after all, it turns out he's just another bastard –'

'Gemma,' Helen had to stop her, 'he said it's up to me.'

'What?'

'Myles, he said it's up to me whether he goes, that the ball's in my court.'

'You mean he won't go if you ask him to stay?' said Phoebe.

'I guess,' Helen said in a small voice.

'So what are you going to do?' asked Gemma.

'I don't know.' Her voice was almost inaudible now.

Gemma was watching her closely. 'What are you so afraid of, Helen?'

She shrugged. 'It's hard to explain.'

'I understand better than you probably think,' said Gemma. 'David died young, so he's going to stay forever young in your memory, always the good guy, never disappointing you, letting you down. I'm not suggesting he would have done, I'm just saying that's bloody hard for anyone to compete with.'

No, she didn't understand at all, Helen sighed inwardly. 'That's not the problem,' she murmured. 'In fact, it's probably the opposite.'

She looked at their expectant faces, waiting for her to spell it out. 'I'm afraid . . .' she began, 'that Myles might be a better

partner, a better lover, more compassionate, interesting, intelligent
. . . that he might turn out to be the love of my life.'

Gemma and Phoebe took a moment to process that.

'I'm struggling to understand the problem here, Helen,' said
Gemma. 'Myles loves you, and you've obviously fallen hard for
him, and the sex must have been pretty mind-blowing –'

'Gem!' said Phoebe.

'She's right,' Helen said glumly.

'You needn't look so miserable about it,' said Gemma. 'Half
your luck, Helen. You should be dancing on the rooftops and
singing hallelujah.'

'That my husband was run over by a bus and I got to meet
Myles?'

'Oh, Helen, no, is that what's bothering you?' said Phoebe. 'You
can't think like that.'

'But I can't help it,' she said. 'The way I feel about Myles . . .
well, I keep thinking that maybe I didn't love David enough. That
maybe if I'd got up to see him off that morning, things would have
been different, he might have been more . . . present in the world
somehow, and he might not have stepped off that kerb. And now I
have this albatross hanging around my neck, and I don't see how I
can ever be happy with Myles because it'll always be tainted by the
fact that we're only together because David did step off that kerb.'

Gemma and Phoebe stared at her, speechless.

'You didn't push him in front of that bus, Helen,' Gemma said
finally.

Now it was Helen's turn to be speechless.

'Could you be more blunt, Gem?' Phoebe sighed.

'Someone has to say it like it is,' she declared. 'You have no
reason to feel guilty, Helen. You would have stayed with David for
the rest of your life, wouldn't you?'

She nodded. 'Of course.'

'Even though the picture I've been getting is that things were
pretty ordinary between the two of you?' she went on. 'Not bad,
just ordinary. But you would have been loyal to the end. And the
thing is, you were. This is the end, Helen. David's gone, till death
you did part. Sure, you wouldn't have met Myles if he hadn't died,

that's a fact. But that doesn't make it wrong. That's like saying Lola's a mistake because I had her with Luke. You don't think that, do you?'

'Of course not,' she said.

'I rest my case.' Gemma got up onto her knees and crawled over to Helen, taking hold of both her hands. 'Do you really think David would have wanted you to live a mediocre life out of some kind of misplaced respect for him? You have a right to be happy, Helen. You have a life. Don't be scared to live it.'

Next day

'Charlie's still not answering his phone,' Gemma said as Helen walked in the house after dropping Noah at preschool. 'Or my messages.'

She nodded vaguely.

Gemma looked at her. 'I take it you're not going into work again today?'

'No,' she said. 'There's a big board meeting,' she added, as though that explained everything.

Gemma wondered if she ought to say something, but enough had probably been said yesterday. Helen was the type who had to sit on things for a while. Gemma, on the other hand, was not.

'Well, if you're not using the car,' she said, 'would you mind if I take it for a couple of hours?'

'Sure,' said Helen. 'Where are you off to?'

'I've decided I'm going to see Charlie and force his hand. I think that pep talk yesterday worked better on me,' she said pointedly. 'I know what I want and I'm not going to wait around any longer. You know what they say – if the mountain won't come to Mohammed . . .'

'I think you got that the wrong way around.' Helen smiled faintly. 'Do you want to leave Lola with me?'

'No, but thanks,' said Gemma. 'I don't know how long I'll be, and she's going to need feeding. Best that she's with me. Don't worry though, I'll have the car back in time for you to pick up Noah.'

*

Gemma turned into the street where Charlie lived in Newtown. She hadn't been there for ages, since before she'd taken off with Luke, and that felt like another lifetime ago. Newtown was as hard a place to find a park in as Balmain, so Gemma ended up blocks away. It was easier to set Lola up in her pram, with all her paraphernalia, than try to carry it all. Of course, that took nearly another ten minutes.

Gemma had lately come to envy the third-world women who carried their babies in simple fabric slings across their backs. Then again, they were usually toiling in the fields at the same time, so perhaps she didn't have it so bad. But she still baulked at all the stuff she had to cart around. And no matter what she brought, she always ended up with too much of what she didn't need and not enough of what she did: Lola would throw up on her only cardigan and the weather would turn cool, or she'd bring seven cardigans and wouldn't need one of them. Thank God she was breastfeeding. If she had to carry feeding equipment as well, Gemma figured she'd need a trailer attachment on the pram.

Finally she was on her way up the street towards Charlie's place. He'd better be there after all this. Gemma manoeuvred the pram through his front gate to the door, which, apart from one small step, was at street level. It was a tiny, single-storey cottage, one in a long row of the same. She remembered when Charlie bought it. They'd known each other a while by then, and Gemma had teased him about becoming a mortgage slave. It seemed like such an alien, grown-up thing to do. What Gemma had failed to appreciate was that Charlie was a grown-up, and so was she, in fact. Pity she hadn't acted more like one.

However, as she often reminded herself these days, she wouldn't have Lola right now if she'd made more sensible decisions back then. Gemma liked to believe there was enough space in a lifetime to make mistakes and live on the edge for a while, as long as you pulled back and took responsibility when it really mattered. And now that she had a daughter, it really mattered. Gemma was finally ready to be a grown-up.

She rang the bell three or four times straight, till she heard Charlie call from inside, 'Okay, okay, I'm coming.'

A moment later the door opened and he squinted out at her. He must have just woken up, but he'd managed to pull on jeans and a T-shirt to answer the door. 'Gemma, what are you doing here?' he said, dazed.

'If the mountain won't come to Mohammed,' she said, pushing the pram into the house past him.

'I think you got that the wrong way around,' he muttered.

'Whatever.' Gemma walked down the narrow hall, glancing into his bedroom, relieved to see his bed dishevelled but empty – an uncomfortable thought had crossed her mind when he'd opened the door half-asleep. She pushed the pram into a corner of the living room and turned around to face him. He was leaning against the doorway, watching her.

'Did you get my message yesterday, about Luke?' she asked.

He nodded but didn't say anything.

'Why didn't you call?'

He shrugged. 'Sorry, I was going to call . . . I've been busy.'

Gemma regarded him sceptically. 'What's going on, Charlie?'

'Nothing.'

'So it seems.'

He scratched his head, ruffling his hair so that a tuft stuck out sideways. 'I need caffeine if you're going to start speaking in riddles,' he said, turning towards the kitchen.

Gemma followed him. 'Okay, I'll give it to you straight.' She paused, choosing her words. 'Luke's not going to have anything to do with Lola, or me. He's completely out of the picture. Okay?'

Charlie was at the sink filling the kettle. 'It has nothing to do with me, Gem.'

'Of course it does.'

'How do you figure that?'

'Charlie, will you please just stop and listen to what I have to say?'

He turned around and leaned back against the bench, folding his arms.

Gemma took a breath. 'Okay, here it is,' she began. 'I don't want my life to be a series of train wrecks anymore, Charlie, and I don't need to wait for my hormones to settle. My hormones are fine. This is not a rash decision; in fact, along with keeping Lola, this is the best decision I've ever made. I want to be with you, Charlie, I want to build a life with you and Lola. You're the best man I've ever known. You're good and you're kind, and you're decent, and you're going to make a wonderful father. And I love you.'

Gemma's heart was beating hard against her ribs. Didn't he have anything to say to that? Apparently not. He just stood there, looking uncomfortable.

Maybe he just needed prompting. Gemma cleared her throat. 'This is the part where you say you love me, Charlie, and we fall into each other's arms, and the closing credits roll and they play some lame song, like . . . I don't know . . .'

'"Will You Love Me Tomorrow?"' he suggested.

Okay, now she could see where he was coming from. 'That depends,' said Gemma. '"Are You Strong Enough To Be My Man?"'

'"You Can't Always Get What You Want",' he countered.

'Well,' said Gemma. '"I Believe In A Thing Called Love".'

'"Love Will Tear Us Apart".'

'"Love Will Keep Us Together".'

'"Only Love Will Break Your Heart".'

'"All You Need Is Love".'

Charlie sighed. '"If Love Is A Red Dress Hang Me In Rags".'

'What?' Gemma frowned.

'It's really the name of a song,' he said sheepishly.

'So what are you saying, Charlie? You don't believe in love, or you don't believe I love you?'

He was quiet for a moment. 'I do believe you think you love me, that you love me in some way, but it's not enough. I'm not in your league, Gem, never have been. And it goes against all the laws of nature to cross leagues. Like crossing the streams in the *Ghostbusters* movie, and look what happened there.'

'I'm so glad you take relationship cues from an eighties sci-fi comedy,' Gemma snapped. 'I happen to think this is serious, Charlie.'

'Sorry,' he said. 'I think it's serious too. It wouldn't work, Gem.'

Her face dropped. 'We could make it work. If we both commit –'

'And what's going to happen when the guy comes along that you really fall in love with?' he said. 'The right one, the one you should hold out for.'

'What if he has, what if he's been there all along and it's just taken me a while to realise?'

'It shouldn't have taken this long,' said Charlie. 'You should have felt it much sooner. You know – the earth moving, the harps playing, all that.'

Gemma had a brainwave. 'So it's the sex?'

'Pardon?'

'If you want the earth to move, then fine, let's have sex,' she said, pulling up her T-shirt.

'Gem, what are you doing?' he said, coming over and taking hold of her to stop her. 'I'm not going to have sex with you.'

She looked at him. 'You don't find me attractive anymore? Since I had a baby?'

Charlie sighed, pulling her T-shirt back down. 'Of course I find you attractive,' he said. 'Incredibly attractive.'

'You do?' she said, looping her arms around his neck.

'Don't, Gem,' he murmured.

'Why not?' she breathed, tilting her head to brush her lips against his.

And suddenly he caught her up in his arms and his mouth came down on hers and he was holding her tight and kissing her frantically. Gemma took a moment to catch up . . . then as suddenly as it had started, it stopped again. Charlie released her abruptly, turning away to lean against the kitchen bench, his back to her.

'What's the matter?'

'I can't do this, Gemma.'

She took a step closer. 'Why not? What's wrong?'

He didn't respond. Gemma nestled into his back and drew her arms around him. 'You kissed me then, Charlie. The other time, I kissed you, but just now, you kissed me. You feel something, Charlie.'

He wrenched away from her. 'Of course I fucking feel something, Gemma!'

She just stared at him.

'I've been in love with you from the start. You knew that, everyone knew that. It took me a long time to get over you, Gem, but I finally did. I'm in a good place now, and I don't want to go back there.'

'What are you talking about?'

'When Luke rang the other day, Jesus, it all came back again.'

'But nothing was going to happen, Charlie,' she cried. 'Why don't you believe me?'

'Because I can't, that's the whole problem, Gem. Don't you see that? It won't work if I can't trust you.'

Gemma was bewildered. 'But I don't want anyone else, Charlie. I've had enough losers. It might have taken me a while to realise, but I know now for sure – I want to be with you.'

But he just looked at her sadly. 'I don't want to win by default, Gemma.'

'Charlie . . .' She didn't know what to say to him. He was standing right there, right within arm's reach, yet he was out of her reach, and there was not a thing she could do about it. It seemed the universe had exhausted its goodwill towards her in giving her Lola. She couldn't have them both. But the void Gemma felt, imagining not having Charlie in her life, was almost more than she could bear to contemplate.

'You know, Charlie, I always thought you were one of the few people in my life who really got me,' she said after a while, the ache in her throat making it hard for her to speak. 'And I was right. You get me so well you don't want to have anything to do with me.'

'Gemma,' he chided gently, taking a step towards her.

'No.' She held her hands up to stop him. She didn't think she could cope if he touched her now. 'You're right, Charlie. We are in different leagues, and clearly I'm way out of yours. I'm really sorry, so sorry, for hurting you . . . for everything. I won't bother you anymore.'

She turned into the living room, blinking back tears.

'Gem . . .'

She ignored him. She had to get out of there. She started to wheel the pram out of the corner.

'Gemma, please wait.'

She stopped, but she didn't look at him.

'I don't want you to go. Not like this. Can't we be friends?'

Gemma turned around then. 'I don't think so, Charlie. You might have your feelings under control, but I haven't got to that point. I can't be around you if I don't think there's any chance . . . I wouldn't care how long it was going to take, but I have to have some hope.'

He stared at her for a while, not saying anything. Gemma could feel her heart plummeting into her stomach. She felt sick as she started to push the pram over to the hall.

'Gemma, stop.'

She sighed, turning around again.

'I, um, I'm still going to need a production assistant.'

'Charlie, I said I can't be around you –'

'Look, are you interested or not?' he said. 'I don't want anyone else . . . for the position . . . and well, I can't make any promises right now . . . It's going to take time.'

Gemma gazed across the room at him. He could take all the time in the world.

'Okay?' he prompted.

'Okay,' she croaked, her voice breaking. A moment later she felt his arms around her, and she melted into his chest, weeping with relief. The universe was going to give her another chance after all, and she wasn't going to screw it up this time.

Charlie drew back to look at her. 'Are you all right?'

Gemma nodded, wiping her eyes. He planted a firm kiss on her forehead, and she smiled up at him.

'So we have a deal?' he said.

'Yes we do,' she said happily. 'Though, actually, I have been meaning to raise something with you.'

'You have?'

'You know me, Charlie, I don't do the "assistant" thing very well. Just ask Myles.'

'So what are you saying?'

'I'm saying that "producer" sounds better. Don't you think?'

His face relaxed into a broad smile. 'I think I'm probably not going to have much of a say in it.'

'Good answer.'

Balmain

Helen was sick of herself. She'd been wandering around the house all morning, restless and agitated. She didn't know what to do with herself anymore. Nothing interested her, nothing seemed to occupy her or keep her mind off her dilemma. Everything Gemma and Phoebe said yesterday made sense, of course it did, but Helen still felt stuck. Whenever she thought of asking Myles to stay, she was terrified by the enormity of it. It was a huge life decision, and it didn't only affect her – she also had Noah to consider, and she didn't even want to think about the conversation she'd have to have with David's parents. Maybe it was easier if Myles went back to Melbourne, let a few months pass. But whenever she thought of him leaving, she felt desolate.

When they'd made love, Myles had touched her so deep down, Helen had glimpsed the hidden, buried grief she realised she'd been suppressing. But the grief wasn't for David, it was for herself, for all the years lost to her mother, her marriage . . . stifled and silenced and suffocated. She'd lost herself under the weight of everyone else's needs, all their expectations. And now Myles said she had to work out what she wanted. But Helen had no idea how to do that.

She was lying on the sofa, swirling in the whirlpool of her thoughts, when the sound of knocking gradually penetrated her consciousness. Helen sat up, listening, but she couldn't hear it now.

As she walked up the hall to investigate, she couldn't see anyone through the frosted glass panel in the door, but when she opened it she saw the hunched figure of a man leaving through the front gate.

'Excuse me,' she called.

He turned around. Helen didn't recognise him.

'Sorry,' she said, 'I didn't hear you knocking right away. I was at the back of the house.'

'Mrs Chapman?' he asked from where he stood. He was late middle-aged, she guessed, and terribly thin and frail-looking, with lank grey hair and a drawn weary face.

'Yes, I'm Mrs Chapman.'

'Mrs David Chapman?' he said solemnly.

Helen took a breath. 'Well, um . . . yes, my husband was David Chapman.'

The man kept his eyes on her as he shuffled back up the path and up the steps to the porch. 'My name is Barry Druce,' he began.

The name sounded vaguely familiar, but for the moment she couldn't place it.

'I'm the . . . well, at least, I was . . . the bus driver who . . .' he said. 'I was the bus driver.'

Helen just stared at him, a million thoughts crowding into her head at once. 'How did you find me?' she asked eventually.

'From the report of the inquest,' he said. 'Transit, they won't give you no information at the time. You have to sign something that you won't try to contact the family.' Then he shook his head. 'A few months later, it's all up on the internet for anyone to see. Addresses, the lot.'

Her head was still spinning. 'What can I do for you, Mr Druce?'

He looked directly at her, and Helen could see the pain in his faded, hollow eyes. 'I hope you'll forgive me, Mrs Chapman, I just had to see, had to know if you were all right. You and your little one.'

Her heart cramped suddenly in her chest. 'Come on in, Mr Druce.'

'No, no, Mrs Chapman,' he said. 'I know I shouldn't of showed up like this. I don't want to bother you.'

'You're not bothering me,' she said, stepping back. 'Please, I'd like you to come in.'

He bowed his head and stepped inside. Helen closed the door and started down the hall. 'This way,' she said to him.

He followed her into the front room and Helen offered him a seat. 'Can I get you anything, a cup of tea, a glass of water?'

'No, no, Mrs Chapman,' he said quickly. 'I'll be right.'

Helen sat in an armchair opposite him. Neither of them said anything for a few moments. 'Um, you wanted to know if we were all right?' Helen prompted him after a while.

'Yes, Mrs Chapman.' She noticed his hands were trembling in his lap. 'It's a terrible thing . . . knowing he left a wife and a young child. Not a day goes past I don't think about it. I pray for you to Saint Louise, every day. Patron saint of widows, you know.'

'Oh,' said Helen. 'Thank you.'

His eyes wandered around the room. 'So, you're okay? This is your house? You didn't have to sell up or anything?'

'No, we're fine.'

'And what of your little one? They don't identify children under age in the inquest.'

'He's a boy, Noah,' said Helen. 'He's only four years old, not quite that when it first happened. He's too young to fully understand.'

He nodded faintly, staring down at the carpet. Helen watched him. If there was ever an example of a shell of a man, Mr Druce was certainly it.

'What about you, Mr Druce?' she asked. 'How are you? Do you still drive buses?'

He shook his head gravely. 'Oh, no, Mrs Chapman. Had to give it away, my nerves were shot. Took to drinking too much for a while there. I couldn't sleep at night, I'd see it happen over and over. It's a terrible thing, Mrs Chapman, a terrible thing.'

'But you were cleared of any responsibility at the inquest,' said Helen.

'Doesn't matter, I'll always feel responsible, Mrs Chapman. I was the one behind the wheel.'

'But do you think you could have stopped, could have done anything different?'

'Oh no, Mrs Chapman, I couldn't of stopped. He was just there, he stepped out right in front of the bus.'

Helen could feel her heart thumping hard. She could ask him. Ask him right now. And then she'd know. Once and for all.

'Mr Druce?'

'Yes, Mrs Chapman?'

'Can I ask you something?'

'Of course, anything.'

Helen took a deep breath. 'Did my husband, David, did he turn to look, was he looking as he stepped off the kerb?'

'Oh no, no, Mrs Chapman,' he said, shaking his head very definitively. 'That was the thing. I've played it over and over, like I said. It all only took a few seconds, but you know how sometimes things happen in slow motion? That's what it was like that day. I was headed along Broadway, coming to a green light. Then there was a loud screech and a bang, further down the road somewhere. I looked ahead, as you do, just for a second. The crowd waiting at the lights, all the heads turned at the same time, towards the noise. Funny how you remember things like that. No one was looking this way, and then one person just stepped off the kerb, just stepped off . . .' Helen was watching him – she knew he could see it now in his mind. 'I couldn't do anything, he was right there in front of me, still looking up the street the other way. It was that quick, he wouldn't of known what hit him, Mrs Chapman.'

Helen had read and reread the report from the inquest, trying to find an answer, a reason, some piece of information that would make sense of it, give her some peace of mind. She'd never been sure if he'd turned his head, never known till now if he'd suffered, even just one moment of horrifying realisation.

Helen felt tears creeping into her eyes. So that was it. A momentary lapse, distracted by something further up the road, stepping off the footpath on autopilot. A life wiped out in a matter of seconds for no reason whatsoever. Nothing could ever make sense of that, ever make it right, or wrong. It was inexplicable. And it just was.

She looked across at Mr Druce. 'But I don't understand, why do you feel responsible, Mr Druce?'

'I don't know, I don't know, Mrs Chapman,' he said, shaking his head. 'Everyone asks me that. I don't know what to tell 'em. Except it's a terrible thing, a terrible thing, for someone's life to end, right in front of your eyes. I can't seem to let go of it. My wife, she can't stand it anymore. She left to stay with her sister. She said I've got to get some help. My kids, they don't want to come and visit . . .'

He was staring down at the carpet, broken. This wasn't right. The poor man just happened to be at the wheel. It could have been anyone.

'Is that him, is that Mr Chapman?' Mr Druce asked, pointing at a framed photo on a side table.

Helen nodded.

He got to his feet and approached it almost reverently, stooping down to look at it. 'May I?' he said over his shoulder to Helen.

'Of course.'

He picked up the photo, examining it closely for a long while. 'He had a good face . . . he looks . . . honest.'

Helen came up behind him. 'So you didn't see him at all?'

'No, no, Mrs Chapman,' he said. 'I couldn't of told you what he looked like. Light hair is all.' He gazed down at the photograph again. 'You have a fine boy there, Mrs Chapman.'

'Thank you.'

He set the photograph down again, being very careful to position it exactly as it had been.

'Mr Druce,' said Helen.

He turned to look at her.

'There's something I'd like you to know. My husband, David, he was a good man, a very compassionate man. He hated to see any kind of human suffering.' Helen paused, choosing her words. 'I can tell you without hesitation that he would never have wanted you to suffer in this way. It was a terrible accident, but there's nothing you could have done, nothing anyone could have done. David would think it was far worse if even more lives were ruined because of it.'

Mr Druce was listening intently, his eyes glassy.

'He'd want you to live your life, Mr Druce. Make the most of every moment. That should be his legacy.'

*

Not fifteen minutes later Helen was running up the hill towards Darling Street. Mr Druce had taken his leave, clutching her hand and thanking her for her kindness, before shuffling back out the gate.

Helen had dashed madly around the house, wasting precious minutes looking for her keys until she remembered that Gemma had taken the car. And so she'd grabbed her handbag and started up the street on foot, walking briskly at first, till she couldn't contain herself any longer and she'd broken into a run. As she came to the corner of Darling Street, a bus was trundling up the block towards her. Helen glanced at the bus stop further up. There were two people waiting. She'd make it. She bolted, arriving breathless at the shelter as the bus pulled up beside her. Helen queued behind the other two, fumbling in her purse for her Opal card. She hoped it still had money on it.

Once on the bus, she swiped her card and it was accepted. Relieved, she made her way up the aisle as the bus lurched off again. There were only a few people scattered around the bus; it was the middle of the day after all. Helen dropped into a seat and sidled over near the window. She gazed out as the bus dipped and bounced its way along the road. She was riding on a bus. And it was okay. Everything was going to be okay.

When they finally pulled up at the back of the Queen Victoria building, Helen was waiting to jump straight off. She started up the street, restraining herself from running this time – she didn't want to arrive all puffed and sweaty. She had remembered she'd need her security pass and had searched in her bag while she was still on the bus, relieved, though not entirely surprised to find it there – it was her only decent handbag, and the only one she ever took to work. Helen slipped the lanyard around her neck as she arrived at the front entrance of the building, and walked inside. She was not exactly dressed for work, but at least she wasn't in her daggy house clothes either. Fortunately she'd had to look half-decent to take Noah to preschool.

The security guard recognised her and smiled, giving her a nod as she hurried over to the lifts. She stepped inside and her heart started to race. It seemed to take an awfully long time to get to the fifteenth floor, but finally the lift came to a stop and Helen dashed out, racing up the corridor towards his office. What if he wasn't there? There was every chance, but at least she could check his schedule from her computer, text him, track him down. Helen had never appreciated modern technology more.

She went around the corner and scooted straight past her workstation to his office. She gave a quick knock and burst in, only to discover Myles was there, but he wasn't alone. She froze as four unfamiliar faces turned to stare at her.

Myles got to his feet immediately. 'Helen?'

She opened her mouth, but nothing came out.

'This is Helen?' said one of the men, also getting to his feet. 'Helen Chapman, I gather?'

He was walking towards her. Shit, now they were all walking towards her. Helen almost flinched as they converged on her, shaking her hand, all talking at once – at least that's what it seemed like. She suspected they were introducing themselves, but they must have been speaking in another language. Chinese? Japanese, perhaps? They didn't look Asian, but Helen couldn't understand a word they were saying. And then Myles was at her side and his hand was on her elbow, the hand with the magic electrical powers.

'Helen, you wanted to see me?' he prompted.

She looked up into his face and managed to say, 'Yes.'

'Excuse us, gentlemen,' Myles was saying. 'I'm sure this won't take long. Help yourselves to another drink,' he said over his shoulder as he led Helen from the room. They walked back out through the door and Myles closed it firmly, turning to face her.

'Helen, are you all right?'

She nodded.

'You seemed in a bit of a daze just now.'

'Yeah,' she said, slipping into a daze again, looking at his face, the face she realised she'd fallen hopelessly in love with, head over the proverbial heels. She could tell him now, if only she was able to put two words together.

'Helen,' he was saying patiently, 'what is it?'

'Oh, um, maybe this is a bad time,' she said, stirring. 'Maybe I should come back?'

'No,' he said, his voice low and steady. 'I want you to say whatever it is you came to say, because I don't want you to have a chance to change your mind.'

He knew. But he had to hear it from her. She took a breath, trying to gather her thoughts. There was so much to say, she didn't know where to start. She'd gone over it all in the bus, but it wasn't exactly polished, nothing like it. It was all over the place, every random thought that had passed through her head in the last twenty-four hours since she'd seen him at the carpark at Brookhaven, since he'd kissed her.

'Helen?' He was gazing down at her with those wonderful eyes, from the face she loved with all her heart. When had she turned into such a hopeless romantic?

There was only one thing to do.

Helen reached up, wrapped her arms around him and planted her lips on his. Myles took only a second or two to respond, then she felt his arms drawing her close to him. And they kept kissing. And kissing. There was an awful lot that had to be said in that kiss. And they both kept right on saying it, and saying it. And after a long, intense conversation, Myles began gradually to pull back, little by little, as their lips played against each other, reluctant to part.

'So,' he breathed, still holding her close, 'that's what you wanted to tell me?'

'Pretty much,' she murmured. 'There's more, but we might have to go somewhere more private for that.'

He smiled, gazing down at her. 'So what brought this on?'

She sighed happily. 'So much, too much for me to go into right now. But I guess the final thing was the bus driver turning up at my house today.'

Myles looked confused.

'The one who drove the bus, you know, *the* bus,' said Helen. 'And he was so depressed and shattered, his whole life was in ruins, and I looked in his eyes and I didn't want that for me, and I knew that David would never have wanted it either. And I finally knew it was an accident, that it was no one's fault. And he's gone, and it's okay for me to be happy again.'

Myles held her face in his hands. 'Well, that's good, because that's my plan, to make you happy.'

'You've made an excellent start.' She smiled, as his lips came down on hers again.

'Myles –'

They sprang apart. One of the Japanese speakers was standing in the doorway to Myles's office, looking embarrassed and a little flummoxed.

'Oh, um, sorry, as you were, sorry,' he mumbled, closing the door again.

Myles turned to look down at her. Helen was biting her lip. 'Uh-oh, is this going to get you into trouble?'

'No,' he assured her. 'But they might not take my glowing recommendation of you on face value now.'

Her face dropped.

'I'm kidding, don't worry about it.' He drew her back into his arms. 'I'd better go back in. Was there anything else you wanted to say?'

'Oh, just, you know . . . I love you. I forgot to say that before.'

'I kind of picked up on that. But it's nice to hear it.' He gave her one last, lingering kiss. 'I'll call you when I'm done here.'

'Okay,' she said.

They drew apart, walking away from each other backwards, their eyes still locked.

'Oh, Myles?' said Helen, as he reached the door. 'There was one other thing.'

He stopped, waiting.

'I guess I'm saying, don't go to Melbourne.'

He was smiling as he took a few steps back towards her. 'You know what,' he said, 'I think I might have a better idea.'

A week later

'Myles asked you to go to Melbourne with him?'

'That's right. Me and Noah.'

Gemma was sitting across the kitchen table staring gobsmacked at Helen. It was to be the inaugural post-Lola Friday night drinks that night and they were expecting Phoebe soon. But Helen had jumped the gun and opened a bottle already; she had a feeling this would go down better with a drink.

'So what are you going to do?' Gemma wanted to know.

'I'm going to Melbourne with him,' Helen said simply.

'Just like that?'

'No,' she said patiently. 'Not "just like that". We've been talking about it for over a week.'

'Oh, wow, a whole week,' Gemma said sardonically.

'Gemma . . .'

'How come when I took off with some bloke, leaving a good job, and I don't know . . . *everything* behind me, people thought I was crazy and irresponsible?'

'I think this is a little different,' said Helen.

Gemma's shoulders sagged in defeat. 'Okay, so Myles is not a total loser like Luke was, and you two actually love each other, for real and everything, but why do you have to move away? You can love each other just as well here in Sydney, can't you?'

Helen sat forward in her chair, leaning her arms on the table. 'I think we need to get away from here to see what we have together.

There are too many memories, too many ghosts. He doesn't expect me to forget David, no way – he's Noah's father – but I think it'll be good for us to start out fresh.' She paused. 'Anyway, it's not like it has to be forever. If I don't like it, we'll come back in a year or so, Myles said, whenever I want.'

'But you won't,' Gemma sighed.

'To be honest, Gem, I've got no idea what's going to happen, and that's a little scary, but it's also pretty wonderful. I've never lived anywhere else my whole life but in this very house,' Helen said, looking around. 'I think if I really want to move on, I have to move out. It's time to finally spread my wings.'

Gemma was watching the look on her face, the light in her eyes. 'You have to do it,' she said resignedly. 'Of course you have to do it.'

'I know.'

'But what will you do in Melbourne? I mean, Myles has a life there, what about you and Noah?'

'Well, he hasn't taken holidays since . . . forever, so he's going to have some time off at first while we settle in. He wants to show me around, introduce us to his brothers. In fact, we're going to have a week or so in Tasmania with Hugo's family on their property. He's got three boys, not to mention pigs and chooks and horses and what have you. Noah's going to flip.'

'All right, so far, so idyllic, then what?' asked Gemma. 'When Myles goes back to work, what are you going to do with yourself?'

'Get a job, of course,' Helen said. 'I've already been looking online. Myles suggested I think about charities, environmental groups, that kind of thing. Somewhere I won't be so ethically challenged,' she said with a grin. 'Turns out there's some interesting possibilities. I was hoping you'd give me a hand updating my résumé actually.'

'Of course, I'd be happy to,' said Gemma. 'You certainly seem to have this all figured out, Helen. Why didn't you talk to me sooner?'

'Because I had to figure it out for myself first. And I wanted to check with Tony before I told you, make sure he was happy to take over responsibility for Mum, and the house. He's totally supportive of you staying here, nothing's going to change for you. He even suggested that Phoebe can move in if she'd like, now that there'll be a spare room.'

'Oh no, Phoebe's flying the coop, trekking to base camp, would you believe? Mad woman doesn't know what a holiday is.' Gemma paused. 'Hey, I've just realised, you're all abandoning me. What am I going to do on Friday nights?'

Helen smiled. 'There's always Charlie.'

'Given time,' Gemma said, nodding. 'I am going to be such a model of patience he'll be begging me to take him in the end.' She stared at the bubbles rising in her glass. 'You know, ever since I began to look at him differently, I can't *stop* looking at him. I finally understand what loving someone's really all about. I'd do anything for him and Lola.'

'I know exactly what you mean.'

Gemma looked at Helen, grinning. 'What a lame, lovelorn pair we are.'

Helen smiled back. 'So, do I have your blessing?'

'Like you need it,' Gemma scoffed.

'No, listen to me,' said Helen as she felt tears creeping into her eyes. 'Damn, I told myself I wouldn't do this.' She sniffed.

Gemma frowned at her. 'What's the matter?'

Helen attempted to compose herself. 'You know what's the hardest thing to leave? Not this house, or this place, not my mum – she won't know the difference. Not even Tony. He'll be coming down to Melbourne in a few months anyway for the season there . . .'

'So what is it?' asked Gemma.

'The hardest thing is that I have to leave you,' Helen said, her voice breaking.

Gemma stared at her. 'Me?' she said. Oh no, now she could feel a lump rising in her throat.

'Do you remember the first day we met, sitting here at this table?' Helen said.

Gemma just nodded. She wasn't game to try to use her voice.

'I remember thinking, what am I letting myself in for? I didn't realise I was getting the best friend I've ever had. What am I going to do without you?'

Oh, why did she have to say that? Gemma's face contorted as she tried to suppress the stubborn lump, but it was no use. She gave up, and pretty soon they were both intermittently sobbing, and laughing, and sobbing again, and hanging onto each other, and sobbing some more.

'They have phones in Melbourne, right?' Gemma said in a strangled voice. 'And the Hume Highway, and aeroplanes flying in and out several times a day?'

'I guess,' said Helen with a sniff.

'And you'll come back for Lola's naming ceremony?'

'Of course,' she assured her. 'We'll be back pretty regularly for Noah to see his grandparents.'

'Okay,' said Gemma, like something was settled. 'Now I need a drink.'

'Me too.'

They picked up their glasses.

'To Melbourne,' said Gemma.

'And to you and Charlie.'

They clinked and drank.

'And to you and Myles and Noah.'

'And to Lola of course,' Helen added.

They clinked and drank again.

'And to David,' said Gemma, 'may he rest in peace.'

'Amen,' said Helen. 'And to friendship.'

They clinked and drank, and then they had to refill their glasses. They sat down at the table, sighing in unison.

'So . . .' said Gemma.

Helen nodded. 'So . . .'

'When are you migrating south?'

'It'll be a few weeks yet,' said Helen. 'There are a couple of things I have to take care of first.'

Garie

Helen took Noah's hand as they walked along the track that led to the headland. It was a warm day; the sky was a clear expanse of blue, and there was barely any breeze to speak of, which was a relief. Noah had insisted on carrying the balloons, but Helen was worried he wouldn't be able to keep hold of them, so she'd tied them to his wrist. He'd picked the colours. Blue for David, because Daddy had blue eyes, and he had lots of blue shirts, Noah remembered. And yellow for himself, and pink for his mother. Helen was carrying the box containing David's ashes. It was a very ordinary receptacle, considering what it held – little more than a shoe box really, made from a kind of plastic-coated cardboard. She remembered being surprised when she'd picked it up from the crematorium, but David would have approved of its simplicity and lack of pretension.

Helen and Noah came to the end of the main track and continued along a path that took them to the spot David had talked about. Helen had phoned the National Parks to make sure she wasn't doing anything illegal, or against health regulations or something, but she had been assured she was within her rights by a very kind man, who had also tactfully suggested she test which way the wind was blowing when she got to the spot, to avoid a potentially distressing outcome.

Helen grabbed a clump of reeds and tore off a few stalks. She held her hand out in front of her and opened it flat. There was barely enough wind to lift the stalks off her hand, but when she brushed them away, they fluttered on the light breeze. She breathed in the salt air, looking out at the ocean. It was calm today, the waves lolling up over the rocks with a gentle splash. David would have liked a day like today.

'Is this Daddy's special place, Mummy?'

'This is it,' she said. 'What do you think?'

Noah looked around and nodded approvingly. 'It's a good place. Are we gunna let Daddy go now?'

'Yes, we are.'

Helen knelt down and placed the box on the ground beside her. 'Hold out your arm, sweetheart.' Noah did as she said and Helen proceeded to untie the balloons. Then she pressed the strings into the palm of his hand and closed his fingers firmly around them. 'You have to hold on tight now, okay, Noah? Until it's time, like we said, remember?'

Noah nodded seriously, his face set in concentration.

Helen picked up the box again and stood up. She took hold of Noah's free hand and they stepped down a couple of rock ledges, close to the edge of the water. 'Okay, Noah, this is it.' Helen took a deep breath and lifted the lid off the box. 'Are you ready?'

He nodded, watching her. Helen held the box out in front of her and hesitated for a moment, before she turned it over. The ashes started to drift out slowly. Helen shook the box gently and more began to fall away. A puff of breeze came from behind her, blowing her hair forward around her face, catching the cloud of ashes and carrying it out further.

'Now, Noah!' Helen cried.

'Now?'

'That's right. Let go of the balloons, sweetheart.'

He held his arm out straight and opened his hand. Instantly the balloons were caught on a zephyr, dancing for a moment before scattering up into the air. Noah squealed with delight, clapping his hands. Helen smiled as she turned the box the whole way over and David's remains drifted peacefully into the ocean below.

She sat down on a flat rock, scooping Noah up onto her lap as they watched the balloons fly away, higher and higher, the ashes gradually dissolving into the water.

'Daddy's all gone now, Mummy,' Noah said, matter-of-factly. If nothing else, he seemed to have inherited his father's pragmatism.

'He'll never be completely gone, Noah.'

'But you gave his clothes to Unka Steve, and now his ashes are sinked in the water.'

'But Daddy will always be in our hearts, won't he?'

Noah turned to look at her, a little unsure.

'What do you remember about Daddy, Noah?'

He thought about it. 'He had big hands,' he said finally.

Helen wrapped her arms tightly around him, resting her cheek against his. 'Bye, David,' she said softly.

'Bye, Daddy,' said Noah, waving as the balloons rose high up into the sky towards the sun, until they couldn't see them any more in the white light.

Acknowledgements

This book would not be here, and I do not say that lightly, without the overwhelming support of a few wonderful people who have helped me through a very difficult time. Their love, loyalty and unrelenting encouragement propelled me to the finish line. And so, before I break into a chorus of 'Wind Beneath My Wings', thank you all from the bottom of my heart:

Diane Stubbings; my brother Bob, sister-in-law Carolyn, and their children, Kane, Tahnee, Olivia and Hayley; Debra Solomon, Desley Hennessey, Robyn Johnson and Lynda Bowden.

And that is not to mention Cate Paterson, brilliant publisher and mentor. If she had doubts she certainly kept them to herself. Her unwavering belief in me inspired me to keep going, and she has given me incredible support on so many levels to get this book published. I can't thank her enough for not giving up on me.

On that note, I am grateful to the entire Pan Macmillan family – specifically, my editor, Kylie Mason, and my publicist, Jane Novak, who I am confident will once again handle things with her customary grace and good humour. Very special thanks must also go to my remarkable copyeditor, Julia Stiles, whose consummate skill and expertise shaped the book into what it is today. I am deeply indebted to her.

Finally, heartfelt thanks to my son, Joel Naoum, and to Jeska Allan, for their insightful feedback and valuable input at the draft stage. And thanks to my boys, Dane, Pat and Zac, for their constant love, support and affection, and for the enormous joy they bring to my life.

More Titles from Dianne Blacklock

About Call Waiting

Of course Meg was a success: she planned, she set goals, she made lists. Ally never made lists.

Ally Tasker is trapped in a dead-end teaching job and a relationship that's going nowhere. Her college friend Meg has a fabulous job in advertising, a doting husband and a gorgeous baby boy. Why did Ally's life seem to be permanently on hold?

When her grandfather and sole relative dies, Ally has to return to the Southern Highlands. As she sets to restoring the rundown home of her childhood, the past unravels, and Ally realises the choice to be happy has been in her hands all along.

Meanwhile Meg's life is not as idyllic as Ally imagines. She longs to inject more passion and spontaneity into her life, but at what cost to her career, and more importantly, to the people she loves most in the world?

Sometimes you have to risk all you have to realise what is worth saving.

Find out more at: books2read.com/callwaiting

About Wife for Hire

When she was a little girl, all Samantha Driscoll ever wanted was to be somebody's wife. She would marry a man called Tod or Brad and she would have two perfect children. But instead she married a Jeff and he's just confessed to having an affair.

Desperate times indeed. Sam has to find a way to support her kids and keep her dream house, but she has no qualifications, having given up any career aspirations she might have had to become the consummate wife. So much for that. Then she finds the job she was born for: Wife for Hire - a service offering everything from domestic help to personal shopping to planning social events for people who don't have the time - people who need a wife.

Surrounded by a gaggle of girlfriends, an eccentric sister, a mother who brings whole new meaning to the word 'demanding', and two teenagers discovering their dad has hormones too, Sam successfully manages a cast of clients from the sublime to the ridiculous, including American businessman Hal Buchanan, who insists he doesn't need her services even if they are part of his executive package. If that's the case, why does he keep hanging around?

Sam may be a born organiser, but there are some things in life that do not go to schedule.

Find out more at: books2read.com/wifeforhire

About Almost Perfect

It's no big deal to love someone who's perfect ... The trick is to love someone despite the fact they're not.

With a beautiful house in an upscale Sydney suburb and two successful careers, anyone would think that Mac and Anna have the perfect life. But their marriage is cracking under the strain of infertility. Consumed by her dream of having a child, Anna cannot see how her pain and disappointment are driving Mac away.

Close by, in a beachside suburb, Georgie Reading and her sister-in-law have made their bookstore, The Reading Rooms, an unqualified success - unlike Georgie's love life. In her thirties, with a deadbeat roommate and no romantic prospects in sight, her beloved brother Nick suggests that maybe she's waiting for someone she was never going to find - the mythical perfect man.

Then Liam walks into the bookstore, and Georgie thinks she has finally found just that. Well, he's perfect for her, anyway. ... At the same time Mac and Anna reach breaking point, putting Mac on a path that will have unforeseen consequences for them all.

Find out more at: books2read.com/almostperfectblacklock

About Crossing Paths

Jo had learned the hard way that life was not mystical, or magical; it was hard and grey and cold most of the time. Much better to see it for what it is than to be perennially disappointed.

It's not as though Jo Liddell never had dreams. She was going to be a journalist and travel the world, but life had a way of stealing her dreams right out from under her. Okay, she had her column, but heaven forbid she had an opinion about anything that mattered. And now that she's saddled herself with a hefty mortgage, Jo has resigned herself to living a less-than-perfect life.

That is, until she crosses paths with Joe Bannister - a celebrated foreign correspondent, returning home to care for his dying father, take the pressure off his long-suffering sister and maybe pull his recalcitrant brother into line. He did not expect to find himself falling for a headstrong woman who seems to resent him.

But after devastating news, Joe is forced to make an impossible choice, and Jo must fight hard for everything she never believed in - success, self-acceptance, and above all, real love.

Find out more at: books2read.com/crossingpaths

About Three's a Crowd

'Well, we're different, we lead such different lives. I'm not sure how we'll go now without Annie. She was like Carrie, you know, in Sex and the City. Annie was our Carrie.'

Without Annie, friends Catherine, Lexie and Rachel are lost. How will they fill the void? Will their friendship survive?

Catherine is characteristically unfazed, forging ahead in her high-flying career while struggling to connect to her unfathomable teenage daughter. But secrets from the past emerge to shatter her carefully constructed image, and threaten all the relationships she holds dear.

Meanwhile Lexie is juggling the demands of her young family and the ego of her hardworking husband, while taking the first tentative steps to achieving her own dreams. She just wished Annie was around to talk to - Catherine is so bossy, and Rachel ... well, her head seems be more in the clouds now than ever.

Rachel knows what her friends think of her - but what they don't know is that she's currently in the thrall of a new relationship. And she doesn't want them to know, because when the truth comes out, fragile friendships will be put to the test all over again ...

Find out more at: books2read.com/threesacrowd

About The Right Time

The Beckett sisters need to shake things up.

Emma has been planning her dream wedding even since she was a little girl, and she's determined to get her happy ending. Just as soon as her boyfriend Blake gets around to proposing …

Liz is a well respected and successful doctor and supposedly the brains of the family, yet she still believes her married colleague will leave his wife for her, one day …

Evie is cheerfully married to Craig, but after three children, things have stagnated. When Craig suggests a way to spice up their relationship, Evie is horrified - but she always tries so desperately to please …

And Ellen, the eldest sister and the anchor of the family, is dealing with the end of her marriage and getting back into the dating game. But she wonders if she'll ever be able to get naked in front of another man, let alone open her heart to love again.

When their parents drop a bombshell that affects them all, and one sister must make a life-changing decision, it's the right time for the Beckett sisters to band together and face the challenges head-on.

Find out more at: books2read.com/therighttime

About The Secret Ingredient

'Taste was such an evocative sense; Andie had closed her eyes, with the scone melting in her mouth, and been transported back to her grandmother's kitchen …'

Nourishment is nurture. That's what Andie learned from her grandmother and what she's always believed, but somehow, since marrying Ross, she's allowed her love of cooking to take a back seat and given up her dream of becoming a chef.

Lately she's been craving more. And as her marriage implodes, deception, betrayal and tragedy lead Andie all the way back to what really matters to her. The new Andie is ready for anything, even a bad-tempered chef who makes it clear he won't tolerate mistakes.

With help from the unlikeliest of allies, Andie uncovers the secret ingredient for a new life, and shows that no matter how many false starts, if you hold on to your passion and your dreams, anything is possible.

Find out more at: books2read.com/thesecretingredient

About The Best Man

Is the best man always the right man?

With American fiancé, Henry Darrow, publicist Madeleine has at last found the yin to her yang - or whichever way round it is. The calm to her storm, the stillness to her constant motion. Balance.

Her boss, Liv, had to be talked into marriage, which predictably ended in divorce. Liv knows that she and her twins are better off on their own anyway. She just wished everyone would stop telling her to 'put herself out there', whatever that's supposed to mean.

However, when Henry's best man arrives from the US to meet Madeleine for the first time, and Liv has a spontaneous chat with a stranger, the settled lives these women thought they had finally achieved are thrown into chaos. Secrets are unravelled and new doors are opened.

May the best man win.

Find out more at: books2read.com/thebestman